BOOK ONE OF THE MACHINISTS

FRACTURE

CRAIG
ANDREWS

ALSO BY CRAIG ANDREWS

FRACTURE

SPLINTER
(forthcoming)

Be sure and follow Craig Andrews on
Facebook and sign up for his Mailing List
to receive exclusive bonus content.

https://www.facebook.com/craigandrewsauthor
http://eepurl.com/IEjIr

For Tiffany,
who sees me at my best, and my worst,
but loves me always.
I love you.

PROLOGUE

BAYLIS EMERGED FROM THE DARK alley with Nyla a couple of steps behind him. The night swallowed the dim light from the flickering streetlamp as he pulled his black coat tight around his shoulders, shielding himself from the rain. He fought to hold back his nervousness—for her sake. It was useless.

The *echo* made them closer than family and more intimate than lovers. It was also forbidden. If any of the Grand Mages ever discovered that he and Nyla had developed one—No, he wouldn't think about that. *Not tonight.*

Nyla glanced at him from the corner of her eye, silently probing his apprehension. He ignored her, instead surveying their surroundings.

"He's home," Baylis said, looking at the three-story apartment complex across the street. Most of the windows were dark, but at the corner of the top floor was an illuminated window.

Nyla's blue eyes narrowed, sharply piercing the night. She seemed to be squinting, but Baylis knew better. She was focusing.

"He's alone," she said.

"Good." Relieved, Baylis sighed. "We made it in time." He waited for a car to pass then stepped into the street. The sound of water spun from the tires splashing against the wheel wells hid the sound of their footsteps.

Nyla jogged to catch up and took her position at his side. Her silver hair was tucked inside her black compression armor, and she wore a hood to hide the rest. Concealed by the rain, they were two shadows hidden in the night.

The gate into the apartment complex was locked, but it was a relic that hadn't been updated since the turn of the last century. Baylis wielded water and projected it into the lock, immediately solidifying it into ice crystals so that it pushed against the correct pins, unlocking the mechanism.

"I wish I could do that," Nyla said.

He smiled at her. It was nothing more than a trick young magi could use to commit pranks. But Nyla was a cleric and therefore had different abilities. "That's why you have me." He held the door as she entered.

The complex was empty. He heard some rustling and a few televisions through the thin walls, but the building was otherwise quiet. Making their way to the third-story corner apartment, they kept their pace and movements controlled to avoid attention. Baylis stopped outside the corner apartment. The metal door was painted a deep red. He gave Nyla a slight nod and grabbed the doorknob.

That's when he heard it—a sound like a match igniting.

Instinctively, Baylis threw his shoulder into the door, barreling into the apartment and yanking Nyla in with him. A mass of blue ice streaked past the door, shattering against the exposed-brick wall at the end of the hall. Small water droplets and ice crystals littered the hallway, quickly melting into the cheap carpet.

"What the hell?" their mark yelled, leaping up from the couch. He was a slender man who was younger than

Baylis, with wide-set eyes and a pronounced chin. "Who the hell are you? Get out!" His voice cracked with fear.

A coward, too, apparently. What could Lukas want with him?

"We're not alone," Nyla said. "Lukas came for him after all."

"I noticed." Baylis glanced at the door, waiting for their pursuer to enter the apartment. The mission was supposed to be simple. They were supposed to grab their mark and bring him under their protection before Lukas could snatch him. And if they met resistance or if Lukas or one of his magi arrived, Baylis and Nyla had been ordered to flee in order to prevent a scene—and to preserve their secret. "Come on!"

The small, single-bedroom apartment had an open concept and was decorated with a mixture of movie posters and sports memorabilia. A well-used couch with sagging cushions and greasy food stains sat in the center of the apartment, facing a thin widescreen television mounted on the wall. Windows, including one leading to the fire escape, lined the north side.

"I said, get the fuck out of my apartment!"

Baylis raced across the apartment then threw open the window to the fire escape. The rain hadn't let up, and a sudden gust of wind carried it into the apartment.

"Baylis..." Nyla said. Their pursuer stepped in from the hall, his face hidden in shadow.

"I told you—" their mark said, voice growing firm. He strode toward Nyla and grabbed her by her shoulders. His grip faltered, and his gaze fell to his chest, where a jagged piece of ice protruded from his torso. Blood dripped from his lips onto the ice, staining its tip pink. He fell, exposing the man behind him.

Lukas had come himself.

That's odd, Baylis thought.

Lukas's thin lips pursed in obvious frustration. Baylis was certain Lukas hadn't expected resistance, and he wouldn't be happy the man he'd come for was lying dead at Nyla's feet—even if the killing blow had been his own.

Short in stature with wide shoulders, Lukas was a human pit bull. Colored tattoos of fire, water, and air rose from the collar of his shirt and extended up his neck. He kept his curly brown hair short and his face cleanly shaven.

Nyla retreated slowly, holding her hands in front of her in submission, like a person trying not to spook an aggressive dog. But Lukas wasn't a man who could be held back with submissiveness.

Baylis darted across the room, stepping in front of Nyla to shield her. "Get onto the fire escape," he said. "Make your way down and run. I'll catch up."

She started to say something, but he pushed her away. She should have known better than to distract him. The metal platform creaked ominously as she lunged through the window, but it held, and she quickly descended.

Baylis met Lukas's eye, weighing the man. Preventing a fight—or a scene—was impossible. The best Baylis could do was keep it confined to the apartment, away from the streets and away from the public and cameras. He wielded fire, projecting it into balls in each of his hands then hurled them at Lukas. Halfway across the room they collided, exploding into a single fireball. Then, wielding again, Baylis hit the fireball with a concussion of air that launched it across the room in a blink.

Lukas clapped his hands together then pulled them apart, stretching a shimmering wall of water between his palms. He caught the fireball, snuffing out the flames as he clapped his hands together again.

Baylis threw a chunk of ice, then a second smaller blast shaped like a chisel. The smaller ice blast cut into the larger, shattering it into dozens of pieces. There were too many for Lukas to counter. They sliced and burrowed into Lukas's flesh, and he stumbled into the hall. Baylis backed toward the fire escape, keeping an eye on Lukas. Nyla was waiting at the bottom. If Baylis raced down the fire escape while Lukas was stunned, he could escape.

"Run!" he screamed.

She hesitated then ran, disappearing into the dark alley they had emerged from before entering the apartment complex.

Lukas wiped blood from his face with the back of his hand. "Why do you fight when you've already lost?"

"I fight for our survival," Baylis said.

"As do I." Lukas stepped back into the apartment. "But as long as we live in the shadows, as long as we hide, we'll never survive."

"It's worked for centuries."

Lukas shook his head. "No. We're bleeding to death, and unless the wound is healed, we'll die."

"You are not our cleric, Lukas."

"No," Lukas said, "I am not." He threw his arms out wide, igniting fireballs in his hands. Lunging forward, he clapped them together, making the two fireballs one, which he flung across the room. "I am your surgeon."

Baylis threw an ice blast, striking the fireball in midair. The flames turned *inward,* and the fireball exploded, hurling Baylis out the window. He was only inches from the pavement by the time he oriented himself. He created a cushion of air between himself and the ground, and it kept him from dying, but not from blacking out from the pain. When Baylis regained consciousness, Lukas was standing over him.

"I'm sorry, Baylis. I wish it hadn't come to this."

Baylis coughed up blood. Hanging off the curb into the street, he was in a puddle of water. The cold was the only sensation he could feel beyond the pain in his chest. He couldn't move his arms or legs. His breathing was weak and sporadic, and he knew the end was near.

Lukas knelt, placing his hands on Baylis's chest. Baylis thought Lukas was going to heal him, but a magi couldn't do that. Only a cleric could.

Where is Nyla? A spasm of searing pain shot through his veins.

The first thing to go was his body heat. Already depleted from his repeated use of fire, he was quickly overtaken by shivers.

No!

The next thing to go was his water. Baylis's lips cracked as water was pulled from his body. His stomach twisted, rivaling the pain in his chest. Then, in a final draw of power, Lukas pulled the air from Baylis's body into his own. The world went black as the oxygen retreated from Baylis's brain. His last memory was of a smiling Lukas standing over him, looking rejuvenated and muttering to himself.

"Now, where is that cleric of yours?"

Nyla...

CHAPTER 1

ALLYN'S PHONE RANG FOR THE third time in as many minutes. His sister, Kendyl, was calling. Again. He knew he was late, but he couldn't do anything about that. Mr. Clarke, *the* named partner at Clarke, Poole, and Associates, was still in his office, so Allyn was still in his. So for the third time in as many minutes, Allyn ignored Kendyl's call, returning to the case file in front of him.

It was pushing eight o'clock—late to be working on a Saturday night—and the rest of the associates in the small but prestigious firm had retired for the evening, but Allyn had a reputation to uphold. He wasn't working a sexy case. *Hell, it isn't even particularly good looking.* But it was important to his client and, thus, important to him. Besides, it was better than chasing ambulances.

Mr. Clarke turned his office light off.

Thank God, Allyn thought. If he left right away, he would only be an hour late. He might still be able to talk his way out of this one.

Allyn watched as Mr. Clarke's silhouette grabbed his coat off the coat rack in the corner of his office and threw it over his arm. Burying his head back in his paperwork, Allyn waited for just the right moment when Mr. Clarke would pass his office on the way to the elevator. He hoped

Mr. Clarke would acknowledge him with a smile or a nod, anything to show him that his efforts were appreciated. When the squeaky footsteps told Allyn his boss was close, he looked up, hoping to catch Mr. Clark's eye.

He stopped in the doorway. His square face was clean-shaven, and his full hair was peppered with gray and parted to the side. He leaned against the doorframe, smiling, his blue eyes as piercing as ever. "You wouldn't be trying to impress me, would you, Mr. Kaplan?"

"No sir." Allyn suppressed a smile. It felt good to be noticed. "I have a lot of work to catch up on."

"A good lawyer can always tell when someone is lying."

Allyn smiled. "Okay. I'm guilty."

Mr. Clarke stepped into Allyn's office and took a seat in one of the leather armchairs in front of his desk. Sitting on *this* side of the desk felt weird.

Allyn's phone rang again. *Kendyl is going to kill me. Of all nights he wants to chat, it has to be tonight.*

"Well, I am impressed." Mr. Clarke crossed his legs. "You've been here for eleven months, and every day for eleven months, you've been the first to arrive and the last to leave."

He noticed. "I have?"

"Don't play coy. You know exactly what you've been doing."

"Sorry."

"Don't apologize, either. It obviously worked. You've caught my attention. Now, the question is, what are you going to do with it now that you have it?"

The leather creaked as Allyn shifted uncomfortably.

"You want to surprise me. Is that it?" Mr. Clarke asked.

"Something like that."

"I'm a lawyer, Mr. Kaplan. I don't like surprises."

Allyn's mouth went dry. His job was to know what to say and when to say it, but he was failing at it miserably.

Mr. Clarke burst into laughter. Allyn didn't know whether to pack his belongings or join in.

"Jesus fucking Christ, son." Mr. Clarke wiped his eyes. "I'm just pulling your leg. You need to get some sleep."

"Someday."

"I've seen a lot of first-year associates, Mr. Kaplan, but not as many second years. And that's the truth." Only a lawyer needed to quantify when he was telling the truth and when he wasn't. "Long hours are one thing. We encourage them. Hell, we expect them, but don't burn yourself out." Mr. Clarke stood to leave.

"I won't, sir," Allyn said. "I'll see you tomorrow."

"No you won't. You're to take tomorrow off. No arguments."

"I'm a lawyer, sir. Arguing comes naturally."

"Then save it for Monday."

"Yes, sir."

"And, Allyn?"

"Yes?"

"I'm still curious to see what you do with my attention." Mr. Clarke strode out of the room.

Allyn smiled. The eleven months leading up to tonight had been rough, but the real work, that was just beginning.

———— ••• ————

Kendyl sipped her drink like a woman who'd been stood up but didn't have the grace to leave. She sat with her back to the door, so she didn't see Allyn as he walked in. Her shoulder-length brown hair, which looked black in the dim light, was thrown over her shoulder. Bracelets and rings covered her wrists and fingers and lightly tapped against the glass as she dragged her finger around its rim. She apparently hadn't changed since she'd returned from the cabin, because she was still wearing a pair of loose-fitting jeans and a dusty black sweater. But that didn't stop a pair of gawkers from attempting to flirt with her from the other side of the bar.

Even at a distance, their resemblance was striking. Growing up, Allyn's buddies had always told him they could never date his sister because it would be too much like dating him. Allyn was fine with that. He was her older brother, if only by seventeen minutes, and protecting her was his job.

The lounge was like any number of bars Kendyl had dragged him to—cramped and filled with generations of hipsters smelling of sweat and patchouli oil. Stainless steel barstools circled the bar in the center of the lounge, and low-backed modern couches and chairs were tucked into the corners, offering feigned privacy.

As Kendyl turned and saw him, the light circling the bar accentuated her blue eyes. Allyn gave her a smile that was all lips and no teeth, and Kendyl turned back to her drink, visibly upset. "I can't believe you made me do that alone," she said as he approached.

Allyn set his briefcase between his feet and took a seat on the barstool she'd reserved for him. "I'm sorry. I got hung up."

"I called you."

"I know."

"Eight times."

"I know."

"What kind of person ignores eight phone calls?"

"Someone who's busy," Allyn said. "If I'm unavailable, then I'm unavailable. It wouldn't matter if you called me *eighty* times."

Kendyl pursed her lips. "You should always be available for family. And you could have called me back."

"You're right. I should have."

The bartender stopped in front of them. He was Kendyl's kind of man, with multiple piercings accompanied by tattoo sleeves on both arms. "Can I get you something?"

"I'll take a scotch, no ice," Allyn said. He'd never been a scotch drinker until the guys at the firm had gotten him started. These days, he didn't drink anything else. He turned back to his sister. "Look, I know I screwed up. I've made a habit out of that lately, and I'm sorry. You're the only family I've got left, so please just stick with me for a little while longer. Things will get back to the way they used to be. I promise."

"I've heard that speech before," Kendyl said, but the heat in her voice was gone.

"It's because I meant it."

The bartender returned, setting the drink in front of Allyn, who nodded his thanks and took a sip.

"How did the meeting go?"

Kendyl bit back a smile. "It was beautiful up there, even more so than I remembered. The trees are bare, so if you climb to the top of the hill, you can see out into the canyon and watch the sun set behind the hills."

"Did the Realtor find it as beautiful as you?"

"She said it was a lovely property."

"Worth?"

"Four hundred. Four-fifty if we do a few things first. She made a list."

Allyn whistled. *Four hundred and fifty thousand dollars.* Kendyl handed him the Realtor's list. "Looks pretty straightforward," he said, scanning the list. "I can pay the upfront costs as long as you pay me back after it sells."

"Allyn—"

"And we'll have to hire someone to do it. I don't have time to be painting and landscaping."

"Hey, listen to me—"

Allyn playfully slapped Kendyl on the back. "Four hundred and fifty thousand! That's more than I thought it was worth."

"I don't want to sell anymore."

Allyn coughed. "What?"

"I said I want to hold on to the house."

"Kendyl—"

"It's amazing up there, Allyn. Magical. I found a piece of myself I forgot a long time ago, and I don't want to lose that again." She took his hands in hers. "Go up there with me and see for yourself."

Allyn shook his head. He couldn't believe what he was hearing. *Who walks away from that kind of money?* Sometimes, he just didn't understand his sister. "When?"

Kendyl shrugged. "Tomorrow?"

Mr. Clarke did tell you to take the day off. "I have to work."

"Who works on Sundays?"

He pulled his hands from hers. "Those of us who want to succeed."

She tried to hide the annoyed look on her face with a smile. "So what are we going to do? I don't want to sell, you do, and we can't do anything unless we both sign off on it."

That's the question, isn't it? They'd inherited the family cabin after their mother passed, with the stipulation that if they ever sold it, they would both have to agree. Allyn could probably fight his mother's will, but he would sooner hold on to the property than try to pry it away from his sister.

"I've got an idea." He took another sip. The scotch warmed his chest. Drinking on an empty stomach was dangerous—his face was already growing tingly. "Why don't you buy me out?"

Kendyl barked a laugh. "I can't afford that."

"The house was appraised at four, four-fifty. If you buy me out at two, that's what? Eleven hundred a month? Twelve? How much is your rent right now?"

"Eight hundred."

"Perfect!" Allyn slapped the bar emphatically. "Get one or two of your artist friends to move in with you, charge them four hundred a month, and you'll actually *save* money." This seemed to give her pause, so Allyn rolled forward. "Or make it an artists' retreat. Rent rooms by the night. Who knows? You might be able to live rent free and keep the house."

"Don't do that."

"Do what?"

"Sell me on it."

Allyn cursed under his breath. He'd misread her. "I'm just trying to find a way to help you keep the house."

"No, you're trying to find a way to walk away guilt free."

How does she do that? "That's not fair. I don't want to get rid of it either, okay? I have a lot of good memories up there, but the house is neglected, and it's falling apart. Let another family buy it and create memories of their own."

"This is the only thing of Mom we have left. You can't put a price on that."

"Apparently, you can." Allyn knocked back the rest of his scotch. "Four hundred thousand."

"Don't be an ass."

"You don't want to be sold. I don't want to be guilt-tripped."

"Fine."

An uncomfortable silence fell between them.

The gawkers at the end of the bar had swooped in on a pair of unsuspecting women. They didn't appear to be having much luck there, either.

Allyn exhaled deeply. He and his sister had always been close growing up, but they had become inseparable after their mother's death. With no one else to turn to, they had turned to each other, but something had changed since Allyn had started at Clarke, Poole, and Associates.

He thought it had something to do with the hours. They'd rarely gone more than a day without talking. Lately, they went weeks, and when they did talk, Kendyl avoided talking about work as though it were religion or politics, which they also didn't see eye to eye on. *What does she think I do? I may not be changing political policy or fighting for social equality, but I'm not chasing ambulances, either. What I do has value to my clients, and that means something to me.*

The bartender came back to drop off their bills. "There's no rush," he said, but the way his eyes flickered to the patrons waiting behind them suggested otherwise.

Allyn pulled his wallet out and grabbed both bills.

"You don't have to do that," Kendyl said, her voice tight.

"I want to."

A moment later, the bartender took the bills and Allyn's credit card. Allyn looked at Kendyl, cocking his head to the side sympathetically. "I'm serious, you know. If you want my half of the house, it's yours. I can cover you until you find a roommate or start renting rooms. So just think about it. I'd feel better knowing you were enjoying it instead of a family of strangers."

Kendyl nodded. "Okay."

Allyn waited until the bartender returned with his card to say goodbye. Leaving the bar, he wondered where he'd gone wrong.

His condo, part of a new housing development that wasn't completed, was three miles away. Tractors and work trucks were parked in front of foundations and framed townhomes, ready to begin work again Monday. As one of the first to move into the neighborhood, Allyn had bought cheap, but he still had to deal with the construction noise and a dirty jobsite—an equal trade-off since he left for the office before the construction workers arrived and returned home long after they'd left.

The garage was on the ground level, with the kitchen,

dining room, and living room taking up the second floor to create an open-concept great room. The third floor had two bedrooms: the master, with an en suite bathroom, and a spare room complete with a double bed, an extra dresser, and its own full bathroom. As a single man in his late twenties who spent far more time at the office than at home, Allyn wasn't overly concerned with furnishings or decorations. He would worry about that later, when he had time to enjoy it or someone to enjoy it with.

He threw his jacket over the arm of the couch and emptied the contents of his pockets onto the coffee table before rounding the corner to the stairs leading to the third story. Allyn gasped, his breath catching in his throat.

Silent and unmoving, an intruder stood atop the stairwell, gazing down upon him. The whites of his eyes burned through the darkness, but shadows hid his face. Allyn's feet felt like they were encased in concrete, too heavy to move. The man crept toward him, making no effort to conceal himself. He had light skin, dark eyes, and curly brown hair.

Not until the man was only two steps in front of Allyn did he realize that he couldn't move. An invisible weight was pushing his feet to the ground, while a similar force pressed against his back, preventing him from retreating.

The man circled Allyn, sizing him up. Even standing a step below him, Allyn was taller. "I expected more," the man said softly, his voice a soft tenor.

"What do you want?" Allyn asked, his voice shaking.

"You."

An invisible force slammed into Allyn's chest, throwing him into the wall. He landed on his hands and knees. The edges of his vision grew dark as blood poured from the back of his head where it had struck the wall. Coughing and struggling to catch his breath, Allyn rose to his feet. His chest hurt as though he'd been punched, and the darkness crept in farther, threatening him with unconsciousness.

Another explosion of air sent him crashing into the dining room table. It collapsed under him. The intruder stepped toward him. Allyn pushed himself up, ready to run. His wrist popped and gave out in excruciating pain. Allyn snatched a broken chair leg and threw it from his knees. It veered off course unnaturally, harmlessly striking a poster on the wall.

Cursing, Allyn rose to his feet and let out a pained breath. Waiting for the inevitable, he watched as the man strode toward him. He didn't have to wait long. When the final blow struck, he crashed through the sliding glass doors and over the railing, to the pavement two stories below. Death rushed up to greet him.

Allyn never felt the impact.

CHAPTER 2

DEATH WASN'T AS PEACEFUL AS Allyn had expected. It was loud, bright, and painful. He had expected eternal darkness, but dreams came in a chaotic mix of sounds, images, and feelings that were all alien to him. He heard unfamiliar voices and tried to call to them, but he couldn't form the words. He could grunt, but even that was difficult and painful, but from time to time, it was received with a gentle touch. Allyn didn't know whom the voices or gentle touches belonged to, but he liked them— they made him feel better.

Death wasn't at all what he'd expected. It was neither love and peace nor pain and misery. It wasn't heaven or hell. It simply *was*. So when the world around him finally coalesced in a blurry mess, he wasn't surprised to find that he wasn't dead at all.

Allyn blinked and wiped the moisture from his eyes, trying to focus on his surroundings. He was in the largest hospital room he had ever been in. An armchair beside his bed faced a large window with deep red curtains thrust open to reveal a dense forest. The hospital was on a hill, which meant it must be OHSU since that was the only Portland hospital that escaped the urban sprawl. He thought that if he leaned forward, he might be able to see over those trees, but the sunlight gave him a headache.

The bed was surprisingly comfortable with a down comforter, fine cotton sheets, and four feather pillows. He didn't have an IV or a heart monitor, so he assumed he must be past the critical stage. Allyn sat up, blankets falling away from his chest. He was *naked*.

What the hell? He searched his bed for the call button but couldn't find it. "Hey!" he yelled. "Hey, I need some help in here!" *And some clothes.*

Silence.

"Hello?" Still no answer. "Hello?" He screamed with more urgency.

The door opened, and a short, slender woman entered. She was roughly his age, with porcelain skin and silver hair. Instead of nurse scrubs, she wore a black compression shirt and matching pants.

Allyn pulled the blanket higher, covering himself.

"You're awake," she said, her voice as cold as her eyes. "How are you feeling?"

"Where am I?"

"You're safe. You were in an accident." She took his wrist firmly, feeling his pulse with her fingers.

He stirred uncomfortably as a tingle shot down his legs. "I remember," he said, trying to focus on something other than the tingling. "A man broke into my condo and attacked me. It's not an easy thing to forget."

"I suppose it's not." She looked at him skeptically but let go of his hand. "I'm going to press against your arms and legs and back to check your muscular response. If it's painful, I want you to say something, okay?"

He nodded.

She started with his feet, squeezing the arch of his foot. Then after he nodded, telling her that he was pain free, she moved on to his heel, then his ankle and calf.

"What's your name?" Allyn asked.

"Nyla."

"How am I doing, Nyla?"

"How do you feel?"

"Honestly? I feel great, considering I was shoved out a second-story window."

She looked at him in a cold, clinical, businesslike manner. "You're lucky to be alive."

"I don't think luck had anything to do with it," Allyn said.

"Oh?" She stopped at his thigh, her eyebrow raised.

"I'm sure you're very good at your job."

She started probing again, moving up to his chest, wincing as she pushed down on his lower rib cage.

Allyn stiffened in pain.

"Sorry," she said. "You've got some bruising."

Allyn exhaled deeply. "It's okay." His eyes drifted down her neck as she leaned over him to check the other side of his chest. He winced but was prepared for the pain that time. A small necklace dragged across his bare chest as she pulled back, rubbing her hands together.

"You're suffering from a minor concussion and have extensive bruising along your chest and upper torso, probably from the impact."

The simple design—a series of intertwined shapes of red, blue, and white—reminded him of something. The red piece looked like fire, and the blue piece could have been a water droplet.

"Your back is worse. The pain in your chest and torso is an impact wound, so to speak, a shock from the impact. The injury on your back is the exit wound, and that's where your most serious bruising is located."

Kendyl liked vintage jewelry and would probably wear something like Nyla's necklace. *Was she wearing something like that during dinner?*

"With some rest and some anti-inflammatory medication, you should be just fine."

No, it wasn't Kendyl. She had been wearing her usual assortment of mismatched rings and bracelets, but Allyn couldn't remember her wearing a necklace. *Then what the hell does it remind me of?*

"We should have you on your way home soon," she said with a lifeless smile. Without waiting for a response, she turned for the door. Her necklace reflected the sunlight, sending small circles of gold dancing across his chest like a tattoo that had come to life.

Tattoos.

The man who'd attacked Allyn had the same symbols tattooed on his neck.

Allyn looked around the room with a renewed interest. It was empty and bland, but not clinical. Where were the white sheets? Where were the railings on the bed? Where was the wash station or his medical chart? Where were the trashcans and hazardous waste buckets? Monitors? Sterile medical equipment?

Where the hell am I? Where was the doctor? Where were the police to take his statement? Nyla had only told him he was safe, not where he was. Something was wrong.

I haven't been saved. I've been abducted.

Allyn sat up and swung his legs to the side of the bed. Touching his bare feet to the cold floor, he slowly put weight on his legs. They strained, shaking with fatigue, but not painfully.

Why didn't I ask how long I've been here? He pulled the top sheet off the bed and wrapped it around his naked body. He held it around himself like a towel as he walked silently toward the door.

He placed his ear against the door. Outside the room, it was quiet. If this were a hospital he would hear patients, nurses, and doctors. Beds would be rolling past, taking people to and from surgery or recovery. There would be commotion, not silence.

Allyn opened the door to a dark hallway. Other doors, identical to his own, lined the walls on either side. Lamps burned softly, like candles, next to each one. The hall ended in a T to his left. To his right, the hall opened into a sitting room partially furnished with high-backed chairs and a brick fireplace.

Faint voices came from the sitting room, but they were too quiet for Allyn to make out. Reckless curiosity overtook him. He slipped out of his room and inched down the hallway toward the voices, and using the corner of the wall as a barrier, he peeked around.

Nyla sat in one of the chairs, engaged in a conversation with another person whose back was to Allyn. The person leaned forward to pat Nyla on the knee. It was a man, older, and clean-shaven with gray peppering his dark-brown hair.

Allyn leaned forward, straining to hear what they were saying, when his ankle popped. Nyla's eyes flashed to him. He ducked behind the corner. "Shit."

"Why don't you come on out, Allyn," the man said, his voice deep and slow. The voice of authority. "This might be a more worthwhile conversation if you take part instead of eavesdropping."

Allyn turned to flee down the hall and ran directly into a wall. No, not a wall—a *man*. Allyn's face hit his chest. The man was a full foot taller than he was, with large round eyes, cropped hair, and charcoal skin. His sleeveless black leather shirt exposed his powerful arms. His expressionless face was hidden behind a closely trimmed beard.

Allyn staggered back, retreating into the sitting room. The man followed him, never breaking eye contract. Allyn's heel caught on a rug, and he tumbled onto his back. Still, the mountain of a man crept toward him like a predator in human skin.

Looming over Allyn, the man reached down with an open hand and waited.

He's helping me up. With a shaking hand, Allyn took the man's arm and was pulled to his feet.

"I'm sorry," the large man said, his voice deep, but warm. "I didn't mean to scare you."

"Why don't you help him to a chair, Jaxon," the older man said. He smiled at Allyn, though it did little to calm his nerves.

Jaxon led him to the high-backed chair beside Nyla then stood beside the older man, his arms crossed. The older man sat back down, watching Allyn, and traced his lips with his finger.

"I assume you probably have a lot of questions," the older man began. "But first, let me welcome you to my home. My name is Graeme. You've already met Nyla and Jaxon. We were hoping you could answer a few questions for us."

"If I answer your questions, can I go?"

"That depends."

"On what?"

Graeme smiled. "On your answers."

Is he serious? Allyn licked his lips. "I don't know." *I don't know if I can trust you.*

"It's only a few questions."

"I need to know that I won't be harmed."

"You have my word." The old man seemed amused.

Allyn looked at Nyla and Jaxon. They both leaned forward slightly, their faces expressionless, eager to hear what he had to say. They didn't strike him as dangerous— well, not immediately dangerous. And both had been kind to him, even if Nyla had been cold. "What do you want to know?"

"What do you remember about your attack?"

How did they know it was an attack and not a burglary?

"I came home and found a man in my condo. He attacked me and threw me out the window."

"Did he ask you anything?"

"No."

"Take anything?"

"Not that I know of."

"Was there anything... unusual about the attack?" Graeme leaned forward even farther. If he moved too much farther, he would fall off the chair.

"Not that I remember." *What about the invisible force that held your feet to the ground? Or the way he threw you against the wall and across the room without ever touching you?*

"You said he threw you..." Jaxon said.

"I didn't jump, if that's what you're asking."

"Are you sure?" Jaxon pressed.

Of course I'm sure. He didn't remember the man *physically* picking him up and throwing him out the window, but he had no other explanation for it. He had to have been thrown. But a small voice in the back of his mind said otherwise. The last thing Allyn remembered seeing before he busted through the window was the man standing in the center of the living room. The man couldn't have thrown him. *But that has to be a symptom of the concussion, right?* Just because he couldn't remember it happening didn't mean it didn't.

"Did he have anything like these?" Graeme asked, rolling up his sleeve. Three evenly spaced scars ran from his shoulder to his elbow. *Not scars,* Allyn decided. They were more like tattoos that rose from the skin. *Brands.* Graeme rolled up his other sleeve, exposing a matching set of brands on his other arm, then looked at Jaxon. He had a similar set on his arms, though instead of the pink like Graeme's, Jaxon's brands looked white against his dark skin. The top one ran across his upper arm and looked like a crude symbol for water, with four wavy horizontal lines stacked on top of each other. The jagged lines of the bottom brand near his elbow looked like fire. Allyn couldn't make out the other. *Air?*

Allyn looked at Nyla. The embellishments on her necklace matched the brands on the men's arms. "I don't know, but he did have tattoos on his neck that looked something like those."

Graeme leaned back, disapproval on his face. He rubbed his chin. "His name is Lukas."

"Who is he?"

"He's dangerous," Graeme said. "To both of us."

"What does he want?"

"I don't know." Graeme stood and walked to the fireplace, clasping his hands behind his back. "You've been thrust into something you don't understand, Allyn. A world you never knew existed. I don't know what Lukas wants with you, but I'm going to find out. Will you help me?"

"Why would I do that?"

"Because we saved you." Graeme's words echoed off the coffered ceiling. "You're a man of the law, Allyn, and I suppose you require proof, but the only proof I have is your own body. You were cast out a second-story window onto pavement, and yet here you sit, talking to me, alive and without any serious injuries. Explain this to me."

Had this man actually saved him? Graeme was right—he should be dead, and Allyn didn't have an answer for that. But he didn't know these people or what they were capable of, and they were somehow connected to his attacker. And that made him nervous. It could all be a ploy to earn his trust. They would act as the savior while really being the opposite.

"I can't explain it," Allyn said, "but that doesn't change the fact that I don't know who you are, either. How do I know if I can trust *you?*"

"We *saved* you, Allyn."

"So you keep saying," Allyn said, "but I don't do business when I don't know all the facts, and you're obviously hiding something."

"What happens when Lukas returns to finish the job?" Jaxon asked.

Allyn didn't have an answer for that. "I'll figure it out." He didn't believe the attacker would come back anyway.

Graeme nodded to Nyla. She got to her feet and placed a hand on Allyn's shoulder.

"If this is business, Allyn, then it's the business of life and death, and you just made a bad investment." Graeme nodded to Nyla again and strode out of the room, Jaxon at his shoulder.

Allyn felt a pinch on his shoulder, and the room went dark.

CHAPTER 3

A SHARP JOLT BROUGHT ALLYN BACK to consciousness. A door slammed, an engine roared, and tires squealed. The hot, muggy air had a dull odor. Sweat beaded on his forehead. He licked his dry lips, his tongue brushing against something rough.

A hood covered his head.

Allyn pulled the hood off, catching sight of a black sedan screeching through a stop sign. He was sitting on the sidewalk of a private street. Mid-level BMWs, Mercedes, Lexus, and Acuras were parked along the curb and in the driveways of condos and apartments. A tractor was parked in the field across the street, ready to continue construction the following morning.

He was home.

Suddenly self-conscious, Allyn looked down at himself. He was fully clothed. At least his abductors—or saviors— had the decency to return him fully dressed. The clothes weren't his, though. They had replaced his black business suit with a pair of loose-fitting trousers and a thin, neutral-colored three-quarter-sleeve shirt. He looked like a hipster, and he hated to admit it was comfortable. More importantly, he found his keys and wallet, complete with all his credit cards, in his pocket.

The garage door to his left opened, and his neighbor wheeled out a green garbage can. Others already lined the street. That meant it was still Sunday. Only a day had passed since the attack.

One day.

It felt so much longer than that. He'd spent most of the time unconscious and the rest of it confused. It felt good to be home, somewhere familiar, where things made sense. Allyn nodded to the neighbor and walked up the driveway to his condo.

It was cold inside. The sliding glass door was open—no, it was broken. Shattered glass covered the floor. He would have to get a tarp or something to cover the door until he could get someone out to fix it.

Memory of the attack flooded back to him: seeing him on the stairs, being unable to move, feeling powerless, and the intruder's apology. What kind of person apologized before trying to kill someone? It didn't make sense, but what did? He was alive, and that was all that mattered. Alive and alone. Or was he? Could the intruder be waiting for him?

Allyn's breathing quickened. Shadows seemed to grow longer and darker, providing an intruder with ample space to hide. What was that dark mass behind the couch? There was a creak on the stairs. Was that someone breathing?

You're paranoid, Allyn told himself. *You're alone. The condo is empty.*

The stairs were empty. Allyn took them two at a time and rounded the corner into his bedroom. The bed was made, and the room was clean—the way the downstairs should have been. The blinds were closed, shrouding the room in darkness. He sat on the foot of the bed and exhaled a long, slow, stress-erasing breath. His head dipped in exhaustion. *How could I still be tired?* He yawned. It felt good to be home.

The room around him disappeared.

Beep! Beep! Beep! Beep! Beep!

Monday. Time for work. *When did I fall asleep?*

For the first time in a long time, Allyn thought about calling in sick. The world had changed, and it was too much to take in. The thought of dwelling on someone else's problems when his own were so much more complicated was frustrating. *Who cares about dog custody agreements or bickering ex-spouses? I just got thrown out a window and was saved by a shadowy group of strangers who hint at being able to do things the rest of us think impossible.*

He needed to talk to someone. He called his sister.

The phone rang several times before the call went to voicemail. It was early, but Kendyl might be in her studio or at work or, more likely, still sleeping. Allyn left a short message asking her to call him back when she got the chance. Then, without knowing what else to do, he got ready for work.

He arrived later than normal, and his boss and a few coworkers were already in the office. Mr. Clarke nodded to him from his office as Allyn entered. *What are you going to do now that you have my attention?* Mr. Clarke had asked the last time they'd spoken. Allyn hadn't planned on showing up late. *He probably thinks I'm slacking off. I'll have to work even harder to make up the lost ground.*

He took a little while to get going. His mind was sluggish and resisted the mental workout, but once he worked himself into a groove, someone else's stress began to replace his. The day became a blur of paperwork and meetings, and with it went his memories of the attack, and the strange occurrences thereafter faded. He needed a distraction, and work was the best kind. Each client was an escape.

He worked through lunch and was well into the afternoon before he took so much as a bathroom break.

He didn't eat. He didn't drink. He just worked. The sun was on the western horizon when his stomach began to gurgle. Scents of spicy chicken and takeout filled the office. Several coworkers were eating in, it seemed, which meant Allyn would, too.

He ordered pizza from a small pizza joint around the corner. They didn't normally deliver, but Allyn ate there frequently enough that they made an exception for him. Before returning to his desk, he made sure to tip the delivery guy, who was a surprisingly muscular high school kid with an acne problem. Grease pooled on top of the pepperoni and mozzarella, and the thin, doughy crust drooped when Allyn held it up, forcing him to fold it in half and eat it like a taco. It was delicious.

Allyn checked his messages, expecting to see a missed call from Kendyl, but she hadn't called. *That's weird.* He scrolled through his contacts and called her again, and for the second time that day, his call went to voicemail, this time without ever ringing. *Payback. She called you eight times, and you never answered. She's proving a point.*

He finished his slice of pizza and got back to work.

Life returned to normal as Allyn settled back into his daily routine. Up early, home late, and life in the office dominated the rest. His clients' problems became his own, and he was once again on the path to becoming a partner. By Wednesday, two days after his return to his normal life, Kendyl still hadn't called, and he got a little anxious. He left her two more messages, each more agitated than the last, pleading with her to call him back. When Thursday arrived without a word from her, he began to worry. By Friday, he was in a panic. He wasn't going to wait for her to call him back. He was going to go over there and talk to her in person.

Kendyl's apartment was in northeast Portland, a single block off Burnside in a trendy, gentrified pocket community with nice boutique ships, small diners, and coffee shops. Allyn hated it. He didn't care how hip the neighborhood was; the surrounding area was plagued with escalating gang activity and violent crime. What Kendyl considered cultured, he considered questionable.

It was well into the evening by the time he made it to her neighborhood. He parked a block away, in the parking lot of a closed coffee shop called A Better Cup. A group of men with soiled clothes and greasy hair stood at the bus stop, talking through missing teeth. They ignored him as he passed by.

Her parking space was empty, but that didn't mean anything since Kendyl didn't own a car. The couple who lived above her rented her space for their second vehicle. Allyn quickened his step so that he was almost jogging through the complex. He sighed in relief when he saw her bike locked to the stairwell. She was home, and knowing she was safe felt good. He almost turned around and left, but he stepped up to the door and knocked. When she didn't answer, he knocked louder. She still didn't answer.

Beating on the door, he called to her. "Kendyl! Kendyl, open up! It's your brother."

Nothing.

He pressed his ear against the door. Maybe her TV was too loud or she was in the shower or listening to music. He didn't hear anything. She could be out for a walk. No, even if Kendyl thought her trendy neighborhood was cultured, she wasn't stupid. *Naïve maybe, but not stupid.* He knocked again.

"Kendyl, please open up. It's me. I just want to talk. Please let me in."

The door behind him creaked open, and a middle-aged woman stepped out. She wore a set of mismatched cotton pajamas, and her bleach-blond hair was tied into a ponytail atop her head.

"Sorry," Allyn said. "I didn't mean to wake you up."

"Did you say you were her brother?" the woman asked. Her voice was thick and raspy, damaged by too many years of smoking.

"Yes," Allyn said. "Do you know Kendyl?"

"Yeah." She pulled the door closed behind her. "I'm Rebecca."

"Have you seen her lately?"

"No. I haven't seen her in almost a week."

Allyn shook his head. "How often do you normally see her?"

"Often enough," she said. "I heard her fighting with her boyfriend the other night."

"Her boyfriend?"

Kendyl didn't have a boyfriend, not that she had told him about anyway. They weren't as close as they used to be.

"Yeah, a shorter guy, stocky, with tattoos on his neck." She nervously rubbed the side of her face with the back of her fingers. "I haven't seen her since."

Allyn's blood froze. Short. Stocky. Tattoos on his neck. He knew exactly whom she was talking about. He turned and kicked the metal door. It didn't move. He kicked again. The wooden frame groaned against the impact, but it still didn't open.

"What are you doing?" Rebecca asked.

Allyn ignored her, continuing to beat the door with his foot. It remained shut, taunting him. He began to panic. The door wouldn't budge, but he had to get into that apartment. He checked for a hidden key under the welcome mat, on top of the doorframe, and in the vase in the corner. Nothing.

"What are you looking for?" Rebecca asked.

Without a key, the door would have to come down. He backed up a few feet and charged, throwing his shoulder into the door. Pain shot through his shoulder, then his arm went numb, and still, the door remained shut. Allyn became furious. Someone was after him. He'd been attacked and abducted, but he'd never told Kendyl. *Stupid.* She was in danger and it was his fault.

Fury spreading through his veins like adrenaline, Allyn charged the door again. This time, he buried his foot inches from the frame. The door burst open, wooden shrapnel exploding into the air, and the door hung awkwardly on a single broken hinge.

"Call 9-1-1," he shouted, charging into the apartment.

The apartment opened into the kitchen. Moldy dishes covered the yellow Formica countertop, and an army of ants marched from the sink, down the cupboard into the living space, and disappeared into the stained carpet. The smell of spoiled meat hung in the air, and Allyn covered his nose with the crook of his arm.

"Kendyl?"

Silence.

Allyn's frantic pace slowed. He became more cautious and observant. The apartment was a small studio with the bed tucked around the corner. Blankets covered the bed, hanging onto the floor in disarray. Clothes had been thrown about and were hanging off chairs, stacked on the couch, and littered the floor. None of the windows or pieces of furniture was broken. He saw nothing that would suggest an attack. And that gave him hope. But she wasn't there. And the same intruder who'd attacked him had been in her apartment.

He was sure she'd been abducted, and it was his fault. He should have warned her. He had to get her back. How? *Think, Allyn. You know who took her, and that's an important first step.*

Allyn exited the apartment, a plan forming in his head.

"Where are you going?" Rebecca called after him. "You're leaving the scene of a crime!"

He knew he was breaking the law, but he didn't care. He had to find his sister, and he couldn't do that while answering police questions. He couldn't go to the police at all. What would he say? *I was recently attacked by a man with supernatural abilities, thrown from a second-story window, only to be saved by another shadowy group of people. No, I don't have any proof. No, I didn't go to the hospital. No, I didn't file a police report.* That wouldn't go over well. They would never take him seriously. The police wouldn't be any help, but he knew who would be.

More of Kendyl's neighbors had gathered outside her apartment. Most were dressed in sweats or shorts with mismatched tops, as though they had been woken up by the disturbance. They grabbed at him, trying to prevent him from leaving. Sirens blared in the distance. Someone had called the police—probably Kendyl's neighbor. He fought through the crowd, slapping back grasping hands and shoving a few of the more forceful people out of his way.

Breaking through the last of them, Allyn quickened his step. From the corner of his eye, he saw a man break away from the crowd to follow him. He was about Allyn's height and build and wasn't wearing pajamas like the rest. His clothes were dark and blended into the dimly lit surroundings. He called out to Allyn.

Allyn broke into a run. The man followed. Allyn cut through the parking lot, slipping between cars and dashing into the street. Instead of turning back toward Burnside, the way he'd come, he went the opposite direction into a residential area.

The man, still following, called out to him again.

Allyn pushed himself harder, sprinting down the street. The man's footsteps became more faint. Allyn rounded the corner onto another street. Just a couple blocks removed from Burnside, the street was quiet and lined with fully grown trees and a small patch of grass between the road and the sidewalk.

Allyn's breathing became heavy. He couldn't remember the last time he'd run so far, and he knew he couldn't keep up the pace. He needed somewhere to hide, and he needed to get there quickly, before the man caught up to him. He chose a dark space in front of a rusty old pickup, where the streetlight had burned out. Crouching with his hands on the oxidized hood, Allyn watched the intersection through the truck's windshield.

He heard the man's footsteps before he saw him. He ran into the middle of the four-way intersection and stopped, whipping his head back and forth, checking all directions. He raked his fingers through his hair then planted them on his hips.

He looked in Allyn's direction. Allyn knew the man couldn't see him, but he crouched farther down anyway. "Go back," Allyn whispered. "You lost me. Give up."

The man looked in the opposite direction, seemingly deciding between the two.

"There you go, go that way, you'll find me over there," Allyn encouraged softly. But the man turned back to Allyn and started down the street. "Damn."

The man walked with a slow, observant pace, hunting. Allyn couldn't outrun him, and something about the man's confident walk told Allyn he probably didn't want to fight him, either. He'd have to wait it out, hope that the man would pass his hiding spot and allow Allyn to double back in the opposite direction.

Allyn quietly stepped around the hood of the truck to the passenger-side door, watching through the window. The man was nearing him, still walking down the center of the street, his head on a swivel as he scanned both sides of the road. A soft rustling noise came from the other side of the street, and the man jerked his head toward it. The sound stopped as quickly as it came, but the man went to investigate. He walked to the opposite side of the road and circled the white sedan where the noise had originated, checking both sides, in front and behind it, even *under* it.

He's looking for my feet, Allyn realized. They were exposed from the knee down under the frame of the truck. If the man just looked... Allyn backed onto the curb and stepped onto a tree root, leaning forward against the truck as though he were doing an inclined pushup. The metal door creaked under the pressure.

The man stood up with a start.

"No, no, no, no, no," Allyn whispered.

The man made for the old pickup, quickening his pace. Allyn followed his eyes up to the burnt-out streetlight.

He knows, Allyn thought, *He knows this is a good place to hide. He knows I'm here.*

Throwing all pretense aside, Allyn backed away from the truck, exposing himself. Damp grass softened his footfalls, but the man saw him. Allyn tried to form a story in his head. Why had he run? How would he explain that to this man? How would he explain it to the police? The facts were on his side, and the law would prevail. It would just be a little awkward at first. Allyn's resolve began to solidify as he built his case in his head.

"There you are," the man said. "I thought I'd lost you." His voice was slow and confident. His dark hair and eyes were a stark contrast to his pale skin. He stepped onto the curb approaching Allyn. "Don't run. I just want to talk."

Allyn backed away slowly. "I didn't break into that apartment. My sister lives there, and she's in trouble. I'm trying to find her."

"It's okay," the man said.

"No, it's not. I need to find her."

The man took another step toward Allyn. "What if I told you I knew where she was? I promise she's safe. Come with me and find out."

Allyn stopped. This man wasn't a concerned neighbor or a well-meaning citizen. He was one of *them*—the same people who'd attacked him. "Stay away from me!"

"Don't you want to see your sister?" He stepped closer to Allyn.

"Help! Please! Anybody!" Allyn shouted.

"What is wrong with you?" The man eyed the surrounding houses. Their windows remained dark. "I'm offering you a chance to see your sister, see that she's okay, help her."

"Call the police! Please! Anybody!"

"Don't. Do. That!" The man leaped forward, his muscles tight, eyes burning.

Allyn shielded his face with his arms, waiting for the blow to land.

"No!" someone screamed.

Allyn was thrown into a nearby yard, landing softly onto wet grass, his elbow slapping against an exposed sprinkler head.

A dark figure landed on top of him. Chin-length black hair hid her face. She was tall and slender, and her clothing was as dark as her hair. "Come on." She rolled to her feet and pulled him up. He didn't have time to ask questions before she pushed him forward. "Go!"

A bright flash of orange light illuminated the street behind Allyn. Two men, Allyn's pursuer and Jaxon, were in the center of the street, fifty paces apart. A ball of orange light, alive, wisps of light clawing away from itself, flew through the air toward the stranger.

No. Not light. Fire.

The man clasped his hands together and opened them again, an opaque blue liquid filling the space between his hands. *Is that water?* The fireball hit the wall of water, making a hiss like cold water running onto a hot pan. Then in one fluid motion, the man spun, whipping his arms around, and threw another fireball. It was smaller in diameter and traveled slower, but it burned brighter. The man swung his hands together, clapping them in front of his chest, and the fireball erupted into a wall, six feet tall and twice as wide, that streaked toward Jaxon.

Jaxon dove behind a parked car, narrowly escaping the inferno. The smoking bottoms of his boots filled the air with the scent of burnt rubber.

The man turned from Jaxon, his eyes flashing to Allyn.

"Go!" Jaxon shouted from behind the car. "Leira, go!"

"Move!" Leira ordered, pushing Allyn away from the melee.

"What about Jaxon?"

"He can take care of himself."

Allyn disagreed. Jaxon looked outmatched. As he emerged from behind the car, his forearms were scraped and bloodied. But what could Allyn do to help? He couldn't compete with that display of... He didn't even know what to call it.

Leira pulled him away from the fray. Allyn turned to follow, and together, they ran for several blocks before turning down an alleyway. Cars parked in front of fences and backyards lined both sides of the narrow alley. Allyn bent over and put his head between his knees, struggling to catch his breath.

"We told you that you were in danger," Leira said. She wasn't even winded. "We told you they would come after you again. You could have gotten yourself killed!"

He couldn't run from it anymore. He couldn't blame head trauma, an unreliable memory, or some sort of trick. These people weren't *normal*. "Who are you?" he asked between breaths. "*What* are you?"

Her mouth opened, but nothing came out.

"I saw..." *What did I see? Fire exploding out of a man's hands? Water? Magic?* He rubbed his eyes. "I'm going crazy."

"You're not going crazy."

"They have my sister," he said quietly. The words hung in the air. He couldn't escape them.

"Who has your sister?" she asked, suddenly alert. "Lukas?"

"What does he want with us?"

"I don't know."

"You were following me. You knew they'd come back for me."

Leira nodded.

"You should have followed my sister."

"We didn't know about her." The words cut deep.

"Who is Lukas? How do you know him?"

Leira winced. "He's... family."

"Family?" He wasn't completely surprised. He had seen dozens of families torn apart by legal litigation. Money was generally the dividing factor. Who deserved what was always in dispute, but he doubted money was the root of this feud. Her story made sense, too. They had to be family. Their abilities would be hereditary, passed down through generations like heart disease or diabetes.

"We need to get back to the car. This changes everything."

Allyn reluctantly agreed. The police couldn't help, but Graeme and his family might be able to. He just worried about what kind of deal he would have to make with them.

Jaxon was already waiting for them by the time Allyn and Leira made it back to the car. It was parked in a similar alley a couple blocks away. He was leaning against the black sedan, wrapping his arm in gauze. The reds, oranges, and blacks of his charred flesh screamed painfully even if Jaxon did not.

Leira strode forward, reaching for Jaxon's arm. "We should do something about that."

"It's fine." Jaxon pulled away.

Leira recoiled. She obviously wasn't used to being rebuffed. "Where's Reyland?"

"Gone."

"You killed him?" Allyn asked. He couldn't believe how nonchalant Jaxon was about it.

Jaxon finished wrapping his arm and tossed the roll of gauze into the car. "He got away."

Leira stiffened and scanned their surroundings uneasily. She had seemed almost relieved by the idea that the man was dead. But now she was on the alert again. "We should go."

"One minute," Jaxon said, pulling away from the car and stepping toward Allyn.

Leira grabbed Jaxon's good arm, stopping him. "It's taken care of."

"I need to know he understands what happened tonight." He turned to Allyn, ready to say more.

"Lukas has his sister," Leira said.

Jaxon turned to Leira. "Sister?"

"He's not the only one in the dark."

"No, he's not." Jaxon rubbed the back of his head irritably. "Get in."

Leira nodded, and Allyn climbed into the back of the car. The black-leather interior was accented with wood-grained panels in the armrests and center console and was as large as it was comfortable. It was the kind of car an old man drove, the kind of car that wouldn't stand out.

Red and blue flashing lights bathed the parking lot of Kendyl's apartment complex as they rode by. What had probably started out as a single police officer responding to a domestic disturbance had grown into a possible robbery and missing persons case. Multiple police officers were on scene, and the local news stations would arrive soon, too, if they weren't there already.

Some of the neighbors had gone back inside, while others had been pulled aside to give statements to police officers. One of them was Rebecca, Kendyl's neighbor.

Allyn wondered how soon he would receive a call from the police. He may not be a suspect, but he would certainly be a person of interest.

The lights vanished behind them as Jaxon turned onto Burnside. A mile down the road, he merged onto the interstate and drove toward the west hills overlooking the city. Driving toward help. Headed toward answers.

CHAPTER 4

GRAEME'S PHONE VIBRATED. HE HATED the thing, or more specifically, he hated his dependence on it. Technology was the greatest scam of the modern era. It had killed his ancestors and sent the rest into hiding. And tonight it brought another end.

The message used a predetermined cypher, but its meaning was clear: Allyn was safe and was returning with Jaxon and Leira. *Why does even good news have to be peppered with bad these days?* Allyn was coming. He was out of Lukas's reach, but he was coming *here*.

The quiet night was a welcome retreat. It left Graeme alone with his thoughts as he wandered the forest that surrounded the manor. Oh, Graeme supposed it wasn't quiet in the traditional sense; it was alive with the sounds of crickets and owls and the soft trickle of water coming from the creek at the bottom of the shallow valley to the north, but it was probably the last quiet night he would enjoy for a long time. Jaxon, Leira, and Allyn had brought something else with them. Something unavoidable. Change.

For the first time since the Fracture, a person from outside the Families was entering their realm. A silent man was entering their world. And he was coming to the manor. It was unprecedented. It was dangerous. It was exactly what Lukas wanted. Even in this victory, there was defeat.

We can't keep going on like this, Graeme thought. The world was a large place, but when the silent men began to look again, Graeme and his family would quickly run out of places to hide. They couldn't let that happen. Lukas had to be stopped, and the first step to doing that was discovering what Lukas wanted with Allyn. Graeme had his ideas, but they were little more than guesses, nothing he could go to the Families with or use to build a Grand Coalition.

Leira said Allyn had volunteered his help. That was important. It meant he would be cooperative, but Allyn would have his own questions, too. He'd seen Jaxon in action, he'd felt Nyla's touch, and he would want answers of his own. *So what do I tell him?*

Graeme couldn't tell him everything. That much was clear. It was as reckless as it was impossible. How could he compress thousands of years of history into a single conversation? It couldn't be done. He would have to give him the basics as a foundation to build on. But what were the basics? *It would be easier if he were a child.* Children are naturally curious. They ask questions and shape their own lessons. Could he expect Allyn to do the same? *Maybe.* Allyn had a thirst for knowledge, which was a necessity in his profession. Allyn *would* ask questions. Graeme didn't need to worry about what to say; he needed to worry about what *not* to say. Everyone was entitled to their own secrets.

They arrived an hour later. Graeme waited outside the manor at the bottom of the main outdoor staircase, where the concrete stairs behind him rose to the manor's double-door entrance. He waited alone. Too many people would be a show of force, which would intimidate Allyn, put him on edge, and make him less likely to answer Graeme's questions. A single man was a show of respect.

The car circled the stone fountain and came to a stop facing the direction it had entered. Graeme couldn't see inside the tinted windows. The door opened, and Allyn stepped out. This was the man Graeme expected to change the magical world. Or end it.

———————••———————

Graeme had aged since the last time Allyn had seen him. His face, clean-shaven before, was covered with the beginnings of a white-and-black-peppered beard. The creases in the corners of his eyes seemed deeper and were bracketed by dark circles. Standing with a slight hunch, he looked how Allyn felt—exhausted.

The manor grounds were enormous, spanning acres. The manor itself—a stone fortress two stories high—looked like something out of a seventeenth-century European countryside. It sat atop a slight hill with cultivated green grass stretching out in every direction around it, disappearing into forest. They had passed through a ten-foot-tall iron security gate half a mile back, and it was obscured by tall, centuries-old evergreens.

Graeme stood silently with his hands clasped behind his back, looking like the embodiment of the manor—secure and imposing—not the type of man Allyn should aggravate. Allyn would have to be patient, let Graeme lead the conversation, and then try to massage it in the direction he wanted it to go.

Graeme's eyes opened wide when Jaxon stepped out of the car. "You're hurt."

"It's nothing," Jaxon said. "Barely tingles."

"That's because there's extensive nerve damage." Graeme gently took Jaxon's arm in his hands and scowled at Leira. "Why wasn't this treated?"

"We didn't have time," Jaxon said, cutting in before Leira could speak. She didn't look grateful for his defense. "Reyland was waiting."

Graeme's eyes darted to Allyn. The piercing gaze made him uncomfortable.

"Get that treated," Graeme said. "It needs to be addressed before the nerves die. It'll scar, but that's a good thing—it'll pose as a reminder that you need to be more careful."

Jaxon's face became hard, his eyes narrowing slightly. "It was luck. A trick. An inferno mine—"

"Which is only dangerous when you're not paying attention," Graeme said. "You were reckless. Get that arm fixed."

Jaxon stormed past him up the stairs into the manor.

Leira started after him, but Graeme caught her by the arm and whispered something into her ear. She nodded and then chased after Jaxon.

"Walk with me," Graeme said, turning down a stone pathway.

Allyn obliged, taking up position beside him. They walked in silence. Only the soft sounds of their feet clapping against the stones interrupted the night. The path led them through a sparse forested area that had been cleaned of fallen limbs and dead foliage. The trees were groomed, and the bushes had been trimmed. The moon, shining brightly in the clear winter night, was visible through the tangle of naked branches.

Allyn struggled to remain silent and not hit Graeme with a barrage of questions. Waiting for the answers to come to him went against everything he was. His job was to seek truth, not wait for it.

Graeme looked at him from the corner of his eye, opened his mouth to speak, and then closed it again.

Nervous people either closed up or rambled on

incoherently. Something told him that Graeme was probably the former. "Jaxon probably saved my life tonight."

"And nearly died in the process," Graeme said. "You may not understand the dangers of this world, but he does. Or at least, he should."

"What world is that exactly?" Allyn winced at being so direct.

Graeme sighed. "I asked you before for your help, and you said no. Now Lukas has your sister, and I don't know what he wants with her or if he'll stop his pursuit of you now that he has her."

Leira said they didn't know about Kendyl. Either Graeme hadn't been entirely truthful with her and Jaxon, or they'd told him on their way back.

"But I do know, Allyn," Graeme continued, "that if you help me answer those questions, I'll do everything in my power to get her back. So I ask you again, will you help me?"

Graeme was playing a game—give me something, and I'll give you something. He was waiting for Allyn to blink first because he knew he had the advantage. Allyn was negotiating from a place of weakness, out of desperation. He had no leverage.

"Yes," Allyn said. "I'll help you."

Graeme's shoulders dipped in apparent relief. He even gave Allyn a small, toothless smile.

They entered a small circular clearing that reminded Allyn of an outdoor study. Tall, solar-powered lamps had been placed evenly around the edge of the clearing, providing soft light. Two seats carved from old tree trunks waited for them in the center, and a stump, which had been cut smooth on top, acted as a table. Graeme took a seat and motioned for Allyn to do the same.

"Then there are a few things we need to discuss first," Graeme said. His voice became quiet, as though he were telling Allyn a secret. "For as long as there have been people like you, there have been people like me. We've been called many things. Mages, wizards, witches, even gods—and, most recently, demons. In the beginning, we worked and lived with non-magic people in a symbiotic relationship. Although greatly outnumbered, we provided the necessities of life, from the warmth of fire to healing and protection. But as men learned to create fire, developed medicine, and built weapons for protection, our relationship began to collapse. So, unneeded and useless to humankind, the ancient magi turned to each other for support, and our first Families were formed."

Allyn looked through the trees toward the manor. Its softly illuminated windows were barely visible through the sparse branches. "Your family lives here? How many of you are there?"

"Not a 'family' as you would define it. Though, today, since our numbers have dwindled to so few, I am related to every magi in some form or another. But no, by 'Family,' I mean we're brought together by a common bond, a mutual purpose that separates us from others. The ability to perform magic."

Allyn leaned forward in his seat, resting his elbows on his knees and clasping his hands together. While he probably looked like an anxious teenager, Graeme looked regal in his throne-like carved seat, strong and formidable. Leira had said she and Lukas were "family." *Does that mean they're related or that Lukas had once lived here with her as a member of Graeme's Family?*

"What can you do?" Allyn asked. "What kind of abilities do you have?"

Graeme held out his hands. At the flick of his wrists, a fireball formed in one hand and a ball of ice in the other. The fire and ice rose into the air, danced around Allyn, and returned to Graeme's hands. The fire dissipated, and the ice fell harmlessly to the ground.

"You can control the elements," Allyn said.

"We call it wielding. And it's not the elements. I'm harnessing—wielding—my body's fire, water, and air."

"How does it work? Do other magi have different abilities?" Allyn asked, thinking of Nyla and Leira.

"Yes. There are two different kinds of magi, those like me who can wield fire, water, and air, and those like Nyla, who is a cleric with the ability to heal."

"Are there magi who can do both?"

"In time, Allyn," Graeme said. "In time. I know you have a lot of questions, but first, let me finish my story. For a long time, our two people coexisted, but as humanity populated and thrived, magi were needed less and less. And they retreated farther and farther. We were sought out in only the most dire of circumstances, usually to aid an ailing spouse or child, though, sometimes, for other darker, more vengeful reasons."

Allyn couldn't help thinking back to the attack at his apartment. A magi would make the perfect assassin. With abilities that nobody knew existed, there would never be a murder weapon or reliable witnesses. Anyone who gave a statement suggesting that magic was to blame would immediately be cast aside and laughed at.

"I know you're thinking of Lukas. But know that, in his heart, Lukas is a good man. He has a different goal than we do, or maybe it's the same goal, but he resorts to different methods to achieve it."

"What goal is that?" Allyn asked.

"Survival. The ancient magi were different from Lukas. They had been cast aside and shunned or worse. Because they became aloof and helped in only the direst of circumstances, they became affiliated with loss, pain, and death. They were resented when they refused help and feared when they did. A parent rejoices when their child is miraculously saved from certain death, but a neighbor sees a sinister force behind it. For every good deed a magi performed, a hundred rumors spread. Magi were consorting with demons, performing sacrifices, and dark deals were made with dark spirits. They were evil.

"Large Families had strength in numbers, but single magi or small Families were easy targets. Their homes were ransacked. Their property stolen or destroyed. Houses burned. Magi died. And a rift formed between magi and humans. So when a human came to a magi with vengeance on their mind, you can see how some would be tempted to accept the offer. It became retaliation on a small scale."

"Which would only make things worse. Strengthen the fears between them," Allyn said.

"The big picture is the last thing on the mind of someone who has been beaten down and broken."

Allyn leaned back in his seat. He knew what Graeme was talking about. People could resort to being sour or petty in a hurry—score a victory right away, even if it meant losing the war later. And he dealt with people who'd only been slightly wronged, nothing to the extent of what Graeme was talking about.

"But you're right," Graeme continued. "Things did get worse. Violence erupted between humans and magi. Hundreds, even thousands, died. Magi fled—small Families first—seeking refuge in a town or city that didn't know their true nature. Larger Families became the target of anti-magic vitriol, and out of a desire to end the violence and protect their loved ones, the Families broke apart, spreading across the land. We call it the Fracture. We adopted human practices, embraced technology and culture and, in the name of survival, hid who we were."

Graeme pulled his cell phone from his hip and held it up for Allyn to see. "That strategy continues today. And because of it, our existence is a rumor. A story or myth, at best."

"Lukas wants to change that," Allyn said. "He's tired of hiding."

Graeme nodded. "Something the rest of the Families don't agree with."

"What does that have to do with me?"

Graeme took a deep breath. "This is where we venture into the unknown. I have an idea, but I want you to understand that it's nothing more than that."

"I understand."

"I believe Lukas thinks you can wield."

CHAPTER 5

ALLYN LAUGHED. IT ALL FELT like a mistake, one big, ridiculous mistake. Graeme didn't look amused. Allyn stopped laughing but failed to wipe the smile from his face. "How would that even be possible?"

"I'll show you." Graeme stood. He motioned for Allyn to follow and, without waiting, walked back down the stone path to the manor.

Allyn followed sluggishly, wondering what time it was. The sky was starting to lighten. Dawn wasn't far off.

Graeme led him up the stairs to the main entrance, grabbed the brass handles, and pushed open the red double doors.

Allyn looked on in amazement.

Two grand staircases curved along the wall on either side, mirroring each other. Hallways painted an ornate red split off in opposite directions at the top of the stairs, and another led forward, deeper into the house. A crystal chandelier that was taller than Allyn hung from the coffered ceiling, and the light reflecting off it made the room feel alive.

Another set of hallways branched off in both directions to his immediate right and left, but Allyn followed Graeme forward, between the stairs, deeper into the house. Sculptures and paintings of various sizes and shapes hung on the walls and filled alcoves. Hand-woven rugs lined hallways and covered the dark hardwood floor. The manor had a history, and Allyn knew without asking that each piece of art told part of the story.

The manor was larger than Allyn had expected. *I should probably stop expecting things to be as they seem.* He was in unfamiliar territory and struggled to make sense of it all. Kendyl would have had an easier time. She was more impulsive, more emotional, and more spontaneous. She believed there was still some magic in the world, maybe not *real* magic, but she would *believe,* while he was still searching for the lie.

They descended two stories into a basement and rounded a corner, where they came to a stop. A sliding-glass door separated them from an enormous chamber lit with lamps hanging from the vaulted ceiling. Mahogany bookshelves, tall enough to require a ladder and overflowing with books, lined the walls. Ancient artifacts set in glass displays were spread throughout the room. It was more than a library. It was a museum.

Graeme punched in a code on a ten-digit metal keypad hanging on the wall, and the door slid opened with a hiss. Graeme waved Allyn forward. The air was dry and smelled... *clean*, strangely artificial, as if it was climate controlled. The door closed behind them.

"Excuse me," Graeme said softly, holding up a hand.

A woman in front of them was hunched over a table, reading a leather-bound book. The fingers of her left hand were buried in her long silver hair, gently massaging the back of her head. It was the same woman who had tended to him in his room. Nyla.

"You should be resting," Graeme said.

She looked up from her reading material as she

became aware of the man approaching her. Dark circles surrounded her bloodshot eyes. Whatever she was doing, she'd been at it for a while.

"I can't rest," she said, returning her focus to the book in front of her. The room was quiet enough that Allyn could still hear their hushed voices.

Graeme glanced in Allyn's direction. He placed a hand on Nyla's elbow and gently pulled her up. "I don't know what you're looking for, but it won't do any good tonight."

Nyla pulled her arm free, never taking her eyes off the book.

"He's gone, Nyla," Graeme said in a comforting tone.

She looked up from her book, staring straight forward. "I know he's gone," she said, her voice cold. "You don't have to tell me. *I* was there."

"How long has it been since you've slept? When was the last time you looked in the mirror? I fear you're intimidating our new guest."

Nyla's eyes flashed to Allyn. "What is he doing here? I thought he left."

"He's helping us."

She looked at him, incredulous. "What does he know? He's the reason Baylis is dead!" She shoved the table forward, rose to her feet, and stormed toward Allyn.

Allyn took a nervous step backward, looking to Graeme for help.

"Nyla..." Graeme said, his voice firm.

She ignored him, powering toward Allyn. She didn't slow down.

Allyn backed into a glass encasement resting atop a pedestal. It rocked perilously. Turning, he caught it as it slid off the pedestal.

Nyla stormed past him and angrily punched the code into the keypad. Before the doors were entirely open, she had vanished around the corner.

"I'm sorry about that," Graeme said. "You'll have to excuse Nyla. She lost someone very special to her recently."

"When you saved me?" Allyn asked, watching the hallway, expecting her to return.

"No," Graeme said. "Before."

"But she said it was my fault."

"She was talking about something else," Graeme said. "Come over here. I want to show you something."

Allyn hesitated. For the first time all night, Allyn felt as if Graeme was holding something back, and it made him suspicious. "I've been wondering, how *did* you find me?"

"I had Jaxon and Leira follow you. I was sure Lukas would make another play, and I wanted them to be there when he did."

"No, that was the second time. I'm talking about the first time, at my condo."

Graeme eyed him for a moment.

He's stalling.

"We have a spy—someone inside Lukas's inner circle. He informed us Lukas was making a play for a human."

"Then why didn't you know about my sister?"

"I don't know," Graeme said. "Either the informant has been compromised, or they were unable to get the information out."

"If they're still there, they can help us get her back!"

Graeme nodded. "In time."

"In time? No! Now! Every second she's missing makes it more difficult to get her back."

"This isn't a normal missing persons case. We know who has her, and we know where she is. We'll get her back, I promise, but we'll move when the time is right and we have a plan with a high probability of success."

He was right. Allyn wouldn't go to trial without a case that he knew front to back, and he would never go if he didn't believe he would win. But that didn't make waiting any easier. He exhaled deeply. "What did you want to show me?"

Graeme held out his arms to either side. "This. This is everything my Family has gathered since the Fracture. Every artifact, every story, every family tree. Our entire history rests before your eyes."

Allyn gaped. He stepped up to the enormous bookcase. There had to be thousands of books containing vast amounts of information on those shelves.

"As you can imagine, it's really quite sparse," Graeme said.

Sparse? Allyn pulled a heavy, leather-bound book from the shelf. The spine cracked and popped as Allyn opened it. The pages were yellow and stiff with age, smelled musty, and were covered with handwritten text.

"Most of the books are similar to the one you hold in your hand, a journal or diary or the like. Together, they make up our history. There isn't an encyclopedia detailing our history through multiple volumes. All we have lies here, in this room, and others like it."

Allyn surveyed the room with a new perspective. While vast, the information on hand would be very limited. Journals and diaries would be great for firsthand accounts, but they would only tell a small part of the story. And what they did have was losing its battle against time. Their history was deteriorating in front of their eyes. Allyn closed the book and gently placed it back on the shelf. "What in here leads you to believe that Lukas thinks I can wield?"

"In all actuality, it's what isn't in here that I believe holds the key. Our records are broken. All we have left are bits and pieces. Entire Families were killed. Others died off or seamlessly transitioned into life with humans. Their history, and *our* history along with it, was lost with them. Magic comes from magic. It has been passed down from parent to child for hundreds of generations. But without the proper ancestral records, entire bloodlines have been lost."

Allyn turned to Graeme, realization forming. "Lukas thinks I'm a long-lost descendant."

"Perhaps," Graeme said. "However, even if you were, it doesn't mean you'd be able to wield. The power would most likely lie dormant inside you, silent, unable to be harnessed."

"Why?"

"To put it simply, you haven't been raised in a way that makes *feeling* it easy."

"But it's possible."

"Yes, it's possible."

"Then I want to try."

Graeme nodded, smiling. "I was hoping you'd say that."

"When do we start?"

"Soon," Graeme said. "But first, I want you to trace your ancestry as far back as you can. And I mean everyone. Brothers, sisters, aunts, uncles, cousins—everyone you can remember. But they have to be blood relatives. No step-relatives or children from a previous marriage. Family by blood."

"I understand. What is your plan? Are you going to reference it with your records?"

"Yes," Graeme said. "And if nothing comes up, I'll contact other Families. We'll find out where you came from."

———————•••———————

By the time Allyn turned in, the morning sun had crept over the horizon. He'd been given the same room as before, only it had been furnished more comfortably. Chocolate-colored drapes covered the floor-to-ceiling windows, and a small seating area had been added in the corner. Looking at it now, Allyn wondered how he had ever mistaken it for a hospital room.

He'd done as Graeme asked and traced back his lineage as far as he could. The first couple generations had been simple, but after that, it became a struggle. Growing up, it had just been him and his sister, and his dad—whom Allyn hadn't spoken to since he was a child—only had a brother. But his mother's side was far more complicated. She was one of five children—one of six if he included Thomas, whom Allyn's grandmother had raised without formally adopting. And her mother had been one of eight kids.

Eight kids, Allyn thought. His sister was enough to contend with. He couldn't imagine having seven other siblings.

Then there were the family secrets or the little-talked-about truths. His grandmother on his mother's side had two kids and then remarried, but refused to talk about her first husband. Then Aunt Becky was really his great-aunt, which means his cousins Jason and Jeremiah were... what? It made his head numb. But he had it on paper, and that was a start. It was also the best he could do running on twenty-four hours without sleep.

The feather mattress enveloped him when he finally lay down. The drapes blocked the light everywhere except for the edges, though, as tired as he was, he probably could have slept in direct sunlight.

CHAPTER 6

JARRELL HARTLINE HID FROM THE woman's screams. Helpless
and frantic, they pierced the walls like an alarm in the
early morning. He heard them, which meant everyone
else heard them, too—and nobody was helping. They
accepted it. He paced along the far wall of his room, as
far from the door as he could get. The concrete floor was
rough against his bare feet. He knew he should be doing
something to help the poor woman. She was a silent and
was being tortured in ways that probably confused her as
much as they hurt.

He didn't know what Lukas wanted with her. Rumor
had it that she was the sister of the man they had tried
to kidnap the week before. *What was his name? Allyn.*
There would only be one reason Lukas was going after
siblings. He had found an ancient line. The implications
were profound. A newly discovered line would bring a
significant number of new magi into the fray and could
tip the number in Lukas's favor, or at least even the odds
a bit.

He's building an army, Jarrell thought.

Jarrell couldn't let that happen. He'd saved the boy by
tipping off Graeme to Lukas's intentions, but he hadn't

been able to do the same for the girl. And now she was here. That was his fault, and he had to do something about that.

He stopped pacing. The screams had subsided—he wasn't sure when—and silence hung in the air, thick and eerie. It wasn't the kind of silence that meant the session was over. She would be crying and pleading for help if that was the case. No, she was unconscious—or worse. And that meant they would come for him next. Jarrell grabbed his book and sat down on his bare mattress to read. The fluorescent bulb hanging from the middle of the ceiling cast a harsh light, creating long shadows and insufficient light to read comfortably, but he had an image to uphold.

The door opened without a knock, and Kaleb stepped into the room, a frown on his face. Jarrell looked up from his book in feigned surprise, sliding his glasses back to the bridge of his nose.

"Lukas requests your presence," Kaleb said.

Jarrell nodded and marked his place with a bookmark, then slowly climbed to his feet with a groan, holding his lower back.

Kaleb shifted impatiently. Lukas's movement had no true command structure, but Kaleb and those who felt especially close to their leader treated Jarrell as if they were his superiors. Jarrell was okay with that. In fact, he encouraged it. It made him less of a threat.

"Sorry. I'm not as young as I once was," Jarrell said, his voice strained. "Where are we going?"

"This way."

Kaleb set a quick pace, probably expecting Jarrell to fall behind and have to eventually ask for him to slow down. Jarrell played his part, following with a slight limp and breathing heavily.

Kaleb glanced back, smiling wryly. He led Jarrell through the compound, which was a private single-level loft above an abandoned machine shop. Exposed ductwork ran along the ceiling, knocking and banging as the furnace kicked on. Stale warm air blew through the vents, offering a temporary reprieve from the cold before escaping through broken windows.

Lukas's quarters were on the far side of the compound, near the barracks, so that he could gauge the pulse of his followers. Only a few had private quarters like Jarrell's, and his privacy would be short lived as more magi flocked to Lukas's cause. Two guards stood outside Lukas's door. They nodded as Kaleb and Jarrell approached.

Kaleb knocked, waited for permission to enter, then opened the door and waited for Jarrell to enter first.

"Thank you," Jarrell said, stepping into the room.

Kaleb closed the door behind them and waited.

Lukas sat in the corner, his back against the exposed-brick exterior wall beside the bed. The bed wasn't his. That was near the front of the room, but a second bed had been brought in for the girl.

Jarrell shivered, not because of the cold winter air blowing through the dusty windows, but because of the woman lying unconscious on the bed. Her wrists and ankles were bloodied from fighting against the bonds tied to the frame. Her dark hair was matted and stuck to her face, hiding the bruises caused by Lukas's abuse.

"Kaleb said you wanted to see me," Jarrell said, tearing his eyes from the woman.

"Yes." Lukas rose to his feet and strolled across the room to a small circular table with two glasses and a pitcher. He filled one of the glasses with water and sipped it without offering any to Jarrell. "She's stronger than I anticipated."

Jarrell knelt beside the bed and examined the woman. She showed few signs of direct abuse, but dried tears sparkled on her flushed cheeks, and her clothes were soaked with sweat, urine, and blood. Jarrell took her wrist in his hand. "She's alive."

"I know." Lukas took another drink.

Jarrell's relief was quickly replaced by anger. *Control yourself. You won't be any help to her if you're dead.* "Then why did you summon me?"

"I want you to wake her up."

So you can continue torturing her. "What do you want with her?"

"I want to bring Graeme to his knees," Lukas said, placing his half-empty glass back onto the small table. "He lied to us, Jarrell. They *all* lied to us, and I'm going to prove it. She is the key." Lukas had been trying to break the girl all night, and every time she lost consciousness, he brought in a cleric to bring her back. It was his way of forcing everyone to play a part. Everyone became responsible for his actions. And now it was Jarrell's turn.

Ashamed, Jarrell placed his hand in the center of the woman's chest. He didn't even know her name. He took a deep breath and held it. He increased his heart rate until it pounded like a jackhammer. His body grew hot, and the hand on her chest glowed red. When it became as bright as the naked bulb above him, he projected.

"I'm sorry," Jarrell whispered.

The glowing energy burst from his hand into the woman's chest, shooting pulses of white light through her body. It ran back and forth from her hands to her feet, then to her chest, where his hand had been. As each wave returned, he learned more about her condition. She was fighting the beginnings of an infection and had a slight fever. Making matters worse, she was significantly dehydrated. The wounds on her wrists and ankles were superficial but needed to be healed, lest the infection return.

Jarrell pooled his body's strength and projected it into the woman. Instantly, the red, irritated flesh under her bindings began to heal, returning to the same creamy color as the rest of her skin. Simultaneously, the same wounds formed on Jarrell's wrists. That was the consequence, the sacrifice. Jarrell gave her more than his strength—he gave her his health and his body, and in return, he took her injuries.

The color in her cheeks faded, and her breathing slowed, strengthening. Jarrell felt his own body temperature rise. He was suddenly thankful for the open windows. His mouth dried and his lips chapped. His sweat disappeared as he gave her his water.

Jarrell felt himself grow weak, but still, he continued. The weaker he grew, the stronger she became. He hadn't been able to prevent her from undergoing this nightmare. He owed her this much—and more. He would give her everything he had to give.

With her physical health returned, Jarrell withdrew. The pulses of energy flowing through her body faded until they disappeared entirely. Jarrell pulled his hand back, rubbing the irritated skin on his wrist. His job was done. He tried to stand, but, dizzy, he staggered to the side and crashed against the wall. Blackness crept in from the edges of his vision. *What's going on? Had she been poisoned?*

No, he thought. She had simply been worse off than he'd realized. He'd taken too many of her injuries and given her too much of his strength—and too much of his water.

Jarrell crawled to the round table that held the pitcher of water. He needed to replenish.

Lukas knelt, the metal pitcher ready in his hand. He set a single glass on the ground in front of Jarrell's face.

Jarrell took the pitcher with shaky hands and tilted it over the glass. Nothing came out. He looked inside. It was empty. He groaned. The back of his throat was dry and cracking. He felt as if he'd swallowed fire. He needed water.

"Thank you, Jarrell," Lukas said. "We need to be

strong. They have the numbers, but we have something more important. Do you know what that is?"

Jarrell barely heard him. His arms buckled under his weight, the empty pitcher crashing onto the ground. Painful convulsions took him next.

"Conviction," Lukas said. "We believe in what we're fighting for, and we're willing to give anything to achieve it. Even our lives."

Jarrell rolled onto his side, inching his face closer to the pitcher. He licked the condensation off the outside of the pitcher. The cool water droplets soothed his blistered tongue, but it wasn't enough. He was going to die from dehydration.

Jarrell rolled onto his back, his vision going dark.

A hand cupped the back of his head and a narrow object was forced between his cracked lips. Cold water poured into his mouth, washing away the stale taste of death.

He coughed. Water ran down the sides of his cheeks and filled in the crevice of his neck. Jarrell reared his head toward the glass, his body running on instinct. More water filled his mouth. This time, his body cooperated and swallowed. Jarrell felt the wave of life flow down his chest. His strength grew with every sip.

"It's going to be okay," Lukas said quietly. "We have the truth on our side. It's going to be okay."

CHAPTER 7

THE CHILLY, LATE-MORNING AIR SLAPPED away Allyn's remaining weariness. The winter sun hung low on the horizon, below thick, high-level clouds, casting long shadows in the forest clearing. Wearing the same office attire he'd worn the night before, black slacks with a white button-down shirt, he wished he'd brought a coat. Allyn had come looking for Graeme. He'd searched the manor, revisiting rooms he'd already been welcomed into, careful not to go where he hadn't. His brief encounter with Nyla the night before had reminded him that he was an unwelcome outsider, and the last thing he needed to do was go opening doors and angering more locals.

Graeme wasn't in the clearing, though. Allyn cursed. Graeme needed the piece of paper in Allyn's hand. He needed to know where Allyn had come from so he could discover who he was. There was one last place Allyn thought to look, but it was truly his last resort. He didn't *dislike* the library. In fact, he thought it was majestic, but Nyla made him nervous, and he got the impression she spent a lot of time there. She blamed him for the loss of "someone important," and Allyn had no way of apologizing because he didn't know what he'd done.

So reluctantly, he returned to the manor. Graeme had made it sound as if hundreds of people lived with him, but Allyn hadn't seen anyone since the night before. Descending the stairwell into the library, Allyn breathed a sigh of relief when he saw that Nyla wasn't there. Unfortunately, neither was Graeme. But *someone* was.

Toward the back, hidden behind a computer monitor, was a skinny young man approaching his teenage years. He sat hunched over a book, typing furiously. He didn't see Allyn.

Before remembering that Graeme had entered a code on the metal keypad, Allyn waited for the glass door to slide open. When it didn't and he realized he didn't know the code, he knocked. The boy's head slid to the side, looking past the monitor, in Allyn's direction. Allyn waved. The boy glanced around the empty room, looking confused, before slowly climbing to his feet and shuffling toward Allyn.

He smiled, seemingly making the boy even more uncomfortable. He stood as tall as Allyn's shoulder and was beginning a battle with acne. He entered the code on the keypad inside the library and eyed Allyn suspiciously as the door slid open.

"Thank you," Allyn said.

"Can I help you?" the boy asked.

"I'm looking for Graeme. Do you know where he is?"

"He's with the others."

Others? "And where are they?"

"If you don't know, then you probably weren't invited, were you?" The boy sneered at Allyn with teeth so large that Allyn wondered if he would ever grow into them.

Definitely a teenager, Allyn thought, amused. It was refreshing to find that even teenagers growing up in a world of magic were still sarcastic little punks. *That*, he was familiar with. "I guess not. I just need to give him this." He pulled the piece of paper from his pocket.

"What is it?"

"Just something he asked me to do." Allyn unfolded the paper.

The boy strained his neck, trying to catch a glimpse of what was on it. "You're *him*, aren't you? The one everyone is talking about."

Allyn shrugged. "Probably. I doubt you get a lot of newcomers around here."

The boy smiled. It was an awkward thing with too much teeth and not enough of... anything else. "That's for sure."

"What's your name?"

"Liam."

"I'm Allyn." He extended his hand. The boy took it and gave him a weak handshake. "What are you doing in here, Liam?"

"Let me see that piece of paper, and I'll tell you."

Allyn laughed, handing him the paper. "Deal."

Liam scanned it quickly, looking disappointed. "What is it?"

"My family tree."

"What are you doing with it?" Liam handed the paper back.

"Trying to find out who I am," Allyn said dramatically.

Liam laughed.

"That's what I think, too. So what about you? What are you doing in here?"

"Working."

"On what?"

Liam looked at his feet. "I'm the Family's Librarian," he mumbled.

"You manage all of this?"

"I'm saving it."

Allyn waited for him to laugh again, but he didn't. Instead, his eyes flickered toward the computer at the back of the room. Allyn walked past him to the table with the computer, Liam lagging behind. An open book rested beside the keyboard. Allyn glanced at the first line of the book then at the computer screen. The text was the same. The boy was retyping the text, and as he was more than halfway through the book, he had been at it for a while.

Mouth agape, Allyn looked back at Liam. "How long have you been doing this?"

Liam shrugged. "A couple of years. I finished that bookshelf over there." Liam pointed to the corner behind him.

Allyn followed the motion of his hand. The next bookshelf over had a hole in the center of it where a book was missing. Liam must have been working through that shelf.

"You did all that by yourself?"

Liam nodded. He was proud. And he had every reason to be. Allyn knew tedious work and transcription was tedium upon tedium. It was also priceless. The decaying texts would be saved forever.

"How old are you?"

"Fourteen."

"That's incredible."

"I'm glad somebody thinks so."

How could anyone not be amazed by this kid's efforts? His work could be the most important undertaking in preserving the magi's delicate history. It would also make him the foremost expert in the field. "There's a faster way to do that, you know. You could just get a scanner and scan it all in."

"I like doing it this way."

"Nobody *likes* doing transcription."

"I do."

Allyn laughed. "Fair enough." He gave his family tree back to Liam. "You might be able to help me with this, then."

"You're serious?" Liam asked. "You actually think you might be some long-lost magi?"

"I don't know what to believe anymore. There has to be a reason why everyone is after me."

"I guess." Liam saved his Word file, minimized the screen, and pulled open another program. He typed furiously. It was code of some kind, and Allyn didn't understand any of it. After several minutes, Liam glanced at Allyn's piece of paper and began typing the names into a column on the left side of the screen. He punched the keyboard and leaned back in his chair, resting his hands on the back of his head.

"What's it doing?" Allyn asked.

"I built a search engine for the names on your list. It'll find any exact matches or anything close. It'll also flag any names that might have changed over the years."

"You did that?"

"Yes."

"Just now?"

"The magi family names were already in a database. Those were the first things we saved. I just built a way to look through them."

Allyn shook his head in amazement. "How long will it take?"

"Not very long. Maybe a few—it's done."

Allyn leaned over the computer. "What did it find?"

Liam slumped in his chair, disappointed. "Nothing. It didn't find anything."

Allyn sighed, kicking himself. Of course it didn't find anything. There wasn't anything to find. He wasn't part of a forgotten magi line. It had been wishful thinking.

"Maybe if we expand the search, include more variables." Liam pulled the keyboard closer.

"It's okay, Liam. I didn't expect to find anything, anyway."

"But I'm sure I missed something. This area here—your

mother's side—it's really vague. If you can fill it in, I'm sure I can find something."

"It's fine." Allyn patted him on the shoulder.

"Please," Liam said. "Let me keep trying." His glassy eyes pleaded with Allyn. The kid was tenacious and confident in his abilities, but there was something else—a longing. He wanted to help and not just with Allyn's search. He wanted to be a part of something.

"All right," Allyn said. "Keep that paper, and I'll see what I can do to get you more names."

"I don't need the paper. I already have those names. If you can get me more, though, that would be even better. I can do this, I promise."

Allyn nodded, smiling. "I know you can, Liam."

The library door hissed open, and Graeme stepped into the Library. Liam's smile vanished.

"There you are," Graeme said. "I see you've met my son."

Allyn looked at Liam. "Your son?"

"My youngest. You didn't tell our new guest, Liam? Why not?"

Liam's face flushed, and he cast his eyes to the floor.

"Liam was helping me with the list of family members you had me make. He built a computer program that allowed us to search through the histories for any sort of connection. He's a computer genius."

"Liam likes his computers," Graeme said, placing his hands on the table. "What did you find?"

"Nothing," Liam said quietly, still staring at the floor.

"Not yet, anyway," Allyn said. "He's going to keep looking, expand the search. Aren't you, Liam?"

"That won't be necessary," Graeme said. "We'll take it from here, but thank you, Liam. It was a good try. Now, I'd like to speak with Allyn in private."

Without a word, Liam headed for the exit. Allyn wanted to say something, but he didn't know what. He watched until Liam rounded the corner, his head hung low.

"Is this the list?" Graeme asked, grabbing the paper from the table.

Allyn nodded.

"I'll get my people on it," Graeme said. "We'll find something."

"Liam didn't find anything."

"I like to do things the old-fashioned way." Graeme pocketed the family tree then tossed a newspaper onto the table. "We're in a bit of trouble."

Allyn scanned the headlines. A small story about a robbery developing into a missing persons case caught his attention. It named him as a person of interest. "Why haven't I heard anything?" Allyn asked, looking up from the paper. "The police should have called me by now."

"That's my fault," Graeme said. "We live in peace here, away from the outside world and all of its distractions. It's better for us that way."

"So?"

"So," Graeme said. "While we sometimes need the aid of technology, we try our best to live without it. This room, for example, is climate controlled and uses a type of light that preserves the artifacts inside it. We do it out of necessity."

"What does that have to do with my cell phone?"

"I had Liam design a jammer that blocks all cell phone transmissions within a two-mile radius."

Allyn pulled his cell phone out of his pocket. "It says I have service."

"And, technically speaking, you do. That's where Liam's design is distinct, where his *genius*, as you put it, shines through. The jammer acts as a barrier, preventing a transmission from entering or leaving, but the signal itself is consistent."

"You keep yourself in the dark."

"It can be turned off, of course, during times of—"

"Then turn it off," Allyn interrupted. "The longer I go without contacting the police, the more I look like a suspect."

"That's of little concern."

"You won't think so when every pair of eyes in the Portland area is looking for me. For someone who does their best to hide, that's not a great strategy for continued success."

"They will never find you here. They have no reason to look."

"I have a life *outside*, one I would very much like to return to when this is over. What do you have to lose from me clearing my name?"

"Everything," Graeme said softly. "But I understand. I wasn't trying to complicate your life. Go back to your room. By the time you get there, the jammer will have been turned off, and you can make your call. I'll give you fifteen minutes."

By the time Allyn returned to his room, his phone was already ringing. He didn't recognize the number, but it was local, and he answered it, expecting it to be the police.

"When I told you I was interested in seeing what you did with my attention, I didn't expect this." The irritated, raspy voice was familiar, and a little amused. Mr. Clarke. "Fucking Christ, son, what the hell happened?"

"You've heard then?" Allyn asked, rubbing his temples. He wasn't prepared for this. The man intimidated him more than any police officer ever could.

"Of course I heard. I've had Portland detectives crawling up my ass since this morning."

"I'm sorry about that. Things got out of hand," Allyn said. "I went to my sister's apartment because I was worried about her. I haven't heard from her in days."

"They say you broke into her apartment, Allyn. They

say you fled the scene once the cops were called."

Allyn sat down on the seat in front of the large window. It looked like it was going to rain at any moment. And when it started, it wouldn't stop for days. Or weeks. "They're not lying. Not technically, anyway."

"You're not helping your case, son."

"I didn't realize I was on trial."

"Having a wanted man working for our firm isn't exactly good business."

"What are you saying? I'm fired?"

"That depends."

"On what?"

"On your defense," Mr. Clarke said. "You're a lawyer, Allyn. Persuade me. Win me over."

Allyn struggled to string together his jumbled thoughts. Too much had happened, too many things that couldn't be articulated easily. Where to begin wasn't the issue. That was easy, but where to end—that was more complicated. And he didn't know how to do it without having Mr. Clarke ask the wrong questions.

"My sister and I are very close," Allyn began. "We've been through a lot together, more than most people. There's rarely a day that goes by when I don't hear from her. So when two days went by, three, then four, I knew something was wrong. I called her. I left messages. I texted her. When I didn't hear back, I went to check on her."

The part about them being so close wasn't technically true—not anymore, anyway. They used to talk a lot more—before law school and his career. Their relationship had developed an awkwardness.

"Her neighbor came out while I was knocking on her door. She said that Kendyl had gotten in a fight with her boyfriend. The neighbor heard them and almost called the cops then, but didn't. I wish she had. The problem is, Kendyl doesn't have a boyfriend. Whoever the neighbor heard shouldn't have been in her apartment. *That's* why there was a fight. Whoever that woman heard is my sister's kidnapper."

"Maybe your sister had a boyfriend and just never told you. Maybe they went on a romantic getaway."

"Never."

"How do you know? Maybe she wanted some space."

"I just know, okay?" Allyn said, a little too heatedly. "I'm the only family she has left. We tell each other everything. If she met someone, she would have been excited to tell me."

"Why didn't you tell the police this? Why the disappearing act? By the way, where the hell are you?"

Allyn winced. "I can't tell you that. I'm sorry, Mr. Clarke. I really am. I know it looks bad, but you're going to have to trust me on this one." He didn't want to say the words because they were so cliché, but he had to anyway. "I'm innocent."

"I'm a lawyer, Allyn," Mr. Clarke said. Allyn didn't need to hear the rest. "Trust doesn't enter the equation, only what I can prove. And right now, you're a liability to this firm."

Allyn tapped the phone against his forehead, sighing deeply. "I understand."

"Good luck, kid."

"Thank you."

"And Allyn?"

"Yeah?"

"If you need legal representation, you know where to turn."

The line went dead. Allyn didn't know if Mr. Clarke had hung up or if the jammer was back online. It didn't matter. Everything he'd worked for had just vanished. And he hadn't had an opportunity to clear things up with the police.

CHAPTER 8

ALLYN HID UNDER THE THICK branches of a nearby pine tree, escaping the rain. The sun had lost its battle with the heavy clouds, and the rain had begun to fall. Something sank inside Allyn. He knew that once the rain started, it probably wouldn't stop. "We're not really doing this out here, are we?"

"Why not?" Jaxon asked with a patronizing smile. "Afraid of a little rain?" He wore a black, sleeveless, formfitting shirt that displayed his defined frame. The white brands on his arms glistened from the water, and Jaxon, ignoring the rain that gathered in his closely cropped hair, refused to wipe away the rest that streaked down his face.

Allyn stepped out from under the tree's refuge, into the downpour. He knew Jaxon was proving a point, but that didn't stop him from feeling inadequate. After Allyn had been fired, Graeme had told him to meet Jaxon in the forest clearing. The time had come to find out if he could wield.

"The water will keep you cool. Its natural rhythm will keep you focused. Of course, if you're too cold, I'm sure we can find a nursery."

Allyn sniffed, wiping his runny nose. "It's fine."

"Good. Have a seat over there." Jaxon pointed to a flat area behind Graeme's carved-tree chairs.

Allyn took a seat, his legs crossed, back straight, and fully exposed to the rain. Looking up, Allyn saw a hole in the canopy. *He's intentionally put me in the most uncomfortable spot he can find. Are they trying to make this more difficult?*

"Before we begin," Jaxon said, walking in a circle around Allyn, "there are a few things you need to understand. First, this is hard. It's not something that can be learned overnight. It can take years of training to wield consistently. And some never master it."

"Then what's the point? If it's going to take me years, why not just help me get my sister back and be done with it?"

"I said *consistently*. We should know if you can wield a lot sooner than that. Second," Jaxon said, continuing before Allyn could ask another question, "I am in charge. You'll do as I say when I say it. Wielding is dangerous, both to you and your trainer. If you die, you won't be helping anybody. And if I die, I'll be very, very unhappy. So listen to what I say and do as I tell you. Understand?"

Allyn shifted uncomfortably. Ignoring the rain was growing increasingly difficult. He would catch a cold if he had to stay out here too much longer. *Could they heal that, too?*

"Third, training is a process. You probably have some twelve-year-old boy's fantasy that you'll be shooting fireballs and ice blasts out of your hands tomorrow. You won't be. Wielding is about control. Controlling your mind. Controlling your body. Controlling your emotions. When we're done, your lips won't turn blue, and you won't shiver like a baby in the bathtub when you get a little wet."

Allyn's face flushed with embarrassment. *I haven't been shivering, have I?*

"Do we have an understanding?" Jaxon asked.

Allyn nodded.

"The first thing you need to know is that magic comes from within. It's the unity of mind, body, and emotion. If the mind doesn't believe, then the magi cannot wield. If the body is injured or depleted, no matter how strong the mind or emotion, the magi cannot wield. If the magi is overcome with emotion, the body and mind become confused, and the magi cannot wield. The three have to work together in perfect harmony to make wielding possible.

"Today, we are going to work on controlling your mind. We are going to strengthen it so that it can ignore your body's impulses." Jaxon pulled something out of his pocket and tossed it to Allyn.

It was a small box, several inches long and a few inches deep, with a hinge on the back. Allyn opened it. A thin gold chain with a diamond pendant the size of a nickel rested inside. Confused, Allyn looked up at Jaxon.

"Pull it out," Jaxon said.

Allyn held the thin necklace in front of his face. The gold chain was tangled in several complicated knots. "What do you want me to do with this?"

"Untangle it."

Allyn looked at the necklace in disbelief. "This is ridiculous. My sister has been kidnapped, and you promised to help me. Instead, you have me sitting in the rain, freezing my ass off, trying to untangle a necklace. What's the point?"

"Tell me how you feel."

"How I feel? I'm fucking pissed."

"Are you cold?"

"What does that have to do with anything?"

"Are you cold?" Jaxon repeated.

"I don't know. Not anymore."

"Then you understand."

Allyn shook his head. "Understand what?"

"That it's possible to control your body."

"I didn't control it. I ignored it."

"What's the difference? They both require a conscious decision. Both are a testament of will. You chose to ignore it, which means your task was more important than your body's impulses. That's control of a sort, and it's a start." Jaxon took a seat in one of the tree chairs behind him and threw his legs up. "I still want you to untangle that necklace, and anytime you get too cold or your hands go numb or you can't stop shivering, I want to you to remember this. Control is a state of mind."

Without argument, Allyn set to untangling the necklace. It was tedious work made more difficult by the weather. At first, Allyn's limbs burned. His pale bare skin turned an irritated red under the rain and harsh wind. White splotches soon replaced the redness, and shortly thereafter, he lost all feeling in his fingertips. They were completely numb. He locked his jaw to prevent his teeth from chattering.

At the end of the first hour, he'd made little progress, and it was hard not to feel discouraged. The center was still wound together in an intricate knot, but Allyn thought there was more chain on each side. *It's like a Rubik's Cube. It will look worse before it looks better.*

Allyn saw marked improvement over the next hour. The knot was noticeably smaller and looser. The rain had let up, and the constant wind had become little more than erratic gusts. The sun even escaped the prison of overcast skies from time to time. It seemed the true winter rain hadn't begun.

Allyn rubbed his nose with the back of his hand. He probably *would* get sick, but his attention was elsewhere. He pulled the end of the chain back through a loop and then pulled tightly on each end. The chain twisted around itself and fell free, letting the diamond pendant dangle back and forth. Blinking in surprise, Allyn looked at the necklace. He'd done it. He turned to tell Jaxon, but the chairs were empty. Jaxon was gone. *Probably inside, where it's warm,* Allyn thought, frustrated. He wiped his forehead with the front of his shirt, and maybe he had a fever, but he wasn't cold anymore.

Jaxon was in the dining room when Allyn found him. He'd changed into dry clothes—so he wasn't as tough as he pretended to be—and was eating a steaming bowl of soup at a table that could seat close to twenty. The room was elegant, with forest-green walls above warm, dark wainscoting. An impressive silver chandelier hung above the center of the table with smaller sister chandeliers on both sides. Tossing the necklace onto the table, Allyn took a seat beside Jaxon.

"What did you learn?" Jaxon asked.

"That you're not against leaving me to freeze to death."

Jaxon snorted. "We haven't even had our first frost. You had nothing to worry about, except battling discomfort. You people are soft and pampered. It's no wonder you're so weak."

"I succeeded." Allyn gestured toward the necklace. "Despite my *weakness.*"

"The necklace wasn't the point. It was only a tool. The lesson was to learn to control your body, that your mind has power over it. You were supposed to learn that when given a task that requires deep focus, your mind could ignore the body's impulses. In this instance, resisting the cold."

"I was only distracted."

"No. You blocked everything out that wasn't a part of the task at hand. In order to wield, you need to focus on the power within and ignore the rest. With practice, you will learn to focus with precision and direct it wherever you need it, even in multiple directions at once. Still, I must say, I didn't expect you to finish."

"Why not?" Allyn asked. "I want to learn."

Jaxon shrugged.

"You thought I'd quit, didn't you?" A sense of pride swelled within Allyn. All he'd done was untangle a stupid necklace, but he found joy in proving people wrong. "I don't know what I've done to make you think I'm worthless or that I give up when things grow difficult, but let me assure you, I don't quit. And I *will* prove you wrong."

Jaxon eyed Allyn for a moment and then nodded. "Good. Then meet me in the clearing again tomorrow at dawn, and we'll begin again."

CHAPTER 9

"**W**HAT'S IT LIKE OUTSIDE?" LIAM asked, peeking over the monitor.

"Cold and wet." Allyn sat across from the boy working on his own computer. Liam had jumped on Allyn's offer to help digitize the library's archives and had lent him his spare computer. It was a battered and bruised relic, but it had a word processor and, after Liam's personal modifications, was able to join the manor's network—another of Liam's growing list of technical accomplishments.

"No, I mean *outside*. What's it like where you live?"

"Well," Allyn said, stalling to find an answer, "it's noisier."

"Noisier?"

Allyn leaned back in his chair. Liam, it seemed, was more interested in asking questions than working, and Allyn was fine with that. They were sitting in the center of the library, working across the table from each other, each transcribing a separate book. It reminded him of studying in his college library, though fewer people came here. Except for Nyla sitting in the back of the library, working on her own research, they were alone. He hadn't seen her since he and Graeme had encountered her in the library on his first day, but she still made him nervous.

"Yeah, you know how it is," Allyn said. "It's a lot busier than your little secluded area in the woods."

Liam's face flushed, and he looked away.

"Wait, have you ever been outside before? Have you ever left the manor?"

"Of course," Liam said, a little too quickly. "Noisy. Busy. I know what you mean."

"Come on, Liam. You're the only one I feel is completely honest with me around here. It's okay if you haven't left the manor. It's nothing to be embarrassed about."

"I've left before. I've just never been to the city."

"Well, like I said, it's busier. There's so much going on, you'll never be able to see it all, with enough people that you'll never be able to meet them all. Which is funny, because compared to other major cities, Portland is actually pretty small."

"Sounds exciting."

Allyn laughed. "It's not some magical fairyland or anything. It's just the way things are. It's actually a little boring."

"How can it be boring with so much going on?" Liam stood and took the book he'd just finished back to the shelf.

Damn, he's fast. Allyn wasn't even halfway through his own book. And his was shorter.

Liam grabbed the next book on the shelf and brought it back to the table.

"It's like life here," Allyn said. "I look around, and to me, it seems like a lot is happening, but to you, it's normal. It's like that for me, too. My average day starts at four thirty in the morning, and I'm at work by five or five thirty and usually work until at least eight at night. I do that seven days a week. It didn't leave a lot of time for excitement."

"That's like one hundred hours a week!"

"Sometimes more."

"Does everyone work like that?"

"No. I was trying to stand out to impress my boss and get promoted. A lot of good it did me, too. I'm an assistant librarian now." Allyn smiled, hiding the bitterness.

"Thanks for the help, by the way. It's nice to have someone talk to." Liam nodded over Allyn's shoulder.

Nyla was sitting at a desk, scribbling something in her notebook. Her white hair was frazzled and tied into a knot on top of her head. In the three days since Allyn had offered to help Liam, Nyla had been in the library, too. She hadn't said anything to either of them—though Allyn often heard her muttering to herself.

"What's she working on?" Allyn whispered.

"I don't know for sure, but I think it has to do with the way Baylis was found."

"Her husband?"

"No, but something was going on between them. I think they were..."

"What?"

"Nothing."

He's hiding something. "What happened to him?"

"To Baylis?" Liam asked. "They found him *dry*."

"I don't understand."

"You're training with Jaxon, right?"

"If you can call it that. Today, he had me separating a bucket of gravel into different groups organized by color, keeping count of how many were in each bucket—all while sitting in front of the fire, wrapped in a blanket. Each time I lost count, he moved me closer to the fire."

Liam laughed. "Mental exercises. Sometimes, I think he finds joy in thinking up new cruel mental games. Has he told you where a magi's power comes from?"

Allyn patted his chest. "Within."

"I mean the actual fire, water, or air."

"No."

"Well, it does come from within, but probably not how you expect. Take water, for example. Have you ever heard the term *water weight*?"

Allyn nodded.

"Okay, well, a normal person has about thirteen gallons of water inside their body, so when a magi wields water, they're actually pulling it out of their bodies. They're not creating it or pulling it out of thin air or anything. It's *their* water. Obviously, our bodies need that water, so we can't pull too much out, or we'll die of dehydration. That's why most magi turn it into ice. Since water expands when it's frozen, they don't have to use as much. Plus, it's more lethal that way, but that's a different point.

"But the same goes for fire and air, too, though fire is a little more difficult to understand. Whatever a magi wields, it comes directly out of their body. Baylis was found *dry*. He had *nothing* left in him. No water, no air, no heat. Someone had pulled it out of him."

"How is that possible?" Allyn asked.

"It's not supposed to be. A magi can only wield from their own body. Even a cleric uses their own body's strength and wellness to heal."

Allyn shifted uncomfortably. Nyla was sitting behind them and could likely hear what they were saying—if she was listening. "Graeme said I was healed. Doesn't that mean a cleric pulled the pain and injuries out of me?"

"No. A cleric doesn't *pull* it from you. They just replace it with their own health. Think of it this way. If you have a cut on your arm, a cleric bandages it with their skin. Your wound will heal, but the same wound will appear on their arm, and they don't have anyone to heal them. They have to heal the natural way. What happened to Baylis shouldn't be possible."

Allyn watched Nyla scribble in her notebook, oblivious to their conversation. He understood her tenacity. She hadn't lost a friend. She'd lost someone deeply important to her—a piece of herself. "No wonder she hates me."

"What do you mean?"

"She's the one who healed me," Allyn said. "She lost Baylis, and then I gave her my pain, too."

Jaxon came for Liam a short time later. Liam never talked about his training, but Allyn assumed it was pretty advanced. Graeme was a grand mage, so like the ability, his proficiency was probably in his blood. If his computer ability was any indication, Liam would be a force to be reckoned with. Liam's departure left Allyn alone with Nyla, but she was in her own world, somewhere far removed from Allyn or anyone else.

Allyn watched her from across the room. She pored over several open books that surrounded her in a semicircle. Scribbling furiously in her notebook, she quietly muttered to herself. He didn't know if she was reading aloud or talking to herself, though neither would have surprised him.

She looked up from her notebook and in Allyn's direction. He threw his head down, feigning concentration on the computer screen in front of him. He'd been finished for some time, but didn't know what to do next since Liam usually chose his projects. When he built up the courage to look in Nyla's direction, she was back to work.

Without knowing what else to do, Allyn returned the book to the shelf. It wasn't a book so much as a journal recounting a magi family's struggle to hide after the Fracture. It ended abruptly, leaving Allyn with a pit in his stomach. He hoped the family had fled and left behind their nonessential belongings, including the book, but something told him that was unlikely. He selected the next book, but it was written in a language using an alphabet he didn't recognize. Frowning, he put the book back but made a mental note so he could tell Liam where he'd left off.

Behind him, Nyla rose to her feet, gathering the books on the table into a stack in her arms. She grabbed the ladder awkwardly with her free hand, using her chin to hold the books against her chest, and pulled the ladder into position. She was halfway up when the books fell. Allyn winced. It was like watching an elderly man fall and knowing something would be damaged. Liam had instilled in him a respect for the text. To respect the text was to respect the author and the life they lived—their struggle, glory and all. In most cases, the texts were the only remaining history of the author's life, and that deserved a gentle hand and honored treatment.

Before he knew what he was doing, he was across the room, helping Nyla scoop up the books. Thankfully, there wasn't any serious damage. "Do you need some help? I could hand them to you."

"I've got it," Nyla said.

"Let me help. You obviously have your hands full. I don't want to see these books get ruined before we've had a chance to transcribe them. For Liam's sake."

"Fine. That one first." She pointed at the bottom book. It was thin, probably a collection of papers that had been bound together at a later date. Allyn handed it to her after she rose to position.

"Where to next?" He grabbed the ladder. She pointed to the far end of the room. "Hold on."

Book by book, Allyn and Nyla returned the books to their rightful places.

"Thank you," Nyla said when they were done.

"You're welcome. I'm in here almost every day. If you ever need help—"

"You can't help me."

"Of course not."

"No. You can't help me because I don't know what I'm looking for."

"You're right. I wouldn't be much help then, would I? But if something changes and you could use an extra pair of eyes, let me know. I'm good at doing research. It's something I do every day at work."

"Why are you being so nice to me?"

"You healed me."

"So?"

"You saved my life."

"It was nothing personal," Nyla said. "It's what I do."

Allyn frowned. "I still appreciate it."

"You're welcome." The words sounded forced and unnatural, as though she were trying them on for the first time, but she wasn't trying to rip his head off anymore. And that, Allyn thought, was important.

———————·•·———————

Liam kicked a rock, sending it cascading off the trail and bouncing off a tree. A squirrel darted out of the underbrush in front of him. Startled, Liam came to an abrupt stop, his feet sliding in the mud. The rain had let up for the moment, though if the black clouds suggested anything, it was sure to return at any time. The squirrel vanished back into the forest. Liam kicked another rock, meaning to send it down the path, but it veered off in an unintended direction.

His training session hadn't gone well. They never did. Jaxon was his reassuring self, telling him that his time would come, to be patient and to keep working. But Liam knew the truth.

He was a failure. A disgrace. An outcast.

He was probably the first son of a grand mage who couldn't wield. He'd spent his childhood like a prince, waiting for the day when his father would pass and he would inherit the crown. But unlike a king, a grand mage could resign the post when he or she could no longer lead. And Liam's ascent to grand mage had never been a sure thing. His Family would have its say. They would choose whom to follow. If he couldn't wield, he wasn't a magi, and he would never become the grand mage. His father would never relinquish command to Liam, and the Family would never follow him if he did.

He wanted to release the festering self-loathing building inside him with an animalistic scream, but a display of emotion of that magnitude would be a lapse in control. And a magi who lost control was a magi who couldn't wield. Or at least that was what Jaxon always said.

The exercise was pointless. Liam couldn't wield anyway, so what would be the harm? *Maybe*, he thought, *I can't because I've already lost control.* The desire might have corrupted him. *Do other magi have self-doubts? Do they struggle for control, too?*

Allyn had started training and wasn't shy about talking about it or asking questions, but Liam had no one to talk to. Jaxon was his instructor, but he didn't seem to understand. And since Jaxon was also the son of a grand mage—albeit from a different Family—talking about it with him was even more difficult.

Leira was a cleric, and they were different, so she couldn't help, and he would *never* ask his father—that would only shame him further. He was on his own and had hoped to find something in the library, but so far, his search had been fruitless.

Liam's pocket vibrated, stopping him mid-stride. He conspicuously checked for onlookers—even several acres from the manor, watchful eyes could be present—and when he was satisfied there weren't any, he slid off the trail and into the forest, where he hid behind the base of a large tree, with his phone in hand.

His father would kill him if he ever found it. The manor's computers, security systems, and jammers were all designed for one thing: keeping the wrong people out. His phone was a gateway to the outside world, and with it came a potential threat of dependency. The day they became dependent would be the Day of Disintegration when the remaining Families splintered into oblivion.

Liam believed otherwise, even if he didn't voice his thoughts. Technology wasn't to blame for their faltering numbers, and it didn't breed out their ability to wield. The real problem was how they straddled the fence between both worlds, using technology while disavowing it, claiming purity but knowing it was a lie. He didn't know who the magi were anymore or who they would become, and that uncertainty caused a splinter in their ranks. Surely it had created a similar splinter in him and the growing number of other magi who couldn't wield. Technology wasn't the problem. Uncertainty was.

But who would listen to him? Who would believe him? He was a technological genius who couldn't wield. He was living proof of his father's ideology. He *had* to learn to wield. Until he did, he wouldn't have a voice.

The touchscreen phone had a mirrored image of a bitten apple on the back. Leira had found it and given it to him after a fair amount of pleading on his end. He still owed her a favor. His father might kill him for having it, but Graeme would destroy her if he ever found out where Liam got the phone.

The words "Search Complete" glowed on the screen. It didn't tell him what the search had found; he would have to check his computer in the library for that, but the search was done. And they would have an answer. Even if the search hadn't found anything, they would have an answer of sorts. In that case, they might be able to finally rule out Allyn being a distant relative. But if it did find something...

Liam smiled. Being useful would feel good.

———————•••———————

"It's not the results I distrust," Graeme said, "but the manner in which they were discovered."

Allyn, who seemed as annoyed as he was, stirred beside Liam. His father sat behind his desk, leaning back in his chair, his hands together in front of his face. Rain streaked down the window, fogging the edges and forming condensation on the inside.

Liam shook his head. Graeme told him that he trusted him but didn't trust the tools he'd used. He wanted his own people to recreate Liam's research by hand to verify the results. But he wouldn't be looking for verification. He would be looking for inconsistencies, mistakes, anything to ignore what was right there in front of his face.

"I'll have Leira organize a team and search through the archives by hand," Graeme said. "Just to be sure."

"To what end?" Liam asked, louder than he intended. "I already searched the archives. I've already done exactly what you're going to do. It's a waste of time."

Allyn shifted. He opened his mouth partway, as if he were going to say something, but he remained silent. Liam was thankful for that. This was between him and his father, and Allyn didn't need to get involved.

"Don't," Graeme said. "I am still your father, and I am still the head of this Family. If I need to confirm someone's story—anyone's story—it is well within my right to do so."

"It's not a story."

"It is until proven otherwise."

"What more do you need?" Liam asked. "Allyn is one of us. His last name shares the same root as two ancient Family names."

"Two Families that were killed off more than a thousand years ago."

"Did we expect to find anything else?" Liam asked. "If he was a member of this Family or any other large Family, we wouldn't be conducting this search to begin with. Why do you always do this? Why don't you trust me?"

"I do trust you."

"Then why do you need confirmation? If you don't understand how I did it, I'd be happy to show you."

"That's not necessary. I wouldn't understand anyway," Graeme said with a smirk.

"It's not that much different than what you'll have Leira do," Liam said. "I conducted a search beginning with basic letter combinations. It's not as easy as just typing in 'Allyn Kaplan' and hitting search. Names change over time, and words can be spelled in multiple ways. So I included a search for basic sound constructions. I got tens of thousands of hits. Anything with those letters or sound constructions was found, even if they had nothing to do with names, so I refined the search until I had a more manageable number.

"From there, I actually went to the source material and searched through it that way. So I guess, Father, if you still feel the need to verify my findings, I can point you to the specific book where you can do so."

Graeme tapped his fingertips together. "That won't be necessary."

Liam couldn't help smiling. It was the first time he'd been able to convince his father to trust him. He turned to Allyn, who gave him a slight nod of approval.

"You know," Graeme said, walking to the bar at the back of the room, "that this still doesn't mean you're one of us."

"I know," Allyn said.

"Names are complicated," Graeme said. "They change. They evolve. Wives assume the names of their husbands. Children are adopted. People change their names legally or simply assume a new identity. You may share a name but not the blood."

"I understand," Allyn said.

"Still, it warrants further investigation." Graeme turned back to Liam. "You said you found the name in a diary?"

"Yes," Liam said. "The diary of Mathieu Latique. He talks about the rumored destruction of the Capalonian Family and fears for his own."

"And you didn't find any other mention of the Capalonian Family?" Graeme asked.

Liam shook his head. "Nothing that was useful."

Graeme poured himself a glass of water and took a drink. "I'm going to contact Darian Hyland, Grand Mage of the Hyland Family, and ask for their permission to search their library."

"Why not have them do it for us?" Allyn asked.

"If you and your sister are of magi blood and can potentially wield, that would shake the very foundation from which we stand. It's not something to take lightly."

CHAPTER 10

LUKAS TOOK KENDYL WITH HIM everywhere he went. She became a fixture at his side, always seen but never heard, like a little trophy wife to be paraded around. Jarrell assumed it was another form of imprisonment, one without walls but constant with supervision. She accompanied him during meals, meetings, training sessions, outside excursions, and even during the night. He didn't know what form of punishment her nightly routine took, and he wasn't about to ask. That could cause a scene and attract attention. That wouldn't help her escape.

Kendyl and Lukas sat at the front of the room between his bodyguards, Kaleb and Reyland. The clatter of forks on plates and glasses on tables, along with general commotion, echoed throughout the large room. In the makeshift dining hall folding tables and chairs were arranged in a chaotic manner, nothing like the formal dining room in Graeme's manor.

Kendyl ate in silence. Jarrell had never heard her speak. He'd heard her cries, her pleas, which she screamed through tears and between sobs, but he didn't know how her real voice sounded. He set down his fork, having lost his appetite.

Still, she held her chin up and gazed through the room, seemingly unafraid to make eye contact with her captors. He didn't know how she did it. Jarrell had seen stronger men break quicker. She had an inner strength that kept her from cracking. And that was what Lukas was after.

"Lukas won't like seeing that go to waste," Keven said, pointing at the half-eaten contents of Jarrell's plate. Keven was one of Lukas's youngest followers. Maybe fifteen or sixteen years old, he was the same age as Jarrell's son. But Simon would never have followed a tyrant.

"I don't have the appetite I once did," Jarrell said. "And I haven't done anything to work one up, either. I haven't left this compound in weeks."

"Our day will come. We need to stay strong. You should eat." The voice may have been Keven's, but the words were Lukas's. Why were the young so easily influenced? So corruptible?

Was I once so naive? "You're right." Jarrell picked up his fork and shoveled in a mouthful. It was easier and less conspicuous than arguing. Keven was soon caught up in a conversation with a member from another table, and Jarrell slid his plate to the center of the table.

He gazed across the room at Kendyl. Her dark hair was pulled back into a ponytail. Her heart-shaped face was the color of pristine porcelain without any bruises or cuts. Her skin showed no evidence of her torture. Those marks were on the faces of the other clerics in the dining room, who, like Jarrell, took turns healing her wounds. They wore bruises, black eyes, and treated cuts, scrapes, and burns, so that Kendyl didn't have to, so she could be beaten again the next day—and the day after. Jarrell was still recovering from the first healing that had almost killed him.

She needed hope. She needed to know that someone in the room was on her side. He was going to tell her, and he hoped she believed him. Her eyes met his and lingered. Even from across the room, he thought he could make out the green of her eyes and the slight imperfection in her right pupil. He nodded.

Kendyl remained expressionless. She had no way of knowing what his nod meant or what his intentions were. He was just another person in a long line of people who had healed her so she could be abused again later. She had no reason to trust him and no reason to assume he was any different from the rest of them.

Lukas touched her arm and stood. Kaleb and Reyland followed suit. With a hand at the small of her back, Lukas guided Kendyl around the table and through the center of the room. Jarrell and the other followers stood and bowed their heads as Lukas's procession passed. Eyes downcast, Jarrell thought he felt Kendyl's gaze as she walked by, but when he looked up, her attention was elsewhere.

Jarrell followed the procession out of the room and through the compound. It was his rotation. Kendyl's well-being would fall to him tonight. His stomach became a gnawing pit, and his hands started to quiver. He hated his part in Lukas's schemes. Graeme needed someone on the inside, and Jarrell had volunteered, but he hadn't volunteered for *this*. He wanted to run, escape while he could, before Lukas caught on. And Lukas *would* catch on. Jarrell would escape as soon as he was sure Kendyl was safe, when he had something to show for his time with the enemy.

The procession stopped outside the storage room Lukas's followers had nicknamed the Range. It had originally housed flammable oils and solvents, keeping them dry and away from sunlight, but now it was used for other purposes. Lukas lifted the lever and swung it aside, opening the large steel door, making the dry hinge squeal. Yellow fluorescent lights flickered on, illuminating a long narrow chamber with concrete walls. Scorch marks discolored the wall at the far end, and large chunks of concrete had been blasted away to reveal the rebar inside.

"Wait here," Lukas said. He led Kendyl across the room to the far wall and grabbed a chain off the ground. Hooking one end around a rod of rebar, he attached the other to a large leather belt, which he wrapped around Kendyl.

Jarrell ran his hands through his hair, feeling more scalp than he used to, trying to find a way to prevent Lukas from following through with his latest atrocity.

Lukas said something to Kendyl that Jarrell couldn't make out then walked back to the procession, his face expressionless.

"What are we doing?" Jarrell asked.

"Training," Lukas said.

"How is this training?" Jarrell was playing a dangerous game by questioning Lukas in front of his closest followers. If he was too forceful, he would be the one chained to the wall to be used as target practice.

"She has the power to stop it," Lukas said, loud enough for Kendyl to hear. "She knows what she has to do. She just won't do it. We're helping her along." Lukas nodded to Kaleb and whispered, "Nothing too strong. I want it to hurt, but I don't want to kill her. Scare her, nothing more. Understand?"

Kaleb's grin faded, but he nodded and stepped forward. If Kendyl knew what was coming next, she didn't show it. She stood tall, her feet firmly planted on the ground, facing them down. Her resolve faded as a cascade of fire erupted from Kaleb's hands. He hurled it toward her. She threw her hands in front of her face and tried to dive to the side, but the chain snapped taught, pulling her back. The wall of fire hit her from the side.

Coughing, Jarrell shielded his nose from the smells of burnt hair and watched as Kendyl rose to her feet again.

Her skin was red, but not scorched or blistered. It looked more like a severe windburn. Kaleb had extraordinary control. His fire burned colder. Jarrell could tell it was painful, even if Kendyl did her best to hide it, but it wasn't fatal.

"Again," Lukas said.

Kaleb brought his hands up level with his shoulders, and with a deep breath, he swung them forward in an exaggerated clap. Dust kicked up from the floor as a gust of wind threw Kendyl against the wall. Her head slapped the concrete with a disgusting crack, and she slumped forward, held by the chain in a half-standing, half-crouching position, unconscious.

"I said to scare her!" Lukas bellowed. "Not kill her!"

Kaleb bowed his head. "My apologies. It won't happen again."

"Out!" Lukas commanded. Kaleb hastily left the room, and Lukas turned to Jarrell. "It's your turn."

Jarrell strode forward as quickly as he could without appearing eager. He took Kendyl's head in his hands. Her hair was matted with blood from a laceration across the back of her skull, and she had a concussion that he would need to monitor, but her pulse and breathing were steady. "She's alive."

"Bring her to," Lukas said.

"She can't withstand any more of this."

"Then heal her."

I can't withstand any more of this. "Even with my healing, she will be weak. How many days has this gone on? She has limits."

"That's what I'm counting on," Lukas said. "Wake her up."

Jarrell shook his head, but did as he was ordered. Two pains formed in his head as Kendyl's wounds healed—a dull ache, probably a symptom of the concussion, and a sharp pain where his skin was splitting apart forming a wound identical to the one healing on Kendyl's scalp. He became dizzy, and fatigue swept over him as her concussion became his.

"I'm sorry," Jarrell whispered in her ear. "I don't like this." He pulled away and noticed her eyes were open. She looked up at him, a puzzled look on her face. Jarrell smiled. "I don't know when, and I don't know how, but I'm going to get you out of this place. Okay?"

She nodded slightly.

He patted her on the shoulder and stumbled back to the front of the room.

"What did you say to her?" Lukas asked.

Jarrell looked back at Kendyl, who watched him with renewed interest. "I told her to do whatever you tell her to, because I don't know how many more injuries like that I can heal."

Lukas smiled. "You see, Kendyl? We're all rooting for your success." He turned to Reyland. "You're up."

CHAPTER 11

"**H**OW FAR IS THIS PLACE?" Allyn asked, looking out the car window. They drove down an empty two-lane highway through a densely wooded forest in the Cascade Mountains. The road had fallen into disrepair and was plagued by potholes and cheap concrete patches. Loose gravel covered the road, offering traction against ice in the coming winter months. It was the kind of scenic highway that was seldom traveled, often forgotten, and otherwise ignored—the perfect place to hide.

"A few hours," Graeme said. "It's along the coastline."

A few hours?

They'd already been on the road for over two hours, having left before sunrise, and the commute was wearing on him. Graeme sat in front of him, facing him, in a black leather bucket seat that butted up back to back with the driver's seat. Jaxon drove, and Nyla sat beside Graeme. Liam sat with Allyn on a long bench seat in the back of the car. Being forced to face two people in such a confined space felt strange. Allyn found himself exchanging awkward glances with Nyla. He would find himself watching her, only to have to avert his eyes when she caught him. Then a few moments later, he would feel her eyes on him, but when he glanced back, it was her eyes that would dart away. It was the type of game lovers played, but today, and within the tight confines of the car, it was just uncomfortable.

"Then I assume it's as far out of the way as your manor?" Allyn asked.

Graeme grinned. "You could say that."

"The Hyland Family lives on forty-five acres of coastal property," Liam said. "Their house, a twenty-thousand-square-foot mansion, backs up to a cliff overlooking the Pacific Ocean. They're actually *more* secluded than we are."

"I thought you said you've never been there?" Allyn asked.

"I haven't," Liam said. "I just like to know where I'm going."

Allyn laughed. "You really are a strange kid."

Liam's face flushed, and he looked at the floor.

Wincing, Allyn wanted to say something. He'd unintentionally embarrassed his friend. He'd meant it as a compliment, but Liam could be a bit... emotional. Saying something else would only make it worse. *Teenagers*, Allyn thought. *They're all the same.*

Jaxon and Leira talked in the front seat. About what, Allyn didn't know—he couldn't hear, but their soft voices were the only noise in the otherwise-silent car. Leira was wearing the same diamond-pendant necklace Jaxon had tasked Allyn with untangling. She played with it, twisting it with her fingers while her other hand rubbed the stubble on the back of Jaxon's neck.

Allyn leaned his forehead against the window. It was a trick his mother had taught him to fight motion sickness. The cold glass felt good against his skin, allowing him to focus on the relief and not the swaying motion of the car. As he'd grown older, his trouble with carsickness had faded, but he always assumed part of it was because he was the driver. When he drove, he had control—something he didn't have at the moment.

"Can I ask you something?" Allyn turned to Graeme.

"Of course." Graeme always seemed to encourage an open line of communication, but it often felt at odds with his direct, sometimes-cold demeanor.

"Why is there so much resistance to what Lukas is trying to do?"

Silence filled the car. Not the silence of before, but complete silence. Jaxon and Leira stopped talking, and five pairs of eyes focused on him.

"I mean," Allyn said awkwardly, "isn't there something to be said about not having to live in secret? Not having to hide who you really are? It can't be easy."

"It isn't easy," Graeme said, "but it is necessary."

"Why?"

"We're different, Allyn."

"So?"

"So," Graeme said, "when was the last time being different was a good thing? When was the last time *any* society of a certain size looked upon someone of a different race, color, or religion and accepted them for what they were?"

"Well…" Allyn stalled, shifting in his seat.

Graeme didn't wait for him to continue. "There are only two things that happen to minority cultures. They're either assimilated into the majority, or they're destroyed."

"That's not true," Allyn said. "There are elements of minority cultures that have entered ours."

"Like what?"

"I don't know. Food? Holidays? I'm not a sociologist."

"That's because there's an overlap between cultures," Graeme said. "Most cultures celebrate birthdays or anniversaries. And holidays are shared by nearly every culture in the world, big or small. It's not a coincidence they all happen to fall at about the same time of year. But what I'm talking about are truly alien cultures. How much of Native American culture has been adopted by American society?"

"I don't know."

"Not much then," Graeme said. "Being different is usually met with violence. Not always physical violence, but emotional violence. Psychological violence. People are afraid of the alien, just as they're afraid of change. They fear it because they're scared it will erase their own traditions. It's an attack on their beliefs. People resist because it's *dangerous*."

"I'd argue people are afraid of what they don't know," Allyn said. "The monster hiding in the closet is scarier than the monster standing in the daylight, where people can see what it really is."

"I don't disagree with you there," Graeme said. "But if people are afraid of the different because they believe that it's dangerous, how will they react when they realize that we truly are *dangerous*?"

"Anyone can be dangerous," Allyn said.

"True, but think of it this way. You restrict access to weapons. You have to have a license to carry one in public, certain kinds are illegal, and you can't bring one into a school, hospital, or government facility. They have to be registered and stowed away properly. I am a weapon, Allyn. And I am every bit as dangerous as the weapons you have created. Will I have to have a license to live? Will my access to schools or hospitals be denied? Will you make me register my abilities? Will I be stowed away in the name of protection?"

Allyn didn't know what to say, so he didn't say anything.

"This debate has raged for hundreds of years, and nobody has been able to solve it."

"It's all happened before, hasn't it?" Allyn asked.

Graeme nodded. "Living openly isn't a new aspiration. Acceptance isn't a modern dream. I told you of a period when we were targeted, persecuted, and killed for what we are. It began when a man named Girak Klay started a movement within the magi order to live openly. By all accounts, Girak was a gifted speaker, and hundreds of besieged magi fled to his cause. The Council, still crippled from the Fracture a century earlier, was convinced Girak and his followers would leave the Order if they didn't heed his movement's demands. It began small. Magi advertised medicinal remedies and health services, hiding them behind flamboyant concoctions of bright colors that foamed, hissed, and bubbled. As the public became used to the relief of these colorful elixirs, the magi stepped out even further. The cycle repeated itself until an ailing person would see the cleric and not the fake potion they hid behind."

"What happened?" Allyn asked. "Why the backlash?"

"Even the most powerful cleric cannot save everyone," Graeme said. "Factor that with the rise of religion and the increased role of the church. We were associated with death and could perform the unexplainable. We were a threat to the establishment. The church called us witches and wizards and convinced the populace we were cavorting with the devil. They called for our heads, and hundreds of magi burned at the stake."

"But they didn't have any proof."

"You don't need proof," Graeme said. "Not as long as you say it loud and say it often. Girak's movement led to the largest massacre since the Fracture, and it was a death blow to our Order."

"Wasn't there something they could do? Some way to defend themselves?"

"A magi's power comes from within. We use our own bodies, our own heat, our own water and air. If we overextend ourselves, we die. But yes, they could have fought, and some did, but most turned themselves in to avoid the stake, only to find their imprisonment a slower, more painful death. Because once captured, the magi were denied food and water, and the convicted witches and wizards more often died of dehydration, malnourishment, or exposure to the elements than fire at the stake."

"They listened to Girak," Liam said, "in an attempt to keep the Order together, but in doing so, broke it apart."

Allyn had forgotten the others were listening.

"It would have happened either way," Graeme said. "Whether this way, or if Girak had fled, it was inevitable. And it's the reason we continue to hide today. It seems, however, that history has a way of repeating itself."

Allyn thought for a moment. "Girak would have left the Order if they didn't listen to him, but in listening to him, the Order doomed themselves. What can you hope to do so that Lukas doesn't do the same thing?"

"We will unite the Families against him," Graeme said. "Where Girak threatened to fracture the Order a second time, I aim to rebuild it and, with our combined strength, pull Lukas back from the edge."

"And if he resists?"

"Then I'll do whatever is required to save my Family."

———————•••—————————

Allyn heard the ocean before he saw it. The steady roar of crashing waves hung in the air like a bass note, swelling and descending with natural rhythm. Its ominous vibrations rumbled against his chest, doing little to ease his nerves. Questions he'd done his best to smother crept to the surface. How much had Graeme told the Hyland Family? What would happen if they weren't as welcoming as the McCollum Family had been? What if they saw him as a threat?

Jaxon followed the bend of the private driveway, passing a mix of pine and bare maple trees. The driveway straightened out, and the Hyland Estate came into view. A massive two-story manor sat atop a single green hill overlooking a perfectly landscaped garden. Even in the early winter months, it was alive with color. Oranges, yellows, and pinks mixed with reds, browns, and greens, all working to make the pale-gray color of the estate more inviting. Behind the estate, the ground dropped away abruptly, and dark-blue water stretched out below an overcast sky until it met the gray horizon. The ocean pounded the rocky cliff with steady crashing waves, blue water turning white, spraying mist two hundred feet in the air and coating the manor windows like a constant rain.

Jaxon brought the car to rest under a covered awning that led to the main entrance. No one was waiting for them. Allyn stepped out, stretching his lower back and trying to shake some feeling back into his legs. Four hours in a car was a long time. Four hours with little to do was an eternity.

He shivered. The cold air was more of a fine mist and smelled of salt and dead fish. Allyn couldn't see another house or building anywhere. If the McCollum Manor was hidden, then the Hyland Estate was truly secluded.

"Graeme McCollum," a high-pitched male voice said. "It's been a long time."

A tall wiry man with short and styled blond hair stepped out of the house. He was young, in his late twenties, with a square face marred by a large nose that looked as though it had been broken more than once. He was wearing a pair of denim jeans and a loose fitting T-shirt instead of the compression armor the McCollum Family wore. His narrow eyes, pale blue in color, scanned the six of them.

"Grand Mage Hyland," Graeme said with a bow of his head. "We appreciate the hospitality."

"Please," he said. "Skip the traditions. We're excited to have you."

"This is Darian Hyland," Graeme said, turning to his group, "Grand Mage of the Hyland Family."

"Welcome," Darian said.

"You have, of course, met my children, Leira and Liam."

Leira and Liam nodded to Darian.

"Of course," Darian said with a smile. "It's good to see you again."

"This is Jaxon, an exchange from the Green Family. He is also our instructor and point man."

Jaxon shook Darian's hand. "Thank you for your hospitality."

"Exchange?" Allyn asked quietly, turning to Liam.

"Every family sends one of their own to neighboring Families and receives one in return," Liam said. "It's a way to keep the bloodlines from interbreeding as well as keep Families in contact. Jaxon is in line to become the next grand mage of the Green Family and came to us to mentor under my father."

"Is there a member of your Family with the Hyland Family?" Allyn asked.

Liam shook his head. "Under Grand Mage Hyland, the Hyland Family doesn't follow many of our traditions."

"Allyn!" Graeme said, his face stern, hiding embarrassment. "Come over here, please."

Darian Hyland smiled as Allyn approached, revealing yellow teeth stained from coffee, tea, and cigarettes or a combination of all.

Allyn left Liam behind and stepped forward to shake Darian's hand. "Thank you for having us."

"He's not a...?" Darian turned to Graeme.

Graeme shook his head.

"Such confidence," Darian said. "Such a presence. Are you sure?"

"That's why we are here," Graeme said.

"Of course," Darian said. "Please, come in. Our archives are yours. They aren't as extensive as yours, but I hope you can find what you're looking for. If there's anything we can do to help, just let us know."

Darian opened the door to let them in.

The Hyland Estate was different from the McCollum Manor in nearly every way. Where the McCollum Manor was a house built prior to modern comforts of electricity and running water, only to have been updated later, the Hyland Estate *felt* new. Instead of private, compartmentalized rooms, the interior used an open concept where people were free to gather and socialize. The main room, a large living quarter with vaulted ceilings, had multiple couches, a bar, and even a TV.

The McCollum Manor felt like a library where occupants were expected to be quiet and have little interaction, but the Hyland Estate felt like a fraternity house. Young magi hooted and hollered, chasing each other through the house, while others lounged on the couches, watching television. Windows were open, allowing the sea breeze to blow through the house, and Allyn could hear music playing somewhere in the estate.

Darian introduced them to the people in the living quarter, and Allyn was quickly lost in the steady stream of names. As he turned to leave, something on the television caught Allyn's attention—a picture of his sister. "Can you turn that up please?" Allyn asked.

The local news anchor, Cynthia Wu, an Asian woman with a nasally voice and a tendency to overenunciate, gave her report from the parking lot of Kendyl's apartment. "...been ten days since Miss Kaplan's disappearance, and authorities are no closer to locating her. In the most recent development, her brother, Allyn Kaplan, who had earlier been named as a person of interest, is now the prime suspect." An outdated college picture of Allyn, probably something taken from Kendyl's apartment, replaced the reporter's image on the television. Then the screen went black.

Allyn gaped, turning to Darian, who held the remote.

"It's a distraction," Darian said. "Focus only on what you can do, not what they're doing."

It's not that simple, Allyn wanted to say. These people didn't understand the complexities of law enforcement or what it meant to be a wanted criminal. Every beat cop, state officer, sheriff, and detective was looking for him. And if this story gained traction—and it looked as though it had—then the police wouldn't be the only prying eyes. Vested citizens taken by Kendyl's story would find ways to help. All it took was one person with one tip to bring Allyn into custody. If that happened, he would never find Kendyl, she would never be saved, and Allyn's only opportunity to clear his name would be gone. Only she could corroborate his story and prove his innocence.

Allyn nodded, realizing he partially agreed with Darian. He needed to focus on his efforts.

The library was on the second floor, in the northern wing of the house. Liam frowned upon the sight of it. Books were thrown haphazardly onto shelves, tables, and chairs. There was no semblance of order or organization. Wherever the books landed was where they stayed. Dust had settled onto the shelves and book covers. Daylight streamed in from the large window, bleaching the texts. The room smelled old and musty, as though no one had set foot in it for years.

"It's not much," Darian said, "but it's what we have."

Liam didn't waste any time. He stepped forward and began pulling books from shelves and flipping through the pages, scanning the content inside. Within a matter of minutes, he had begun to create his own organized mess—diaries with diaries, histories with histories, and parchment with parchment.

Graeme and Darian offered them well wishes and turned to leave. Jaxon and Leira left a short time after, leaving Allyn alone with Liam and Nyla.

"This is a mess," Liam said when they were safe from prying ears.

"It's sad," Allyn said. He held up an old newspaper. The paper was stained and yellowed, and the faint text was impossible to read. "How much do you think was lost, just in this room alone?"

"Hopefully, nothing important to our search," Liam said lightly, but Allyn could hear his pain. Liam had made preserving the library at the McCollum Manor his mission—without thanks or show of appreciation from his Family—only to see so little care taken in another library. Allyn imagined he must have been feeling a mix of pain, frustration, and helplessness.

Nyla ignored Liam's organized piles and began sifting through books of her own choosing. She had asked to come, and Graeme had obliged. Allyn thought her interest had little to do with their search.

"I found the reference to the Capalonian Family in a diary," Liam said. "So I think we should start by looking in other diaries. We don't have time to read them all, so just skim them. If anything jumps out, take a closer look. When you're done, make a pile over here, and I'll go through them a second time to see if you missed anything."

Allyn cleared a spot on a leather armchair, then sat and slid one of Liam's piles of diaries in front of him. They varied in size and binding. The first one was a thick leather tome with elegant cursive script on the inside. The first entry was dated April 22, 1784, and the flowing handwriting made it difficult to skim, so Allyn found himself reading entire entries.

From what he could tell, the author was a woman in her early adult years, living in New England. In one particular entry, she wrote of having kept a secret from her husband. Their young boy had fallen and broken his arm, and after the local doctor struggled to set the bone, he told them that it wouldn't heal correctly and that the boy would never have full use of his arm again. The woman had the ability to heal her son, mend the bone, and provide a more hopeful future for him, but doing so would risk exposing her secret and putting her life and the life of her son in danger.

Allyn flipped the page and read the next entry, then the next, and the next, hoping to find out what she did. But there was no further mention of the issue. Whatever she decided, she hadn't written about it.

The next volume was a thin book held closed by an elastic band that snapped apart like a dry twig as Allyn tried to slide it over the cover. The content held little that supported their search, but it offered another gut-wrenching portrayal of the struggles of underground magi trying to assimilate into the world of humans. Halfway through it, Allyn had to put it down.

"I can't do this," Allyn said. "It's all death, struggle, and more death. Are they all like this?"

Liam put down his book. He'd stopped organizing and started scanning with Allyn. "Not all of them, but they will all tell of some sort of struggle."

Allyn pinched the bridge of his nose.

"What would your diary look like?" Liam asked. "I'm sure your own life has had its share of problems."

"Nothing like this."

"Maybe not."

"How do you do it?" Allyn asked. "How do you read these without becoming an emotional wreck?"

"I'm a teenager." Liam smiled. "I'm already an emotional wreck."

Allyn laughed, the tightness in his chest easing a bit.

"They're just words on a page," Nyla said, never looking up from her own book. She sat straight backed and cross legged in the corner.

"They're more than that," Liam said.

"Not if we don't read them," Nyla said.

Liam looked at Allyn with a confused look on his face.

"What she's saying," Allyn said, "is that only when we read these books do the words become real and the authors live again. That's how you can read them without having a nervous breakdown. If you don't read them, if you don't preserve them, then their struggles were meaningless."

Liam smirked. "Makes sense, I guess."

Nyla watched Allyn from the corner as he opened his book again. A small smile appeared on her lips. Allyn smiled back and started to read. After a while, the air, trapped within the confines of the small room with three occupants, became hot and stale. Allyn removed his coat and threw it across the back of his chair. Liam's forehead glistened with sweat, and Nyla had even rolled up her sleeves. Allyn thought about suggesting opening the window, but he already knew what Liam's answer would be. Besides, the window didn't look as though it had been opened in years, and Allyn doubted it would open at all.

Allyn's stomach growled, letting out a slow, drawn-out cry that could have been heard from across the room. Liam didn't look up. He looked invested in the text in front of him. *What time is it anyway?* Dawn had arrived hours ago, and they'd missed breakfast. The dull-gray overcast sky didn't offer much in the way of suggesting the time, but it had to be past lunch. Were they supposed to find Graeme when they were done, or was he planning to come get them?

"Look at this," Liam said. He sat on the ground with his legs crossed in front of him, hunched over a red hardback book.

"What is it?" Allyn asked.

"I don't know, but it's old." Liam climbed to his feet, his knobby knees popping as he shuffled toward Allyn. "There's no way it can be an original text. It's too old. It would have to be a copy of a copy."

"How can you tell?" Allyn asked, taking the book from Liam. It looked unremarkable. It lacked an author, title, engraving, or other identifying mark. Allyn would have probably skipped right over it. He handed it back.

"It speaks of a time before the Fracture," Liam said. "Which means it's at least a *thousand* years old. They wouldn't have used a cover or binding like this, and it has obviously been printed, even if it was on a primitive printing press."

"That would have been expensive," Allyn said.

"Very. If someone took the time and money to print this book, then it must be important." Liam's eyes glazed over as his mind went to a different place. "I wonder where the other copies went..."

"What does it say?

Returning from his faraway place, Liam looked at Allyn. "Things I've never heard about. Listen to this. 'The air was thick, a byproduct of the tense atmosphere. It wasn't an open forum, but that didn't mean the Council was free from prying ears. Their vote would determine the fate of all magi, present and future. One decision brought death, a slow drawn-out affair that would span generations. The other offered salvation. At a price. To grant the ray of hope, the Council would pay with a Great Sacrifice—their Great Sacrifice. To grant life, they died. To sentence death, they lived—'"

The door opened, interrupting Liam. Four people

walked in, led by a young man with sandy-blond hair and fair skin. Shorter than Allyn by nearly a full head and not particularly muscular, he strode in with his arms at his sides, almost flexing. Behind him, three more young magi fanned out in a V formation.

"Can we help you?" Allyn asked.

"My name is Cason," the man with the blond hair said. "Grand Mage Hyland sent me to request your presence in his study." For a Family that ignored tradition, Cason was overly formal.

"But we just started!" Liam protested.

Cason frowned. "And you can return when Grand Mage Hyland deems it so. Until then, if you will please follow me." He held his hand up to the door, pointing the way.

"Fine," Liam groaned, grabbing his coat dramatically. He folded it over his arm, hiding the book. Liam caught Allyn's eye. His face was expressionless, but his eyes pleaded with him not to say anything. "Let's go."

"All of you," Cason said, nudging Nyla with his foot.

"I'm busy," Nyla said, her eyes buried in her book.

"Grand Mage Hyland requested all of you."

"I'm sure it doesn't concern me. Take them." She pointed to Allyn and Liam. "They're distracting me anyway."

The slender man with spiked black hair behind Cason snickered. The other two struggled to hide their amusement. Cason strode forward, trying to reestablish his authority, and yanked the book from Nyla's hands. She reached for it, but he tossed it across the room. "He said all of you."

Nyla chewed on her bottom lip, glaring at Cason. He stood over her, unflinching.

Allyn watched nervously. This wasn't how he'd expected things to go. He'd expected a familiarity among the Families, a special bond like seeing a distant cousin for the first time in a long time. He hadn't expected the friction or the pissing contests between jocks. But these jocks weren't all bluster.

Nyla stubbornly got to her feet, making it clear she didn't like it.

Cason led them out of the room, Spike, the man with the spiked black hair, and Scarlet, a beautiful woman with auburn hair, forming up behind them. They rode their heels, never more than a step behind.

We aren't being summoned, Allyn thought, *We're being herded*. They didn't go back the way they'd come in. Instead, Cason took them to a new section of the estate.

Cason gave a curt nod, and the man beside him broke formation and disappeared down an adjoining corridor.

"What are you going to do with that book?" Allyn asked Liam under his breath.

"I don't know what you're talking about." Liam shot a nervous glance at Scarlet. She kept her eyes ahead, seemingly unaware of their conversation.

"I saw you hide it under your coat. What are you thinking? If you get caught, they'll kick us out, and we won't find anything."

"This is too important." Liam patted his coat.

"Nothing is more important to me than my sister."

"You don't understand. This book describes events prior to the Fracture. Do you know what that means?"

"It could be fake."

"We'll never know until we read it. What did you say? Words are just words until they're read? Besides, I can't leave it behind to be destroyed like the other books in their library. I'm sorry, Allyn. I just can't."

Allyn shook his head. "Don't get caught."

"Don't tell on me."

Descending a stairwell, they emerged at the basement level. Unlike the rooms and hallways above, these were quiet and empty, and they lacked windows and natural light. Scarlet and Spike eased off their heels a bit, allowing Allyn to relax, not feeling like he had a dog nipping at his heels. They rounded the corner into a long corridor. At the end stood two large double doors whose dark wood was a stark contrast to the light-gray concrete walls. They looked old—and strong.

Nyla slowed, falling into step between Liam and Allyn. "Something's not right," she whispered. "Don't let them touch you, especially her." She nodded toward Scarlet.

Liam's back stiffened, and he looked at Allyn from the corners of his eyes. A chill ran through Allyn, causing the hair on his arms and the back of his neck to stand. If Nyla was uneasy, if Liam was nervous, he should be terrified.

"What's wrong?" Allyn asked.

"That's a holding room," Nyla said, nodding to the doors ahead.

"A what?"

"Shhh," Nyla said.

Cason turned on his heel and nodded. A firm hand grabbed the back of Allyn's neck. A powerful wave of exhaustion followed. His body became weak, his legs buckling under him. Darkness crept in from the edges of his vision. He'd been through this before. He was being forced unconscious.

As quickly as the hand had grabbed his neck, another slapped it away. Nyla—in a single, fluid motion—drove her palm into Scarlet's chest, throwing her backward into the wall. She spun, whipping her leg into Spike's face. He fell to the floor.

Allyn staggered, relief flooding through his body. He felt as though he'd been woken up from a deep sleep. His body reacted slowly, and everything took a half-second longer to process.

Nyla bolted forward, driving her knee into Scarlet's

face as she tried to get up. Blood splattered the concrete floor, and Scarlet landed in a heap atop Spike.

A concussion of air threw them backward. Allyn bounced off Liam, and they each skidded to a stop several feet down the corridor. Nyla yanked them to their feet and huddled them up behind her, shielding them from Cason.

Cason waited, watching. Allyn looked down the corridor behind him; it was long and narrow with nowhere to hide. Spike and Scarlet got to their feet, each taking up position at Cason's shoulders. Scarlet, her face bloodied, rubbed her chest where Nyla had hit her. A bruise was already forming on Spike's cheek.

"Stay behind me," Nyla said.

"What are you going to do?" Allyn asked.

"Just stay behind me."

"There's nowhere to go," Cason said. "Be good boys and girls and play nice. There's no need for this to continue."

"You're a traitor," Nyla said.

Cason laughed. "To what? A traitor to who?" He waved the two magi forward. They split up, strolling down each side of the corridor, while Cason took the center.

"You're working with Lukas," Nyla said.

Cason smiled.

Allyn stepped aside, outside Nyla's protection.

"No," Liam said, grabbing Allyn's arm.

Yanking it free easily, Allyn kept his eyes on Cason. "What do you want?"

"I think you know what we want," Cason said. "We want you to reach your potential."

"Is that what you're doing with my sister? Helping her reach her potential?"

"Perhaps," Cason said, smiling wickedly. Spike and Scarlet circled, blocking off their only escape. "I do wonder, though, if she is so important to you, why are you *here* and not trying to save her?"

Allyn's hands balled into fists.

"I'll tell you why," Cason said. "They don't *want* to find her. They don't want to lose you."

"That's not true," Allyn said.

"Yes it is. They know that as soon as you find your sister, you're leaving, and they'll lose something special."

"What am I?"

"Come with me and find out."

Allyn took a tentative step toward him.

"Allyn!" Liam shouted. "No!"

Ignoring Liam, Allyn stepped forward, offering his hand.

Cason smiled, reaching for Allyn's hand.

Allyn slapped it away and drove his shoulder into the man's chest. Cason collapsed. Tripping, Allyn fell on top of him.

"Get down!" Nyla screamed.

An explosion sent him and Cason crashing into the double doors, throwing them open. They tumbled into the holding room.

It was surprisingly well furnished with several armchairs and modern couches spread throughout. A large ornate rug stretched from one end of the room to the other, and landscape artwork hung from the walls, giving the windowless room a feeling of warmth.

More explosions thundered behind them. Liam and Nyla were in a pitched battle with Spike and Scarlet. Allyn grappled with Cason, trying to pin his hands to the floor. Jaxon had taught him that hand motions weren't necessary to wield, but they did make it easier.

Cason drove his forehead into Allyn's nose.

Blinding pain shot through Allyn's face. He rolled onto his side, blinking in quick succession, trying to regain his vision. The room was a blurry mess. A blob of color in his vision was accompanied by more pain in his chest. Allyn rolled into a ball, protecting his head with his arms as blows rained down. Cason hit him, kicked him, and beat him until he was nearly unconscious, nearly dead.

The blows stopped, and Allyn was only faintly aware of a crash behind him. He uncurled, his muscles screaming in agony. Someone touched him. He fought the hand away. Then a voice was yelling at him.

Why are they yelling?

The hands became more urgent—more violent.

Allyn balled his hands into fists and swung indiscriminately.

"Allyn!" the voice said. "It's me!"

I know that voice. Liam.

Allyn stopped fighting, and Liam tried to pull him up, but as Allyn tried to stand, his legs collapsed. His left eye was swollen shut, and he couldn't move his left arm.

Liam wrapped Allyn's good arm around his neck and held him up. With his good eye, Allyn watched as Nyla landed blow after blow to Cason's mid-section and face. But the man never went down.

Cason blocked a punch and, with his off hand, sent Nyla stumbling backward. Without missing a beat, he spun into a crouch, blasting her with a concussion of air. Nyla cascaded through the air into the wall, then fell to the floor, motionless.

Wiping blood from his lip, Cason refocused his attention on Allyn. He tossed a softball-sized fireball back and forth between hands. The flame burned brightly but gave off little light and didn't flicker in the air. Cason tossed it high into the air, and then catching it with his right hand, he spun and threw it at them with a powerful overhand pitch.

"No!" Allyn screamed. He hooked Liam's head between his forearm and chest and spun him around so Allyn was between him and Cason. Searing pain screamed across Allyn's back.

The room went dark.

CHAPTER 12

"LUKAS IS BUILDING AN ARMY," Graeme said as he entered Darian's study.

Darian motioned for him to take a seat on a couch beside the door. The cold leather creaked as Graeme sank into it. Darian's private study was decent sized. A black-and-white mural of a snowy landscape covered the opposite wall, and a third was filled with windows overlooking the cliff and the ocean beyond. Floating shelves held books, photographs, and other personal belongings, while a large desk with a computer monitor sat in the center of the room.

"That is a very serious accusation," Darian said, grabbing a decanter from a small bar in the corner. He filled a wine glass with a deep-red liquid. He held it to his nose, breathing in the aroma, before taking a sip.

"It's not one I make lightly," Graeme said.

Darian nodded to an empty glass, silently asking Graeme if he would like one.

"Please," Graeme said.

Darian filled a second glass. "I assume you have evidence to back it up?"

"The man sitting in your library isn't enough?"

"A man nobody knows, who cannot wield, or has any known ties to any surviving Family? That's not a lot to hang your hat on."

"Then perhaps you can tell me what Lukas wants with him and his sister," Graeme said.

Darian stared out the window in silence, tapping the side of his glass with his fingernail. He seemed distant and distracted. "We live in dark times. He might be using the sister as bait."

"The thought crossed my mind, but I have reason to believe otherwise."

Darian's blue eyes opened wide in surprise. "You have a spy."

"I never said that."

"How else would you know?"

"I have my secrets."

Darian sniffed. "It does seem to answer a lot of questions," he said quietly, almost to himself. He looked down, seemingly noticing for the first time that he still held two glasses of wine, and brought the second to Graeme. "Do you know where he is hiding?"

"No," Graeme said. "I don't."

Darian watched him, his eyes narrowing. "I'm not sure I believe you."

Graeme shrugged. "That's unimportant."

"On the contrary." Darian leaned against the corner of his desk. "It's very important. If you want to unite the Families against him and fight a war, you'll need us to believe you."

Graeme sipped his wine. The merlot evaporated on his tongue, leaving behind a dry, chalky residue. "I don't want to start a war. I want to prevent one."

"War is easy to prevent. You don't fight it."

Graeme pinched his forehead. Darian was the youngest grand mage in the Families and the first in a growing trend of anointed young leaders, but Graeme hadn't thought he was naive. *Why is he being so flippant?* "Sometimes, you don't have a choice. Our way of life is being threatened, and our very existence lies in the balance. Isn't that worth fighting for?"

"We lived on the brink long before Lukas divided your Family," Darian said. "Our numbers have dwindled since the Fracture. We're hanging on by our fingernails, and the world only continues to get smaller. There will come a day when there will be nowhere left to hide. What then? I'm not saying I agree with Lukas, but maybe it is time to try something new."

"Then that is something that should be agreed upon by the Families," Graeme said. "Not by a rogue magi who doesn't have the responsibility you and I do."

"He has a responsibility to his followers."

"That's not the same thing."

"Maybe not," Darian said. "But maybe it's more difficult. He promises change, a brighter future, and that he's the one that will lead them to a better world. His followers expect that from him and nothing less. And they expect it quickly. He's put himself in a precarious spot."

"He's done it to himself."

Darian grimaced.

"What?"

"It's just that—" The door to the study opened, and a young magi stepped into the room. "Yes?" Darian asked.

"The, uh, the shelter is full," he said, refusing to look at Graeme.

"Thank you," Darian said.

The young man nodded and turned to leave.

Darian closed the door behind him. "My apologies. I was just saying that your Family has been through a lot. A splinter is never easy. It suggests a lack of leadership, a lack of direction, or both. Lukas left *your* family,

Graeme. Can you honestly tell me this isn't a personal crusade to squelch a mutiny within your Family to avoid embarrassment?"

Graeme sat motionless. "How dare you."

Darian held up his hands in surrender. "I meant no offense."

"This has nothing to do with me. Do you understand? Nothing."

"I just had to be sure."

"I hope I made myself clear." In one swallow, Graeme drained the wine glass.

"Crystal." Darian exhaled deeply, his head and shoulders dipping slightly. "I was also afraid you might say that."

Darian opened the door, holding it open as four magi entered the study.

"What's this?" Graeme jumped to his feet.

"It's necessary, I'm afraid." Then, with a weak, sympathetic smile, he added, "I'm sorry."

Graeme didn't resist when the men grabbed him and bound his hands behind his back. Fighting so many magi inside the small study was suicide. "How long? How long has Lukas had you in his pocket?"

"I told you I thought it was time for a change," Darian said. "I can't sit back idly any longer and watch as our people die."

"You're digging your own grave."

Darian shrugged. "We'll see." He turned to the magi holding Graeme. "Where are the others?"

"Cason has them in the shelter," the magi said. "We're still rounding up the other two."

"Excellent," Darian said. "Once they're secure, I want them separated from each other, understood?"

Nodding, the man started to respond when a distant boom interrupted him. The floor shook, knocking the decanter off the stand, spilling red wine across the dark hardwood like blood spilling from a corpse.

"I thought you said they were secure?" Darian said.

Before the man could answer, more explosions rattled the room, each bigger and louder than the last. Graeme's thoughts went instantly to Liam. Was he all right? Had they bound him, too, or did they get him into the shelter by some other means? He struggled to control his emotions. Getting angry would make him rash and stupid. They were greatly outnumbered and in enemy territory. If they had any hope of escaping alive, Graeme needed to keep his wits.

"Get him out!" Darian yelled, pointing at Graeme. "And find the other two. They'll no doubt be heading for the others."

The other magi shoved Graeme through the doorway.

Allyn woke violently. His back arched as though he'd been hit with a defibrillator. He gasped, his eyes bulging as volts of energy spread through his limbs. He felt the skin of his back stretch as his wounds healed. Burns were replaced by soft, tender skin. Soon, the sharp pain vanished entirely. Breathing became easier and less painful as his insides rolled and ribs popped back in place. The pressure around his swollen eye subsided, and his shoulder felt as if it had been guided back into place by invisible fingers. The energy surged through him, comforting him, addressing his most dire injuries, and then... it was over. His body relaxed as he lay on his back, breathing rapidly.

Nyla stood over him with her hand against his bare chest. "How are you feeling?"

Allyn blinked. He could see out of *both* eyes, and his left arm, while sore, was back in its socket and functional.

He rolled onto his side and probed his ribs, which were bruised but not broken. He was in remarkably good shape.

"Thank you." The words sounded hollow. *What do you say to someone who makes a habit of saving your life?*

Nyla nodded. Her cheek was red and puffy, and her left eye was nearly swollen shut. She held her left arm tightly against her body, keeping it immobile, swaying as she struggled to keep her balance. He didn't know how many of the injuries she had sustained during her fight with Cason and how many of them were a result of healing him, but she was a mess.

Cason's body lay motionless in the center of the room. Blood streaked down his face, and more pooled behind his head. He didn't look as though he would ever get up again.

"What happened?" Allyn asked.

"We survived," she said. "For now. Can you walk?"

Allyn planted a shaky leg on the ground and stood. He was weak, his muscles were pained and tight, and he would have to move slowly, but he could walk.

"Good," she said. "We need to leave before others arrive."

Liam stood at the double doors, looking down the corridor. "We're clear."

"Then lead the way," Allyn said.

Nyla quietly led them down the corridor, with Liam a couple paces behind her. Allyn moved slowly, struggling to not fall behind. His legs felt mechanical, moving and bending on command but not adapting to the terrain. He tripped over his own feet more than once.

They passed Scarlet, her skin red and blistered. Her neck was twisted backward, and her leg was folded awkwardly underneath her. One of Spike's fireballs seemed to have gotten the better of her. Spike didn't have any noticeable injuries, but his chest rose and fell weakly. Allyn knew if he didn't get immediate help, the man wouldn't live to see tomorrow.

Nyla peeked around the corner and winced.

"What is it?" Allyn asked quietly.

"There has to be another way out," she said.

"Why not just go out the way we came in?" Liam asked. "It's the fastest."

"It will also lead us directly into their reinforcements," Nyla said. "We need to find another way."

"Liam's right," Allyn said. "We don't know if there is another way out, and this way, we can move more quickly."

"Fine," Nyla said. "But at the first sound of *anyone* coming, both of you will hide. No arguments."

They didn't have to wait long. Beyond the entrance to the stairwell above them, Allyn heard the sound of people running. And they were getting closer. Allyn froze. He wasn't in a condition to fight, and he wasn't sure how far he could run. They had only one option.

"Hide!" Allyn whispered forcibly. Without waiting for a response, he darted back into the maze of corridors. Their footsteps echoed off the bare walls, and maybe it was the adrenaline kicking in again, but Allyn started to feel better. His ailing limbs grew more responsive, and the pain subsided.

Liam blew past him, fleeing like a frightened animal. He stopped abruptly at the intersection and looked around frantically before rounding the corner and vanishing. Allyn recognized the corridor.

The holding cell. The Hyland magi would be going there, and they would find Cason, Spike, and Scarlet.

"Wait!" Allyn shouted after him.

Liam didn't listen and charged into the room.

Allyn cursed and followed. He couldn't leave him. After jumping over the scorched remains of Scarlet, he landed softly then rushed toward the holding cell. He really *was* feeling better. *What did Nyla do to me?* He'd always assumed healing was instantaneous and that once it was done, he was as good as he was going to get. But he was growing stronger. Did that mean she was growing weaker?

Allyn planted his foot, skidding to a stop.

The corridor behind him was empty.

Where's Nyla? She had been right behind him. *She could have got turned around*, he thought, though that wasn't likely. She might be lying in wait, ready to spring an ambush on their attackers and give him and Liam a chance to escape. That was more likely. She was a warrior and would fight until the bitter end.

Torn, Allyn looked back at the holding cell. Somewhere inside, Liam was hiding, and unlike Nyla, he wasn't a warrior. Liam needed his help. But something wasn't right. His body felt better—better than it should. Nyla wasn't waiting behind to spring a trap. She would have said something. She would have told them to go on and to save themselves while she did something to help. No, she'd disappeared because she was in trouble and didn't want to be saved. She was like a laboring animal finding a quiet place to die.

Liam needed his help, and Nyla didn't want it. He doubted that he could find her and still have time to help Liam. But he had to try.

He owed her.

He found her stumbling deeper into the compound, holding onto the wall for support.

"Nyla!"

She didn't stop.

"Where are you going?"

"Go back," she said.

"No." *She is trying to lead them away!* "I'm not going back without you." He grabbed her arm. She tried to pull away but was too weak.

"Please," she said softly. "I'll lead them away, give you a chance."

Allyn shook his head. "The only chance we have is with you." He pulled her to him, and she collapsed. After hoisting her up over his shoulder, he raced back to the holding cell. He heard whispers and footsteps on the stairs when he rounded the corner to the long hallway. His steps became labored. His injured body was running out of strength. They weren't going to make it.

Liam appeared in the doorway. "Come on!" he called out, waving them on frantically.

The terror in Liam's eyes urged Allyn on. Nyla stirred, and a fire ignited inside him like a shot of pure adrenaline. He charged forward with renewed intensity, rushing past Liam into the holding cell. Liam kicked the door closed behind them.

"Block the doors," Allyn said, gently laying Nyla on the floor. Her breathing had grown frantic, and her eyelids fluttered. Her body trembled. "Nyla. Nyla, stay with me. Stay with me, Nyla."

Her eyes opened.

"There you go," Allyn said. "Stay with me."

She looked at him, her eyes narrowing in confusion.

"I'm not leaving you," Allyn said. "Okay? You saved me. It's my turn."

Nyla whispered something inaudible.

"What?" Allyn put his ear close to her lips.

"I didn't... do it... for... you."

Allyn pulled away. Her eyes locked onto his, and a silent understanding passed between them before her eyes rolled back. He watched helplessly as the convulsions took her.

Footsteps echoed through the corridor.

"Help me!" Allyn yelled, running to the wall and grabbing one end of a large desk. Liam grabbed the other end, and together, they slid it in front of the door. It wouldn't stop them from getting inside, but it would give him time to build a more proper barricade. "Get ready. The moment that door opens, blast them with a fireball."

Liam looked to the floor.

"What?"

"I can't," Liam said softly.

"You don't have to kill them," Allyn said. "Just scare them. Make them think twice about coming in here."

Liam rubbed the top of his foot with his heel. "I can't," he said again. The echoing footsteps nearly drowned out his voice.

"We don't have time for this. Just do it." Allyn ignored Liam's response and checked on Nyla. The convulsions had subsided to a sight tremble in her hands and feet that was masked by her labored breathing. Her skin was cold and clammy as the life flowed away. Allyn propped her head up with a fringed throw pillow from the couch. "Don't quit on us now."

He exhaled. *What now?* They were in a room without windows or exits, save for the one they just barred shut. The barricade would have to slow their entry and allow Liam to take care of them one by one as they tried to enter. Liam would have to get over his fear. They didn't stand a chance without him.

"Liam, I know—" Allyn came to an abrupt stop when he saw him.

Liam stood in the center of the room, tears streaming down his face. "I can't," he said between sobs. "I'm sorry." Shame, embarrassment, and pain hidden behind tears boiled to the surface. "I can't wield."

Bang! The door rattled against its hinges.

Graeme's procession received more than one confused look as they escorted him through the estate. Since the explosions had stopped several minutes before, Graeme supposed it looked as if he had attacked the Hyland Family. The handcuffs and heavy guard didn't help.

Darian planned this well, Graeme thought.

His guard picked up two additional escorts as they exited the main living quarters and entered a private wing at the north end of the estate. The additional guards took up position in the rear behind the two who were already on his heels. He had six escorts in total. Darian was afraid of him.

As he should be.

Darian favored intimidation and brute strength with his procession. Each of Graeme's guards was a magi. *Why not use a cleric's abilities and subdue me by forcing me under?* Graeme's blood boiled as the realization came to him. *He's going to use my son against me.*

Graeme wielded water and fire, using the fire to draw the heat from the water, and projected it onto the steel handcuffs binding his wrists. They were a European design with a thick hinged steel plate instead of a chain—more of a shackle than a cuff and far more difficult to break out of.

The private wing of the estate bore few of the decorative adornments the main living area displayed. Simple runners lined the floors, and the old singled-paned windows were left without drapes. Paint flaked away from the bare walls, and the baseboards were dented and scratched. Where the front rooms felt new and modern, this felt old and dingy.

Graeme continued to pour his efforts into the cuffs. The silver cuffs were coated in thick frost, and the cold steel bit into his wrists. His escort paid him little mind, but he pulled the cuffs closer to his body anyway, partially obscuring them under his shirt. He projected the building ice crystals into the locking mechanism. Baylis had been able to pick locks this way, using slivers of ice to push against the correct pins and then reinforcing them with air to turn the mechanism, but Graeme had never been very good at it. Making matters worse, the cuffs were an unfamiliar design with a locking mechanism that he was unaccustomed to. Graeme quickly gave up on the idea.

He continued to fill the lock with ice and focused his efforts on freezing the areas where the cuffs were weakest. If he projected fire and air into it, expanding the ice crystals almost instantaneously, he could create a miniature blast and blow the cuffs off—and maybe his hands along with them. *Better to use that as a last resort,* he decided.

The procession stopped outside a nondescript door, which the lead escort opened and then ushered him inside. The two magi at the rear took up station in the hall on either side of the door and pushed it closed.

The lead guard, a thick man who kept his hair long in an attempt to hide his receding hairline, strode across the room and yanked open the burgundy floor-to-ceiling curtains, allowing daylight to enter the room for the first time in a long time. Dust billowed from the curtains, making the air heavy. Mothballs had gathered in the corners of the room, and still more dust covered shelves, tables, and lamps. The furniture—a simple loveseat and an armchair with matching ottoman—were hidden under white sheets.

The guard in front of Graeme visibly relaxed as the door closed. Graeme lunged forward, throwing his hands and wrists over the man's head. He pulled back viciously, choking the man with the centerpiece of his cuffs. They fell backward into the door with a loud crash.

The other three guards watched in horror as Graeme strangled their fellow magi. The man struggled to pull the cuffs away from his neck. He kicked, scratched, and clawed, but Graeme had the leverage. The guards in the hall banged on the door, trying to get in, but Graeme and his hostage pushed against it, keeping it closed.

The magi to his right charged. Graeme wielded fire and projected it into the cuffs. They burned orange, swelling from the mix of ice and water inside, and exploded against the man's neck. Shrapnel scattered through the air, taking out the incoming magi's eye and dropping him to the ground, dead. The man he was strangling went limp against his chest, and Graeme pushed him aside, letting the body collapse to the ground.

The magi at the window sent a fireball hurtling in his direction. Graeme dove aside, and the fireball struck the door, blowing it to splinters and knocking the magi in the hall to the floor. In a matter of seconds, Graeme had cut the procession of six down to two, and the remaining magi waited nervously, watching Graeme with wide eyes.

Graeme got to his feet, rubbing his wrists. "I didn't want it to come to this, but I will protect my Family by any means necessary. You can either let me walk through that door, or you can join your comrades on the floor."

The two men exchanged looks before holding their hands in front of them in surrender.

"Where are you holding my son?" Graeme asked.

"The holding cell," one of the men said. "In the basement."

"Is there another entrance?" Graeme asked.

The man shook his head.

"Get on the ground, facedown, noses touching the floor."

Graeme took a deep breath and held it. He wielded air into a solid wall that he placed directly behind each of their heads. The barrier would keep them from looking up, or so they would believe. "Do you feel that?"

The men grunted.

"Good," he said. "That shield will dissipate as I get farther away. Do not try to watch, do not try to get up, or else I will know and have to come in here and deal with you. Understood?"

Again, the men grunted.

It was a lie, of course. The barrier would hold only as long as Graeme focused on it, which wouldn't be long. But if they believed it to be true, then it was as real as steel. The two men wouldn't move until Graeme was long gone.

Graeme backed into the hall, stepping over fragments of wood. A hole had been blown open in the wall, exposing pink insulation and electrical wires. Both guards were lying dead on the floor. The one nearest to Graeme lay slumped against the wall, with a large piece of wood buried in his chest, and the other was facedown, with blood matted against the back of his head.

It's a shame it had come to this. Two dead out here, two more inside, and who knows how many more down in the basement. They'd come to the Hyland Estate looking for answers to prevent war, but instead, they had started one. Lukas was one step ahead of them, and he obviously had other plans. They had walked straight into a trap. Graeme kicked himself for not having seen it coming. He should have known Lukas would already have reached out to Families that might be sympathetic to his cause. And who better than Darian Hyland, the youngest grand mage of all the Families? He led a weak fledgling Family that had shed many of the ancient customs and traditions. They had much to gain by being the first to join Lukas's movement.

He had no excuses and no one to blame but himself. Even as Graeme went through all of it in his head, he knew that Allyn was the key to the trap. He wasn't a magi, and he wasn't a savior. He was just a man, another pawn in Lukas's game, nothing more than a distraction meant to divert him from focusing on the real problem—stopping Lukas.

Was the Hyland Family the first to form an alliance with Lukas or just the latest and the first to make a play? Word would be out as soon as Graeme made it known to the other Families. He would find out who stood with whom. Lukas wouldn't surprise him again.

Graeme charged forward, ready to take on the entire Hyland Family. He was going to find those stairs, enter the basement, and find that holding cell. He was going to protect his Family—by any means necessary.

Allyn threw a broken table leg at the door. The rest of the table lay in shards on the floor, having been destroyed when Nyla tackled Cason. The leg bounced harmlessly off the door. Their barricade—a collection of tables, chairs, rugs, and anything else they could pile in front of the door—had held so far. The dead bodies in the hallway probably had something to do with it, too. When they figured out nobody in the room could wield…

It won't come to that, Allyn thought. *We will get out of here before it comes to that.*

"She's getting worse," Liam said. He sat on his knees, holding Nyla's hand. If the tenderness around Allyn's ribs and stomach were any indication, she'd suffered severe trauma to her internal organs, a few broken ribs, and possible internal bleeding—all because she had healed him.

I didn't do it for you. Her words haunted him. "I know," Allyn said, picking up another table leg. He didn't know what he would do with it, but he felt better armed with something.

"What are we going to do?"

"I'm working on it," Allyn said. *How do you tell someone you don't know? That they were probably going to die?*

"There aren't any windows or doors or another way out. And they know we're in here, so we can't hide."

Allyn closed his eyes, trying to hide his annoyance. They'd already been through this. "Can you try to wield?"

Liam shook his head.

"You're a magi. Your father is the grand mage. And you're telling me you can't?"

Liam's face flushed with anger and embarrassment.

"What about the conversations we had about my struggles?" Allyn asked. "You gave me advice, gave me things to try. Were you just full of—" He realized he was taking his anger out on Liam. The kid may have misled him, and his timing couldn't have been worse, but he didn't deserve Allyn's wrath.

Liam refused to look away from Nyla. "I just told you what Jaxon always told me."

"Can you try? Maybe it will be different this time."

"It won't be."

"Will you just try?" Allyn asked. "For me?"

Liam looked up at him, hurt in his eyes. Allyn was asking him to knowingly humiliate himself in front of him, and he hated himself for it, but he didn't have any other ideas. If Liam could accidentally hit the wall with a fireball, it would give them more time. *And then what? Give Graeme more time to rescue us. Is that my plan? Wait to be rescued?*

Liam gently placed Nyla's hand on her chest and stood. He rolled his shoulders and neck, and with a long, deep breath, he closed his eyes.

Shuffling and indistinguishable whispers came from outside the door. They were planning something. He was running out of time.

The air shimmered around Liam, and his skin somehow seemed brighter. *He's doing it.* All he'd needed was the stimulation of being in a real-world situation, like an athlete performing during a big game. Liam had what it took when it counted. The lights in the room flickered and then shut off entirely, plunging the holding cell into darkness. They were definitely planning something.

Liam opened his eyes. The lights flickered on a moment later. He sighed with frustration. "I can't do it. I can *feel* the power inside me. I just can't do anything with it. I can't project it. I don't know why."

"It's okay." Allyn sat down, wondering what else they could do. At least this way, when Hyland's magi broke through the barricade, he and Liam wouldn't look like a threat. They might spare them.

Nyla coughed. A thin red line streaked down her cheek. Allyn rushed over to her. Taking her chin in his hand, he rolled her onto her side. Blood poured from her mouth like wine from a tipped glass.

"We need to get her help," Allyn said.

Liam nodded. It was time.

"Stay with her," Allyn said. He walked to the door and knocked. The shuffling in the hall stopped. "Can you hear me?"

Whispers.

"Parley." Silence. "You hear me? We want to parley." Allyn waited for several excruciating minutes. *What's taking so long?*

"Allyn?" a new voice called out. "This is Grand Mage Hyland. I'm told you wish to speak."

"I do."

"It's very simple," Darian said. "Come out peacefully, and you won't be harmed. I apologize for any injuries you may have sustained, but we can prevent more from occurring if you come out peacefully." Darian sounded genuine.

"What assurances do I have that you won't kill us on the spot? I need an act of good faith."

"What do you propose?"

"I have someone who needs medical attention," Allyn said. "Once they're treated, I'll come out. I'm yours."

"No!" Liam shouted.

"It's me you're after anyway," Allyn shouted over Liam's protests. "You heal my wounded, and you can have me. Let the others decide for themselves."

"What are you doing?" Liam demanded.

"Nyla needs help," Allyn said. "I don't know what else to do."

"They'll kill you!"

"I don't think so," Allyn said. "If they wanted us dead, we'd be dead. They've had plenty of opportunities."

"They tried! Nyla *stopped* them from killing you. She nearly killed herself trying to *save* you!"

"I don't think those were Cason's orders."

"I don't care what you *think*. As soon as you leave, they're going to kill us."

"What do you want me to do, Liam?" Allyn asked. "What other choice do we have?"

Liam looked down at Nyla's helpless form. More blood had streaked down her cheek. "I don't know."

"Me, neither," Allyn said. "This is all I've got."

Liam took a deep breath. "All right."

"Do we have a deal?" Allyn shouted through the door.

"Yes."

"Give me a hand with this," Allyn said to Liam, gesturing to the barricade. Together, they pulled off the loose stuff first. As they pulled the last of it off, they got to the bulk of it—a dense wine rack that doubled as a serving table. It probably weighed more than the two of them combined and was bottom heavy, making it difficult to tip over. After some grunting and a little sweat, they managed to slide it away from the door.

Allyn walked to the center of the room, Liam standing at his shoulder, and waited. Liam gave him a small, reassuring nod.

"All right." Allyn took a deep breath. "It's open."

The door opened slowly, and a hand, palm toward the sky, slid through first. A short woman with bobbed blond hair combed to the side gingerly stepped into the room. A nervous expression on her face, she quickly scanned the room. Her eyes came to rest on Nyla's body.

"I'm in," she said to someone in the hall.

"Close the door," Allyn said.

"I'm here to help," the woman said, but she kicked the door closed. "My name is Elisa."

"She's over here," Allyn said, gesturing to Nyla.

"What happened?" she asked.

"She saved my life," Allyn said bluntly, his eyes flickering to Cason's motionless body.

Elisa gave him a sidelong glance before placing a slender hand on Nyla's chest. "She's hurt."

"We know that," Liam said as he knelt and took Nyla's hand.

"Her left lung is collapsed," Elisa said. "She has multiple broken ribs and a lacerated spleen. She's bleeding internally."

"Can you heal her?" Allyn asked.

"Not completely," Elisa said. "The best I can do is stabilize her condition. The rest is up to her."

Liam wiped her cheek, washing away the blood streaks. Save for her swollen eye and the bruising on the left side of her face, she looked normal. Peaceful. She had attempted to sacrifice herself when she healed Allyn. She'd acted like a woman who wanted to die—a woman who wanted peace with her lost husband. *I didn't do it for you.* Did she *want* to be saved?

"Do what you can," Allyn said. He would rather have her be alive and ungrateful than dead and not be able to tell him.

Healing was a surprisingly violent affair. Allyn had been on the receiving end of it, and it hadn't been pleasant, but he hadn't expected such intensity. A glow emitted from Elisa's hand, and a similar wave of light rippled through Nyla's body, expanding outward. Nyla convulsed, her back arched, and arms and legs waved frantically in the air, as she raged from side to side in what looked like a violent seizure.

The swelling around her left eye remained unchanged, as did the bruising on her face and side. In fact, she looked completely unchanged as the glow dissipated. Elisa withdrew and stood, cradling her stomach. "It's done." Her voice was soft and pained.

"She doesn't look any different," Allyn said.

"The bruising and swelling are superficial wounds," Elisa said. "I've done what I can to address her most dire injuries." She lifted her shirt to the bottom of her ribcage to show the newly forming bruises on her stomach and chest. They were identical to those on Allyn's own midsection. "Any more, and I would risk my own life."

"Thank you," Allyn said

Elisa nodded to him. "It's done," she called out in a hoarse voice. "We're coming out." She held out an arm, directing Allyn to start walking.

Allyn waited. "Liam..." he said, his voice failing him.

Liam didn't say anything. He just watched as Elisa escorted Allyn out of the room. The last image Allyn had was of Liam sitting alone beside Nyla. A small figure in a large room, ever present, always loyal, he was unwilling to leave his friend's side. *What have I done?*

Four magi stood with their backs against the wall as Allyn entered the hall. Several more, maybe ten in all, stood at the ready behind the smiling Darian Hyland. He patted Elisa's back and gently guided her along. "Good work," he said. "Go get some rest."

Elisa slowly shuffled down the hall, stooped over and holding her midsection.

"It's a good thing they heal faster than we do, isn't it? What would we do without them?"

"We'd become less careless," a voice boomed from around the corner.

Darian whipped his head around. The hallway—with the exception of Elisa, who stiffly stood at attention—was empty.

"How do we learn from our mistakes if we don't understand the pain of failure?" Graeme strode into the hallway, passing Elisa without second thought, Jaxon and Leira at his side. Confidence radiated from them like steam from boiling water.

"How did you...?" Darian said. "Take him!" he shouted, shoving Allyn toward the nearest magi.

The man shoved Allyn face first against the wall, knocking the wind out of him.

"I'm here for my Family," Graeme said.

"I have you outnumbered five to one," Darian said.

"Your numbers don't intimidate me," Graeme said. "Not when I know that half of them can't wield, and the other half can barely keep from lighting their shoes on fire."

Some of the onlookers looked at their feet, while more wore angry expressions. Darian tapped his foot nervously.

"Dad?" Liam stood in the doorway, supporting Nyla, who had an arm thrown over his shoulder. She watched groggily through half-open eyes.

"Liam—" Graeme said.

"Grab them!" Darian shouted.

Two guards seized Liam and Nyla. Liam, whose resolve must have steeled from the sight of his father, fought. He flailed his arms, kicked at the man's shins, and tried to pull away.

"Let him go!" Graeme shouted.

The man grabbed hold of Liam's wrist and twisted it behind his back. Liam cried out in pain, falling to his knees.

"Stop!" Graeme shouted. "Don't let it come to this, Darian. You won't like the result."

Jaxon stepped forward, but Graeme held him back.

"You won't win," Darian said.

"I just want to take my Family and go," Graeme said. "But I *will* kill every last one of you if you try to stop me." The words echoed through the hall, severing Darian's hold over his men. More than one of his magi retreated a step and exchanged nervous looks with those closest to them. This wasn't their fight. They weren't willing to die over it.

The man holding Allyn was a different beast. His grip tightened, and he pushed Allyn into the wall harder.

"Let them go," Darian said. The hallway rang with the murmurs of relief and surprise, but the hands holding Allyn didn't loosen. "I said, let them go."

The man slammed Allyn against the wall one last time then shoved him aside. Allyn rushed to Nyla, who had collapsed under her own weight. Allyn grabbed her, slinging her arm over his shoulder. "I've got you."

They staggered toward Graeme. Jaxon and Leira met them halfway. Leira took Nyla, and Jaxon guarded against any dissenters.

Graeme took the top of Liam's head in the palm of his hand and checked him over. "Are you all right?"

"I'm okay," Liam said.

Graeme pulled him close and glared down the hall. "If one of you so much as takes a step in our direction, I will burn this place down with all of you in it."

Satisfied that they had taken his threat to heart, Graeme started for the exit. They didn't meet any resistance on their way out, though they did receive confused looks from other members of the Hyland Family. Allyn committed their faces to memory. They hadn't been part of the attack. They hadn't been part of the attempted abduction, and they might not support Darian's actions.

He still had hope they were good people.

CHAPTER 13

SLEEP BROUGHT ITS OWN HORRORS. Allyn ran the halls of the Hyland Estate, frantic, searching for something— what exactly, he didn't know. The walls shook with the echoes of explosions beating with a steady rhythm like a heartbeat. He found a set of stairs and descended into the belly of the estate, beyond the basement level, past the holding cell, continuing downward until, at last, there wasn't a house at all.

Darkness surrounded him. Silence enveloped him. His feet didn't even make noise against the empty abyss that was the floor. *This* was the solitude he had sought upon lying down.

A dim light shined ahead, beckoning Allyn like a lonely streetlamp. As Allyn approached, it seemed to solidify. A single brick wall sat in the darkness, like a stage prop. An invisible spotlight bathed it in a circular light, highlighting a familiar body crumpled on the floor.

Scarlet.

Her neck was bent awkwardly, and her leg was folded under her, just as she had been in the Hyland Estate, but her eyes were open. She *moved*. Allyn crouched in front of her, speaking in a comforting tone. He was there to help. A deep hurt filled her eyes. Betrayal. It wasn't Scarlet anymore.

It was Kendyl.

"Why?" she asked. "Why did you do this to me?"

"I didn't."

"Why, Allyn?" she asked more forcibly.

Kendyl stood up, her left leg still bent at an unnatural angle. She limped toward him, her arms outstretched, reaching for him.

"I didn't know," Allyn said, stumbling backward as she drew closer. "I didn't know it was you. I'm sorry."

She reached for him, fingers extending, *growing* in length.

"I'm sorry!" Allyn slammed his eyes closed, cringing at her inevitable touch.

But it never came.

Allyn opened his eyes. A sturdy double door replaced the wall. Kendyl had disappeared, too. He pushed open the door and found himself in the holding room. Only the room was completely bare. The furniture was gone, as well as the lamps, shelves, books, rugs. Everything was gone, except Cason's lifeless body. Two hand-shaped bruises marred his neck. Allyn placed his hand on one. His own fingers were shorter and thicker than the ones that had marked Cason's neck. He gripped the other side of Cason's neck, placing his other hand over the second bruise. Strangely, his hand fit this bruise perfectly.

Turning to leave, Allyn found Kendyl in the doorway. She looked at him with the same cold, lifeless eyes. Her mouth moved, but no sound came out. Allyn backed away, tripping over Cason's body. As Allyn hit the ground, Cason sprang up and snatched at him with quick, snake-like movements. Allyn shuffled backward in a crab walk away from Cason—only now Cason's face had been replaced with Kendyl's. The Kendyl at the door continued to limp toward him.

Panicked, Allyn slid backward until he hit the closets. With nowhere else to go, Kendyl-Cason easily caught up to him and grabbed his foot with a powerful hand. With one arm, she slid him toward her. Allyn kicked, trying to break free, but Cason's grip was too strong. He continued to fight as Cason's hands clasped around his neck. Allyn beat against the hands, kicking wildly as the powerful grip lifted him from the ground. As blackness crept in, the Kendyl in the doorway repeated her question...

"Why?"

Allyn woke clawing his away across the bed, his heart on the verge of beating out of his chest. The room was dark, moonlight obscured by the window dressings. Images of crumpled bodies lying in unnatural positions, scorched skin, and strangled victims stuck with him. It was probably his imagination, but the putrid smell of burnt flesh clung to him. Rolling out of bed, he opened the window, allowing the cool breeze to wash it away. It didn't. The smell of the dead and dying continued to tickle his nose, distracting him, reminding him of all the things he wanted to forget.

He leaned his head against the window frame. A thin layer of frost covered the grass and shrubs, turning leaves and branches into crystalline wonders. The dense layer of fog forming beyond obscured his view of the forest, leaving him alone with his thoughts and his memories. The room suddenly felt very confining, stifling his thoughts like a thick sweater on a warm day.

The halls were empty in the early morning, even emptier than usual. The solitude was nothing like the bustling activity at the Hyland Estate. *No*, Allyn thought, *don't think about that.* He laughed a self-deprecating laugh. The man running from scary dreams was the same man who, only a few hours earlier, had sacrificed himself to save the others. *Who am I? Am I the self-sacrificing hero or the cowering wimp?* But he hadn't sacrificed himself expecting to die. In fact, he had known they wouldn't kill him. They wanted him. Everyone did. *And instead, they have my sister.* Whatever happened to her was his fault. He had failed to protect her. He had failed to get her back. Liam and Leira had showed him how *real* family took care of each other.

The ride back had begun with Leira checking Nyla's injuries. To Allyn's surprise, Elisa had told the truth and treated them with care. Leira said Elisa had gone further than she would have expected another cleric to go—that didn't stop her from doing more herself, though. She patched her up, aiding Nyla by shouldering her pain. Leira even healed the wounds Elisa had called superficial, stroking Nyla's cheek even as the injuries appeared on her own face. But Leira wasn't just another cleric. She was a friend. She was family.

A clock chimed in another room, interrupting the silence with a familiar tune that he couldn't put a name to. Allyn roamed the house, exploring rooms and admiring art and decorations with a freedom he rarely felt. During the day, he was an outsider, the first silent to be invited to live among a magi Family in centuries.

The notoriety didn't make Allyn feel comfortable. Graeme and Liam had tried to make him feel at home, but they couldn't be with him all day, every day. Allyn still appreciated it. The truth was, he valued Liam's friendship and had grown to consider him a real friend.

Graeme had probed them about their capture, often stopping them midsentence to clarify a small detail or even to have them repeat certain parts as he committed them to memory. When there were mild inconsistencies between their two stories, he took great care to listen to each one. Allyn admired the older man's ability to listen. In his own experience, a person's memory of an event always veered from the truth. This wasn't intentional, of course, just a byproduct of how the mind copes with painful experiences. Graeme wasn't attempting to find out who was right and who was wrong, because he knew the truth lay somewhere in the middle.

Graeme was brief in his own retelling—he had allowed himself to be taken captive, and then, when the situation presented itself, he escaped. He refused to answer questions and dodged others by saying he needed time to think. When it became apparent that he wasn't going to answer any more questions, Allyn stopped probing.

The ride was long and quiet after that. Likely mad at him, Liam refused to look at Allyn, while the rest withdrew from one another. On a few occasions, Allyn caught Graeme watching Liam with a fatherly look. They'd nearly lost each other, and Allyn hoped that after being faced with that reality, their relationship would improve. Then at least something positive might come from an otherwise-terrible event.

Deep in thought, Allyn entered the foyer. Nyla turned to look at him, a surprised expression on her face. Moonlight poured through the window, reflecting off her silver hair, which she had pulled over her shoulder so it draped down her chest. She was sitting sideways in an armchair, with her knees pulled up close to her chin, letting her feet dangle over the arm.

"Sorry," Allyn said, backing out of the room.

"It's okay," she said. Her gaze lingered on him, inviting him to stay.

Leaving felt wrong, but he'd never been comfortable around Nyla. Then she had saved his life. Twice. He leaned against the wall. "You can't sleep, either?"

She shook her head. "I slept all day."

"How are you feeling?"

She shrugged.

It was a stupid question. "Well, you look better."

She gave him a small smile. "Are you all right?"

"I am. Thanks to you."

"Good." Nyla turned her attention back to the window. The entire back wall of the foyer was lined with windows, and a folding door opened onto a balcony, beyond which a large grassy field disappeared into the forest.

"You shouldn't have healed me."

"Why not?"

"You could have killed yourself," he said. "You would have if one of Darian's clerics hadn't healed you."

"I'm fine," she said. "I heal faster than you do. You're the one who should be resting."

Allyn shrugged. "I can't sleep."

"It's a lot to take in, isn't it?"

"Which part?" Allyn stepped inside the room, stopping beside Nyla's chair. "The part where I'm being hunted and my family is being kidnapped, or the part where I'm watching people die around me? I don't know what to do. Every time I try and help, things get worse."

"Not everything."

"Really?" he asked, challenging her. "What's gotten better since I've been here?"

"Liam."

Her words slapped him like a switch in his mother's hand. "What about him?"

"Before you got here, he lived in his cave, working on his library. He didn't leave. He didn't talk. He rarely trained. But since you arrived, he's changed. It's not just that he's stepped out of the library. It's that he's wanted to."

"I can't take credit for that," Allyn said. "I didn't do anything."

"Yes, you did," she said. "You took an interest in his work. You took an interest in him."

"That's because it's pretty damn impressive. You don't

know what kids are like outside this place, but I guarantee you, they aren't like Liam."

"You made him feel special."

"You're making this sound bigger than it is."

"Sometimes, the smallest gestures make the biggest impact. Graeme was going to leave him behind today. You stuck up for him—"

"And nearly got him killed."

"Maybe," she said. "But you couldn't have foreseen that, and besides, that's not the point. I'm sure he appreciates the gesture."

"He's probably traumatized."

"Why do you think that?"

"Because I am." Allyn took a deep breath. "I'm not used to watching people die."

"I'm sorry."

"Don't apologize. It's not your fault, and if you hadn't killed them, I don't know what would have happened."

"No," Nyla said. "I'm sorry because I didn't think about how you felt. Your wounds are healed, but I didn't think about the wounds inside. Death is never easy."

Allyn sat down in a second armchair beside Nyla. "I've never seen someone die before. Not like that. I've never seen a dead body."

"I hadn't either, until..."

"Baylis."

She pursed her lips. "We grew up together, lived as members of this Family for over twenty years, but the only memory that sticks with me is him lying in that alley. Skin dry and shriveled like leather. Blue lips. Skin as white as cotton. He looked like a monster. No matter how hard I try, I can't forget."

"What was he like?" Allyn asked.

"Stubborn." Nyla laughed to herself, remembering a better time, her eyes sparkling in the moonlight. It was the first time Allyn had seen her genuinely happy. "He was goal oriented. *Very* goal oriented. The world was a set of achievements to him, like a staircase, each step leading to something bigger. He said it helped keep him motivated since he was able to look behind and see everything he had achieved, but also kept him focused since he saw what lay in front of him. Everything had to be planned. Everything. Even our—" She stopped abruptly as if she was about to say something she hadn't meant to.

Nyla was finally opening up to him, and he wasn't about to let her close up again. "Even your... what?"

"Nothing. Forget it."

"You were married, weren't you?"

Nyla laughed. "No."

"Then what?"

"I said to forget about it."

"That doesn't come naturally for me. If it's a secret, I promise I won't tell anyone." He gave her his best smile.

"Okay." Nyla leaned in closer, dropping her voice to a whisper. "But this stays between you and me, understand?"

Allyn nodded.

"We weren't married, but you were closer than you realize." Nyla took a deep breath. "We shared an echo."

"A what?"

"An echo."

"I don't understand."

"It's a connection between two people in both mind and body. That's why it is forbidden." She paused and then continued. "When a cleric heals someone, they're using themselves to heal. My strength becomes their strength. My energy becomes theirs. I'm quite literally giving myself to someone, but I change in the process, too. I take on their injuries, their pain. I take *them*. Over a period of time, after many, many healings, so much of myself is in the other person and them in me, that we actually become a part of one another. The same person."

"What does that mean?" Allyn asked. "You can hear their thoughts and feel their pain?"

"No. That would have been nice sometimes. We certainly would have had fewer arguments," Nyla added with a laugh. "But no. It's more of a sixth sense, an instinct. I could *feel* somewhere deep inside myself that something was wrong, and I was drawn to it. Drawn to him. And he, me."

"That sounds like it could be really helpful. Why would it be forbidden?"

"Because, as we change, as we meld together and the echo grows, we cease to be ourselves. We become something different."

Allyn sat silently for a while. The horizon was beginning to show signs of the coming sunrise, turning to a dark purple that hid the stars behind the new light. He felt Nyla watching him, and his ears burned as the question formed in his head. "That's why you want to die, isn't it? When Baylis died, so did a piece of you."

Nyla's eyes narrowed. "Why do you think I want to die?"

"Because of what you said when you healed me. 'I didn't do it for you,' you said. You did it for yourself. You knew that if you healed me, you would probably die."

Her eyes growing moist, Nyla turned away. "You don't understand. He died to protect *me*. That's not how it's supposed to be. I was supposed to protect *him*. We were stronger together, but I ran. And he died." Her voice quivered, and she fought to hold back tears. "I didn't heal you to help *you*. I didn't heal you so I could die. I did it for *him*. Because that's what I should have done that night."

"Oh... Nyla, I'm sorry. I didn't know."

"It's okay." She wiped away a tear.

"I promise I won't tell anyone."

"Thank you."

"Is that what you're looking for in the library? An explanation to what happened to Baylis?"

Nyla gave him a confused look.

"Liam said they found him dry—that it shouldn't be possible."

Nyla shook her head. "No. It's not impossible, it's just *wrong*—an abomination."

"Then what are you looking for?"

Nyla bit her bottom lip. "I'm trying to find out who I am."

"I'm not sure you are going to find that in the library." He meant it as a joke, but within the context of their conversation, it fell flat.

"I feel myself changing, and I don't know what I'm changing into." There was fear in Nyla's eyes. "Now that Baylis is dead, that part of me is gone, too. I don't know if I'll revert back to who I used to be, or..."

"Become something else entirely."

She nodded. An understanding—a closeness—grew between them. Because of the forbidden nature of the echo, she hadn't been able to talk to anyone and had been forced to dig through the archives to discover what would happen to her. Allyn was the only person who understood the depth of her loss. She had shared her deepest secret with him and was now bare and vulnerable.

"Can I tell you a secret now?"

Nyla nodded.

"My sister and I have a connection like the echo, too." Nyla sat up a little. "I know it's not the same thing, and it's not even real. Actually, it's always been kind of a joke between us, but we've always been able to tell if something was wrong with each other. I would have a really bad day and need someone to talk to, and the phone would ring, and it would be her. Or I would get a sudden urge to go see her, and I'd find her in tears, having just broken up with a boyfriend or lost her job. One time, when we were kids, I found her at the bottom of a hill after she fell off her bike and broke her leg. We've grown apart, and it's not as strong as it used to be, but even now, I can feel that she's hurting. She's alive. And she needs me."

"You said you were twins?" Nyla asked slowly.

"Yeah," Allyn said.

Nyla stood up abruptly. "Come on."

"Why?" Allyn asked. "What's going on?"

"I think we just found out why Lukas is after you."

Nyla stopped outside Graeme's study. A thin ray of light shone under the crack of the door. It seemed he, too, was awake. She knocked and, without waiting for a response, walked in. Graeme looked up sharply from his desk.

"Nyla," he said, shielding a piece of paper with his arm. He pulled his glasses off. "Is everything all right?"

"We need to talk," she said, glancing back at Allyn, who was waiting outside the door.

Graeme set his glasses on the desk and motioned for them to sit. As confused as Graeme was, Allyn walked into the study and took a seat in an armchair beside Nyla.

"What's going on?" Graeme asked.

"I think I know why Lukas is after Allyn," Nyla said. "And why after we helped Allyn escape, he went after his sister."

Graeme leaned back, his leather chair reclining against his weight. Nyla clearly had his attention. "Continue."

"We originally thought he abducted her as bait," Nyla said.

Allyn wanted to stop her. *They thought Kendyl was bait? How long have they suspected that? Why didn't they tell me?*

"Then we thought maybe she was a distraction. I don't think that's the case. Allyn and Kendyl are twins, and they share a connection very similar to the echo. Graeme, he *feels* her distress."

Graeme studied Allyn, his dark eyes probing. "Is this true?"

"Yes." Allyn nodded. "I can feel something isn't right."

"Be more specific."

"It's like..." Allyn struggled to find the words. "It's like when you feel a cold coming on. You're not sick yet, but you know you're not right."

"Suppose this is true," Graeme said. "That doesn't mean Lukas isn't using her as bait."

"He would only do that if he knew about the connection," Nyla said, "and how would he know about that? We didn't find out until tonight, and Allyn is living with us."

"Lukas could have suspected it," Graeme said. "Twins have always been associated with magical abilities. The ability to hear each other's thoughts, even see through each other's eyes."

"True," Nyla said, "but everything involving a telepathic connection between twins is anecdotal at best."

"Yet also very historical," Graeme said. "Twins are prevalent in almost every major myth and legend across every major culture and religion."

"If that's the case, then you should have suspected it," Allyn said.

Graeme looked at Allyn with a leveled gaze. "It doesn't change anything. Twin, or not, you still need magi blood to wield."

"According to you."

"No," Graeme said. "That's the way of it."

"Your son has magi blood, but he can't wield."

Graeme's face turned to stone. "His abilities will

manifest in time. He can feel the power. He just can't project it, which is more than you can say."

"I think what Allyn is trying to say," Nyla said carefully, "is that it doesn't matter what we believe. Lukas might think Allyn can wield simply because he's a twin. It wouldn't be the first magi experiment intended to discover the ability in others."

Graeme tapped his finger on his desk.

"He's building an army, Graeme," Nyla continued, "and he's already built alliances. Now he's looking for a new weapon. We need to act."

Graeme sighed. "I know." Graeme sent Nyla to bring Jaxon, leaving Allyn alone with him.

Tapping his foot nervously, Allyn looked around the room in an attempt to hide from Graeme's gaze.

"I really thought you would be able to wield," Graeme said after the awkward silence became nearly unbearable. "Or at least have some magi blood in you."

"I was nearly convinced myself," Allyn said.

"If Lukas is truly after you because you're a twin, then I owe you an apology. I should have gone after your sister sooner."

Allyn leaned forward, resting his elbows on his knees. *Is he actually apologizing?* "I appreciate that, and I understand why you were reluctant to attempt a rescue. You're looking out for your Family, and by helping me rescue my own, you'll likely have to hurt people you've known for a long time. It will start the war you've been trying to prevent."

"It's more than that. Lukas splintered *my* Family, and I fear that was just the beginning. Everything that happens after today—the pain, the loss, the bloodshed—it will all be because of me."

Allyn opened his mouth to tell him that it wasn't his fault, but he was interrupted by Nyla returning with Jaxon.

Jaxon wore his usual loose-fitting brown cotton pants and a sleeveless black leather vest that exposed his powerful build. With alert eyes, Jaxon didn't look like a man who'd been asleep.

Does anyone sleep around here?

He nodded to Allyn as he entered, then stood at the edge of Graeme's desk. Nyla returned to her chair.

"We're going to strike Lukas's compound," Graeme said. "Tonight. Lukas has no doubt heard of the failed attack at the Hyland Estate and knows there will be repercussions, so time is of the essence. He will expect me to round the Families up against him, build an alliance. He will believe he has time. He doesn't. If we strike tonight and catch him by surprise, we will have the advantage."

"What is our objective?" Jaxon asked.

"His sister," Graeme said with a nod in Allyn's direction. "I made him a promise—help me discover why Lukas wants him, and I'd help get his sister back. He's held up his end of the deal, and now it's my turn." If Jaxon disapproved, he didn't show it. "I may have also given Lukas information about our mole," Graeme added with a wince.

"How?" Jaxon asked.

"I didn't realize it at the time, but Darian was probing for information. I said too much, and he inferred the rest. Lukas will begin questioning immediately."

"He'll also be looking to flee," Jaxon said. "If he hasn't done so already."

"Another cause for speed," Graeme said.

"Then it's decided," Jaxon said. "We go in tonight."

"It's decided."

It feels good to be alone, Liam thought. The library was empty in the early morning, just him and his books. Other than Nyla, who had only recently begun digging through the histories, nobody spent time in the library. It was the only place in the manor that was truly his. Even though Allyn had helped for a time, he was likely asleep, recovering. Things were returning to normal, and that was great as far as Liam was concerned.

The purified air, dry and odorless, smelled of musty paper when he cracked an old book open. Liam imagined libraries on the outside, several stories high with floors and floors holding thousands of books, newspapers, and magazines. He wondered if they smelled like his library. One day, he would find out for himself. He would walk the aisles, picking up random books, skimming the pages to see what secrets they held, spending days and weeks within the majestic library walls.

Some day.

Some day after he finished his work. The book in front of him was the next in the long line to be digitally transcribed and salvaged for future magi generations. The words flowed from the page, through his fingers, and onto the screen. Liam paid them little attention, occasionally checking his work for spelling errors or missing words. He didn't fix "mistakes" in the original text because preserving the original text was important. Sure, he could have used a high-end scanner and scanned the pages into the computer. It would have been a lot faster, but doing so would bypass his internal search and tagging programs that allowed him to pull up specific information and related material within seconds—as long as he knew what to look for. And every now and then, something would catch his eye—a heroic story, a gut-wrenching struggle, an interesting piece of information previously unknown within the magi community. Scanning might have been easier, but this way was more fulfilling and turned him into the most knowledgeable young magi in all the Families. It was a nice side effect. He smiled at the thought.

That will be my life's work. He would finish digitizing his own library, improve its search and tagging capabilities, and then move on to the next Family's library and do the same. He would work alone because that was the way he worked. People wouldn't tell him he was avoiding them anymore. They wouldn't tell him that he was antisocial or call him a hermit. They would just leave him to his work because it was important. And if they *wanted* to talk, or if they needed his help, they knew where to find him.

By the time he was done, every Family's library would be preserved for future generations. When he was done, he might link the information together on a central server somewhere, so that anyone in the magi community could have access to any Family's library whenever they wanted. They would thank him and honor him with the title "The Librarian," and nobody would remember that he was the only son of a grand mage who couldn't wield.

But all of that started with the open book in front of him, so he kept working. *Yes,* he thought, *it feels good to be back.*

Liam was finished with almost half of it when the door opened. He didn't know how long he'd been working or what time it was—time had a way of disappearing in the library—but if the dark circles around his father's eyes were any indication, it was still early, not even a full day since the attack.

He was alone, which was strange. After recent occurrences, he expected Jaxon or Leira to be with his father at all times. And where was Allyn? Liam hadn't seen him since they'd returned to the manor—not that he had sought him out, either.

Since Allyn had learned that Liam couldn't wield, something had changed between them. The image of Allyn's face would be forever burned into his memory. It was an expression his father had the grace to hide, but no doubt felt—an expression of disappointment. Why would Allyn care so much anyway? It was none of his business. Liam hadn't told him he couldn't wield. *But why should I?* Some things didn't need to be common knowledge.

"We need your help, Liam," his father said.

There's a first! "With what?"

"I need you to search the archives and find any mention of twins. Who they were, what they did, rare abilities, anything odd or out of the ordinary."

"For what?"

"There's no time to explain right now. Do you think you can do that?"

Liam shrugged. "Shouldn't be too difficult."

His father nodded approvingly. "How long do you need?"

"A couple hours, maybe longer. It depends how deep you want the search to go."

"I want everything."

"Then the more time, the better."

Graeme nodded. "Thank you. Call for me as soon as you find something. Anything."

"Okay."

Graeme turned to go but stopped at the door. "And Liam? Best we keep this between us, okay?"

Liam nodded, and his father left, leaving him to his self-imposed seclusion. *Twins? That was the best they could come up with?* It was busywork, of course. His father meant to keep him occupied and out of the loop while the rest of them did something important. *Probably something to retaliate against the Hyland Family.* He'd proven how worthless he was outside the library, so they would do whatever possible to keep him cooped up. He ignored the order and returned to the work in front of him. He would eventually do as his father asked, but it would be done on his own time. If anyone asked how it was coming along, he would just say that it was a complicated search, but he was making progress.

They wouldn't know any better.

———————••••————————

A hushed silence fell over the manor as word spread of the ambush at the Hyland Estate. War was coming. No longer a distant threat, it had arrived, and people were going to die. Preparations began, not in the form of a call to arms of battle preparations—the manor was already in full lockdown and had been since Allyn's arrival. No, these were emotional preparations between loved ones—extra hugs, loving looks, even a few tears when nobody was supposed to be watching.

Goodbyes.

Allyn kept his head low as he left Graeme's study. The normal quiet, laid-back atmosphere had transformed into an active swarm of intense looks. Hushed whispers became shouts and walking turned to running as peace was replaced by war. His war. The mothers, fathers, husbands, and wives preparing for death would do so because of him. He didn't want them to see the guilt in his eyes, because while a somber mood hung over the manor like an Oregon winter, Allyn's insides roared with excitement.

By this time tomorrow, Kendyl will be safe.

Allyn bit the insides of his cheeks, fighting the smile that threatened to spread across his face. This wasn't a time to smile. He nodded to a pair of magi rounding the corner. They were in the middle of a conversation and didn't stop or acknowledge Allyn. *How long has it been?* Allyn asked himself. *Two weeks?* Even after they'd grown distant, he hadn't gone that long without seeing Kendyl. *Since when? Her vacation?*

"Not a trip," she had told him. "A *once-in-a-lifetime* trip." But even then, they had spoken to each other almost every night. She would tell him of her travels, the interesting towns, and amusing locals, all the while ridiculing him for not going with her. She called him old.

"Not old," he told her. "Responsible."

"Same thing," she said. Allyn imagined her sticking her tongue out for effect. After their mother's death, they each collected survivor's benefits until they turned nineteen and drew from the remaining money in her life insurance. He had used it to attend college, but Kendyl had planned a sprawling three-continent, four-month backpacking trip. "What better way to celebrate Mother's life than by doing everything she never got to do?" she had asked him.

"By earning a degree that will allow me to give back for my entire life." What he didn't tell her was how tempted he was to join her. In truth, he envied her ability to focus on the present, not years down the road. While he had the career, the car, and the condo, she had the fun. She had the memories. *We could each die tonight, and she would have lived the fuller life.*

He trembled at the thought. The possibility of that outcome had never entered his mind. He always believed she would return safely. On two separate occasions, Graeme and Jaxon had told him that he'd entered a dangerous world, but until the recent ambush, he'd never felt it.

It won't come to that. We have a good plan and the advantage. Graeme was planning to strike that night, under the cover of darkness and, Allyn hoped, in surprise. Graeme had mobilized every magi available, calling on every magi and cleric in the manor to be prepared, and used others already out on Family business to spread misinformation. Some would tell of a future strike, others of Graeme not attacking at all, while more would spread talk of an attempt to form a Grand Coalition. As information rolled in via Lukas's spies, so would the varying reports. Lukas wouldn't know what to expect, so Graeme said Lukas would prepare for everything except for what they would actually do—strike before those preparations became reality.

Allyn entered his room and closed the door and curtains, shutting himself away from the world. He had his own plans to make. The conflict was about to blow up into full-scale war, and he had no intention of being around for it. He and Kendyl needed to be long gone by the time anyone noticed they were missing. They couldn't go home, not if they intended to get away. They needed to vanish. Maybe he could take her back to Europe, meet her friends, see the sights, and heal by getting away from it all. It wasn't much of a plan, but it was a start. But first, he needed to get Kendyl out—alive.

CHAPTER 14

J ARRELL HARTLINE MARCHED THROUGH THE concrete corridors of the compound with Lukas's other followers. Whispers and rumors spread through the disorderly group like dandelions in an overgrown field. Darian Hyland had attempted to capture Graeme McCollum and Kendyl's brother, Allyn. The young fool was unsuccessful, and a handful of his Family was dead, but nobody knew if Lukas had ordered the attack.

"Graeme is building a coalition."

"He says he won't retaliate. He doesn't want a war."

"I heard he was already planning a strike."

Each person said something different, something that contradicted what the last person had said. Jarrell wanted to laugh. They were clueless. Lukas was too. *Unless he's marshaling us together to address the rumors and tell us what's really going on.*

They entered the cafeteria—a large open room with a matching concrete floor and walls unadorned with decorations. The tables were pushed against the walls, chairs resting on top, keeping the center of the room open. Bare but functional, nothing flashy—that was Lukas. He was about structure, strength, and unity. Most of the

Family had already arrived, leaving Jarrell at the back of the room, struggling to see over the rest. He pulled his glasses off and breathed onto the lenses, then rubbed them clean with the hem of his shirt. More than one person asked what was going on, but most waited patiently, at least as patiently as could be expected. Answers were coming. Why else would they have been summoned there?

Lukas entered a few minutes later, accompanied by his two bodyguards. Kaleb, the younger of the two, strutted beside his leader, a wicked grin on his face as if he reveled in knowing something the rest didn't. Reyland, always expressionless, stalked on the other side of him, his back straight, eyes darting, and muscles tight, ready to strike. He wasn't just a man prepared for a fight. He was a man looking for one.

Ever present, Kendyl brought up the rear. Silently pleading for help, her eyes flickered toward Jarrell as they always did when he was near. He'd offered it, but had so far been unable to make good on his promise. He had to be patient and wait for the right time. Jarrell looked away, in part because it made him feel helpless, but also because those pleading eyes might lead to unpleasant questions. She didn't look at anyone else like that. She didn't so much as make *eye contact* with anyone else. If someone was paying attention... the weight of her gaze subsided as she passed, its incrimination staved off for another time.

Lukas leaped onto a table at the far end of the room, and the crowd fell quiet. He stood silently, scanning the crowd. "Here we are. Look around. The men and women standing beside you are the men and women who are going to change the world. Men and women who already courageously stood with me and left behind a philosophy that saw our numbers decline year after year, decade after decade, generation after generation. The same men and women who are willing to stand, willing to fight, willing to die so that this philosophy is replaced by one that not only ensures the survival of the magi race but one where it thrives. One where we don't have to cower or hide. One where we can once again be *proud* of who we are and what we can do. You are the men and women of change."

He fell silent again, watching the audience. He exhaled, and his voice took on a somber tone. "So it pains me to inform you that some of those who stood with me, with us, are gone. Slain by the very hands that held us back, by the man who holds a foot at our necks and watches as we suffocate. Graeme has acted against us, without the consent of the very magi Families he suggests *we* rebel against. He's a traitor and has always been a traitor, and now his hands are bloody from an unprovoked attack."

Murmurs spread through the followers, then shouts for action and calls for retaliation. Jarrell shrank back, wishing he could hide. Lukas was inciting a mob whose devastation would be more catastrophic to the stability of the magi community than any other internal conflict. There would be no going back from this. Lukas was placing the blame squarely at Graeme's feet, and the mob wouldn't rest until they had spilled his blood.

The provocation was as illogical as it was unfair. The magi numbers had been declining long before Graeme's rise to power. They'd been declining since the Fracture. He was just the biggest target because he was Lukas's loudest opposition. Jarrell didn't stand for everything Graeme believed in, but he didn't want to see the Families go to war. He worked with Graeme not only because he believed in him but because it allowed him to keep the peace by bringing balance. Through his information, Graeme could counter Lukas's moves and ward off war for another day. This business with the Hyland Family was an extension of the truth at best and a complete fabrication at worst.

"But fear not." Lukas raised a hand, interrupting the

growing discussion among the masses. "Our day to right those wrongs is quickly approaching, and to help aid our cause is Darian Hyland and his strongest and most loyal magi." Lukas pointed to the back of the room, where the young Darian Hyland entered, followed by ten of his magi. They were dressed in black battle attire embroidered with intricate gold patterns along the sleeves and chest. Four clerics wearing similar muted-gray garb made up the rear guard. Applause broke out, and the Hyland Family received pats on the back and nods of encouragement as they strode through the crowd.

Lukas pulled Darian onto the tabletop with him and shook his hand. Darian smiled and said something to him that was too quiet for the crowd to hear. Lukas patted him on the back and gave him a smile of his own. "If any of you have doubts about what I say, I offer Darian Hyland himself as proof."

Darian stood there, hard and unflinching, silently agreeing with Lukas's account. He was younger than even Lukas. Even from across the room his pale-blue eyes were striking. If he spoke with the same conviction that his eyes suggested, it was obvious how he'd become the youngest grand mage within the Families. People were born to follow such a man.

"Everything he says is true," Darian said. "I welcomed Graeme and his Family into my home and offered my assistance. They were looking for something, a book of some kind. When they didn't find it, they accused me of keeping it from them. Said I hid it. Graeme knows he's fighting a losing battle. Already, the Families are lining up against him, and he's becoming desperate. He's power hungry, and he's willing to do whatever it takes to hold on to what little of it he has left. When I told him I didn't know what he was talking about, he became violent, attacking my magi. We were forced to protect ourselves, and after a tragic battle where we repelled them from the house, six of my magi and one of my clerics were dead. We're here not for revenge, but to ensure that no more magi need to die senselessly at the hands of this desperate man."

Darian's voice was quickly drowned out by cries from his audience.

"We won't let it happen!"

"We're with you!"

"Kill the traitors!"

Lukas motioned for the crowd to settle down, but the corners of his mouth hinted at a smile. "Please," he said. "Please." The calls for revenge didn't stop, but Lukas spoke over them. "I hope it doesn't come to that."

The crowd booed.

"I really don't. Graeme's followers are not all bad. They're scared. Scared of change, scared of what they would do with the freedom we strive for. But even as I say this, my spies tell me that Graeme is mobilizing. I can't tell you when he'll be here, but I can tell you that it will be sooner as opposed to later. He is coming. And he's coming for our blood."

"He's not going to get it!"

"Let him come!"

"We're not afraid!"

"As of right now," Lukas yelled over the restless crowd, "we are at war. We are not fleeing. We are not seeking it out. But if it comes to us, we will be prepared. I've assigned each of you to a squadron, complete with a squad leader and a second. This information will be distributed along with orders. If they come for us, we're going to blow them back to Graeme's doorstep in pieces."

The crowed roared.

It was over. There was nothing Jarrell could do except try to contact Graeme, tell him not to attack and that he was entering a trap. But that would only delay the inevitable. If Graeme didn't attack, Lukas would. He had fear on his side, and it was as powerful an ally as any. Jarrell had failed. All he could do was cut his losses and run. But he still needed to make good on a promise.

CHAPTER 15

THEY APPROACHED ON FOOT, USING the shadows to hide their advance. Allyn crept along in the middle of the file, behind a handful of magi. The magical S.W.A.T. force totaled more than twenty in all and was one of two storming Lukas's compound. Graeme led this force, Jaxon the other, each approaching from different areas with separate objectives.

Jaxon's force was tasked with creating a diversion, assaulting the elevator that led to the top floor of the abandoned warehouse where Lukas made his compound, and then entering through the main entrance. Meanwhile, Graeme and his force would ascend the fire escape and slip in among the chaos, using it to find Kendyl and retreat with minimal casualties.

It was a sound plan.

Allyn shivered against the wind. His compression armor did little to repel the rain that poured down in sheets. A river of rainwater flowed down the street against the curb and into a drain in front of them. Save for the hollow sound of splashing water echoing through the open grate, the streets were quiet. Lukas's compound was in an industrial part of town two blocks south of the Columbia

River where more buildings were vacant than occupied. And as late as it was, all the buildings were quiet, their working inhabitants having long since called it a day.

Lukas's compound wasn't much to look at and certainly not what Allyn had expected. Yellow light poured from the grimy top-floor windows of the otherwise-vacant building. Some were propped open, and others were broken. It looked... normal, hardly the sinister building of a psychopath bent on death and destruction.

Graeme ordered them to a halt, and they slid off the main street into the shadowy recesses of stoops, alleys, and corners, where they waited for their cue to advance.

Hold on, Kendyl. We're on our way.

The lookout's eyes widened in terror as Jaxon slipped from the shadows in front of him, driving his large fist into the man's face. Leira caught him as he stumbled backward. White light flared as her bare hand touched his face, forcing him unconscious. Together, they dragged him into the alley where the rest of their force waited.

Erik, a young bright-eyed magi, handed him the rope. The kid's hands were trembling. Embarrassed under Jaxon's gaze, Erik withdrew, joining the others in a silent circle watching Jaxon and Leira bind the lookout's wrists and ankles. Having trained so many of the magi under his command was an odd feeling. Things weren't supposed to work that way. Those who did the training weren't supposed to command. It was too personal.

Jaxon knew each of them. He knew their strengths and weaknesses. He remembered how quickly some had learned and how some had been blocked for years before finally being able to wield. Most, though not all, were younger than he was, but they were all *his* magi. And he would have to order some of them to their deaths.

It's not supposed to work this way.

He pulled the rope tight in a complex knot that would likely have to be burned off. In reality, the rope would do little to hold the man once he regained consciousness, but that wouldn't happen until they were ready. The knot was merely a symbolic gesture. He nodded to Leira and tossed the man over his shoulder.

She waited, her honey-colored eyes seeming to glow a bit brighter for a moment. Nobody else seemed to notice. Perhaps it was his mind playing tricks, but he felt as if he noticed things about her that nobody else did. *Does she notice things about me?* The thought scared him more than what waited for him inside that compound.

"It's clear," Leira said.

He took her word as truth. As a cleric's abilities grew, they could probe for energy and feel when another person was close. Proximity was important. Not even Leira could feel how many magi were waiting for them in Lukas's compound. Four guards were all they'd found outside. How many magi had Lukas drawn to his cause?

Jaxon stepped out of the alley. The limp man was dead weight on his shoulder. He jogged along easily, and the rest of his force followed, with Leira bringing up the rear. The man's face bounced against Jaxon's shoulder. He would probably wake up with a broken nose, but he would wake up. He would survive. Jaxon was relieved Graeme had ordered him not to kill unless they couldn't help it and only if they were provoked. They were there for Allyn's sister, nothing more. Graeme still held out hope that war could be prevented, though neither of them believed it could.

Still, it was good to hope.

Laying the unconscious man on the ground, Jaxon selected the clerics, eight of them in all, and silently counted to three with his fingers. On three, he slid into the deserted warehouse, clerics streaming in behind him, as silently as possible. Dust hung heavily in the air, and pools of standing water spread across the concrete floor. Obscured by the dirty windows, dim light came from streetlamps across the street. A metallic smell mixed with exhaust from large metal fabrication equipment.

They fanned out, searching from corner to corner, ready to force more guards into unconscious submission. Fire and air concussions were dramatic, even intimidating, but would prematurely alert Lukas to their presence. They didn't find any other guards, confirming his expectations that Leira would have alerted him if more guards were waiting.

Even in almost complete darkness, Leira's eyes seemed to glow. There was no way it was a trick. He could tell when she was wielding.

"Clear," he said in a forceful whisper. Magi swarmed in behind him. Erik and another young magi carried their captive inside by his hands and feet.

Jaxon found a metal folding chair tucked away in a corner. Metal shavings covered the seat, but it would do. It didn't need to be comfortable. He carried it to the back of the warehouse, where a freight elevator sat open. A wave of relief flowed through him. They'd passed the first known variable in this operation. He shuddered to think of what they would've done if the elevator hadn't been waiting. He just hoped it was operational.

Jaxon placed the chair in the middle of the large elevator then climbed atop it, probing the ceiling for the maintenance hatch. When he found it, the dry hinge squealed as he propped it open. The rooftop was three stories up, and it would be tight, but they should have enough room. Satisfied, he stepped down.

"I found it," Leira whispered, stepping toward him.

"The breaker for the plant or the floor?" Jaxon asked.

"An emergency shutoff. We pull the lever, and the lights go out in the entire building."

"Good work." He turned to Erik. "Follow Leira. When we give the command, I want you to pull the lever. Understand?"

Erik nodded and left with Leira.

"Tie him to the chair," Jaxon said, pointing at the unconscious guard. "We're going in."

———•••———

The compound bustled with activity as magi under the watchful eyes of Lukas and Darian Hyland built makeshift barriers, bunkers, and traps. They used whatever they could find: chairs, tables, buckets, even a broken toilet, tossing them onto heaps meant to slow an incoming attack. They quickly ran out of things to build barriers with. When someone brought this up to Lukas, he looked at him incredulously.

"We're on the top floor of an abandoned warehouse," he said. "Go downstairs and find something!"

The young man paled then vanished, likely rushing downstairs to gather more supplies. He was one of the last to seek Lukas with a problem. He found the rest on his own.

"You've funneled them this way but haven't left yourselves anywhere to retreat," Lukas said, observing one of the makeshift bunkers. "What happens when they advance and your backs are against the wall?"

"We'll kill them all."

"I like the sentiment," Lukas said. "But it's not going to work. Turn this into a false trail. Back there by your second barrier, leave a small opening against the wall where you can double back and get behind the enemy. Turn this into a bunker facing that way, against the wall. They'll be like prisoners in a shooting range."

The revision meant removing hundreds of pounds of

broken bricks and cinderblocks, but the men followed Lukas's orders without question. Elsewhere, Lukas sent a team of magi to gather discarded drums of oils and solvents, which they positioned outside doors, in well-trafficked hallways, and exposed rafters.

"All this oil won't be easy to put out," Jarrell said, rolling a barrel into place.

"It's not supposed to be."

So Lukas isn't intending on staying here. He's willing to bring the whole building down on us as long as it means killing Graeme in the process.

Lukas hadn't divided the men into squads as he'd indicated he would—he probably hadn't expected the men to jump straight to work. But once they did, he wasn't going to stop them. Without a squad or someone telling him what to do, Jarrell was left to his own devices. Having long since learned that the worst jobs often went to those who waited to be told what to do, he did just enough to look busy. It gave him an opportunity to see the layout, and what he saw sent chills down his spine. If Graeme assaulted this compound, it would be a bloodbath.

He had to get word to him somehow. But the compound was on lockdown. He couldn't slip out like he had before. And Graeme's estate was across town. He couldn't just slide a note under his door. Jarrell didn't have a cell phone, and even if he did, he would have to contend with Graeme's cursed jammer. He had only one way to get word to Graeme—in person.

He had to flee. But he wouldn't do it alone.

Jarrell strode through the chaotic halls like a man in the middle of an important task, pushing past other workers, dodging looks, and refusing to make eye contact with anyone. The last thing he needed was to be summoned by someone in charge or someone who thought they were.

"You," a voice called out. *Kaleb.* He was exactly the

type of person Jarrell was avoiding. Jarrell kept walking. "Jarrell!" Kaleb yelled above the commotion, too loudly for Jarrell to act as if he hadn't heard him.

I'm an important man on an important errand, Jarrell told himself, steeling his confidence. Not missing a step, Jarrell turned to him and held up his finger. "One minute," he said and kept on, continuing his pretend task.

Kaleb blinked. He wasn't used to being blown off and would likely find a way to punish Jarrell for the public swipe at his authority.

Jarrell slipped into his room and closed the door, muffling some of the commotion outside. He observed his room. What would take with him? What did he need?

Nothing. I don't need to bring anything. He rubbed his forehead. Beads of sweat poured down from his thinning hair, the moisture fogging up his glasses. *When did I start sweating?* Was it the nerves or the work? It didn't matter. The only thing that mattered was... *Lukas is alone.*

Alone.

Where is Kendyl? Lukas never let her out of his sight. She was like an abused pet, always cowering but never raising a fuss. Lukas didn't keep her at his side for that reason alone, though. It was a mind game. She was the embodiment of the war against Graeme and a walking example of their first victory—a trophy to be admired. As long as she was the center of attention, she couldn't escape. And a trophy would be locked up safely in only one place.

Jarrell strode through the halls toward Lukas's private chambers before he realized what he was doing. This area of the compound was deserted and the sounds of battle preparations distant. Reyland, Lukas's most trusted bodyguard, stood outside the door, and Lawson, a newer guard, stood at attention beside him. Reyland's disheveled black hair clung to his pale forehead, and his eyes, which were even darker even than his hair, latched onto Jarrell as he approached. He scared the death out of Jarrell.

His mind told him to stop, turn, and run, but his body disobeyed and continued forward purposefully. *Get control of yourself, old man. You are a trusted member of Lukas's followers and were sent here for a specific reason.* "I'm here for the girl," Jarrell said, stopping in front of Reyland.

"Lukas said nobody in or out," Reyland said. They were the most words Jarrell had ever heard the man utter—Reyland would rather kill a man than talk to him.

"Now I'm telling you different," Jarrell said. "Let me in."

"No."

"Do you really think I'd be here if Lukas didn't send me? What business do I have with the girl?"

"Nobody in or out. Those are my orders."

"Look," Jarrell said irritably. "I understand the good-soldier routine, okay? I'll even tell Lukas about it, but right now, I need to get into that room."

"I can't let you do that."

"Then you're going to have to stop me because I'm not going to find Lukas just so he can tell you different." Something about acting tough and talking tough actually made him feel tough. Jarrell pushed his way forward and was immediately met with a hand to his chest. Reyland's eyes bored into Jarrell's, probing for something. *Fear,* Jarrell realized, setting his jaw and meeting Reyland's gaze.

"Find Lukas," Reyland said, his eyes still set on Jarrell's.

Lawson obeyed without a word.

Once Lawson was out of sight, Jarrell snatched Reyland's hand and wielded. Reyland's fatigue was like a vast underground lake, deep and hidden from the surface, but still present. Lukas was riding them hard, those closest to him the hardest of all, and for once, Jarrell appreciated it. He gathered his own fatigue to the surface and projected it into Reyland. Almost immediately,

Reyland fell to the floor, unconscious. Checking the halls for onlookers, Jarrell grabbed Reyland's arm and dragged him inside Lukas's chamber. The lack of guards would be suspicious, but one lying unconscious outside would be even more so.

Entering Lukas's chamber, Jarrell immediately found Kendyl. She was in the corner where the concrete wall met the brick exterior wall, gagged. A single naked light dangled above her. Rope held her hands behind her back, and her ankles had been tied to the legs of a metal folding chair. If she saw him, she didn't acknowledge him. Jarrell dropped Reyland and rushed to her.

"Can you walk?" he asked, kneeling in front of her, working at the knots that bound her ankles. She grunted something inaudible. Jarrell cursed himself and removed her gag, a dirty piece of worn cloth soaked with saliva. She was fortunate she hadn't suffocated.

"What are you doing?" she asked, panicked.

"We're leaving."

"No!" Kendyl shouted, thrashing, pulling the knots from Jarrell's hands.

"Stop. I can't untie you if you keep doing that."

"Please," Kendyl pleaded. "Just go."

"Don't you want out of here?"

"He'll catch me."

"No, he won't," Jarrell said. "That's why I'm here."

She stopped thrashing, and Jarrell restarted on the knots.

"My friends are coming, and when they get here, Lukas is going to kill them. I have to get out of here. I have to stop them. And you're coming with me." The ropes fell limp, and Jarrell unwrapped them from her legs. The skin around her ankles was raw. He would have to heal them before they got infected—it would help him earn her trust—but it would have to wait until they reached safety.

"Why are you doing this?" Kendyl asked.

Jarrell walked behind her to begin on the knots that bound her wrists. "I told you I would get you out of here.

"That was you?"

What have they done to her? He was likely the only person within the compound who had expressed kindness toward her, but she had no idea who he was. Head trauma and concussions could be healed, but the memory loss that followed couldn't.

"I remember... but it's foggy, like a dream. I thought it was."

"It wasn't," Jarrell said, finishing untying the knots at her wrists. "Can you stand?"

She didn't get a chance.

The door opened behind Jarrell, bathing the room in light from the hallway.

Lukas stepped inside.

The dark elevator shaft was claustrophobic. It was lined only with dim service lights and a track that held the elevator car in position. The ceiling, hidden in the darkness above, already weighed down on him, forcing him to crouch lower, almost hugging the steel bracket to which the car itself was attached. He prayed he wouldn't be smashed between it and the ceiling. He could have used a small fireball for light, but that might alert the magi to his presence. Even alone and riding atop an elevator car, he needed stealth.

The three braided steel cables that pulled the car upward slowed as the car approached the third floor—Lukas's compound. Assuring himself one last time that he wouldn't be smashed, Jaxon peered through the vent into the car, where the unconscious magi sat tied to the folding chair.

Here we go, Jaxon thought as the car came to a stop. A bell rang, and the doors opened. Shouts of alarm rang out, and four magi streamed into the elevator car to assist the incapacitated guard.

"It's Jared," one said.

"Get Lukas," said another. He must have been yelling at someone outside the elevator, because nobody inside left. They were already working at the knots that bound Jared.

"He was supposed to be outside," the first man said. "What happened to him?"

The second man stood up with a start. "They're here."

They know we're coming. What are we running into? He was thankful to be atop the elevator car so that his squad couldn't see his uneasiness.

The bell chimed again, and the doors began to close. One of the magi hit a button on the panel, and when the doors continued to close, he slapped it again, this time more irritably. Jaxon smiled. He'd cut that wire himself.

As the doors closed, Jaxon wielded water and fire then projected it into the doors. Ice filled the crack between the doors, sealing them shut. Satisfied that it would hold, Jaxon stepped to the edge of the car and sent a small beam of flame down the shaft to signal his squad below.

The elevator shaft went dark as they cut the power.

———————•••———————

"I was hoping it wasn't you," Lukas said, entering the room, a handful of magi following closely behind. Lawson must have found Lukas faster than Jarrell had anticipated.

Someone kicked Reyland, bringing him to. He stood, woozy, fighting the vast ocean of exhaustion Jarrell had steeped within him, watching Jarrell with murderous eyes.

Jarrell wanted to apologize to Kendyl, but the words caught in his chest. His nerves had finally caught up to him.

"I wanted the spy to be someone... intimidating," Lukas said. "Killing you will only look pathetic. Though, I must admit, I admire the strategy. I didn't take you for the mole. You're too soft, too skittish, too much of a... cleric."

The magi behind him snickered.

"What am I going to do with you?"

"Kill him," someone said. "And throw his broken body onto Graeme's doorstep."

"That's exactly what I was—"

The room went black.

Someone shouted a curse, and fire ignited around Lukas's arm. The magi behind him followed his lead and also wielded fire. Jarrell couldn't make out much, but the confusion on Lukas's face was evident. Whatever was happening hadn't been by his design.

The door burst open, and a young magi barreled into the room. "They're here! Jared is in the elevator, dead or unconscious. I don't know. He's tied to a chair."

Lukas grabbed Jarrell by this shirt and shoved him toward his bodyguards. "Take him!"

Reyland stepped forward, a dark smile touching his lips, and grabbed Jarrell by the neck.

"Don't kill him," Lukas said. He rubbed his temples. "Not yet. I have other plans for him."

Reyland ushered Jarrell out of the room. The last thing he saw was Kendyl crying as Lukas yanked her from the chair.

"There it is." Nyla pointed to the sky above the compound, where a large orange fireball burned through the low-hanging clouds. It was their sign to move forward. Things were going according to plan. There was still hope.

Graeme ordered them forward. Allyn wondered what they looked like—a group of men and women dressed in black, emerging from shadowy recesses and thick fog. They were a mix between a street gang and a military unit. Either way, he was certain it was an imposing sight.

Nyla leaned close to Allyn. "Are you ready to get your sister back?"

On Graeme's command, the magi unleashed destructive creations of fire and ice, assaulting the compound. The soot-stained windows exploded, dropping the unsuspecting magi inside, and the compound rang with shouts of confusion, orders, and pain.

A fireball erupted from the compound, shooting toward them. It was met midair with ice, and the flame was snuffed with the sound of cold water pouring onto a hot skillet. Lukas's followers hurled fireballs and shards of ice in their direction, but they countered each before it became dangerous. As Graeme's magi continued their assault on the compound, fireballs and ice blasts shattered against the building's brick exterior, forcing the enemy magi inside to take cover.

Fighting broke out inside the compound, and the magi at the windows turned to fight someone else. Jaxon's squad had arrived.

An explosion rocked the building, blowing out more windows, and a man was thrown into the night, falling three stories to the concrete below. Allyn turned away, but he still heard the man hit the ground to the sound of an egg cracking. He shuddered. That had been him. But unlike this man, Allyn had lived to tell the tale.

Graeme jogged forward, his magi in close pursuit. He led them around to the back of the building where it butted up against another unattractive warehouse. Graeme wheeled a dumpster over and used it as a step to reach the ladder to the fire escape. He pulled himself up, and without waiting for the next person, he began his ascent. One by one, they climbed onto the fire escape, and by the time Allyn's turn came, the steel brackets that fastened it to the brick building groaned under their combined weight. Nobody slowed. Allyn cursed under his breath, continuing upward, praying they didn't fall.

From the top of the metal stairwell, Graeme called for Allyn, and he squeezed his way through the others to kneel beside Graeme. Locking eyes with Allyn, Graeme stood slowly, peering into the compound through a cracked window. Allyn followed his lead.

The upper floor was a mix of concrete and thin walls that didn't reach the ceiling. Allyn had worked in a similar building as a cleanup kid during high school and remembered the way conversations drifted throughout the floor, seeping through uninsulated walls, only obscured by the banging of exposed air ducts. On the deserted floor, the sounds of workers' voices and blowing fans had been replaced by the sounds of battle from the front of the building, where the battle raged.

"I don't know where she is from here," Graeme whispered. "It's likely she's with Lukas, or he might have hidden her somewhere he thought she would be safe. We're going to search the back of the compound first. If she's here, we'll get her and slip back out the way we came in."

"And if she's not?" Allyn asked.

"Then we'll be paying Lukas a visit." Graeme slipped a leg through the window and crawled inside.

Dirt and dust fell from the ceiling as explosions rocked the front of the compound. Outside, they were only loud and uninviting, but inside, Allyn felt them in his chest and under his feet. They seemed to blow through him. If Graeme was concerned, he didn't show it. He stopped outside a door, waited for a couple of the nearest magi to take up position at his shoulder, and kicked it open. Magi streamed inside, ready to attack. The room was empty. Seven or eight bunks lined the wall, meaning Lukas was packing the magi inside like children in a classroom. They probably shared personal belongings, too.

No wonder Lukas is playing the instigator. Tensions were brewing inside his compound. Cram too many people into a tight space, and fireworks would follow. It was only a matter of time before he had his own splinter to contend with.

After they found the next two rooms empty, Allyn grew increasingly agitated. They were supposed to be able to sneak into the compound, grab Kendyl, and sneak back out, but as the minutes ticked by, the chances of that happening became smaller. "This isn't working. We're searching the compound when we need to be looking for Lukas's room. That's where Kendyl will be. Do we know which one is his?"

"The one with the guards?" Nyla asked.

Graeme shook his head. "Too obvious."

"His room will be the biggest," Allyn said. "He's not going to share a room with fifteen other people, regardless of how full the compound is. The question is, is it close?"

Graeme traced his lips with his fingers. "He's worried about detractors, and by presiding over their sleeping quarters, he could quell any growing dissent."

If Graeme was right, then this hall was like a barracks, and Lukas's room would be private but near, allowing him to come and go as he pleased without probing eyes. It would have a back door.

"The fire escape," Allyn said.

"What?" Nyla asked.

"We walked right past it," Allyn said, doubling back. He stopped at the window where they'd come in and poked his head outside, looking in both directions. The fire escape platform ran parallel with the hall, extending in both directions. "The platform runs that way until it ends at a window."

"But there isn't a window over there," Nyla said, looking in the direction Allyn pointed. "It's just a wall."

"That's because it's on the other side," Allyn said. "That's Lukas's room."

There weren't any guards stationed outside the door, but that didn't mean no one was waiting inside. Allyn stepped aside as Graeme came up behind him, and magi lined up, ready to storm in like a trained police force. Graeme held up his fingers in a silent count. On three, he kicked in the door, and the magi swarmed inside, Allyn with them.

The room was sparsely furnished with a double bed, bedside tables, a dresser, and even a desk. Against the back of the room, along the exposed brick exterior wall, was the window he'd seen from the fire escape. In front of it was a metal chair with frayed ropes at the legs. Allyn felt a small glimmer of vindication push against his overwhelming sense of frustration. It was Lukas's room.

But it was empty.

Allyn knelt in front of the chair, taking the ropes in his hands. They were oily and slick with sweat and blood. "She was here. She was *here*." He threw Kendyl's bonds to the floor.

"Lukas will have her," Graeme said.

"Then our paths will finally cross." Allyn's voice was firm. "You can put your Family in order while I get my sister back." Allyn strode past Graeme and back into the corridor. His plan was simple—follow the noise.

He ran wildly, throwing stealth aside, as the rest of the unit struggled to keep up. He entered a large open room, startling a young man tasked with guarding the space. The kid squealed, and Allyn drove his fist into his face. He winced. The boy couldn't have been much older than Liam and had the same awkward look of an adolescent trying to grow into his body. Allyn felt bad for the kid. He obviously wasn't a threat, otherwise Lukas would have used him in the battle, and he was probably too young to have chosen to follow Lukas, but they couldn't be slowed.

Nyla forced him under before he could make more noise, and Allyn continued through the room. Tables and chairs were stacked on top of each other and pushed off to the edges of the room. Breadcrumbs, wrappers, and plastic silverware littered the floor. It smelled of cheap cafeteria food. The sounds of battle were getting louder.

It has to be on the other side of—

An explosion rocked the building. His ears ringing, Allyn found himself on the ground, metal splinters in his hands and arms, white dust blanketing his shirt. The chairs and tables that had been neatly stacked atop each other were scattered across the floor, and a four-foot hole had been blown in the concrete wall.

Through the hole, red and blue lights flashed against the concrete walls like light from a police car. Magi on both sides of the room attacked from behind makeshift bunkers of brick, stone, and furniture. Within the confined space, the magi didn't have time to counterattack, and fire exploded against bunkers and walls with a steady rhythm. This was the kind of battle where the more aggressive force won, and Graeme's forces, who had been ordered not to kill unless necessary, were tentative, confused... and losing.

"They're pinned down." Graeme's voice trembled. How long had he tried to avoid this? "Stand back." He formed something in his hand—a flame that burned inside a globe of ice the size of his fist. He hurled it into the room.

The wall exploded, throwing unsuspecting enemy magi on the other side of the wall to the ground. Others dropped to the floor, shielding themselves from flying debris, while even more turned in shock to see a new force assembling behind them. The magi pinned down at the far end of the room charged forward, using the lapse in the battle to their advantage. They struck hard, using air to throw debris at the backs of their attackers. It was less accurate, but when it connected, enemy magi fell with a sickening crunch. Blood and broken bones replaced burns.

Pinned down between two groups, Lukas's force fought like a cornered animal—ferocious and with nothing to lose. Never surrendering, they forced Graeme's magi to kill them to a man, cursing them until the end.

The battle over, Graeme knelt beside the last of the fallen enemy magi, taking his hand in his own and whispering something to him.

"That was well-timed." The leader of the squad approached. Wisps of his shoulder-length black hair stuck to his tanned face, partially hiding his bloodshot left eye. His arms were covered with dozens of cuts and small burns. "Thank you."

"He was my nephew," Graeme said, closing the fallen magi's eyelids with his fingers. "His father believed in Lukas, and children believe in their parents. He never had a chance, Trevin. Please don't thank me."

Allyn stepped over fallen bodies and debris. The floor was slick with urine, water, and blood. Worse than the sights of the battle were the smells. Small fires smoldered in scattered patches, and the smoke, smelling of burned hair and flesh, mixed with the nauseating smell of feces. A magi lay in front of him, his lifeless eyes open and gazing toward the ceiling.

"They're all family," Trevin said. "It's a terrible thing."

Allyn looked closer. Something about the dead man felt familiar, but he'd seen so many new faces that it was tough to be sure. He might have seen him anywhere. Or his mind could be playing tricks on him. After seeing enough people in a short period of time, anyone was bound to think he'd seen someone before. But something *pulled* Allyn toward the man.

"A terrible thing," Graeme agreed.

Allyn barely heard him. Pinching his forehead, he closed his eyes. He still saw the man's face, only this time—"He's one of Darian's."

Graeme turned to Allyn. "Who?"

"I've seen this man," Allyn said. "He smashed me against a wall during our escape from the Hyland Estate."

Nyla, who'd been probing the fallen to search for survivors, stepped toward him. "Are you sure?"

"I'm positive."

Graeme circled the room, looking at fallen bodies. "He's right," he said. "Darian is here."

"What does that mean?" Allyn asked.

"It means," Graeme said, "this operation just got a lot more difficult."

Water poured from the elevator doors like a stream running down a rocky hillside. It puddled under Jaxon's feet and around the bodies behind him. They'd pulled and pried, doing everything they could to open the doors, never realizing they were frozen shut. Jaxon had slipped in behind them, driving his elbows into the tops of the two men unfortunate enough to be standing directly under the service hatch. The two who had been prying the elevator doors open turned just in time to see Jaxon's fists pummeling into their faces. All four lay motionless but not dead. He wouldn't kill unless he had to. That wasn't his mission. Death would destroy any hope they had of healing the splinter.

Jaxon's legs were weak. Freezing the doors shut had required more water than he'd expected, and water wasn't as easily replenished as air. He was severely dehydrated and would have to take care not to wield too much more of it. He hoped he wouldn't have to use it at all, but since water was the counter to fire, which was a magi's favorite method of attack, he didn't think that was likely.

The sounds of battle had waned, as both sides were undoubtedly regrouping, digging into the trenches, and securing their positions. Jaxon worked his fingers inside the crack between the elevator doors and pulled. When they didn't open, he put a foot against the doorframe for leverage and tried again. This time, the seal popped, and the doors opened.

The compound was dark. The exterior streetlamps and the remains of small fires inside provided what little light they could. The concrete floor was cracked in places and missing altogether in others. Bodies filled the corridor. Some were burnt and scorched, while others with gaping wounds lay in pools of water left behind from the melted ice blasts. Others didn't have any noticeable injuries, but their cracked lips, odd skin coloring, and popped blood vessels in the whites of their eyes told Jaxon everything he needed to know. Magic had limitations, and they'd pushed themselves too hard.

There was movement in front of him. Jaxon froze, watching the dark corridor intently. Someone had run through an intersecting corridor. Approaching warily, Jaxon peered around the corner. The person was gone, but Jaxon followed in silent pursuit. At the very least, this corridor should lead back toward the main entrance where Leira would be.

The battle roared again as the respite ended. Jaxon continued on, ignoring the sounds of destruction and the cries of pain. He had his orders—find Jarrell. He rounded the corner and nearly tripped over a young fellow who was hunkered down behind a makeshift bunker. Another lookout waited across the hall. It was a trap, and they were waiting for someone to spring it on. Jaxon drove his knee into the first man, and a concussion of air exploded between his knee and the man's chest, sending him flying down the hall. He'd learned the trick a long time ago. Air wielded with kicks, punches, and elbow jabs increased their strength tenfold.

Jaxon spun on the other one, wielding more air just in time to smother a fire blast. Air could be just as effective as water at combating fire. The man fell to the ground, his jaw unhinged, after Jaxon landed another air-aided blow.

Jaxon raced onward. Any magi within the vicinity would be drawn to him now. As if on cue, a group of magi appeared in the corridor in front of him. They stopped short, watching Jaxon in surprise. Maybe they hadn't been drawn to him. Two men held up a third, his arms draped across their shoulders, his feet dragging on the floor behind him.

Jarrell.

Was he a wounded soldier or a captive? Did they know he was the spy? The way they dropped him to the floor suggested they did. How had he been caught? The man leading the group cocked his head to the side, weighing Jaxon. *Reyland.* His dark features against his pale skin made the man look like a walking corpse. He sneered at Jaxon with yellow teeth behind black lips and stepped forward.

Jaxon didn't wait. He was outnumbered five to one, and Reyland was as powerful as he was, maybe more so. And already, his muscles were cramping from dehydration. He wouldn't win this battle. Jaxon shot five quick blasts of fire in their direction, and without waiting to see if they hit their target, he ran straight for the wall to his right and drove an air-aided shoulder *through* it. He found himself on the floor of a room lined with bunks. Jaxon quickly climbed to his feet and ran toward the door. A bolt of fire struck the bunk behind him, blasting the wood frame to pieces and igniting the sheets. Reyland wasn't about to let Jaxon escape.

Charging through another wall, Jaxon lost all sense of direction. He was in another corridor with a brick wall and windows overlooking the river. He tripped, fell, and rose to his feet. Something exploded *above* him. Thrown down the hall, he hit the floor with a crack and slid into a wall. Ears ringing, his vision blurred, Jaxon struggled to his feet.

Embers fell from the ceiling, coming to rest on the shoulders of his compression armor, burning the exposed skin on his neck and scalp. Something else fell from the rafters. *Cold. Wet. Water. A hole in the roof. What just happened?*

Reyland stalked toward him, smiling.

Smiling. Jaxon gritted his teeth. With men like this, men who sought blood and enjoyed spilling it, there was no hope of mending their splintered Family. Reyland was a cancer, and the only way to cure it was to remove it or destroy it.

Jaxon charged. His temper flared, fueling the fire pouring from his hands. How many times had he told his students to leave their emotions behind? Emotion led to death. It would burn him out, sap his body of everything it needed. But not today. A wall of flame filled the hall, spurred forward by Jaxon.

Reyland stepped through it. The flames singed his body but were stamped out. By what? It didn't matter. Jaxon was nearly on him now.

Reyland prepared to wield.

Jaxon jumped, driving the bottoms of his air-aided feet into Reyland's chest, crushing his ribs. The impact threw Reyland onto his back and whipped his head into the concrete floor with a crack.

Landing on the floor on his side, Jaxon rolled to his feet, ready to attack again, but Reyland lay motionless, staring through the open expanse in the roof with lifeless eyes, his chest caved in with the shape of two bootprints. Jaxon spat and stepped back into the bunk-filled room, making his way for the hall, ready to find Jarrell.

The detonation shook the building to its foundation. The floor rolled, nearly buckling. Windows shattered, and people dove for cover as air ducts and metal piping fell from the rafters. Over it all, Allyn heard a scream. It shook him more than the explosion did.

"Kendyl!" he shouted, darting out of the room in the direction of her voice. Someone called after him, pleading with him to wait, but Allyn barely heard. The part of him that did didn't listen. The hallway became a dark tunnel as the world around him disappeared into shadows. He ran blindly, using only his ears to guide him. "Kendyl!" he called out again. No answer. But somewhere ahead of him, he heard the scraping of labored steps. Then voices. A whimper. A shush. He pushed forward.

Allyn slid around the corner, barely catching sight of a group of people. He didn't recognize all of them, but he did her.

Kendyl wasn't chained or bound, dragged or pushed. She followed the group like an abused pet, out of fear, not loyalty. Her dark hair, normally bordering on black except for a warm-brown sheen in direct light, was knotted and faded as though it hadn't seen a brush in weeks. A gaunt face with bloodshot eyes looked at him and... nothing. She had no expression, as if she didn't even see him. Her face heavy and slow, she watched him like someone who'd taken too many painkillers.

This wasn't the Kendyl he knew. That Kendyl, his *real*

sister, was a warm, inviting person. She didn't bring just sunshine into a room; she brought the sun. She burned with positive energy, warming even the worst of days. She didn't get down. She didn't get depressed. She smiled and waved at the difficulties in her life. It would take true horror to turn her into the cold, lifeless shell of a person that Allyn saw.

They disappeared around the corner.

He stormed ahead, rage filling him, burning so hot that he could feel his body growing warmer. The pain from the splinters in his arm, the ache in his back that had never quite healed since the fall, and the dull headache from the building stress all faded as the burning anger swelled through him. He felt almost as if he could grab it.

"Kendyl!" Allyn rounded the corner.

They stopped and turned to meet him. Lukas arched an eyebrow. He wasn't what Allyn remembered. He was shorter and skinnier. His curly hair was thinner, but he held his shoulders high and his back straight. His chin was slightly elevated, exuding supreme confidence. If it weren't for the pulsing aggression inside him, Allyn might have wilted under such confidence. Lukas pushed Kendyl behind him, and one of his magi took her by the shoulders.

Kendyl watched Allyn, recognition slowly forming in her eyes.

She still doesn't believe it's me. What have they done to her? They were back in the barracks hall of the compound, outside Lukas's room. *He's trying to slip out the back door.* Allyn cursed himself; he should have left a couple magi behind in case Lukas returned.

"Allyn," Lukas said, his voice a soft tenor. "I wish we could have met under better circumstances. Your sister has been kind enough to tell me so much about you. Defender of the weak, protector of the innocent, speaker for the voiceless. It's ironic for a silent man like yourself, is it not? Or has Graeme finally unlocked the power that resides in you?"

"You're a liar," Allyn said. "I can't wield, and you know that. That was never your game. You used me as a pawn to distract Graeme while you built a coalition behind his back."

Lukas raised an eyebrow. "I'm many things, but a liar isn't one of them. That is your problem, Allyn. You don't *believe.* It's easier for you to believe in an evil master plan than it is for you to believe that you're something special."

Footsteps rang down the hall, and Allyn turned to see Graeme, Nyla, and the rest of their squad racing to catch up. *Was I really that far ahead of them?*

Lukas took a step back, shielding himself behind a couple of his bodyguards as the squad gathered around Allyn. They outnumbered Lukas two to one.

"Let her go, Lukas," Graeme said.

Lukas ignored the command, keeping his attention on Allyn. "Let me guess. He's had you searching for lineage. Building family trees, tracing your ancestry, trying to find out what you can do by finding out where you came from."

Allyn frowned.

"I'm not surprised," Lukas said. "Graeme believes we are who we *were.* It's simple that way, but that doesn't make it true. You are who you are because of *you*, not because of the dead and buried. Each of us is different, and we can change. We live in a new age, Allyn. The world has changed, and we have along with it."

"Do all of your followers believe in empty words?" Allyn asked. "Because you do a great job of saying a lot without actually saying anything at all."

"The ability to wield isn't hereditary," Lukas said. "If it were, our numbers wouldn't be shrinking."

"Our numbers decline because we forsake our old ways," Graeme said. "We're too quick to embrace new ideas, new cultures, new technologies. They make us forget who we are."

Lukas waved his hand. These were tired arguments between adversaries.

"If you've unlocked the powers of the universe," Allyn said, "then show me. What can my sister do that I cannot?"

Lukas grinned. "You really are a lawyer, aren't you? Always needing proof. I'll show you what I'm talking about. We'll conduct a little experiment. You can be my guinea pig, if you don't mind, and I'll let your sister go. You can take her and leave without ever having to worry about me again, but you have to do something for me first."

"What?"

"Wield."

"I already told you, I can't."

"And I already said you could." Fire sprang to life in Lukas's hands.

Graeme leaped forward, wielding his own fire, ready to strike.

"Give me fire." The fire in Lukas's hands was replaced with ice. "Give me water. Give me air. Heal someone in your group. Do anything. Just prove me right."

Allyn watched him, unsure what to do. Something needed to be done quickly, while they had numbers, before Lukas did something desperate. Attacking would risk hurting Kendyl. Maybe if Lukas saw him try and fail to wield, he would finally understand that it wasn't possible and that he and Kendyl were normal. At the very least, it would distract Lukas so Allyn or Graeme could formulate a better plan. Allyn closed his eyes, ready to try. And fail. Again.

"I know you can feel it," Lukas said. "Something inside, something you've never felt before, a writhing storm, a torrent of emotion. Harness it."

Allyn frowned. The truth was he *did* feel something. *It's my anger.* Anger and adrenaline could do strange things to the body.

"Stop trying to talk yourself out of it," Lukas said. "It's there. It's real."

Against his better judgment, Allyn focused on it. He was enticed by it, mesmerized by it, and drawn to it. He poked at it, prodded it, approaching from different directions, never able to get any closer. It slipped from his grasp like water through his fingers. After a time, it dissipated, growing smaller and harder to find. He focused harder and tried to excise his emotion, but it still withdrew until it was entirely gone.

He opened his eyes.

Everyone was watching him. Even Graeme watched with renewed interest. He didn't believe Lukas, too, did he?

"Pity," Lukas said. "I might be wrong about you." He turned to Kendyl. "About both of you."

He's going to let her go. Allyn took a couple steps forward.

Lukas's eyes narrowed in thought.

Do it. Don't talk yourself out of it. "Let her go."

Lukas shook his head. "I'm sorry," he said. "This is too important." He turned to the magi holding her. "Kill them."

He pulled Kendyl away from the bodyguard and pushed her into his chambers.

CHAPTER 16

"**N**o!" ALLYN SCREAMED, RUSHING FORWARD. He knew there was nothing he could do, but he was tired of that excuse. He was going to get his sister back, or he was going to die trying. He wasn't going to lose her again. Someone caught him by the neck of his compression armor, trying to pull him back, but he was too strong and too determined. He heard a curse, and then he was free, stumbling forward.

The bodyguards took a defensive stance, guarding the door, wielding. A concussion of air detonated in front of Allyn, flattening the four enemy magi against the wall. They slumped, dazed. One coughed as if he'd had the wind knocked out of him. The others threw wild attacks from their knees.

A fireball flew forward, striking the chest of the man who had held Kendyl, throwing him through the door he was charged with protecting. His skin was charred and blistered under singed clothing. He didn't get up.

Allyn slid under another wave of enemy attacks. This time, they were more precise, forcing Graeme's magi to dive for cover. Painful screams filled the hall. Someone hadn't been quick enough. Reckless and desperate, Allyn tackled the magi nearest him, wildly throwing his fists into the magi's face. Someone grabbed him from behind. Allyn turned just in time to see a blast of ice drive through the man's temples. He fell on top of Allyn, pinning him to the magi he'd tackled.

After another concussion of air and another crash, the hall fell silent, save for the scraping and clawing of Allyn struggling to untangle himself from the enemy. Someone pulled the dead weight of the fallen magi off him, and he rolled free. The last enemy magi remained on the floor, holding his hands up in surrender, warily eyeing his fallen comrades.

Allyn rushed inside the room, Graeme at his shoulder. The magi who'd held Kendyl lay just inside the door, his wound steaming, black clothing still smoldering around the wound like a burning cigarette. Cold, fresh air blew in through an open window where Lukas was trying to push Kendyl onto the fire escape. She saw Allyn and planted her foot against the window frame. As hard as he tried, Lukas couldn't force her through the window.

That's the sister I know, Allyn thought. *Give him hell.*

Lukas let go of her and stepped away. She fell, crying out as she landed on her shoulder. Favoring it, she rolled onto her knees, cupping it with her hand. She seemed unable to move it.

"Step aside, Allyn," Graeme said.

Allyn complied, throwing himself against the wall. Graeme and Lukas stood face to face, ten paces from each other, each waiting for the other to strike.

Lukas struck first. A flash of blue light streamed toward Graeme, too quickly for Allyn to tell what it was. Blue was usually ice, but the burst looked alive, like blue flame.

Graeme blew it aside with air. The blue flame hit the wall behind him, blowing a four-foot hole in the sheetrock, leaving flames around its edges. Graeme retaliated with his own attack, and the duel began in earnest. Red and blue flashes of light illuminated the tight confines of the room as each man attacked, defended, and retaliated. Loose paper from Lukas's desk blew into the air when one of Graeme's fireballs struck it, leaving behind the sweet smell of smoke as they gently fell to the floor.

Keeping to the edges of the room, Allyn tried to work his way around the two men and get to Kendyl, but they were all over the place, diving in all directions, narrowly avoiding each other's attacks. Another of Graeme's errant fireballs nearly struck Kendyl. She screamed as it flew over her shoulder, striking the brick wall behind her. Fallen bits of brick and mortar rattled against the ground, where she sank down, pulling her knees close. She watched the two men, flinching each time a blast shook the room.

Graeme and Lukas fought with an intensity Allyn had never seen. They wielded faster, with larger blasts of ice and fire that burned brighter. The brightness, it seemed, was related to power—the brighter the attack, the more powerful.

A fireball burning as brightly as the sun shot toward Lukas. It was mere inches from his chest when a ribbon of water appeared between his hands, dousing it. It hissed, but something *inside* continued forward, striking Lukas in the shoulder. He stumbled backward, holding his shoulder where a sliver of ice protruded from it. He must have wielded fire, because it quickly melted, leaving behind a small hole that bled onto his white shirt.

His confidence growing, Graeme pushed harder, unleashing attacks in quick succession. With his left arm pinned against his chest and useless, Lukas struggled to ward Graeme off. He was being pushed back—toward Kendyl.

Allyn took a tentative step forward, and when Lukas paid him little heed, he took another and then another.

Within moments, he was halfway across the room. He caught Kendyl's eye and nodded to the side, silently telling her to move. He hoped she understood. She slid to the side, narrowly avoiding Lukas's feet.

Just a couple more steps. Allyn warily looked in Lukas's direction. Graeme had him pinned in the corner. This was the moment he was waiting for. He leaped forward, grabbing Kendyl's outstretched hand, and yanked her to her feet. He didn't wait or glance in Lukas's direction. He pulled Kendyl behind him, running for the door, toward safety.

Kendyl tripped.

He tried to pull her up, but her feet slipped. A concussion of air shattered the windows and threw them to the ground. Lukas leaped out the window.

"No!" Graeme jumped to his feet and rushed to the window.

Allyn ignored him, instead grabbing Kendyl under her arms and pulling her up again. She was limp, and blood dripped from her lips. Something clear protruded from her stomach. *Ice. No! I won't let you go again.* Allyn readjusted his grip and backpedaled out the door, catching a glimpse of Graeme climbing onto the fire escape as he entered the hall.

"Nyla!" Allyn yelled. "Nyla!" She was there in a heartbeat, taking Kendyl from his arms. The remaining magi charged into the room, ready to assist Graeme. Why hadn't they gone in there with him? Lukas wouldn't have escaped if they had.

Nyla gently laid Kendyl on her side and looked her over. A jagged piece of ice the size of Allyn's forearm stuck through her abdomen. Bright-red blood pooled around her on the pale concrete floor.

Allyn took her hand and held it to his chest. "It's okay, Kendyl. It's going to be okay."

She didn't respond.

"We need to get the ice out of her before I can do anything," Nyla said.

Allyn grabbed the shard of ice with his free hand, but his fingers barely made it around it.

"No," Nyla said. "We can't pull it out. It might break or splinter. We have to melt it."

Allyn looked around the hall. They were alone. The only magi who had been with them were in the room with Graeme.

"Can you do it?" Allyn asked.

Nyla shook her head.

Allyn tightened his grip on Kendyl's hand. He wasn't going to leave her side. He wasn't going to lose her again. Nyla rubbed his back. She probably meant it to comfort him, but it only stoked the anger inside him. Lukas didn't need to kill her. They weren't who he thought they were; he'd nearly admitted to that himself. *Then why kill her? Always questions. Never answers.*

With no other option, Allyn took the ice in his hand and yanked it free. Kendyl groaned and clutched her stomach as Nyla sprang to action. Placing a hand against the wound on Kendyl's stomach and another on the hole in her back, Nyla closed her eyes. A soft-white glow shimmered above Kendyl's body. Nyla grimaced.

"What?" Allyn asked.

"The ice punctured her stomach. She's bleeding internally."

"What can you do?"

Kendyl met his eye. "Nothing."

"No," Allyn said, shaking his head. "No."

Nyla watched him, her lips parting as if she was going to say something. She didn't. What was there to say?

"How long?" Allyn's voice was weak.

"Not long."

"Can you make her comfortable?"

"She is comfortable," Nyla said. "Her body's natural responses have taken care of that." She stepped aside. "I'll give you a moment." She left them behind, walking to the other end of the hall.

Allyn brushed the side of Kendyl's face with his thumb, and tucked strands of dark hair behind her ear. Only then did he notice her lips were moving. He bent down, turning so his ear was near her mouth. It was quiet, but she was definitely saying something.

"It's okay," Kendyl said.

It was the worst thing she could say to him. It was too much. "Kendyl..." He had so much to say, so many apologies.

"It's okay," she repeated.

He blinked away tears, fighting the emotion that threatened to show itself. He swallowed the lump in his throat and exhaled softly. He had to be strong and exude confidence. She had to be scared enough as it was.

"It's going to be okay," he repeated her hollow words. *Why do people always say things they know aren't true?* "It's going to be okay." Maybe they were more for him than her.

Kendyl said something that Allyn couldn't make out.

"What was that?" he asked.

"I can hear it," she said. "It's getting louder."

What's she talking about?

"Here it comes."

Allyn gripped her hand. Tears fell from his eyes, splashing gently on the floor. He squeezed his eyes shut, holding back more. A strange calmness washed over him. Maybe death *was* peaceful.

Urgent footsteps echoed through the hall. Voices. Sharp words. Yelling. Allyn opened his eyes to see someone pushing past Nyla, racing toward him. He'd never seen the man before. He was pudgy, with a hairline that looked like a cul-de-sac, and he wore thick lenses that magnified his frantic brown eyes.

The man came to a stop beside them. He hunched over Kendyl, reaching for her wounds. Allyn started to stop him, but he noticed Nyla wasn't chasing after him. Jaxon was at her side. They watched as the pudgy man performed his work. They trusted him, so Allyn would, too.

As the white glow dissipated, the man's shoulders hunched. He apparently had drawn the same conclusion Nyla had. Then, oddly, the man steeled himself, his posture becoming erect and his eyes determined. "You're Allyn, I assume?" His voice was friendly.

Allyn nodded.

"I promised her I would get her out of here. She didn't believe me."

"You're Graeme's mole," Allyn said.

The man winced. He didn't seem to like that distinction. "My name is Jarrell."

Kendyl's eyes drifted closed. Her breaths became shallow. Allyn squeezed her hand tighter.

"Tell her I'm sorry I didn't do it sooner," Jarrell said. "I need you to let go."

"That's not going to happen."

"Please," Jarrell said.

Something in his voice told Allyn it was okay. He squeezed Kendyl's hand a final time and placed it on her thigh.

"Whatever you do," Jarrell said, "whatever you see, do not interfere. You will kill her." With that, Jarrell took a deep breath and placed his hands back over Kendyl's wounds. Allyn had seen people healed before, but it had never been quite like this. The normal soft-white glow became something so bright that Allyn couldn't look at it directly. Even the air around it seemed to shimmer. He could almost *feel* it, tender and therapeutic. Jarrell's hands started to shake, and sweat beaded on his brow as his pale face turned red with strain.

Kendyl stirred, but her wounds did not change.

Jarrell continued, seconds turning into minutes. His eyes were closed, and a permanent wince marked his face. His breathing became sharp, ragged breaths. The glow around Jarrell's hands dimmed as he appeared to get weaker. Still, Kendyl's wounds hadn't changed.

Jarrell cried out. He was pushing himself too far. His body was giving out. Nyla took a couple steps toward him, ready to aid him. He couldn't continue like this for much longer. Short, ragged breaths became nothing more than Jarrell sucking in air and holding it for as long as possible. Exhaling sharply, he blew spittle from his mouth. His tongue, red with blood, snaked out to moisten his cracking lips.

Face pale, skin dry, Jarrell looked as though he would fall over dead at any moment. Then Kendyl's wounds began to close. Tender pink skin stretched across the hole in her back until it was closed completely. More did the same over her stomach. Jarrell began to shake violently, his hands barely able to keep the connection between their bodies. He coughed, flinging a thick ball of blood and mucus from his mouth. At last, he withdrew his hands and collapsed on the ground beside her, looking into her eyes.

Her eyes are open!

Jarrell convulsed violently, his eyes never leaving Kendyl's.

Nyla arrived and took him into her arms. His body relaxed. Nyla didn't probe. She didn't have to. Jarrell's eyes had lost their sparkle. Allyn had seen the blank expression on the faces of men and women throughout the compound. Death.

"What just happened?" Allyn asked softly.

"He just did the impossible," Nyla said. "He saved your sister's life."

But something wasn't right. Kendyl wasn't moving. Allyn cupped her face, rubbing her cheek with his thumb. "Kendyl. Kendyl. Can you hear me?" She didn't respond. He turned to Nyla, pleading with his eyes.

Nyla slid over to Allyn, probing Kendyl again. Confusion spread over her face.

"What?" Allyn asked.

She didn't respond.

"What?"

"He was too late."

Hot anger swelled inside him. It was a carnal thing spewing forth from the deepest recesses of his body. Anger at Lukas. Anger at himself. Anger at Graeme. Anger at being abandoned. Anger at the cancer that had taken his mom. Anger at the responsibility that lay at his feet. Anger at the death of his hopes and trampled dreams.

He focused on that anger, surprised by some of it. How long had he been carrying it? He had to get it out. He centered on it, adding his grief, pulling it from within, trying to get it *out*. He rolled it into a ball inside, allowing it to swell, pulling it from that place, pulling it *through* himself, washing it off his skin into his hands. He had to get rid of it!

Instinctively, he placed a hand on Kendyl's chest. He held it there, pushing his anger into his palm. It spewed forth, growing into red coils of electricity that wrapped around his hand, stretching out across Kendyl's exposed skin. Then he released. Kendyl convulsed. Her back arched, and her body grew rigid, as if she had been hit with a defibrillator. Then she fell limply back to the floor.

Nyla shrank back.

Allyn drew the anger out again, and more red coils of electricity wrapped around his fingers. When he released it, Kendyl convulsed again. Ready to do it a third time, Allyn dove deep within himself. The emotion was growing harder to grasp.

"Wait!"

Allyn withdrew.

Nyla had drawn closer. She held Kendyl's hand in hers. "How did you do that?"

Only then did Allyn realize what he'd done. He felt it in his hand. It was weak, but there. A pulse.

"I don't know," he said. But it didn't matter. Kendyl was alive.

CHAPTER 17

KENDYL WOKE TWO DAYS LATER. Graeme had put her in a spare room near Allyn's. It was smaller than his, barely large enough for the four-post bed, single bedside table, and the leather armchair Allyn currently occupied, but it also had a clear view overlooking the forest behind the manor. Hidden behind a steady drizzle and low-hanging clouds, the trees were difficult to make out, though. Winter had officially arrived, and it was going to be another wet one.

Kendyl awoke slowly, as if she were waking from anesthesia, and Nyla had told him the process wasn't all that different. Kendyl's body needed lots of rest, so she was kept unconscious in a form of magic-induced coma. Nyla checked on her every hour, even through the night, tracking her body's healing process and making sure she didn't wake prematurely.

Allyn was there for all of it. He had barely left her side and felt guilty when he did, but some things couldn't be done in the bedroom. Meals were brought to him when it became obvious he wasn't going to adhere to a normal eating schedule. Nyla was especially accommodating, checking in on him as often as she did Kendyl, and she kept his spirits up by updating him with her progress. Kendyl's pulse was stronger. Her breathing was more stable, and her body was beginning to fight the magical anesthesia. All were good signs, according to Nyla.

"Why can't you just heal her?" Allyn had asked.

"There's only so much we can do," Nyla said. "Her body needs to do the rest."

He didn't understand, but he didn't argue. Nyla had her reasons, whatever they were. She would make the final decision. She would allow Kendyl to wake when she felt she was strong enough. That decision had come hours ago. Now it was up to Kendyl.

Her fingers moved first, then her toes. Her eyes opened next, slowly blinking away moisture and squinting at the daylight shining in through the window. Nyla closed the curtains as Allyn knelt beside the bed. Confused, Kendyl looked at him.

"Hey there," Allyn said. "How are you feeling?" When she didn't respond, he asked, "Can you hear me?"

Kendyl groaned.

"It's okay, take your time." *She never did like to wake up.*

Kendyl blinked a couple more times and shook her head, trying to clear her it, before resting her gaze back on him. "Allyn?" Her voice was soft and weak.

"Yeah, it's me. I'm here."

She nodded and scanned the room. "Where are we?"

Allyn looked to Nyla for help. She shrugged and sat down on the other side of the bed.

"We're with friends," Allyn said.

"Friends?" Kendyl gave Nyla an appraising look. She didn't seem to believe him.

"That's right," Nyla said. "Friends of Allyn's. I've heard a lot about you. It's nice to finally put a face to the name. May I take your hand to check your vitals?"

Kendyl pulled away.

"It's okay," Allyn said. "She wants to help."

Reluctantly, Kendyl offered her hand. Nyla took it and placed her fingers on Kendyl's wrist. Kendyl was oblivious to the faint glow around Nyla's fingers.

"Well, you're not going to be running any marathons anytime soon," Nyla said as she withdrew her touch. "But given the circumstances, you're doing remarkably well. Try to take it easy tonight. Work on getting your feet under you. Walk around the room. But don't push yourself too hard. You should feel even better tomorrow."

Kendyl didn't respond. When had she become the rude one?

"Thank you," Allyn said.

Nyla smiled and stood. "I'll leave you two alone. I'm sure there's a lot to talk about, but I'll be back in an hour with lunch."

Kendyl suspiciously watched her go. It was out of character. Kendyl wasn't the suspicious type. If anything, she was too trusting, always willing to give someone a chance—or two. "We need to go," she said, kicking her legs over the edge of the bed as the door clicked shut.

"Easy," Allyn said. He took her heel in the palm of his hand and rolled her legs back onto the bed. "You heard her. Don't push yourself too hard."

Kendyl kicked Allyn's hands away. "What are you doing?"

"I'm listening to the doctor's orders."

"She's not a doctor."

"Close enough."

"You don't know who these people are, Allyn. You don't know what they're capable of. We need to leave."

"No."

"Allyn! Listen to me!"

"They saved your life."

Kendyl stopped fighting.

"They're not who you think they are."

She glanced at the door. Someone walked past, their footsteps muffled behind the door. "Who are they, then?"

Allyn told her everything. He started with the attack at his apartment. He told her how he survived a fall that should have killed him and woke up in a room just a few doors down without any injuries. He told her how Graeme had asked for his help, how he'd said no, and how he'd regretted it. The man who had attacked him didn't come for him again and had gone for her instead. Allyn talked, and she listened, never interrupting.

He told her about going to her apartment and finding one of Lukas's magi waiting for him. He explained his agreement with Graeme, who'd promised to get her back if Allyn helped him, and how Graeme had kept that promise.

The nagging pit of guilt in his stomach slowly dissipated as he recounted his story. It felt good to get it out.

"It's not your fault," she said.

"I should have said something," Allyn said. "Warned you."

"What good would that have done?"

"It would have given you a chance to get away."

She shook her head. "Something is going on here, something bigger than both of us. I don't think we could have escaped it."

Allyn sighed. "I'm one of them."

"What do you mean?"

"I can wield. It's not like the rest of them. It's electricity, I think."

"Let me see."

Allyn grimaced. "It's not that easy." His knees cracked as he stood up. *How long have I been in that chair?* He paced in front of her bed. "I've tried to do it again, but I can't. I feel a void inside me where the power came from, but it's empty, and something is keeping me from filling it again. I think I have some kind of block."

"Do you think it's something somebody did to you? A shield of some kind?"

"I don't think it works like that."

"What is it then?"

"I didn't have a choice," Allyn said. "You were going to die if I didn't do something. I was frantic, scared, willing to do anything to save you. I think I just broke through it before."

Kendyl sat up in the bed. "Then maybe it's been there all along, and only when your need was more powerful than the block were you able to wield."

Allyn nodded. "That makes sense. Graeme said that even if I had descended from an ancient magi line, I probably still wouldn't be able to wield. The ability would have been bred out of me because I'd lived apart from it for so long."

"That explains why *I* can't."

"You tried?"

"What do you think Lukas was trying to get me to do?" Kendyl asked. "He was trying to break through my block. He..." Her eyes grew distant, and her expression became dark.

"Hey," Allyn said, shaking her foot. "It's okay now."

Kendyl's eyes looked wild. "Do you think the block is permanent?"

"I don't know. It might be. I haven't been able to wield since."

"You haven't had to. But you broke through it once, so you should be able to do it again. And it should be easier next time."

Next time? Allyn hoped there wasn't a next time. "Maybe."

"Then all I have to do is get past it once."

"What are you planning?" Allyn asked.

"Nothing," she said. "I just want to know what I'm capable of."

"It doesn't matter," Allyn said. "As soon as you're healthy, we're getting the hell out of here."

Kendyl started to respond, but Nyla stepped into the room, carrying a tray of roasted garlic chicken over steamed rice with an assortment of greens. Allyn's stomach growled as she placed the tray beside Kendyl.

"You look like you're doing better," Nyla said.

"I'm feeling better," Kendyl said.

"Good," Nyla said with a smile. "Is there anything else you need?"

Kendyl shook her head.

"I think we're good," Allyn said.

"Okay," Nyla said. "I'll leave you be."

"Do you want some?" Kendyl asked as Nyla left. "I can't eat all of this."

"They wouldn't have given it to you if you didn't need it," Allyn said. "I'll just run down to the kitchen and get something. Do you want anything else?"

"I'm good," Kendyl said, her mouth full.

"Okay," he said. "I'll be back."

He left, guiltless for the first time in a long time.

The funeral procession began the next day. Allyn and Kendyl filed out of the back of the manor along with the McCollum Family into the gardens, where twelve bodies wrapped in white sheets lay atop a pyre. A single body was elevated on a platform above the rest. As he drew closer, Allyn noticed personal effects had been placed upon the chests of the fallen, visible for all to see, identifying each body. The one on the elevated platform had a pair of glasses resting atop a leather-bound book. Jarrell.

Kendyl held on to Allyn's arm as they continued forward. This was the first time she'd left her room, having insisted on being present out of respect for the man who had saved her life. She owed Jarrell a lot more than she could ever give. Exhaling deeply, Allyn hoped his respect was stronger than his stomach. The idea of burning the dead didn't seem right.

How is it any different than cremation? he wondered. *It's not done in front of me.*

Kendyl squeezed his arm. *Am I really that easy to read?* He squeezed her back. It felt good to have her back. Nobody else understood him the way she did or could make him feel at ease like she could. *But even she's not comforting enough for this.*

The rain had slowed to a sprinkle, and the raindrops, small and fine, hung in the air. The smell of mold and decay accompanied the moisture, and the mist that had formed in the forest at the edge of the gardens swallowed tree trunks and low-hanging branches. *A somber mood for a somber day.*

They gathered in a crescent shape around the pyre, never more than three people deep so everyone had a clear view. They were a colorful, if silent, group dressed in shades of red, blue, even yellow, bringing the garden to life with color.

Graeme stood in front of the gathering group, watching with his hands clasped behind his back. He wore a thick white robe with gold embroidery around a matching shirt and vest. He had come to see Kendyl while she was in her coma and once since she'd woken, but the visit had been more business related than personal. He wanted to know how Allyn had done what he did. He wanted him to do it again so he could see it with his own eyes. Allyn had been unable to duplicate the feat.

Dressed in white garb similar to Graeme's, Liam and Leira stood on either side of him. Leira had tucked a green flower into her hair that matched the color of her eyes. Around her neck hung the pendant Allyn had untangled for Jaxon. It had been cleaned and buffed until it sparkled brilliantly.

Allyn tried to catch Liam's eye, but any time he looked in Allyn's direction, his gaze seemed to slide past him. He hadn't spoken with Liam in a while, and he was hurt that he hadn't come to see Kendyl. He may not have known her, but he and Liam were friends, and that was the type of thing friends did.

Once everyone was in audience, Graeme extended his hands out to the side, bowing his head, and hummed a single, steady note. The congregation followed by bowing their own heads and humming. Allyn's chest vibrated, and the humming stirred the void inside him. It started small, like Graeme's lone voice, but grew in strength as the congregation matched his tone, rippling through him with waves of energy.

A group of twenty-four magi stepped slowly down the path in a pair of parallel lines, splitting the gatherers down the center. They were dressed in black robes, with their hoods drawn to hide their faces as they looked at the ground. Each person held more of the fallen's personal belongings. "A memento of the dead that had a deep sentimental attachment," Nyla had told him. More than one was crying.

The families of the dead.

The funeral procession stopped in front of Graeme. One by one, he took their hoods in his hands and pushed them back, exposing their faces. He whispered something to them and kissed each person on the forehead. The first pair stepped around Graeme, walked up to the pyre, placed their belongings on the body of their loved one, and then turned to face the audience. The next two did the same.

Allyn was surprised when Graeme pushed the hoods back on the final two. They were *young*, maybe in their late teens—a boy and a girl. Siblings. The boy's resemblance to his father was striking. He was thinner than Jarrell but had the build of someone who would put weight on later. He wore a pair of large, black-rimmed glasses similar to his father's, and his hair was already showing signs of thinning. The girl had inherited her father's small mouth and poor posture. Each wore the mask of strength. Allyn admired their courage.

The humming faded as Jarrell's children placed their belongings on his body. Graeme began to speak. At first, Allyn thought there was something wrong with his ears, but by the confused look on Kendyl's face, he wasn't alone. Graeme wasn't speaking a language either of them recognized.

"Latin?" Kendyl mouthed to him.

Allyn shrugged. He had no idea what Latin sounded like. How would anyone? It was a dead language. If anyone else in the audience was confused, they didn't show it, though more lost their battles with their emotions, bursting into tears. Nobody offered them a hug or even a compassionate smile. They were alone with their grief.

Graeme spoke for several minutes, his voice strong and compelling. He looked each of them in the eye as if pleading with them, strengthening their resolve. Allyn may not have understood the words, but their effect was obvious. All around him, magi stood a little taller and held chins a little higher. Expressions became firmer, growing more resilient.

His Family had been through a lot: living in seclusion out of fear of the world outside, splinters within their family, war, and death. But still Graeme held them together. He was a true leader, whom Allyn, if he didn't have other responsibilities, might've found himself following.

"I ask at this time," Graeme said, slipping into English, "if there are any who wish to speak final words of the fallen?" Whispers rippled through the crowd. This, it seemed, was not with tradition.

An odd time to break with custom, Allyn thought.

Kendyl stepped forward.

Allyn started to call after her, but stopped short. What did she have to say about people she'd never known? Allyn thought he saw the smallest of smiles creep across Graeme's face as he took Kendyl's hand and led her into position. He stood behind her left shoulder.

Kendyl looked over the crowd, her eyes growing wider, probably second-guessing herself. Allyn couldn't help but smile. She saw him and must have taken it as encouragement, because she opened her mouth to speak.

"Hi," she said nervously. "I obviously don't know most of you or even many of them." She pointed to the pyre behind her. "But I wanted to tell you about the person I did know. My captivity was... dark. I was beaten, burned, beaten again, and nearly drowned. I cried, pleaded, begged, but it never made any difference. It never stopped. And that was only the first day. Lukas thought I was one of you. He thought he could beat the ability out of me, force me into wielding. He was wrong.

"But the pain continued, and as Lukas grew more desperate, so did his methods of torture. I wasn't going to last long. I didn't *want* to. That's how Jarrell found me. At my weakest. My lowest. After a particularly brutal session, Lukas forced him to heal me, and with compassion in his eyes, Jarrell did. It nearly killed him. But that day, I saw a promise in his eyes. He was going to help." Kendyl's eyes were wet, but she held her emotions in check. Allyn struggled to do the same. Kendyl hadn't told him all of this. He'd asked, but she said with that haunted look in her eyes that it was too soon. Perhaps she was right.

"The torture continued, but every day, I had something to hold on to. I could hide inside that little ball of hope.

It kept me from breaking, probably from death itself, and then two nights ago, when eleven other people made the ultimate sacrifice, Jarrell did the same. I was mortally wounded by a desperate attack from a desperate man trying to save himself. Lukas tried to break me. Instead, he broke my brother."

Allyn shifted uncomfortably, feeling his face grow hot as the congregation's attention turned to him.

"It's true," Kendyl said. "He can wield. I was saved by two people that night. My brother and Jarrell."

Whispers spread through the crowd. Rumors of his ability had spread since that night, but hidden away in Kendyl's room, Allyn hadn't been forced to face them. His silence had turned some magi into believers and others into skeptics, but now that it was in the open, he would have to face them.

"Jarrell knew that saving my life would end his own. That it would be the most excruciating pain he would ever endure and that it had little chance of success. But he did it anyway. 'Tell her I'm sorry I couldn't do it sooner,' he told my brother. His last words."

The whispers stopped. Silence.

"Lukas tried to turn me into one of you. Where he failed, Jarrell succeeded. No, I cannot wield, but I make this pledge to you. As long as you'll have me, I'll be here. As long as you ask for my help, I'll give it. Because this is a family, and Jarrell made me feel like I was a part of it." She nodded to Graeme before striding across the wet ground, reclaiming her place by Allyn's side.

"We need to talk," Allyn whispered.

"There's nothing to talk about."

At Graeme's silent command, the mourners in black stepped forward. With Graeme in the middle of the line that extended around the edges of the pyre, they turned to face it. Fire ignited in the hands of the magi in black, and together, they lit the pyre. Flames quickly engulfed it. Blown by a gentle eastern breeze, the smoke billowed toward the mourning families. A collective deep breath was followed by a gust of air, pushing the smoke away. The flames flickered against the gust, and oddly, the nature of the fire changed. It burned differently, casting smoke away from the crowd.

They watched until the pyre was reduced to ash.

***

Allyn pushed Kendyl into his room and kicked the door closed. "You should have told me you were going to do that."

"I didn't know I was going to," Kendyl said, rounding on him. "What difference does it make anyway?"

"I've spent weeks trying to save you so I can get you away from these people."

"Why?"

"For your protection. As long as we're intertwined with them, we'll never be safe. We'll never be able to go home or have a normal life."

Kendyl smiled condescendingly. "You think they'll leave us alone if we run away? That we'll be safe and return to our lives like nothing ever happened?"

"No—"

"Then how exactly were you planning on accomplishing that?"

"We hide."

"Where?"

"Far away," he said and then added in a quieter voice, "I don't want to talk about it here."

"Are you afraid someone is listening?" she asked, her own voice growing louder. "Let them. I'm not leaving."

"Kendyl—"

"No, Allyn."

"Stop being so impulsive!"

"Stop being so impractical!" She lowered her voice. "I know you mean well, but you can't protect me like they can, and you shouldn't have to."

"It's my job," he said, playfully nudging her shoulder. "You're my little sister."

"By seventeen minutes. That hardly counts." She smiled. "I'm also an adult, capable of making my own decisions."

"Have you ever dreamed of a fresh start?" he asked. "Just pack up what you can carry and go?"

"Of course."

"This is that opportunity."

"I know." She sat on the foot of the bed and drew her knees to her chest. "I'm nothing out there, Allyn. I can make a difference here."

He sighed and sat down beside her. Her mind was made up. He would stand a better chance of convincing a dog that it was a cat than he did of changing her mind.

"*You* should go, though," she said. "You have a life out there."

Somehow, he'd known that it would come down to this. He felt like a parent having to choose between two children. Kendyl was right. He *did* have a life outside, and he'd worked his butt off to build it. Turning his back on that meant turning his back on the years of early mornings, late nights, and the career that he'd begun as a tribute to his mother. It meant walking away from her memory. How could he explain that to Kendyl? She hated his career.

He looked at her. Those soft eyes that looked so much like his mother's were pleading with him. He smiled. It made sense now. Leaving his career behind wasn't disgracing his mother's memory, but leaving his sister behind was. *They* were her memory. They kept her alive.

"You're the only family I have left," Allyn said. "Everyone else has either been taken from me or left. I'm not going to do that to you. I'm staying."

CHAPTER 18

ALLYN WATCHED AS THE YOUNG girl dug in her heels, forcing her mother to drag her. Kendyl stepped forward, ready to intervene, but Allyn stopped her.

"Please, Mother," the girl said, tears streaming down her innocent face, "don't make me go."

"Michella," her mother said, "we've already been over this. We're leaving. Now come on!" She adjusted the bag slung over her shoulder and gave the girl a sharp tug. Michella stumbled forward and gave up her fight. She walked down the hall with her head hung low to where a man, presumably her father, waited.

He tousled her hair, gave her an encouraging pat on the back, and offered the girl's mother a small shrug.

For an adult, moving was opportunity wrapped in inconvenience, but for a child who was leaving behind everything she'd ever known, it was terrifying.

They're leaving because of us, Allyn thought. And they weren't the only ones. He and Kendyl had passed others in the halls. Allyn wondered if Graeme would actually allow them to leave. And if he did, how many more would follow?

Nyla had come with word that Graeme wished to see them in his study and then promptly left to attend to errands of her own, leaving Allyn and Kendyl alone to deal with the looks and whispers. Most of the magi were courteous, smiling and nodding to them, opening doors or holding them open to pass. The majority of the unhappy magi just scowled at them, but a few openly mocked them.

"Being able to wield doesn't make you one of us," an older magi had said before spitting at Allyn's feet.

"Make way for the future!" another had patronized. He even went so far as to run in front of them and push people aside. "Make way for the future!"

But the ones who made Allyn feel the worst were the ones who didn't say anything at all—the families that just left. It takes a lot to make someone uproot their lives.

Could our presence really be that threatening?

"Maybe I made a mistake," Kendyl said. "Do you think he's summoning us to tell us to leave?"

"You spoke from your heart," Allyn said. "You won more people over than you lost, Graeme included, I'm sure."

She shrugged. She didn't believe him. Allyn wasn't surprised. He wasn't sure he believed himself. Now that Kendyl was safe and they hadn't found any conclusive evidence as to who they were, Allyn's deal with Graeme was done. He had thought it would be his choice to stay, but what if it wasn't? Now that it was done, what if Graeme *wanted* them to leave? Where would they go? How would they hide? His original plan seemed woefully inadequate when faced with reality.

The door to Graeme's study was open when they arrived. Graeme sat at his desk, and Liam sat cross-legged in one of the two armchairs. The curtains were open, revealing the last smoldering embers of the funeral pyre glowing orange in the distance. Jaxon was out there somewhere, overseeing it.

Allyn knocked as they entered. Graeme stood when he saw them, but Liam didn't acknowledge them. He had a

222

different air about him lately, quieter, more reserved, less interested in the outside. He hadn't been the same since the ambush at the Hyland Estate.

"Ah, Allyn, Kendyl," Graeme said. "Thank you for coming. Liam, let our guests have a seat."

"It's okay—" Allyn started, but Liam stood with a huff and stepped aside. He leaned against Graeme's bookcase, resting his foot on the edge of the desk. Graeme promptly knocked his shoe away with the back of his hand. "Thank you," Allyn said, sitting down, Kendyl beside him.

Liam responded with a flick of his hand.

"You gave a lovely speech today," Graeme said. "It must have taken a long time to prepare."

Kendyl shook her head. "It just came to me."

"Impressive," Graeme said, his eyebrows raised. "You're a gifted speaker."

Nudging Allyn, Kendyl said, "It runs in the family."

"Your brother might have told you that he and I had something of an agreement. He would help me discover why Lukas wanted you, and in return, I would help him get you back."

"He did."

"Then he probably told you we never discovered why Lukas was after you."

Here it comes, Allyn thought. *He's going to say he fulfilled his end of the bargain and kick us out.*

"Without knowing why he attacked you, we have no way of knowing if he'll do it again. That, among more recent developments, is why I think you two should stay under our protection."

"What?" Allyn asked, shocked.

"Lukas was right," Graeme said. "You are able to wield, and Kendyl likely has the ability, too. That alone makes you a target. More than that, you're a danger to yourself and those around you. You need to be surrounded by people who understand that danger and can help you master it. Wielding requires restraint. Control. And I'm offering a safe environment for you to master your abilities. One that will allow you to nurture them.

"In return, I need to know how you are able to wield. How did Lukas know of your abilities? And what is the nature of your magic? It's something different, something new. Our numbers are declining, yet here you stand, something unique. How is this possible? Help me answer these questions, and you'll have a safe home here with us."

"We accept." Kendyl extended her hand.

Allyn shook his head. Kendyl always jumped first and then wondered how deep the water was.

"This decision needs to be made by both of you."

Allyn leaned forward, rubbing his hands together. "While I'm not as quick to act as my sister, I agree with her."

"Excellent," Graeme said, sinking into his chair.

He's relieved. He thought we were going to run. He wanted us to stay.

Liam looked annoyed.

Did he just roll his eyes?

"After our discussion with Nyla, I had Liam conduct a search looking for twins within the magi history," Graeme said. "His search hasn't yielded any results, but I promise to keep looking."

Looking guilty, Liam glanced at his father from the corners of his eyes.

"You still think he's after us because we're twins?" Allyn asked.

"I do," Graeme said. "If you were a part of a forgotten hereditary line, he'd go after your other family members— cousins, aunts, uncles. Instead, he's focused solely on you."

"There are other twins," Kendyl said. "Hundreds of them in the city alone. Why not go after any of them? Why continue to pursue us?"

"He's already hedged his bets on you," Graeme said.

"He's not going to stop, is he?" Allyn asked.

"No. He's not." Graeme sighed and stood to look out the window. The glass reflected his tormented expression. He had been a different man since the assault on Lukas's compound—and Lukas's escape. After the desperate attack that nearly killed Kendyl, Lukas had fled the compound and lost Graeme and the rest of the McCollum magi in the dark streets of the industrial district. And without Jarrell's inside information plotting his every move, Lukas had become a ghost. "You're a symbol of power to him. Capturing you means taking you from me and winning a battle against his greatest adversary. It adds credibility, legitimacy to his new Family. But most importantly, if he proves you can wield, he proves he was right and that the magical world has changed. That the old ways are outdated. Extinct." He bowed his head.

Allyn couldn't imagine what Graeme was going through. He knew how important tradition was to him. To Graeme, preserving the past was the most powerful tool in preserving the future, but because of Allyn, he questioned that past, and his future was unclear. Graeme didn't fight Lukas out of spite or to keep him silent. He fought him because Lukas's methods were immoral, but it put Graeme in an awkward position. He had held on to his beliefs, enforced them, and fought for them. And now he would fight to protect the living embodiment of his mistakes. It was an exercise in humility that would have destroyed a lesser man.

But how much of this is about us? Allyn wondered. *If Lukas can use us to gain legitimacy, why can't Graeme? His family has splintered and is doing so again. He has a lot to gain by keeping us here and being the one to discover a new kind of magi.*

"We do have one advantage," Graeme said. "Lukas *suspects* you can wield, but he doesn't *know* you can."

"What are you saying?" Kendyl asked.

Allyn took his face in his hands, rubbing his cheeks. "He wants me to kill Lukas."

Kendyl's mouth hung open, but nothing came out. She tapped her teeth together—a nervous habit.

Even Liam stirred uncomfortably.

Graeme turned to Allyn. The soft-orange glow of the pyre reflected in his eyes. "Or distract him long enough so I can."

"What of healing the splinter?" Allyn asked. "Reuniting the Family?"

"An infection needs to be stopped before the wound can be stitched back together," Graeme said. "Until Lukas is gone, the wound will fester, the splinter will deepen. Only when he's gone can the healing process begin."

"My brother isn't a killer," Kendyl said.

"He was prepared to kill for you," Graeme said. "Everyone is a killer if driven far enough."

"What do you want me to do?" Allyn asked. "Cuddle up next to him? Tell him what he wants to hear? Earn his trust and stab him in the back?"

"No," Graeme said, either unaware of or ignoring the dash of sarcasm in Allyn's voice. "We're beyond that. It might have worked before we rescued Kendyl, but not now. Besides, I wouldn't know where to find him."

"You don't think he's returned to the Hyland Estate?"

Graeme shook his head. "It's the obvious move."

"Which Family stands to gain the most by sheltering them?" Allyn asked.

"Any of them."

"How many live in the area?"

"Enough to make our search nearly impossible."

"You've enlisted my help," Allyn said. "At some point, you'll need to trust me."

Graeme looked puzzled. "I don't understand."

"You swipe away my questions only to answer them with something vague and hazy."

"I apologize." Graeme returned to his desk and sat down. "It's not my intention. It's an old habit." Graeme hesitated before continuing. "There is a large concentration of Families in the Northeast, but our greatest population lies here in the Northwest, around the fringes of larger cities like Portland, Seattle, and Vancouver, B.C., primarily."

"Why?"

"Let's just say that the Northwest is more accepting of alternative lifestyles."

Allyn laughed. He knew what Graeme was alluding to. Portland was an interesting mix of eclectic personalities, making it the alternative capital of the world. People there didn't just accept diversity. They celebrated it. Flaunted it. Reveled in it. The backs of cars, old and new, luxury and clunker, proudly displayed Keep Portland Weird bumper stickers. The magi Families were hiding in plain sight.

"There are four other Families within fifty miles of the Portland area," Graeme said. "And another six if you double that."

"Including the Hylands?"

Graeme nodded.

It was less than Allyn had expected, but more than he'd hoped. "You're right. We won't be able to find him, so we make him come to us."

"How do we do that?" Liam asked quietly.

Liam had been so quiet that Allyn had almost forgotten he was still in the room. "We appear weak."

"That shouldn't be difficult," Graeme said. "We *are* weak."

"You're going to let them leave, aren't you?" Allyn asked. "Those who want to?"

"Yes." Graeme's voice was heavy. "Limbs need to be trimmed back from time to time, to protect the tree." He didn't seem to believe his own words. He wasn't pruning the tree. He was cutting it in half.

"Where will they go?" Kendyl asked.

"It's not my place to ask."

"How will they get there?"

"I don't know."

"You're not going to help them?"

"I'm letting them decide for themselves. That's all the help I can give."

"They're alone with nowhere to go without protection. If something happens to them, it's your fault!" Kendyl said.

"Their blood is already on my hands," Graeme said softly. "This *is* protecting them." Graeme's decision to let the defectors leave meant he was facing another splinter. It left them weak in numbers and vulnerable enough to make them question their leader.

"That's it!" Allyn said. "A splinter. Lukas is a predator. We need to play the part of the wounded animal. Lure him to us."

His face hard, Graeme leaned forward over his desk. "I won't use my Family like that."

"They won't be in any danger," Allyn said. "They're leaving and will be long gone by the time Lukas arrives. But the people fleeing are families—mothers and fathers with children, not the people who fought to save Kendyl. For this to work, we need someone significant, someone indispensable to lead the splinter."

"Jaxon," Liam said.

Graeme was silent.

"He wouldn't really be splintering off," Allyn said. "We'd orchestrate a public argument between the two of you.

Afterward, he would storm off and lead a group of followers away, only to lie in the weeds until Lukas takes the bait. It's the type of thing that would give us the advantage."

"That's a desperate plan," Graeme said. "You would bring Lukas here. If we lose, we lose everything."

"It's only a matter of time until he's bold enough to attack the manor. This way, it happens on our terms. This way, we can prepare."

Graeme tapped the top of his desk with his knuckles. "I'll have to think on it."

"Think fast," Allyn said. "It needs to look like Jaxon is leaving with the others. Leading them."

Deep in thought, Graeme didn't respond. His eyes had already glazed over.

———— •••• ————

Allyn ducked just as the tree exploded into splinters. Pain shot up his arm as wisps of flame kissed his flesh.

He's trying to kill me! He darted through the forest, using the pine trees and foliage for cover, running in a perpetual state of self-preservation with his hands and arms held in front of his face to protect his head. Fireballs and blasts of ice slammed into trees all around him. A concussion of air detonated against his back, sending him tumbling face first over the ridge. His tumble came to an abrupt stop against a fallen tree. The rotten trunk was soft, but the impact shot pain through his shoulder.

Wincing and rolling his shoulder to make sure it wasn't broken, Allyn stood and looked up the embankment. Jaxon watched from the top. *What the hell is he doing?* Graeme had told him to meet Jaxon in the forest for a training session, but Jaxon hadn't been there when he had arrived. And when he *did* show up, he'd attacked Allyn. Jaxon stepped away from the ridge and vanished. *Great.*

Allyn scanned his surroundings. He hadn't been in this

part of the forest before. He was in the middle of a small valley that was maybe a quarter mile across at its base, where a shallow creek meandered through it. The foliage was thick with bushes as tall as his chest, some with briars and brambles. Others had leaves that left painful white welts on his skin that stung until he rubbed cool mud over them.

In the distance, a branch snapped and fell with a crash onto the forest floor. Save for the trickling water, the forest returned to silence. Allyn started upstream, climbing over the fallen tree that had stopped his tumble and using the underbrush for cover while keeping the creek in sight. He planned to follow the water until he was convinced he'd escaped Jaxon—who was hopefully going in the opposite direction—before climbing the ridge and doubling back to the manor from the north. Then he could find out what the hell was going on.

Even while attempting to be silent, Allyn trampled through the underbrush like a wounded deer. He couldn't remember the last time he had been deep in the forest. That was more Kendyl's thing. His favorite hiking trails were paved. This was wet and dirty and smelled of decay and death. Wasn't nature supposed to be clean? Fresh?

Allyn hid his hands in the sleeves of his long-sleeved shirt to protect them from the stringing nettles that were everywhere. He quickly gave up trying to hide in the underbrush and made for the creek. The cold water sucked the air from his lungs and threatened to numb his feet up to his calves, but it was quieter. In most places, the creek was less than ten feet wide and rarely deeper than his ankles. It flowed gently, except for a few places where the water funneled between narrow banks, growing deeper, tugging at his legs and almost pushing him over.

Allyn walked for what felt like an hour—the time was difficult to tell with the trees blocking out the sunlight—

before beginning his trek back up the ridge. His shoes squished with each step. His feet tingled as feeling slowly returned. Trees protruded from the hillside and offered aid as Allyn climbed the ridge. One branch snapped free, and Allyn nearly tumbled back down the hillside. After regaining his footing, Allyn tossed the branch aside and started up the ridge again.

His legs weak and shaking, Allyn crested the tree line at the top of the ridge and entered a meadow with knee-high wild grass. The manor was nowhere in sight. He didn't have time to be disappointed. A concussion of air hit him in the chest.

Blinking away tears and double vision, Allyn found himself on his back on the moist earth. Expressionless, Jaxon strode toward him with a baseball-sized ball of ice in his hand.

Allyn pushed himself backward, unable to stand. "What are you doing?"

Jaxon hurled the ice at him and shot it forward with air. It closed the distance between them in a blink.

Allyn threw his hands up and screamed. Red coils of lightning as thick as his finger sprang from his palms, twisting around themselves almost as if they were battling each other then shattering the ice into hundreds of harmless pieces. Another ice blast was already streaking toward him. He rolled to the side and shot it out of the air, too. Breathing heavily, Allyn held his wrists in front of him. Red bands of electricity wreathed around his arms, alive, twisting, radiating power—ready to be unleashed again.

"I don't think anyone really believed me, and I almost doubted myself, but I knew it. I saw it with my own eyes." Jaxon looked satisfied.

"It was a game?" Allyn asked angrily. The coils burned brighter. "You could have killed me!"

Jaxon dismissed Allyn's anger with a wave of his hand.

"It was weak fire and ice with dulled edges. Bruises maybe, but it wouldn't kill you. And look what you did. You don't have control over it. It's instinctual. But you can do it. You can wield."

Allyn held up his arms in front of him. The coils crackled and hissed when they touched one another. "What is it?"

"Some kind of electrical charge. I've never seen anything like it. I'm more curious where it comes from. Magic has a cost, Allyn, and without knowing what it is, I don't know how safe it is to wield."

"If it's electricity, then my body should replenish it, shouldn't it?"

"Perhaps. But your heart runs off an electrical system. Can you inadvertently wield too much and send yourself into cardiac arrest? Or can you unintentionally electrocute yourself?"

The charges continued to coil around Allyn's arms, never going higher than his shoulder. They emitted a soft red glow and tingled his skin, but they didn't burn. "They don't hurt."

A ball of fire formed in Jaxon's hand. "When I wield fire, it doesn't hurt me, either, but that doesn't mean it's not a danger to you." He let the fire burn out. "Can you let the charge dissipate?"

Allyn looked at his arms, *willing* the charge to dissipate. Nothing happened. He looked to Jaxon for help.

"Electricity must be severed," Jaxon said. "Pull the plug."

It was easier said than done. The energy didn't emit from a singular place. It flowed through his body, radiating from his toes to his fingers. Like an ocean of power, its depths were limitless. He thought back to the first time he'd wielded. The ability had begun in the void, so Allyn returned there. But it was no longer a void. It had become a ball of writhing energy, hot to the touch. Severing it was like smothering the sun—impossible. Instead, he *pulled* it back. Allyn imagined himself pulling on the energy like a rope, bringing it back under his control one yank at a time. As he reeled the electricity back into the void, the tendrils lost their glow until, at last, they dissipated entirely.

"Good," Jaxon said.

It didn't feel good. Allyn was exhausted as if he'd lost a wrestling match with himself.

"As you practice, it'll get easier."

"Why are you telling me this?" Allyn asked. "If it's instinctual, I can't control it."

"You will be able to in time. Soon, I hope, if Lukas takes your bait."

"Graeme agreed to it?"

Jaxon nodded solemnly.

Another weight suddenly fell on Allyn's shoulders. He'd expected Graeme to move forward with his plan, but the reality was heavy. And even in victory would be destruction and death.

"Leira and I will be leaving tonight," Jaxon said. "I wanted another session with you."

"Tonight?" *So soon. Leira, too?* Graeme envisioned a deep splinter. Allyn hoped it didn't make them look *too* vulnerable.

"Most of those leaving have already left. If we don't leave with them, it will look suspicious, maybe even cause Lukas to question it. It's better this way."

Allyn didn't disagree. They wanted Lukas to be bloodthirsty and chase them into a dark hole, not wonder if a trap waited for him inside. "I've got a lot to learn before Lukas strikes."

"Nothing is preventing you but your own doubts. Ease those, and there's no reason you cannot wield at will. The more you know, the more you immerse yourself in our world, the quicker that day will come."

"Then tell me what you can."

As Allyn and Jaxon returned, the sun slid slowly behind the pine trees along the western edge of the manor grounds. Its long rays streaked through bare branches to warm the frosty ground. The leisurely walk had taken hours, and Jaxon had used the time well. He listened to Allyn explain his block and offered ideas to overcome it. He was particularly encouraged when Allyn told him that he felt the empty space inside him.

"It is the key to wielding," Jaxon had said. "It is also the most difficult to teach. Liam cannot wield because he can't find the emptiness. Without it, he cannot pool his body's elements into it, and he has nothing to project. But with you, we have the container and just need to fill it up. What did you feel that night at Lukas's compound?"

"I felt helpless," Allyn said.

"And how did *that* make you feel?"

"Are you my psychiatrist now?"

"A what?"

"Never mind," Allyn said. "I was mad. Angry. Livid. We had finally saved Kendyl, and then, for no other reason but to save himself, Lukas lashed out and nearly killed her."

"He *would* have killed her if not for you."

Allyn nodded as his emotions from that night flooded back. "Everyone I've ever known has been taken from me. I wouldn't let it happen again."

"You used your anger as fuel."

Allyn shrugged. It hadn't been a conscious decision. It had simply happened, and he didn't know how. If he did, he would have been able to wield on command.

"Emotion can be used in such ways," Jaxon said. "But you must be wary of using it. Anger is particularly useful in wielding fire because it makes our hearts beat faster, blood race through our bodies quicker, our body temperature rise, which we then pull from to create fire. I imagine it helps with your ability, too. You can feel it now, can't you?"

Allyn reached inside, probing the void. It had been a blazing ball of energy before, but now a shell protected it, and Allyn couldn't get inside. He chipped at it, testing for weak points, but it was impenetrable. Growing frustrated, Allyn used his anger as a chisel to break away at the shield. The shell cracked, and energy seeped through the cracks like light through holes in a wall. Then as Allyn continued to break the shield apart, it burst, and energy flooded through him, causing his body to tingle. He directed it through his porous skin and let it coil around his arms like writhing snakes. It warmed his hands and arms but didn't burn him.

"Not bad," Jaxon said. "Strike that tree over there." He pointed to an elm tree atop a small rise in the middle of the meadow.

Allyn projected the energy forward. It struck like a long band of electricity using him as an anchor. The tree exploded, and Allyn was thrown backward as the red bands winked out. Coughing, Allyn rolled onto his knees. He felt as though he'd been kicked in the chest. "What happened?"

"My best guess? The tree is denser than you are, so it, not you, became the anchor. So you were pushed from it, not it from you. How do you feel?"

Allyn staggered to his feet, wincing. "How do you think I feel?"

Jaxon laughed. "Can you wield?"

Allyn shook his head.

"Fueling yourself with anger comes with a cost. Your body can only maintain its heightened metabolic rate so long before growing tired, and when it's gone, you're left weak and depleted. And anger fades. As it does, so does its effectiveness. More importantly, anger makes us irrational, blind to our surroundings. If you can only wield when you're angry, you won't be much of a magi."

Jaxon began to walk again. Allyn followed, struggling to keep up.

"But," Jaxon said, "in your instance, I'm not against it. You were not trained to listen to your body as we were. In fact, you've grown to ignore it. So controlling it is impossible. You need a stimulant, for a time at least. But use old anger, latent anger, the kind you've lived with for years. It will give you the spark without the inconsistencies."

"I'll try," Allyn said. "Do you think I'll ever be able to wield fire or water?" He'd seen how useful water was to countering fire, and he doubted electricity would do anything to stop the magis' favorite weapon.

"I don't think so. You're a new kind of magi, Allyn. You won't be able to counter fire with water, but nobody will be able to counter you, either. If you can master your ability, you will be the most powerful magi in a generation."

Allyn couldn't help but feel elated. It meant he wouldn't have to live in fear. He could make good on his promises. But he would have to train, learn to wield on command, and master his ability. He would. By the time Jaxon returned, Allyn would amaze him with his improvement.

The sky was a combination of white and dark clouds, and the sun had disappeared entirely behind the hillside as they rounded the side of the manor.

"You forgot my session."

Liam sat at the base of the manor stairs. There was hurt in his eyes. He held a twig in his hands, breaking it in half, then breaking *those* pieces in half. He dropped them into a pile that sat at his feet. He'd been at it for a while.

"Liam—" Jaxon started.

"It's okay," Liam interrupted. "I'm not important. I can't wield like *he* can."

He's been avoiding me because he's jealous. "Liam, it's not like that."

"I thought we were friends!" Liam's voice cracked. "I thought you understood."

"Understood what?"

Liam shook his head and stood, then turned to leave.

"Liam, wait!"

Liam ran up the stairs, two at a time, ignoring Allyn.

Jaxon took a step toward him, but Allyn stopped him. "This is about me. Not you. I'll talk to him."

Jaxon exhaled loudly. "That could be the last time I ever see him."

"It won't be."

"I hope not."

Me, too.

CHAPTER 19

L IAM WAS EASY TO FIND. Some people seek the comforts of their bed when they're upset, while others find peace with close friends and family. But like Allyn, Liam escaped into his work. Regardless of what the kid thought, they *were* friends, and like all good friends, they knew each other well.

The glass door was closed, and the digital pad blinked red. Liam was sitting at the back of the library, with his face hidden behind his computer monitor. When he saw Allyn approach, Liam promptly ignored him.

Allyn knocked on the glass. Liam didn't move. He was going to be difficult. After Allyn punched the code into the pad, it turned green, and the sliding glass door hissed open. Allyn stepped inside.

Liam looked up in surprise. "How did you...?"

"Your father's trust isn't without its benefits," Allyn said.

Liam turned back to his computer. "Go away."

"I'm not going anywhere."

"I don't have to talk to you."

"You're right," Allyn said. "You don't have to do anything. But if you want to, I'm here and willing to listen." He dragged another chair over and sat down across from

Liam. An uncomfortable silence filled the room as Liam continued to ignore Allyn. He seemed bent on proving that he didn't have to talk. That was fine with Allyn. He would wait as long as necessary. Something told him that the kid's patience would wear out before his did.

Allyn got up and strolled through the room. He'd spent hours in the library, most of them helping Liam with his transcription, never paying much attention to the artifacts beyond the books. Most of them rested atop pedestals while the oldest and most fragile were protected within glass encasements. A leather jerkin hung stiffly on a wire mannequin's torso. It was dark, almost black, with weathered elemental symbols sewn into the chest. Allyn wondered if it came from a time when magi weren't required to hide or if it was something worn in the privacy of home.

Another embroidered jerkin, this one encased in glass, hung beside it. The clothing reminded Allyn of ceremonial military fatigues. The torn edges of the white leather were frayed. Stitched in what had probably originally been a vibrant red, flames circled the hem of the jerkin, and blue embroidered water droplets dripped from the shoulders. Between the fire and water was an ivory band that was several inches thick. Neither the fire nor the water penetrated the band.

Allyn continued through the room. Cases and pedestals held weapons—swords, maces, spears, and a particularly elegant six-foot staff with intricate lacework gilding its dark, smooth wood—and more tattered clothing. A wool pair of breeches with holes and slices stained with blood hung on the wall beside paintings and tapestries. A few evenly spaced sculptures filled out the room. They told the same story, each a different portrayal of the same event—the Fracture.

Houses burned. The soil was stained red with blood as

the living magi fled in opposite directions. For the first time, Allyn thought he glimpsed Graeme's fear of what would happen if they were discovered. Violence and bloodshed would follow. If hundreds had died during the Fracture, how many would die during a modern-day version? Instead of swords, maces, and spears, they would face guns, gas, and bombs. And they were greatly outnumbered. It wouldn't be a battle. It would be a massacre.

It was only a matter of time before the magi community would be found again. Lukas's ideology was pure—as long as they lived in the shadows, they would never regain the glory they had before the Fracture. But his methods would prove disastrous. They pitted magi against magi and Family against Family. His strategy broke the Families, making them weak. He used fear and violence as tools against his own people when they should be united.

Surrounded by weapons, shields, and armor, Allyn realized the magi were more vulnerable than ever before. Solidarity wasn't enough. They needed an edge. They needed modern weapons, contemporary armor, an updated strategy, and someone who knew the world outside. They needed him. Allyn laughed, silently thanking his sister. Unwittingly, Lukas had given the magi Families the tool they needed. Kendyl had been right, again. They couldn't leave, not when they were needed. She'd *felt* it, where Allyn had to *reason* it. How did she do it?

"That's my favorite piece in here." Liam watched him from his seat at the table.

Allyn had stopped in front of a golden dress of chain mail. "It's beautiful."

"It's been in my Family since its founding."

Allyn lifted the bottom of the skirt. It was surprisingly flexible though heavier than he'd expected.

"I used to dream about wearing it," Liam said. "Feeling the weight of it. Basking in its protection. But I realized it could only make a man *feel* more powerful. It can't actually make him so."

"Maybe making someone believe he's stronger actually makes him so."

"Feeling invincible is a quick way to find yourself dead."

"You sound like Jaxon." Allyn laughed. "But you have a point." Allyn returned to his seat. Liam's voice had lost its edge, but awkwardness still stretched between them. "I remember my first case. It wasn't anything real exciting, but it was *mine*. I went in all bluster and flash, wrapped in my own armor of self-confidence, and I got my butt handed to me."

"What happened?"

"I was unprepared. I didn't understand how hard I needed to work, how many variables I needed to prepare for. It was an important lesson, and I'm thankful to say I haven't made the same mistake since."

"I like to think I work hard."

"You do." *You work harder than any kid I've ever met.*

"And that's what's so frustrating. I try. I practice. I do everything I'm supposed to do. But I can't wield."

"I'm not so different," Allyn said. "I can't wield on command, either."

"But you *can* do it."

"I did it by accident."

"That doesn't make me feel better."

Allyn sighed. "You can't compare yourself to everyone else. There will always be someone who can do something you can't do or someone who can do it better."

"You don't understand. I'm the *only* one who can't."

"That's not true. There're more magi today that can't wield than ever before."

"I'm the only son of a grand mage who can't."

"You're just the first," Allyn said. "There will be more."

"Yeah," Liam said. "My kids. My family's magical line ended with my father."

"Now you're just being morose," Allyn said. "Don't kick yourself for who you aren't. Celebrate who you are."

"And who's that?"

"The most intelligent kid I've ever met. Sure, you can be a bit emotional at times, but you're always honest. You care more about the artifacts in here than anyone else does, and you're the only person actively trying to preserve them. That alone makes you special. And don't get me started on what you can do with computers."

"I am pretty good with them," Liam said sheepishly. He smiled, his face flushing with color.

"Pretty good?" Allyn asked. "Liam, you're a *wizard* with computers. I've never seen anything like it."

Liam's smile vanished.

Damn it, Allyn thought. He'd accidentally reminded Liam of what he *couldn't* do. *Kendyl was always better at this sort of thing.* "I'm sorry, I didn't mean—"

"No, you're right." Liam dashed away from his chair, racing to the bookshelves. He piled several books in his arms, then carried them over to the table and sat down.

"What are you doing?" Allyn asked.

"I'm looking for something."

"Obviously."

"There have been periods in our history where our numbers have shrunk unexpectedly. I'm looking for dates." He didn't sound upset. His speech was quick and excited as each word rolled into the next.

"Can't you do a search in your computer?"

Liam shook his head. "I haven't gotten to these yet."

"Can I help?"

Liam grabbed the top book off the stack and slid it to Allyn.

"What am I looking for?"

242

Looking up from his book, Liam thought for a moment. "Actually—" He snatched the book from Allyn. "I've got a better idea." Liam quickly typed something on his computer and then turned the monitor to face Allyn. "I need dates of technological advancement. A time when technology has grown by leaps and bounds. The railroad, cars, space exploration, computers, all of it."

Allyn pulled the computer closer and got to work. Liam worked more furiously than Allyn would have believed possible. He flipped through pages in a blur.

He doesn't actually read that fast, does he? Allyn's own search was slower. He didn't know where to begin to research the technological advancement of the modern world, so he started with what he knew: recent things, like the first home computer, telephone, and automobile. Then he worked his way back to electricity, the combustion engine, and the Industrial Revolution.

"Hmmm," Allyn said to himself, jotting down the date and inventor of the telegraph.

Liam looked up from his book. His finished pile was taller than the unfinished one. "What?"

"It's going to sound stupid, but I've never looked at it like this. The world's evolved more over the last three hundred years than it had over the previous three *thousand* years combined."

"Keep going," Liam said, unimpressed. "We need to go further back. We need everything."

He didn't understand what Liam was looking for, but Allyn didn't question him. When Liam was on a roll, questions fell around him like rain from a wet umbrella. So Allyn kept going. He wrote down dates for the first gun, the earliest known uses of antiseptic, and early-modern water purifiers. The advancements came fewer and farther between, and as a whole, they were less world changing than the previous ones. If modern advancements were the signs of cultural maturation, these were its foundation.

Liam returned to the bookcase for more books. His eyes were beginning to glaze over and his hair was more disheveled than usual, but he was smiling. It warmed Allyn. He couldn't remember the last time he'd seen Liam smile. Allyn's own endurance was wavering, and he wasn't sure how long they'd been at it. His original paper was full, front and back, with notable advancements, their dates, and discoverer or inventor. He remembered study sessions similar to this during college, but those were always group sessions and almost always involved alcohol, which meant they usually devolved into small parties. Studying had been more fun in college.

"That's weird," Liam said, going over his notes. All of his books were in the finished pile. "I've always been told our numbers have declined since the Fracture."

"They haven't?"

"Oh, no, they have, just not as sharply as I'd expected. And it's not the declining rate of magi I'm investigating. It's the declining rate of magi who can wield. It was a slow, steady decline until about the eighteenth century, when it spiked. And then it did it again at the turn of the last century."

"That is weird." Allyn grabbed his notes and walked around the table to stand over Liam's shoulder. His legs were beginning to cramp, and standing felt good. "Any idea why?"

"Did anything momentous happen around the eighteenth century?"

Allyn eyed him curiously before reading his notes. "The Industrial Revolution."

Liam nodded with a knowing smile. "And more recently?"

Allyn didn't have to consult his notes. "The digital revolution."

"Exactly."

Allyn rubbed his forehead with his thumb and index finger. "The magi's declining numbers directly coincide with major advances in technology."

"No," Liam said. "Not our declining numbers. The number of magi who can wield."

"What are you saying?"

Liam's smile split his face in two. His eyes grew moist. "I'm a *wizard* with computers."

Comprehension struck Allyn in the chest like one of Jaxon's concussions of air. It was the answer he'd been looking for.

"Your magic isn't dying," Allyn said. "It's evolving!"

CHAPTER 20

L IAM CRASHED INTO ALLYN. CRYING and laughing, he wrapped his arms around Allyn in a tight embrace. Allyn returned the embrace, patting Liam on the back. He knew what it was like to cry tears of joy, and of relief. He'd done it after passing the bar exam, which had closed a door to that chapter of his life. He assumed that was how Liam was feeling.

"What now?" Allyn pulled away, still holding Liam by his shoulders.

Liam wiped his tears. "We tell everyone."

Their excitement was quickly quashed as they entered the main level of the manor. The halls, which had been a chaotic mass of people earlier, were deserted and quiet.

"Where is everyone?" Concern filled Liam's voice.

"I don't know."

Doors were ajar, exposing empty rooms, where belongings had been cast aside haphazardly as if the manor had been ransacked. *If we'd been attacked, we would have heard something in the library, wouldn't we?* The library was essentially an enormous vault, both heavily insulated and climate controlled—a bomb shelter for ancient artifacts. The manor could crumble around it, but the library would remain intact.

Allyn entered a room. It was larger than his own, actually two rooms in one with a small eat-in kitchen. A crib rested at the foot of a queen-size bed, its blankets half on the floor. The separate room was hidden behind a half wall that extended just far enough to hide a second bed. Both were empty. Other than various nonessential items strewn about the room, nothing was out of the ordinary. No sign of a struggle or forced entry. Though very disorderly, the rooms were free of bodies, blood, or signs of battle. The occupants had fled.

Hurried footsteps echoed down the hall. Allyn quickly made for the door in time to see two men about his own age rushing down the hall with bags thrown over their shoulders. The one in the lead, a lanky man with shaggy brown hair, called out to the other, egging him on.

"Come on! They've already left!"

"Who left?" Liam called after them. Without answering, they continued to the end of the hall. Liam looked at Allyn, his face worried. "Something isn't right."

"Come on," Allyn said, darting after them. Unencumbered by baggage, Liam and Allyn easily caught up to the two men then followed them through the main hall and into the grand entryway. The two men slowed as they stepped through the double doors into the night. Outside stood a figure masked in darkness. The men maneuvered around him like water flowing around a boulder then picked up their pace once they were beyond him.

Allyn and Liam stepped out onto the cement patio overlooking the grounds in front of the manor. It was a dark night with the moon and stars hidden behind a clouded sky. The wind had picked up into a steady gust that whipped through Allyn's clothes as though he wore nothing at all. Rain hadn't yet begun to fall, but if the cold, damp air was any indication, it wasn't far off.

Motionless, Graeme stood outside the manor doors,

his arms folded, watching as the two men raced down the gravel driveway, trying to catch up to a larger group ahead. "It's done," Graeme said, his voice nearly as dark as the night.

"Who is that?" Allyn asked, trying to make out the leader of the group.

"Jaxon."

Jaxon? He was supposed to join a group of fleeing magi, not lead one.

"I should have known this would happen," Graeme said. "Feigning weakness can expose where it already lies. Jaxon's departure swayed those who were undecided, convincing them to flee. We lost another twenty after our... disagreement."

They had agreed that for the splinter to appear authentic, the argument would need to be public. Not a play in the hall in front of an audience, but something loud enough to be heard by one or two magi. Rumors would spread from there, and Jaxon's departure would confirm them, but the public spat seemed to have done more than they had anticipated. Jaxon was leading magi who thought they were involved in a real splinter. The plan was already falling apart. It was supposed to give them an advantage. But *this* left them weaker. "How many do we have left?"

"Fifteen," Graeme said.

"Fifteen?" Liam asked, his voice cracking.

Allyn ran his hands through his hair. *Fifteen against two Families. We don't stand a chance.*

"Fortunately," Graeme said, "those who cannot wield were the first to leave. We have fifteen *true* magi."

True magi. Those words would have once soured Liam and made him defensive or reclusive. Even still, confident and defiant, he scowled openly at his father, but Graeme didn't seem to notice. What Graeme thought was good fortune was actually a liability. Graeme didn't know what Allyn and Liam knew.

"They *can* wield," Liam said.

Graeme turned to him.

"*I* can wield."

Graeme blinked. "You can? Liam, that's wonderful!" He reached for his son.

Liam backed away. "But not how you think."

"I don't understand," Graeme said, lowering his arms.

"Our magic isn't failing us. It's evolving. I can't wield the elements like a *true* magi or heal the sick and wounded like a cleric. My abilities are different."

"How so?"

"I can speak with computers."

Allyn winced. It sounded ridiculous.

"Or more specifically, I can build computer code."

Graeme scowled. "This isn't a time for games."

"It isn't a game. It's true. The number of magi who could wield, the number of *true* magi"—Liam obviously had serious disdain for that distinction—"declined substantially in the mid- to late-eighteenth century. There was another deeper decline in the late-twentieth century. Don't you see? The world is changing, and so are we! Like all dominant species, we're adapting. Evolving."

"Working with computers is a skill, Liam, not an ability."

"A skill is something that's acquired," Liam said. "It takes thousands of hours to master, but from the first time I touched a computer, I could do incredible things with it. Ability is born inside us. Just like this was born inside me."

This seemed to give Graeme pause. Allyn had long wondered how Liam had acquired his first computer and why Graeme hadn't promptly taken it away.

"And what about Allyn's abilities?" Liam continued.

"They're something new. Jaxon and Nyla said they're a form of electricity."

"Suppose this were true," Graeme said. "What then?"

"Then it's likely that some, if not most, of the magi who cannot wield have another ability," Liam said. "Something that mirrors the technological world."

"And they just fled for another Family," Allyn added.

The group of magi had traveled out of sight. Intermittent drops of rain began to fall, more surely to follow. Graeme continued to watch, as if willing the fleeing magi to return. "This is a disaster."

"I don't disagree," Allyn said slowly, "but we are the only three people in the world who know the truth. Defeat Lukas tonight and lead the evolution of the magi race tomorrow. Die tonight, and the truth ends with us."

"They're our absolution," Graeme said contemplatively. "This can heal the splinter, not just within our Family but within magi Families everywhere. This is the answer." He took Liam's face in the palm of his hand. "You're our redemption. Our future."

Liam swallowed a lump in his throat. "We need to finish Lukas first."

Graeme nodded. "Assemble the magi."

Fifteen of Graeme's most trusted and loyal magi gathered with Allyn and Kendyl in the main entryway. They had bled for Graeme, they *would* bleed for him and, if necessary, they would die for him. They would say it was for the Family, but in Allyn's estimation, Graeme was the only thing that held what little remained of the McCollum Family intact.

At a full head shorter than every male magi in the McCollum Family, Mason weighed no more than Liam did and was the least physically intimidating person Allyn had ever seen, but he was also one of the most powerful. Jaxon said the strongest magi weren't usually the most physically endowed, and Mason was the living testament. His strength came from his depth of focus, his ability to listen to his body, and knowing just how far he could push himself.

Then there was Ren, the only female magi in the room and one of only two Allyn knew of. She was of average height and build, and she had pulled her sleek black hair into a tight ponytail. A deep scar ran down the bottom of her ear to the edge of her mouth, a blemish on an otherwise-porcelain face. She was quick to smile and quicker to wield. Her bravery was well known, and she was said to have saved Graeme on more than one occasion. She and Mason had been present during Kendyl's rescue. They waited with the others for Graeme's announcement.

Wearing compression armor that Leira had given her, Kendyl stood with Allyn. The black formfitting clothing looked like athletic gear, but it was tough to tear, water resistant, and flame retardant—modern armor for a modern war. Allyn would soon change into it, too.

Two people stood out from the sea of black—Nyla and a man Allyn had never met. But Vincent's reputation preceded him. Despite his broad shoulders and even thicker neck, Vincent was softer than most. Clerics tended to be thicker, more filled out than the magi. Allyn suspected this was a symptom of their duties. Vincent and Nyla wore navy compression armor that separated them from the others in black.

Only two clerics, Allyn thought. *Leira left with Jaxon, but where are the rest?* Nyla and Vincent would be run ragged and overwhelmed if forced to heal a group that outnumbered them by so much.

Raindrops tapped the roof and windows in a steady rhythm, an ambient noise behind the murmurs of magi.

The room smelled of sweat and fear as rumors spread through the gathered force faster than they would in a locker room. Including Graeme, Liam, Allyn, and Kendyl, the group was only nineteen strong, and the consensus was that Graeme would flee. Jaxon's departure had shaken their confidence more than Allyn had expected. Graeme's false splinter was deep enough to create a real one. Only Nyla was quiet because she knew Graeme wasn't the type to run. He wouldn't leave the manor and all its belongings to the man who would destroy it.

A collective gasp overtook the crowd as Graeme strode in under the arch of the grand staircase, wearing a sleeveless leather doublet. A deep red with a series of silver buckles running up the chest, it was emblazoned with the magi symbols of fire, water, and air—each displayed in vibrant yellows, blues, and whites. It was bold and traditional. If anyone had doubts about Graeme's intentions, this answered them. This was war apparel.

Liam was at his side—as his equal. He wore black compression armor embroidered with silver and gold, and his grim expression matched his father's. The murmurs grew silent as they stopped in front of the gathered Family members. Graeme surveyed them, holding each of their gazes for a short span, nodding subtle encouragements to a few before moving on.

"I stand before you a humbled man," Graeme said as a gust of wind howled outside. "In my attempts to hold this Family together, I've broken it apart. My grip was too firm. Our numbers are dwindling, our power declining, our influence dissipating. Worse, the world and the technological ideology I rejected may hold the key to our redemption, but I've cast them aside, unwanted, unneeded, unaccepted. And now they're with the enemy. I don't deserve to stand in front of you tonight, nor do I expect you to stand and fight with me."

Allyn shifted uncomfortably. He wasn't the only one. Confused, the magi around him looked at each other. Was Graeme trying to push away the only people he still had on his side?

"Yet, for the first time in a long time, I stand here hopeful."

Liam stood a little straighter and took a deep breath. *He can't be comfortable being the center of attention.*

"Our numbers are *not* dwindling. Our power *is not* declining. Our influence *will* return. I know this because I've learned of a secret. A new breed of magi has been born. They've lived among us undiscovered, unaware of their abilities, thinking themselves failures. *Machinists*, I've come to call them."

Eighteen sets of eyes locked onto Allyn, and it was his turn to feel uncomfortable.

"It was Liam who brought reason to my doorstep, knowledge to my chamber, truth to my soul. *He* is a machinist, perhaps the first of his kind, and his abilities aren't anything like ours. Ours are from a different age when we lived with different struggles, needed different abilities. Fire and water, once vital for survival, are now plentiful, simple to produce. The ability has become redundant, one we do not need anymore and are thus losing. The world is changing, and so shall we. So we are.

"The machinists are the magi race's response to the digital age. Computers are the new fire, the Internet the new water, electricity the new air. And so we've evolved. The scope of the machinists' abilities are unknown, but their presence is undeniable."

Liam stepped forward, taking center stage, his phone glowing in his hands. He held it in front of him so that the screen faced the group, and even though he hadn't touched a button, the demonstration began. First, the light above the chandelier flickered on and off. Then the lights on the wall followed suit. Table lamps and stand lamps in nearby rooms were next. The home phone rang in the distance. Even the smoke alarm went off. Every electronic device within sight or earshot came to life.

Cries of disbelief and shouts for it to stop echoed through the chamber. Annoyed magi covered their ears. Others were frightened, some bewildered, but most were encouraged. Liam had given them an impressive display. And as abruptly as it began, it stopped.

Graeme stepped forward, placing his hand on his son's shoulder. "Here we stand, nineteen strong, but fighting for the magi future. If we die tonight, this secret dies with us, and so too will our race. I won't let that happen. When this threat is neutralized, we will tell the Families of our discovery, and we will be hailed as heroes. We will thrive. But first, we have to live."

Collective agreement rippled through the assemblage, along with a couple shouts of support as magi nodded to one another.

"Tonight, we fight. Tonight, we win. Tonight, we preserve our place in history." The shouts grew louder and more enthusiastic, becoming a battle cry. "Let's get to work."

The thunderous reception shook the floor. If Lukas was anywhere near the manor grounds, he had heard it.

Graeme quickly organized them into various groups assigned with defending the manor. With over one hundred rooms, six entrances and exits, and countless windows, securing the manor was an impossible task, so they would channel Lukas's force through the manor in a predetermined path. The teams would lay traps and construct barriers. They boarded up windows, barricaded doors, and blocked entire hallways from wall to wall with furniture, appliances, and anything else that was bulky and heavy. When that ran out, they moved outside, using lawn furniture, firewood, and boulders. At one point, Allyn even saw two magi carrying what was left of a tree trunk on their shoulders.

Graeme sent Allyn to train with Mason.

"You'll be of no help to anyone if you can't defend yourself," Graeme had said.

Jaxon had instructed him not to use hot anger as a catalyst, but with Mason as his instructor, Allyn found that difficult. The short man made up for his small frame with a big mouth. Loud, direct, and condescending, Mason was a terrible instructor. They were on the second floor deck, under the overhang and hidden from the rain, but their breath billowed into the cold air like smoke. Mason, who only came to Allyn's shoulder, paced around him in a tight circle.

"No! No!" Mason said, his voice high-pitched, almost whiney. Allyn wished he could gag him with air. "Don't close your eyes."

"It helps me focus," Allyn said.

"Close your eyes to focus, and you'll open them to find yourself dead."

"I'll be dead if I can't wield to defend myself, too."

"There are other ways to defend yourself."

"Graeme isn't interested in me running and hiding, and neither am I. Let me try my way before trying yours." Allyn started to close his eyes again when Mason slapped him across the face.

"As long as I'm charged with instructing you, you'll do it my way." The man's voice went up an octave as he grew more angry. "No closing your eyes."

Allyn refused to give him the satisfaction of rubbing his cheek, but it burned in the cold air.

"Now do it again, this time looking into my eyes."

They went on like that for over an hour before Mason ended the session. It had hardly been the safe, nurturing learning environment Graeme had promised. And Allyn, too caught up in his disdain for Mason, hadn't been able to successfully wield. As frustrated as he was, he was even more disappointed. It was like picking up an instrument years after putting it down. He knew he *should* be able to play it, but his body had forgotten how.

Mason sent him to the kitchen for water and a hearty meal of red meat and bread, then to the second-story sitting area where the rest had gathered. Nobody expected Lukas that night. Jaxon had left only a few hours ago, and the word would need time to spread, but preparations had been made and defenses had been set. They wouldn't be undone so he could sleep in his room. Now that the chairs, couches, and tables had been used for barricades, the sitting area would comfortably sleep nineteen—though, because a handful of people would always be on watch, it wouldn't need to.

Liam sat cross-legged beside Kendyl, who was sprawled out on her side, propping her head up with her elbow. Their laughter washed away Allyn's irritation. He tried to recall the last time he'd heard that sound.

"What's so funny?" he asked as he approached.

"Nothing," Kendyl said, but Liam gave her a guilty look, and they burst into uncontrolled laughter. It made Allyn's face burn.

"Come on," he said. "Tell me."

"We're just trading childhood stories." Kendyl's grin suggested the stories were about him.

"You aren't going to tell me, are you?"

"You don't want to know," Liam said.

He probably didn't, but it didn't help satisfy his curiosity. "Just remember," he told Kendyl, "I have plenty of embarrassing stories about you, too."

"The difference is I'm not as easily embarrassed as you are."

His face grew hotter, and he longed to change the

subject. He sat down beside Liam. "That was an impressive display earlier."

Liam checked to make sure no one nearby was listening then leaned in closer and whispered, "It was a trick."

"A trick?" *Too loud.* He asked quietly, "How?"

"It was pretty simple really. Everything in the house is part of the network. I can open and close breakers or turn power on or off with the push of a button."

"But you didn't touch anything."

"A timer," Liam said. "Like I said, it was really simple. You just believed because you wanted to believe."

"What *can* you do?" Kendyl asked.

Liam shrugged. "I'm still trying to figure that out, but they needed something to fight for other than survival. Something real. Something they could see. Feel. Hear. Hope only goes so far."

Kendyl looked at Allyn. He laughed. "I told you he was an incredible kid."

"You weren't exaggerating."

Liam's face flushed. "Please stop," he said. But there was pride in his voice. "Tell me something about her."

"What do you want to hear?" Allyn asked.

"Something funny." His words hinted at something else. *It felt good to laugh.*

Allyn thought it was strange that with battle imminent and death all but certain, they would sit around telling funny stories, but it *did* feel good. And so they went on trading embarrassing stories far into the night. Some were about others, but most were about themselves. They laughed, cried, and held their stomachs while gasping for air, pleading for the storyteller to stop. They discussed secrets, longings, and ambitions, and for the first time in as long as Allyn could remember, he was happy.

He knew it wouldn't last.

CHAPTER 21

"WOULD YOU PUT THAT DOWN and help me?" Allyn asked.

Liam sat beside him on the burgundy-cushioned window seat, his back against the wall. He was *supposed* to be helping Allyn watch the northern grounds of the manor. Instead, he was reading the leather-bound book he'd stolen from the Hyland Estate. Liam sighed and carefully closed the book. He didn't use a bookmark because he said doing so would damage the tattered pages. Opening his phone, he punched in something on the digital screen and pulled up the surveillance cameras from the front gate. Empty. He cycled through the other six, surveying each of the five entrances and the eastern and western edges of the grounds. All were still. Content that nothing was amiss, Liam returned his attention to his book.

"You know that's not the same," Allyn said.

"I know," Liam said. "But I can only look at the same empty field for so long."

The manor grounds were still. Graeme's magi had barricaded themselves inside the manor when the sun disappeared behind the tree line. The first stars were appearing in the sky, and with the moon but a sliver, it would be a dark night. Allyn had endured another long day of training, if it could be called that. It felt more like failing. Mason forced him to do things his way, and it wasn't working. It wasn't *going* to work. Mason—as stubborn as he was short—refused to let him try something different.

"At least he could have given us something interesting to watch," Liam said.

Allyn smiled. Liam had a point. Watching the tree line was challenging. The darkness played with his eyes, and shadows moved every time the wind blew. If he squinted, half of the trees could be mistaken for a man. "I'm content with it being uninteresting. That means the battle hasn't begun." Two days had passed since the McCollum Family had splintered, and they hadn't heard or seen anything. No sign of Lukas or his intentions.

"The wait is killing me," Liam said.

"It's better than someone actually trying to kill you."

"You like to argue, don't you?"

Allyn laughed. "I do it for a living. Or did."

"You miss it, don't you?"

"It's complicated."

"How?"

"It's not as simple as missing it," Allyn said. "I don't really know how to describe it. My life had a purpose, and I don't know who I am without it. But it's more than that. I lost my mom when I was just a little older than you are now, and I got a job that I thought my mom would be proud of. So turning my back on it isn't easy for me because it means turning my back on everything that made me who I am."

"I think I know how you feel," Liam said softly as though he were sharing a secret. "I lost my mother, too. I wish she didn't have to die, but I wouldn't be the same person I am today. And I like who I am."

"What happened to her?"

Liam pulled his knees close. "She got sick."

Allyn studied him for a moment. He knew how hard it was to open up. Some wounds never healed entirely. "What kind of sick?"

Liam shrugged. "My father refused to take her to a specialist. Refused to let anyone other than our clerics treat her. If he'd taken her to a doctor, then who knows, she might be here today. But he didn't."

It clicked. His wife's death had backed Graeme into a corner. He wouldn't use technology even to save her life. Embracing it later would trample her memory. But Liam hadn't been a part of Graeme's decision. He saw how helpful it could be and how their lives could benefit from it. That was when he embraced it. And that also had to be why Graeme never pulled Liam away from it. Sure, he would rail against it, but deep down, where no one was privy, Graeme was encouraging his son because Liam could right his wrongs.

Beep! Beep! Beep! Liam's phone sounded the alarm. Liam stared at the screen, his eyes growing wide. "Allyn?"

A sinking feeling grew in Allyn's midsection. "What is it?

Liam turned the phone so Allyn could see it. Four police cars with flashing lights were parked outside the front gate. Officers crouched behind open doors, guns drawn, while another was hooking a cable to the gate.

This can't be happening. Of all the things they'd prepared for, this had never entered the conversation.

"They've found us," Liam said.

"No," Allyn said, watching the cable grow taut. The gate bent, then ripped off its steel hinges, and a stream of police cars raced through the opening. "They've found *me*."

"Step back!" Graeme shouted. He was in the grand entryway with a handful of his magi. "Get away from the doors and windows. Keep your hands in front of you and don't do anything stupid!" Gray dust billowed as police cars raced up the gravel driveway. "Find everyone. Find them and bring them here."

"Wait!" Allyn shouted, rushing into the chamber, careful to stay away from the windows. "It's me they're after."

"I know," Graeme said.

"Let me go out there, surrender myself. You don't need to be involved in this."

"It's too late," Graeme said. "They're already here."

"You're herding everyone up together," Allyn said. "They're going to run background checks on everyone, and when they don't find *anything* on *anyone*—no drivers licenses, no student ID cards, not even a library card—they're going to think that's more than just a little odd."

Graeme looked at Allyn dead in the eye. "I know."

"Do you?" Allyn asked. "They're going to arrest me for kidnapping. They will arrest you for harboring a fugitive and probably arrest everyone else until they know what to do with them. Even after Kendyl clears our names, the damage will have been done. We'll be broken apart with nowhere to go, nowhere to hide, and Lukas will pick us off one by one. Meanwhile, the police will storm the house and find a treasure trove of historical artifacts belonging to a previously unknown race of men. The magi existence will be discovered. And Lukas will win."

"What would you have me do?" Graeme asked.

The first cars outside screeched to a halt, and officers jumped behind opened doors, their guns raised.

"Run," Allyn said. "Have the magi hide in the forests. The police don't know these woods like you do. They won't be able to follow, not at night. But you and I need to be here when they crash through those doors. When I'm in custody and Kendyl is presumed safe, the case is closed. They will have what they came for, and it should give the others the time they need to escape."

More cars screamed to a halt. Teams of police gathered outside, ready to storm the house. Graeme tapped his foot, thinking.

"Whatever you're thinking," Allyn said, "think fast."

"Do it," Graeme said. His magi fled the room in an instant, racing to the common room where the rest of the magi were gathered.

"Find my sister. Hide her in a bedroom. Bar the door. Make it look... make it look bad."

Nodding, Graeme rushed out of the room.

"And Graeme?"

He stopped and turned. "The first opportunity you get, break free of your cuffs and find her, okay?"

Graeme nodded and disappeared into the manor.

Shadowy figures slipped past the windows as Allyn knelt in the center of the entryway. He placed his hands behind his head and waited. Muffled footsteps preceded a knock. Then the door crashed inward. Armed officers wearing flack jackets and wielding shotguns, Glocks, and assault rifles streamed into the manor. "Get on the ground! Get on the ground!"

Allyn went to the ground, face first, keeping his palms on the back of his head, barely glimpsing a team of officers climbing the stairwell. He hoped the magi had enough time to flee. Someone took his hands, wrenching them violently behind his back, nearly ripping his shoulder out of its socket. Allyn cried out in pain, instinctively trying to roll away.

"Stop resisting!"

Allyn gritted his teeth, trying to keep his body relaxed. He felt the cold steel of handcuffs slip around his wrists before he was hauled to his feet.

"It's him."

"How many are with you?"

Allyn remained silent.

"Get him to the car."

The first officer passed Allyn off to another officer, Grimes, who led him outside. With his thinning blond hair parted down the middle and kept long enough to cover his ears, Officer Grimes looked like the kind of man who refused to admit he wasn't as young as he used to be. He didn't wear a coat, and his sleeves were rolled up, exposing arms that could have been carved from stone. Officer Grimes gently led him down the stairs.

The manor grounds were a flurry of activity. There were close to twenty squad cars outside, and more officers poured into the manor while others searched the grounds with flashlights and spotlights, looking for anyone who might have slipped out the back. *They're not going to make it.* Too many magi were trying to hide, and too many officers were looking for them. They would be found, hauled back, and thrown into squad cars.

Grimes opened the back door of his car and guided Allyn inside. "Watch your head." He closed the door, spoke into the walkie-talkie on his shoulder, and joined a nearby circle of officers.

Allyn shifted, trying to find a spot that would allow him to watch without having the cuffs dig into his lower back. He caught a glimpse of Graeme being shoved into another squad car on the other side of the driveway. Kendyl was led out sometime later. They'd thrown a blanket around her shoulders, and a woman dressed in a gray pantsuit, probably a trauma specialist or psychologist of some kind, was saying something to her. Kendyl didn't appear to be listening. She scanned the grounds, looking for something.

Me, Allyn realized. *She's wondering if I'm okay.*

He tried to think of some way to get her attention.

But the door was locked and could only be opened from the outside, and its glass was thick enough to muffle anything he shouted. *We'll see each other soon enough*, he thought, resigned.

As the minutes wore on and nobody else was escorted to a squad car, Allyn began to feel a little better about his plan. The magi, it seemed, were better at hiding than he'd given them credit for. He shouldn't have been surprised. They'd been hiding for centuries. He imagined them hidden deep in the forest, cold and wet, not knowing how long they would have to hide. All because he had been too stupid to march straight into the police station with his sister and clear things up. He'd tried, of course, as soon as Kendyl was healthy enough to walk, but she'd insisted on staying for the funeral, after which they had been caught up in the magi conflict.

The car rocked to the side as Officer Grimes climbed behind the wheel. The car was already running, so he gave the siren a quick chirp and made a U-turn through the grass and back onto the driveway. An officer at the end of the driveway waved them past the mangled remains of the gate.

The winding, two-lane country road was cut directly into the hillside. Overgrown branches stretched over the road like long, weathered fingers, and fallen limbs littered the edges of the road. A small ditch cut between the road and the hillside, and the road fell away into a deep ravine on the other side. Because the country lane had no streetlamps, Officer Grimes turned on his brights and drove slower than the posted forty-five-mph speed limit, carefully avoiding the potholes that plagued the neglected road.

They rounded a bend and—

"Shit!" Grimes bellowed.

Allyn jerked forward. The seatbelt caught and ripped

into his chest as the brakes locked. The car slid forward with a screech. A black sedan was parked in front of them, blocking an entire lane. A fireball appeared out of the darkness, streaking toward the car. Grimes swerved, but the fireball hit the underside of the car, flipping it onto its side. The world turned upside down as the car rolled onto its top, coming to a stop in the ditch.

Fighting with his seatbelt, Grimes kicked open his door.

"Don't!" Allyn yelled. "Run!"

Grimes didn't respond. He crawled out of the car, pulling his gun out of its holster.

"He's not who you think!"

Grimes shouted something inaudible as he raised his gun. A dark figure stepped forward. Allyn didn't need to see his face. He knew that confident walk. *Lukas.* Allyn thrashed in the back of the squad car. He had to get free. But his hands were still cuffed, and the seatbelt held him upside down. Pressure built in his eyes and nose as blood rushed to his head. He had trouble seeing.

Pop! Pop! Pop! Grimes shot at Lukas.

A concussion of air blew Grimes against the squad car. He looked down in shock where a twisted piece of metal stuck through his abdomen. He didn't suffer long. He didn't even have time to look up again before Lukas hit him with a fireball.

Lukas walked over to the car and knelt, peering inside with an amused look. "That worked out rather well, wouldn't you say? Come on, let's get you out of there." He reached for Allyn's buckle, drawing closer to Allyn.

Allyn drove his forehead into Lukas's nose. Lukas fell back with a curse. Blood poured from his nose, dripping off his chin. Allyn thought about wielding, but his poor training sessions with Mason gave him pause.

"You piece of shit!" Lukas screamed, flashing white teeth that were stained red. He kicked Allyn, aiming for his head, but the angle was awkward, and his legs were too short to land anything but a glancing blow. "Get out here!"

Again, Lukas reached in, this time projecting fire into the belt. The belt gave way, and Allyn crashed onto the roof of the car, landing on his head and rolling onto his side. Lukas grabbed his foot and yanked him through the shattered window, dragging Allyn over glass that sliced into his arms and back. Lukas drove his foot into Allyn's chest again and again.

Allyn groaned and tried to roll away, but Lukas continued. "Okay!" Allyn screamed between kicks. "Please!"

Lukas growled and stood over Allyn with his hands on his hips, breathing heavily, but he stopped.

Headlights rounded the bend, coming directly at them. Allyn was filled with hope, followed by dread as he remembered the fallen officer. Allyn tried to yell for the car to stop, turn around, go back the way they came, and save themselves. But he struggled to make his voice any louder than a whisper.

The car came closer. The orange headlights were blinding. Lukas cursed, diving to the side. *No. Not headlights—*

A pair of fireballs soared over Allyn's head and crashed into Lukas's car, bathing the lonely road in an orange light. Two figures raced toward him. He squinted, trying to make them out. Another fireball shot forward, quickly followed by a blast of ice.

Someone grabbed him by his armpits and dragged him away. "It's okay. I've got you," Leira said.

That meant the other person was Jaxon. Relief flooded through Allyn. They hadn't left. They'd kept their promise. Allyn could see him, a shadow in the night, stalking Lukas with fists wrapped in air. Leira dragged Allyn behind the overturned squad car and probed him, her hand glowing softly on his chest.

"Nothing serious," she said, relaxing.

"Get the cuffs off me."

Hidden behind the squad car, Allyn could no longer see the battle. If Jaxon could divert Lukas's attention long enough, Allyn might be able to hit him with an electric charge.

Leira found the officer and reached inside his pockets.

"On his belt," Allyn shouted. "Beside his radio."

Leira found the keys, unhooked them from his belt, and ran back to unlock Allyn's cuffs.

"Thank you," Allyn said, gently massaging his wrists where the cuffs had rubbed him raw.

"We need to take care of that before it gets infected," Leira said.

"In a—"

An explosion rocked the night, shattering the remaining windows of the squad car.

Jaxon was on the ground, blood pouring from his forehead. Lukas was several feet away, rolling to his feet. His car was on its side. One of his fireballs must have struck the gas tank. Stumbling toward Jaxon's motionless body, Lukas, with a wild look in his eye, formed something in his hands.

"No!" Leira shouted, bolting toward him. She would make it to Jaxon before Lukas did, but what did she hope to do? Die with him? She couldn't fight Lukas. Twenty feet before she reached Jaxon, she skidded to a stop, grabbing Grimes's gun from the pavement. It surprised Lukas as much as it did Allyn.

A shot rang out in the night. Lukas dove behind the smoldering car. Leira continued to shoot, striding forward as bullets clanged against the scorched metal.

Allyn made a wide arc to flank Lukas from the side. He calmed his breathing, trying to steady his nerves, and dug inside. He found the void easily, but without anger, he didn't have anything to fill it.

Leira shot two more rounds, keeping Lukas at bay behind the overturned car.

Allyn struggled to wield. *I should be the one with the gun.*

Pop! Pop! Pop! Leira shot. Then *click, click, click.* She looked at the gun, confused, seemingly unaware she was out of ammo.

Lukas rose from behind the car, his face a mix of relief and amusement. "Technology always pales in comparison to what we can do."

Leira hurled the gun at him.

Allyn reached out with a yell, wishing he could stop her. The officer would have more magazines on his belt. The gun flew harmlessly over Lukas's shoulder, skidding to a halt on the blacktop.

Allyn fished inside for something—anything. Frustration began to build. He tried to quell it before the anger took him.

"How many people have already died because of you, Allyn?" Lukas asked. "Your selfishness has cost others everything."

Anger rippled through him like a shiver in the night, its heat suddenly surrounding the void.

"Fuck it." Allyn succumbed to the anger, drawing from its power like a turbine sucking water from a river. Red coils of electricity wrapped around his arms, alive, ready to be unleashed.

Lukas took a step backward.

Allyn hurled electric bolts at Lukas. *Those are new.* Before, the electricity had come out as a long connected charge like a lightning whip, but these were separate charges, like electric bullets. Lukas met them in the air with ice, creating a sparking miniature blast when they hit. Allyn cursed. Jaxon had said his charges wouldn't have an elemental counter, but ice could apparently be used to slow his attacks, and because he was unable to attack with anything but electricity, Lukas quickly quelled his advance.

"Good!" Lukas shouted. He looked proud. "You have the ability to become a powerful magi. Let me show you how."

Allyn growled and continued to throw charges in Lukas's direction, but nothing came close to landing.

"You hate me, but you shouldn't," Lukas said.

"You've taken everything from me!" Allyn said.

"I've *given* you everything. Without me, you wouldn't know what you were capable of. Without me, you wouldn't be able to wield. You're *special* because of me. You should *appreciate* it."

"Why me? Why my sister? What is so special about us?"

"You're twins," Lukas said.

Allyn shook his head. "There has to be more."

Lukas smiled like a cornered child. "Okay, Allyn. I'll tell you as a gesture of good faith. I want to heal the Fractured Families, end this life of hiding, live as we were meant to."

"Then end the war."

"It's not so simple. If it weren't me, it would be someone else. Mine is a noble cause, and for that, I'm justified. With you, I can prove that there are more magi in the world. That their abilities are only dormant. That we are not as weak as we appear to be."

"That won't heal the splinter you've created. It won't heal the splinters developing in other Families or bring back the magi you've killed."

"What is a magi Family, Allyn?" Lukas asked. "It's a group of people that are only distantly related, if related at all. We're held together by a common purpose and similar goals. What better way to unify the Fractured Families than a new common purpose? Don't you understand? You and your sister are *proof*. Symbols."

"You believe the Families will unite around you to

search for more like us."

"Is it really so hard to believe? Magi went into hiding after the Fracture, but their abilities didn't die. They just went into hiding, too. As generations went by, the ability lay dormant until it was forgotten entirely. But there are still echoes of it—a connection between siblings, a parent doing the impossible to save a child, someone surviving an impossible fall. You call them miracles but ignore what they really are. I sought you out because you were the perfect combination: a set of twins from a broken family. After a terribly emotional childhood full of heartache and loss, you're more in tune with your bodies and your feelings than most. If anyone were capable of finding their dormant ability, it would be you."

"It was a guess," Allyn said almost to himself, not believing his ears. "You didn't know I could wield. You only *hoped* I could."

"And I was right."

Allyn didn't know whether to laugh or cry. *A guess.* Lukas would never understand what he'd cost Allyn, because he'd never cared about anything more than himself and his own ambitions. He didn't do it for a greater good. He did it for *his* greater good.

"We weren't the first twins you tortured, were we?" Allyn asked.

Lukas smiled. "Why does it matter, Allyn? We found you. Our line will continue. The magi race won't die out. It'll thrive!"

"It matters because you destroyed lives and families. Your Family didn't splinter because of what you believed. It splintered because of how you proved it. You abducted and tortured innocent people under the false pretense of the *greater good*." He almost spat those last words.

The smile melted off Lukas's face. "Don't think yourself too important to kill, Allyn. There are thousands more like you. You are not the last, only the first."

"I'll never join you." Allyn watched as understanding grew on Lukas's face. Allyn would always be the enemy. Lukas had created a monster who wouldn't be satisfied until his creator was dead.

Fire burned in Lukas's hands. Allyn had no counter to it. If it struck him, he was gone. He steadied himself, ready to attack, and surveyed his surroundings, searching for cover. The car was a good fifteen paces behind him, and the road fell away to his right, but he had no idea how far down it went. The hillside was to his left, but it was steep, and he could never scale it in time.

Lukas blasted fire at him. It burned brightly, radiating heat like a bonfire. A killing blow. Allyn dove, narrowly avoiding the blast, then rolled to his feet, but Lukas was already wielding a wall of fire ten feet wide and almost as tall. Heaving it forward as if he were shoving a boulder, the wall of fire slid toward Allyn faster than he could run.

Allyn threw his hand forward as if reaching for Lukas. A red rope of electricity shot out, arcing through the air and lassoing Lukas. Flames continued to race toward him, reaching for Allyn to pull him into their glowing abyss. Even ten paces away, the heat stung his face. Allyn yanked on the electric lasso. Arms pinned at his sides, Lukas flew toward him, slamming against the ground, unable to soften the impact. The wall of fire began to dissipate, but it wouldn't do so in time. Allyn crouched, throwing his arms over his head to protect himself from the incoming fire.

Something wet and cool covered him.

The fire, scalding hot, passed over him, hissing upon contact. Once the fire was beyond him, Allyn stood, his clothing steaming.

Jaxon was on his feet, too, barely. Leira was at his shoulder, helping him walk. Their faces were an identical mess of torn flesh. *She healed him, and he saved me.* He didn't know who to thank. There would be time to figure that out later.

Lukas, no longer bound by Allyn's electric lasso and visibly weak from creating his wall of fire, was on his feet, teetering at the edge of the road. He looked down the steep hillside, weighing his options. Something shot into the air across the valley. Bright and orange, it looked like a flare.

Jaxon rushed forward suddenly. Lukas disappeared off the road.

Rushing to the side of the road, Allyn and Jaxon peered down. It was dark enough that they couldn't see the bottom, so Jaxon dropped a weak fireball from the edge. It hit the ground, briefly illuminating the bottom of the valley before being doused by the wet ground.

Lukas was gone.

Jaxon breathed a sigh of relief.

"Thank you," Allyn said.

"Don't thank me," Jaxon said, looking out over the valley. "It isn't over. Lukas has taken the manor."

Jaxon hadn't sighed in relief, Allyn realized. He'd sighed in despair.

CHAPTER 22

UNSHOTS SPLIT THE NIGHT. NOT distant, over the valley like before, these were closer, outside the manor. Liam crept forward, staying low to the ground. Officers had searched the forest, sticking mostly near the tree line, scared to venture too far inside. They had flashlights and floodlights capable of illuminating large portions of the forest, but the light also made shadows. The officers were so focused on what they *could* see that they didn't think about what they *couldn't*. They'd passed by, sometimes mere feet from Liam, never seeing him. The forest was quiet now, the officers having long since returned to the manor empty-handed.

As the night had worn on, the police presence had thinned. Allyn was in custody, his father had been arrested, and they'd taken Kendyl. The manor was empty since the magi had fled just before the front doors came down. When they didn't find anyone else, the police had finished their business inside and left.

Liam walked through a spider web. Its fine, sticky threads tickled his nose and lips. *No spiders,* he told himself, wiping the web off his face. *There aren't any spiders.* He fought the urge to brush his shirt and run his fingers through his hair again. *I hate the forest. It's so... dirty. It even smells dirty.*

Nearing the tree line, where the manor was visible beyond the foliage, Liam dropped to all fours. The manor was so dark, quiet—and dead. Seeing it so lifeless was eerie. Only a single squad car remained to protect the crime scene. A husky officer bent over its hood, pointing his gun at the tree line.

A fireball shot out from Liam's right. The officer dove for cover, narrowly avoiding being torched as the fireball exploded against the hood of his squad car. His cry of pain and confusion was quickly replaced by the sound of gunshots being fired blindly into the forest.

Bullets whistled through the air, catching dead limbs and embedding into trees but never finding a human target. When the clip was empty, a mass of magi rushed out of the forest, storming the grounds. The officer was quickly dispatched with an ice blast to the neck as magi ran past, climbing the stairs and darting into the manor. Darian Hyland stopped atop the landing, turning to overlook the grounds.

Like he wants to be seen, Liam thought, slowly creeping back into the forest, unsure of whether Darian could see him. *Probably not.* But his steady, confident gaze unnerved him.

Darian shot a fireball into the air. It burned brightly in the darkness, a flare that would be visible for miles as it reflected through the thin clouds. Darian turned and strode into the manor, closing the door behind him.

Liam pulled his phone out of his pocket, shielding the LED screen with his hand so that it didn't expose his position. He sent out a one-word text message to every member of the McCollum Family with a phone. *Homestead.* Anyone who received it would know where to find him. It was a risk. Someone might have left a phone inside the manor, or in his father's case, the police might have collected it, but it was a risk he needed to take.

He meant to retake the manor.

———••———

Nestled deep within the forest, the homestead was nothing more than a crumbling foundation that stood three or four feet above the ground. The dwelling had been small—only one room with a single door that was currently recognizable only as a rectangle cut out of the foundation. A chilly wind whined through the naked branches as Liam approached. It had taken him nearly an hour to arrive at the heart of the forest.

What do I do if nobody comes? Liam shivered at the thought. Somebody would come. *Won't they?* He sat down in the corner of the homestead, the rough porous foundation against his back, and pulled out his phone. He smiled as he toggled up the security cameras. His network was still up. That meant he had an element of control.

Liam drew his knees close to his chest. The night was cold, and while his clothing was flame resistant, it wasn't particularly warm, and the ground was soggy from an afternoon of rain. Teeth chattering, Liam set his phone on a broken piece of foundation and rested his forehead on his knees, fighting to keep his eyes open. It was late, closer to dawn than dusk, and this was the first time he hadn't been running or hunted for hours. Fatigue had finally caught up with him.

I can close my eyes, Liam thought, *just for a second. Just... for... a...* Sleep washed over him.

A branch snapped in the distance.

Liam's eyes popped open. "Who's there?" He stood, his muscles aching, his left arm asleep, preparing to wield. *Wield what?* He still didn't know what he was capable of, and deep in the forest, he was far away from a computer.

I hate the forest.

Straining his ears, he thought he heard something in the distance—voices or whispers. Maybe it was the forest playing tricks on him again. That shadow over there looked like a man. It moved. It *was* a man! "Stop!" Liam commanded.

"Liam?" The deep voice was powerful if slightly strained, and it came from that towering shadow.

"Jaxon?"

The forest came alive with activity as several people stepped forward: Jaxon, Leira, Allyn, and the group that Jaxon had led away. Jaxon strode directly toward him, then picked him up and... gave him a hug. "Are you hurt?"

"No." Liam's voice was strained from being squeezed so tightly. What had gotten into him? Jaxon let him go, and Allyn stepped forward, tousling his hair and smiling at him as Leira reached out to probe him. She could have just asked if he was okay.

"This was smart, Liam," Jaxon said. "Only those of us who live here would know of this place."

"Or anyone who has lived here," Leira said, clearly implying that Lukas might also recognize the code.

"A risk I would have taken, as well," Jaxon said.

Liam swelled with pride. "They've taken the manor."

"How many?"

"Twenty? Thirty?" Liam said. "It was hard to tell."

Jaxon winced. "That's more than I hoped."

"It's Darian," Liam said.

"And Lukas."

Liam gave him a puzzled look.

"You didn't see Lukas?" Jaxon asked.

"No."

"He's there," Jaxon said, turning to Allyn. "This was his plan all along. Have the police divide us and take us into custody so he could take us one by one."

Liam scanned the group. It was everyone Jaxon had left with, save for Allyn—where had they found him? Hadn't he been taken into custody? His father wasn't among them. Neither was Kendyl, Nyla, or anyone who'd fled into the forest. "Where's my father?"

"We don't know," Allyn said. "Lukas was waiting for me. He ambushed us on the road and killed the officer who had me in custody. It looks like they tried to do the same with your father, only Lukas's magi is dead, and your father is missing. He's alive. Somewhere."

"He'll be here," Liam said, surprised by the assuredness of his voice. He didn't *feel* that confident.

Jaxon nodded.

"Did you see if Darian had my sister?" Allyn asked.

Liam shook his head. For someone who had stayed behind to watch the manor, he wasn't able to answer very many questions.

"You said Graeme promised to protect her," Leira said. "If Graeme is safe, then so is Kendyl. He'll bring her."

Allyn didn't appear entirely convinced, but he didn't argue.

"We need to take back the manor," Liam said.

"They have thirty magi inside a building we spent two days fortifying," Jaxon said. "We don't have the firepower."

"More will come."

Jaxon looked at him skeptically.

"Everything we have is inside that house. *Everything.* I haven't spent the last three years preserving our history so we could hand it over to Lukas."

"The police will be back, too," Allyn said. "As soon as they realize their officers are missing."

"How long do we have?" Jaxon asked.

"A couple hours," Allyn said. "Three, four at most. And when they come back, they won't leave again. We've either lost the manor to Lukas or the police. Take your pick."

"We need to try and salvage as much as possible," Liam said. "To do that, we need to get Lukas out."

"We won't have a lot of time."

"It will be enough," Liam said. "It has to be."

"What makes you so sure?" Jaxon asked.

"They don't know we have this." Liam pulled up the security cameras on his phone. "Knowledge is power. We know where they are and where they're the weakest. If we hit them right, they won't know we only have twenty. It will feel like fifty."

"What else can you do with that?" Allyn asked.

"As long as they don't disable the network, I can do almost anything. Cut off power, lock mechanical doors like the one in the library, and create general havoc." Liam smiled wickedly.

"You can do all of that with a phone?" Jaxon asked skeptically.

"He doesn't know..." Allyn said. Jaxon had left before he and Liam had made their discovery. He didn't know about the machinists.

"There isn't time," Liam said. "Yes, I can do all of that with a phone. We have a distinct advantage. The only question is, do you want to use it?"

Jaxon took a sharp breath. "What do you need?"

———————•••———————

Graeme arrived with Kendyl a short time later. His arm was slung over her shoulder as he used her for support. Dried blood matted his hair, burns and scrapes covered his arms and face, and he walked with a noticeable limp, but Kendyl was unharmed except for a tear in the back of her compression armor. Graeme had obviously gone to great lengths, including personal harm, to protect her.

Relief flooded through Allyn as he saw her. He hadn't realized how worried he had been. She staggered forward, likely exhausted from having to support Graeme through the forest, and tripped over an exposed root, sending them both crashing into the homestead's foundation.

Allyn rushed to help them up. And that's when he saw the others.

A group of almost fifteen magi were close in tow. Unlike Graeme and Kendyl, they appeared entirely uninjured, though tired and disheveled, after having to run frantically out the back door when the police arrived. It was no wonder Graeme was late to arrive—he'd spent half the night rounding up the splintered magi.

"Thank you," Kendyl said with a wince as Allyn helped her up.

"Are you okay?"

Kendyl nodded. "They were waiting for us. It was an ambush."

"I know," Allyn said. "They came after me, too."

"Where is Lukas now?" Graeme asked.

"He's holed up in the manor with Hyland and perhaps thirty others."

Graeme cursed. "What's your plan?"

Jaxon turned to Liam. If Graeme was surprised that Jaxon had deferred to the boy, he masked it well.

"It just got a little easier with you showing up," Liam said. "But our plan is to create a diversion at the front entrance and sneak our magi in through the second-floor terrace. From there, we'll break into three assault squads, flanking them from multiple positions."

"After that," Jaxon said, "it's as simple as mop up."

"What kind of diversion?" Graeme asked.

Allyn smiled. "A big one."

CHAPTER 23

CRASH!

Allyn burst from the tree line, dashing for the manor. Running under only the cover of darkness, he felt exposed. He focused on the back of the manor, where Liam said Lukas had positioned two magi guards on watch, ready to drop and hide in an instant or dodge an attack.

Graeme and Jaxon were with him, but the rest of their squad stayed hidden among the trees, waiting for their signal to advance. The back of the manor was dark and silent, an indication the diversion was working.

Crash!

Allyn imagined the diversion in action. Mason was hammering the front of the manor with ice like a battering ram. They had hoped Lukas would draw his forces together in the grand entryway, ready to repel their attack from a fortified position. As he did, Allyn and the others would slip in the back.

Allyn slipped on a rock and fell to the ground, catching himself with his hands so he didn't faceplant into the soggy grass. Someone grabbed his arm and yanked him forward. It did little to help him regain his balance, but it kept him moving forward. There still wasn't any activity in the back of the manor. The guards must have moved to the main entrance with the rest of Lukas's force. Their plan seemed to be working.

Allyn was the last to make it to the manor, throwing his back against its stone exterior, hidden under the first-level windows, beyond the view of anyone inside. Graeme raised his fist into the air, giving the signal for the others to advance, and five more magi broke from the tree line racing for the manor.

With the next wave of magi approaching, Jaxon slipped up the spiral stairwell to the second-story balcony, valuing silence over speed. Allyn was close behind. They arrived at the back door as the other magi neared the manor. Inside, the room was empty. Sofas, armchairs, and a bar had once been arranged neatly around the living space, but the furniture had been used for barricades. There were no signs of the guards Liam had seen on his monitors.

Jaxon counted silently, and on three, he pulled the door. It didn't open. Allyn cursed. Breaking into the manor wasn't going to be as easy as they had hoped.

Crash! Shouts echoed deep inside the manor. Allyn found the security camera protected under the eave of the roof and gave a thumbs-up. Liam said he could loop the feed so that anyone inside watching the monitors would see only old footage from before they had gathered on the balcony. Liam, however, would be watching the live feed.

I hope he knows what he's doing. Allyn had faith in the kid, but he wasn't sure it was enough to trust him with his life.

"Noise," Jaxon whispered, handing Allyn his cell phone. It was a product of the early century, a bulky flip phone without a touchscreen. A few months ago, Allyn would have been embarrassed to carry it around, but it had become his lifeline.

We need noise, Allyn texted Liam. *Five seconds.*

Moments later, a series of explosions and concussions pounded the night, drowning out the sound of shattering glass as Jaxon drove his elbow through the glass door. When nobody came to investigate, Jaxon stepped into the room.

Allyn looked down from the balcony, nodding to Graeme. The five magi waiting nearby ascended the staircase and streamed into the vacant room with Jaxon as the last group advanced upon the manor. As the group of twelve, including Nyla and Leira, closed in on the manor, Allyn entered.

How long until Lukas realizes the attack in front isn't an attack? No time for that. The sooner they got their force inside, the less time Lukas would have to discover the truth.

Graeme led the last squad into the sitting room.

We're in, Allyn sent Liam, exhaling softly. They'd cleared the first hurdle.

The east and west wings are quiet, Liam sent back. *Don't know from there.*

The security cameras only covered the entrances to the manor. It was the glaring flaw in their plan. Once inside, Liam was blind. Allyn showed Jaxon the message.

"East wing," Jaxon whispered to Trevin.

Trevin nodded and led a team of five magi toward the east wing, where they would wait for the order to advance.

"We'll take the west wing," Jaxon said before turning to Nyla. "You've got the center hallway of the second floor."

That meant Graeme would take the center hallway of the first floor, where he stood the best chance of encountering Lukas. There had been some debate as to whether that should be Graeme, but he had eventually won out. It was his Family, and therefore, Lukas was his responsibility.

Allyn sent Liam the final message: *Moving out.*

With nothing but the occasional squeak from the hardwood floor or creak of a hinge, the magi squads filed out of the room. Jaxon waited for the rest to shuffle out before nodding to his squad and leading them to the western wing. Allyn brought up the rear while Leira fell into position behind Jaxon. This was a stealth mission, and they would rely heavily on Leira's ability to silently incapacitate enemy magi.

The western wing of the manor was made up largely of bedrooms, bathrooms, and a handful of sitting rooms. They had intentionally closed the doors when they were fortifying the manor, and they had remained closed. Jaxon had the rooms searched anyway—he didn't want anyone sneaking up behind them—and after discovering them empty, they continued on.

A sharp gasp was followed by muffled scream, and then silence. Jaxon walked back through the hall toward Allyn, their first victim slung over his shoulder. He carried the man into one of the bedrooms and gently laid him on the bed, more for the sake of silence than respect. Allyn knew what came next.

Jaxon placed his hand over the man's chest and buried ice through his heart. The man lurched chest-first into the air, eyes bulging, and Jaxon held him down as he thrashed and cried. Then, as quickly as it began, it ended. His body slumped, going motionless, as his eyes glazed over.

Allyn swallowed the bitter taste in his mouth. The man would have killed them, but something didn't feel right about killing a man in his sleep. Jaxon didn't look as though he had enjoyed it, either. He patted the man's chest and whispered something to him—a final goodbye between Family.

Jaxon closed the door and stepped past Allyn. "It had to be done."

"I know," Allyn said. *But that doesn't mean I have to like it.*

Allyn had barely recovered when the manor shook under the thunder of explosions. He braced himself against the wall as boarded-up windows shattered. Dust fell from the high ceilings, and a painting crashed to the floor in the distance. Shouts of alarm were followed by more giving orders. One of their squads had met resistance. The time for stealth was over.

Liam ordered the magi reserve unit forward, marveling at his sudden rise in influence. Yesterday he'd been an outcast and a symbol of their dwindling power. Today, he was their hope—and commander. That power also meant he was ordering men to their deaths. He wasn't sure how he felt about his newfound respect. Sometimes, reality struggled to live up to the dream.

Mason led the reserve unit out of the forest in a frantic charge for the front of the manor. Light flashed behind obscured windows, and the sound of explosions was muffled by the stone walls of the manor. Wisps of smoke rose over the roofline from the south end of the manor. A soft breeze kept the sweet smell away, but Liam would have to keep an eye on it. If it grew too thick, he would have to signal a retreat—a fire could kill more than a battle with Lukas. And if they lost the manor to fire, why continue to fight?

Mason and his squad dropped behind the protection of the garden's retaining wall and waited for Liam's signal. The three-foot-tall concrete wall rose with the stairs up to the double-door front entrance, giving the elevated entryway its own lush garden full of shrubs, flowers, and small trees.

Liam checked the security feed. Once the battle had

begun, the cameras had done little to aid them, but some eyes were better than none. And sometimes, knowing where someone *wasn't* could be as important as knowing where they *were*. The entrances were quiet. Nobody was trying to sneak out the back door, so Liam waited. His signal was really a *lack* of one. By doing nothing, he told Mason that he was clear to proceed. If Liam ordered someone to blast the entrance with more fire and ice, then Mason was to hold his position.

Five seconds passed, then Liam watched Mason storm the stairs. Fortunately, they weren't met with resistance, which was a sign they hadn't been seen. Liam didn't see how he did it, but he *heard* it. Louder and more powerfully than any of his previous attacks, Mason blew the double doors off their hinges.

From the distance, Liam couldn't see inside the manor, but he did see Mason dive to the side, narrowly avoiding an enemy attack. The man behind him wasn't so fortunate. It sent him sailing through the air, landing unnaturally on the concrete at the base of the stairs.

He didn't get up.

Liam's stomach churned. *Who was it? Kevin? Rory? Anderson?* The motionless body was too far away for him to tell. A strong hand grabbed him by his shoulder.

"There's nothing you can do." Andrew stood a head taller than Liam. With closely shaved blond hair and the patchy beginnings of a beard, he was only a few years older than Liam, but he always made Liam feel like a child—something made worse by the fact that Andrew was the only magi whom Graeme had ordered to stay behind to protect Liam, the children, and magi who were unable to wield. He pulled Liam back into the cover of the forest.

When did I step out from the trees?

The fallen magi remained motionless, and no one came to his aid. Someone should have helped him. All of the clerics were inside the manor. *But someone should do something!*

"I know," Liam said. "I just wish I knew who it was."

"Would that make it any easier?"

Liam sighed. "You're right." He let Andrew pull him deeper into the trees, where the rest waited nervously. Mostly children and adolescents, they were gathered in a semicircle, sitting on fallen logs, pacing, or crying while the few adults in their group did their best to calm them.

Liam struggled to get the image of the fallen magi out of his head—the way his leg was folded unnaturally beneath him and how his arm was bent awkwardly at his side. Liam hoped that despite the odds, the man was alive, but that also meant he was dying alone.

Slapping Andrew's hand off his shoulder, Liam darted back to the manor. Andrew yelled for him to stop, but Liam charged ahead. Family didn't leave Family behind. They didn't run away when things looked bad. A Family fought with each other, for each other, and for as long as it took, until victory was at hand. He broke from the trees into the open and, without having to worry about tripping over the underbrush, pushed forward with renewed vigor. Andrew cursed behind him. So he *was* following him. *Good.* Liam would need his help dragging the fallen magi to safety.

A fireball sailed through the air above him. Mason's squad was having difficulty entering the manor. They were lined up against the exterior, shooting quick attacks inside before ducking behind the wall. Two more magi had fallen.

Liam cursed. Was he going to carry them to safety, too? *One thing at a time. Grab the closest one first. Get him to safety. Then worry about the rest.*

Liam slid to a stop beside the fallen magi. It was Rory. He was worse than Liam imagined. He'd taken a fireball to the chest; his face and arms were red and blistered, and the edges of the burns were dark and crispy. His tattered shirt was completely missing below his chest.

But he was breathing.

"Damn it, Liam," Andrew said, closing in behind him. "What are you doing? You're going to get yourself killed."

"Help me." Liam took Rory below the armpits and waited for Andrew to take his legs. "He's alive. We need to get him back to the forest." Andrew harrumphed but grabbed Rory by his waist. Rory's broken leg swayed nauseatingly under him. "I couldn't leave him."

Carrying Rory through the forest proved to be more difficult and slower than Liam had expected. Liam's feet seemed to catch every root, vine, and rock. He almost fell twice, once bouncing Rory's bad leg off the ground. Rory stirred at that, moaning and rocking his head back and forth. Liam winced, apologized, and kept moving.

"Make way!" Liam ordered. The group of nonwielding magi cleared, allowing Liam and Andrew to lay Rory on the ground. "Fetch some water," he said to no one in particular. "We need to get a splint on that leg."

Andrew nodded. They found two branches that were mostly straight and butted them up against the sides of Rory's leg. The way they'd laid him down, it was mostly straight, though bent slightly to the side at the knee.

"Hold him steady," Liam said.

Andrew held him by his shoulders.

Liam exhaled softly and took Rory's foot, placing his other hand above Rory's kneecap. He lifted it about six inches above the ground and rotated it. Rory's knee twisted without resistance, nearly making Liam sick. Rory barely moved, his unconsciousness acting as a natural anesthesia. Once the knee was in place, they repositioned the branches and bound them together with their belts.

Exhausted, Liam sat back.

Pepper, a young boy whose hair couldn't decide if it wanted to be light or dark, returned with water.

"We need to clean his wounds," Liam said. The boy paled.

"I'll do it." Joyce stepped forward. In her early thirties, her hopes of wielding had died long ago, and with them, so had her dreams of becoming a cleric. But she had found her place in taking care of the clerics' wounds as they healed. She took the canteen from Pepper and gently poured its contents over the wounds on Rory's arms, slowly washing away the dirt and debris.

Rory might live, or he might not, but he stood a better chance than he had at the base of the manor. And if he didn't survive, at least he would die with Family.

"I don't like that look on your face," Andrew said.

"There're more," Liam said. "There were two more fallen outside the doors on the landing."

"I can't let you do that," Andrew said. "It's suicide. I'm supposed to protect you."

"Unless you tie me up, there's nothing you can do to stop me," Liam said. "If you want to protect me, come with me."

Andrew eyed him, weighing him. "Fine. But we need to get them in one pass. We can't be running back and forth. It exposes us too often and might invite an attack."

Liam smiled. "Do we have any more volunteers?"

The vase in the alcove above Allyn's head shattered. He retreated down the hall as colorful hand-blown glass peppered the wall. The table was next, tossed aside like a twig in a windstorm, the rest of its contents crashing onto the floor, leaving Allyn exposed.

"Here!" someone called from the bedroom across the hall. Ren beckoned Allyn toward her while sending fire, ice, and more fire in quick succession toward the enemy at the end of the hallway, where Lukas's group was using the McCollums' own fortifications against them.

Under Ren's cover fire, Allyn darted across the hall and into the room. "Thank you," he said, his voice almost a whisper. He leaned against the wall, exhausted and short of breath. Ren stood above him, continuing to attack. Her compression armor was torn in places and burnt in others, but she didn't seem to notice.

The grand entryway was just beyond the enemy magi at the end of the hall. Equal in number to Jaxon's squad, they were fortified behind the bunkers while Jaxon's unit was split up and disorganized, with four magi in three different rooms. Carefully made plans had been thrown to the wind the moment the first fireball flew. Once Lukas realized his enemy was in the manor, he had quickly dispatched his own squads to repel them.

Caught off guard, Allyn had watched helplessly as Christopher, one of the magi at the front of the squad, took an ice blast in his chest. He was still on the floor, bleeding. The rest had dove into nearby rooms as discipline was replaced momentarily by self-preservation.

"I need cover," Allyn said. "Something to keep them down as I make for Jaxon."

Ren nodded and counted silently. On three, she stepped into the hall, sending a volley of air-propelled ice blasts that spread through the hallway like birdshot from a shotgun. Though they were perhaps too small to kill a man, they would knock him unconscious if they struck him in the head. Lukas's people ducked behind the barricades.

Allyn dashed into the hallway, running to Jaxon's room, which was two doors down and on the other side of the hall. Jaxon saw Allyn rushing toward him and made room for him to slide inside.

"This isn't going well," Allyn said once he was inside.

The sounds of Ren's attacks stopped after Allyn was safely in Jaxon's room. "We need to get to Lukas before you drain yourself. What can I do?"

"Make me invisible," Jaxon said sarcastically.

"I think I can do that." Allyn smiled at Jaxon's confused expression. *Blackout*, Allyn texted Liam. They'd purposely left the lights on prior to their assault. Shutting them off would have alerted Lukas to their attack. "Liam is going to kill the lights. When he does, you'll be invisible."

A fireball sailed past the door. It was bright enough to destroy any advantage the darkness would provide.

"Hold!" Jaxon shouted. His squad's attacks stopped almost immediately. The enemy's followed suit shortly after. An eerie silence fell over the hallway, broken only by the sounds of battles in other areas of the manor—not as many as Allyn had expected. Only two of the other squads had encountered resistance. That meant two had not. *Why?*

Ten seconds, Liam texted back.

"Be ready." Allyn showed Jaxon the text.

Jaxon took a series of deep breaths and rocked his head from side to side, stretching his neck. There was a distant click, followed by a brief hum, and then the room went black. Allyn couldn't see Jaxon, but he felt him slip past, like a massive predator seeking its prey.

Unintelligible and confused, whispers from the enemy magi carried down the hall. *Good*, Allyn thought. There was a shout of alarm and—

Flash!

Jaxon leaped over the barricade as something blue shattered against the ceiling. Someone cried out in pain, and the hall went dark.

Flash!

Jaxon's fists, wrapped in air, drove into a magi's face. He crumpled against the wall. The darkness came again.

Flash!

Jaxon's air-aided fists discharged light as he struck an enemy magi.

Flash!

Two more magi slid down the hall toward the rest of his squad, Jaxon's hulking body a distant shadow.

Flash!

An orange ball of dim light flickered in Jaxon's hand as he wielded fire, illuminating the dark hall. Bodies were strewn around him like petals circling the center of a flower. The way Jaxon fought embodied elegance. No extra movement. Nothing unnecessary. He did what he had to do, and he didn't relish it.

"Let's go," Jaxon ordered. His squad emerged from their positions, falling in line behind him. Leira immediately checked Christopher's vitals then shook her head solemnly.

The hallway ended in a landing directly above the grand entryway. Bodies littered the floor, but the darkness made it impossible to tell how many were theirs. Allyn swallowed the bile in his throat. The smell of fresh death lacked the potency of decay, but it was enough to make him gag. It hung heavy in the air, sticking to him like thick syrup. A different smell, something sweet and familiar, undercut it.

"Do you smell—" Allyn flinched, catching sight of an ice blast flying toward them.

Jaxon saw it, and a wall of fire formed in front of their squad. When it dissipated, Jaxon blindly launched a concussion of air into the center of the entryway, scattering bodies toward the walls.

Below, four magi using a makeshift bunker battled Trevin, Nyla, and Mason's forces. The interlopers were outnumbered but held a better position than Graeme's magi did—or they had until Jaxon's squad had arrived. Pinned between the two squads and forced to battle a new force with an elevated position, Lukas's squad retreated.

Sending a volley of wild attacks, they raced down the center hallway deeper into the manor.

Graeme was supposed to be in that hallway.

Mason's force chased after the retreating magi.

"Hold!" Jaxon shouted.

Mason held up a fist, and his force stopped, watching the deserted hallway, prepared for another battle to flare up.

The floor was slick with blood and melted ice as Allyn stepped over a host of bodies and into the entryway. Most had gaping wounds in their stomachs or chests. None were scorched or blistered. Their methods were the opposite of those they'd used during their assault at Lukas's compound, where most of the dead had burned to death.

The magi squads filed into the entryway. Each bore the marks of battle. They had lost seven people, most coming from Mason's squad, who had attempted to enter the manor before enough of the other squads were in position. He had lost more than half his men.

"Where's Graeme?" Jaxon asked.

The rest looked around as though they expected to see him behind them.

"How many did Liam say he saw enter the manor?" Nyla asked.

"Between twenty and thirty," Allyn answered.

"There aren't enough bodies," Nyla said. "There's twelve, maybe fifteen in here. Where are the rest?"

Allyn's phone vibrated in his pocket. It would be Liam. Probably wondering if they had won since the fighting had stopped.

"Something isn't right," Mason said.

"Arm the barricades!" Jaxon ordered.

Allyn pulled his phone from his pocket and looked at the message. *Run!*

Before he had a chance to say anything, a fireball, bright

and raging, streaked into the room. Caught off guard, they couldn't extinguish it. It struck the underside of the staircase, and flames leaped from its center, climbing the wall. Another fireball struck the opposite wall, splashing like liquid. In an instant, the entire entryway was aflame. More raced across the walls as though they had been doused with accelerant.

The smell. They put something on the walls!

Coughing, Trevin rushed outside with two magi on his heels. Allyn followed. Scrambling onto the patio, Allyn tripped, and something sailed over his head.

Allyn fell on top of Trevin. Ice poked him in the chest. It stuck out of Trevin's back. The other two magi lay beside him, each with fatal wounds.

Allyn frantically crawled back into the entryway. "Trap! Run!"

They didn't have a choice. They ran deeper into the manor—into the flames.

CHAPTER 24

LIAM WATCHED HELPLESSLY AS TEN of Lukas's magi stood in a semicircle around the base of the manor, hurling fire inside. It had happened so quickly. He had been checking his phone, ready to turn the power back on, when they had appeared out of the forest. As the manor burned, they killed anyone who attempted to escape. It was a massacre.

He had already done what he could to help by telling Allyn to run. He hoped Allyn had received the message in time. Not knowing what else to do, he did the only thing he had left. Punching buttons in quick succession, Liam sealed off the library. It was climate controlled, sealed below the manor itself, and designed to withstand anything short of a natural disaster, but Liam wondered if it could withstand the weight of the manor collapsing on top of it. He was about to find out.

Who am I saving the library for? he wondered. Within minutes, the manor would be reduced to ash. He and his Family were homeless. Nowhere to sleep. Nowhere to hide. Nowhere to protect their history. And the police would return. *I'm handing them the evidence we have fought so long to keep hidden. Our identity. Our history.* It made Liam sad, sick, and angry. A people's history belonged with *them*, not in a storage facility, where it was catalogued and hidden from those who needed it. But it was better than the alternative.

"Prepare to move." He and Andrew withdrew into the clearing, where the rest of their group waited. After rescuing Rory, Liam and Andrew had brought back four more. Each had serious injuries, half of which were likely fatal if they didn't receive treatment soon. Joyce had done what she could, but her skills could only accomplish so much.

"You can't be serious," Andrew said.

Liam beckoned him closer. "They've torched the manor. The battle is over. We lost. We need to get the rest of them to safety."

"Look at them." Andrew surveyed the group. "They won't last a mile."

"They don't have to," Liam said. "The injured can't walk. We can't carry them. And if we are somehow able to retreat into the forest, they won't receive the medical attention they need."

"What are you suggesting?"

"They stay behind."

"With who?"

"Me."

Andrew shook his head. "If Lukas comes looking, you're signing up for a death sentence."

"If someone doesn't stay behind, then I'm sentencing *them* to one," Liam said, looking at Rory. Joyce held a canteen to his lips, willing him to drink. He wouldn't last an hour. "If we win this battle, we'll need someone who knows where you are."

"I thought you said the battle was over."

Liam sighed. "It's not looking good, but I'm not going to give up."

"If you're staying, then I'm—"

"But," Liam said, interrupting, "if we *lose*, they will need someone to protect them." Andrew gave him an appraising look that said he still wasn't entirely convinced. "They're important, Andrew. I know they don't look it, but they are our future."

"Fine," Andrew said, "but at least allow someone to stay behind with you. Help you look over the injured."

Liam agreed and pulled Joyce aside. He wouldn't order her to stay behind, and thankfully, he didn't have to. She volunteered.

"It's my duty," she said, her voice tight with fear.

Courage grows from the ashes of fear. Another one of Jaxon's favorite sayings.

Since the wounded were staying behind, preparing the magi to move was done in short order. Liam organized them into small groups, dividing the children evenly among them and assigning each a guardian. After giving his initial orders, Liam allowed Andrew to take over. Liam thought it best to wait until the last moment to tell them that he and the wounded were staying behind. When the time came, the group put up the fight he'd expected, and like his short argument with Andrew, Liam eventually won. More volunteered to stay behind with him, and though he was tempted, he rejected the idea. He needed to get as many as he could to safety.

"Where are we going?" Andrew asked.

Liam blinked. He had been so focused on locking down the library and organizing the magi's departure that he hadn't thought of where to send them. They could return to the homestead, but that meant being outdoors for an extended period of time, and some in the group were already concerned about the elements. That plan also relied on the idea that someone would return for them. If they lost the battle, or if Liam fell before he could get word to the survivors, then his group would wait at the homestead until one of their own decided it was time to leave.

They could make for the city, but what would they do when they arrived there? They had no one to take them in. Having the group walking the empty streets late at night didn't feel like a legitimate alternative to leaving them at the homestead.

"Liam?" Andrew prompted.

They want an answer. "I'm open to suggestions," Liam said quietly to Andrew.

"I thought you had a plan?" Andrew asked loudly enough for his voice to carry to the group. A few turned to look at them.

"My plan," Liam said in a forceful whisper, "is to keep you safe, and I'm trying to decide the best way to do that. We don't have a lot of options, and I was hoping you could think of something I couldn't."

He couldn't, so Liam sent them back to the homestead. There was some grumbling about how they had just left there, but Liam did his best to ignore it. "Wait until midday tomorrow. If nobody arrives... do what you think is best."

Andrew nodded.

The plan wasn't very good, and Liam was sure that given enough time, he could think of something better, but time was another thing he didn't have.

The group filed down the trail and deeper into the forest. Liam gave them what he hoped was a reassuring smile. "I'll see you soon." Watching them disappear, Liam was left with a new worry.

What now?

———————•••———————

Allyn's lungs were on fire. Each breath was agonizing as the thick smoke burned him from the inside. He coughed. It made the pain worse. In the middle of a coughing fit, he instinctually took a deep breath, which only made him cough more. It was a vicious cycle.

Holding on to the wall for guidance and stability, Allyn stumbled down the hall. He was moving too slowly, and the flames were spreading too quickly, already racing ahead of him. Bodies littered the floor. Too many to only belong to the enemy. Allyn stepped on something—a hand. He bent down to help the person up, but the arm was limp. Whoever it was wouldn't get up ever again. The body would burn to ashes with the manor, buried under its rubble.

Someone pushed him. Allyn was only faintly aware of the others jostling around him, trying to escape the inferno, each too absorbed in his or her own misery and will to survive to worry about others.

Allyn slipped and fell in something wet. Nobody stopped to pick him up. They ran over his back, trampling him, pinning him to the floor. The force drove the air from his lungs. He took a slow, timid breath, expecting the pain, but he was welcomed with cool air. In disbelief, he drew in another. He wasn't hallucinating. The air was still tinged with the taste of smoke, but it was faint. He started to stand, then stopped.

Stay low! Old training seeped into his consciousness. *Smoke rises. Stay low to the ground.*

Allyn crawled forward. It was a slow process that forced him face to face with the dead. Instead of faceless souls, they had names. Vincent. Griffin. Ari. More he didn't know. Too many that he did. It was the last time anyone would ever see them. Allyn etched their resting faces into his memory.

Crash! A support beam fell behind him. The house was collapsing. Allyn pushed forward harder, hand over hand, slipping, sliding, and clawing, but always moving forward. Even low to the ground, the oxygen was quickly replaced by smoke.

I'm not going to make it.

Another beam crashed to the floor.

That was close.

Staying as low as possible, Allyn rose to his feet and rushed forward. *There!* He entered the sitting room. His team had entered on the second floor directly above this room. The far wall was nothing but glass—french doors sandwiched between floor-to-ceiling windows. The doors had been thrown open and the windows shattered, likely from frantic magi doing what they could to escape. They were outside, maybe fifteen paces from the manor, most on their hands and knees, coughing and crying, but alive. Others stood over them, helping.

No. Not helping. What are they doing?

Lukas stood over a man on his knees. The others held him down. They were taking prisoners.

Allyn ducked behind a velvet armchair. The fire roared around him, drowning out the voices outside. Allyn caught only a few words, and none of them made sense. There was another, closer crash. Burning embers billowed into the sitting room. If he ran outside, Lukas would have him and maybe kill him. Allyn didn't know what Lukas wanted with him anymore. He was stuck between certain death and a probable one.

"It's over," Lukas said to the kneeling man.

Graeme!

He screamed. The primal sound was agonizing. His body lurched forward, head thrown back, face toward the sky. The magi at his sides struggled to hold him down. They turned their heads. Whatever Lukas was doing to Graeme, they didn't want to watch. The captives around Graeme fought to break free, but Lukas outnumbered them more than two to one. More of Graeme's screams cut through the air.

What is Lukas doing to him?

Graeme coughed, gurgled and then spat. A light formed in the middle of his back, dim at first, then brighter as it burned through his compression armor. A white-hot fireball the size of a sand dollar passed through Graeme. He slumped forward then hung motionless in the grip of the guards. The magi holding Graeme let go, stepping aside. One threw up as Graeme fell face first into the ground as the hole in his back still smoldered.

He killed him! He just killed Graeme!

Satisfied, Lukas stepped over Graeme, toward someone with chin-length black hair. Leira was on her knees, fighting the hands that held her in place, trying to get to her father. Lukas knelt in front of her and stroked her chin, almost consolingly. He whispered something in her ear then turned to the man at her side.

Jaxon fought the four magi who gripped him. His muscles were clenched and straining. Even outnumbered, Jaxon nearly broke free. A concussion of air shook the air, sending two magi to the ground. He was on his feet in an instant, turning to attack his remaining two captors, when another concussion ripped the air.

Jaxon was on his back, dazed.

"On your knees," Lukas commanded.

Lukas's magi swarmed Jaxon, pulling him up, then shoved him to his knees. Jaxon continued to fight, pushing them away, trying to pull free, but it was futile. Lukas meant to kill Jaxon the same way he had Graeme. Something stirred inside Allyn—something he could use.

Anger.

Flames at his back, Allyn raced for the open doors, wielding the electricity. He jumped out of the manor, hit the ground, rolled, and threw a static charge at Lukas.

Lukas looked up in surprise and took the static charge in the shoulder. The force threw him away from Jaxon. Allyn turned, shooting two more static charges at Jaxon's captors. The magi holding Jaxon's left arm took the charge in the face. His eyes rolled back as he crumpled to the ground. Allyn hadn't intended to kill the man. The charges were powerful enough only to stun, not kill.

But maybe since it hit him in the head...

Jaxon ripped free, driving air-aided fists into the magi around him. Bones cracked, jaws unhinged, and magi fell. Leira threw her head back, driving her head into the nose of the magi behind her. Then she spun, taking the other man's face in her hands. He fell unconscious almost instantly. One by one, the remaining members of the McCollum Family fought back, each fighting for their lives, their Family, and their grand mage.

Allyn found Lukas across the battlefield, shedding his coat and patting out the flames at his shoulder. Allyn felt as if only he and Lukas existed. Graeme was dead. Jaxon and the rest were battling Lukas's magi. Lukas seemed to realize this, too. His eyes locked onto Allyn, his dark expression unnerving him. Allyn had no idea how he could kill Lukas when Graeme and Jaxon had failed.

The flames at Allyn's back gave him a good view of the battlefield. The McCollum magi were outnumbered, though the odds grew in their favor. Jaxon was fearless, like a berserker. He rushed a group of magi, sliding under a fireball, then spun around another and launched a concussion of air toward the group before driving two ice blasts into the dazed magi. With fists encased in air, he quickly dropped two more and charged another squad.

Nyla and Leira worked together. Quick and nimble, they danced around attacks, sweeping close to their attackers, then drawing on their fatigue to subdue them into unconsciousness.

Allyn found Lukas stalking around the edge of the battle toward him. Lukas threw three fireballs in quick succession. The first missed, Allyn dodged the second, and the third took one of Lukas's magi in the chest. He hit the ground, eyes glazed, never knowing the man he followed had been the one to kill him.

That will be me, Allyn thought. Lukas always wielded fire, and Allyn couldn't counter it. Careful not to hit one of his own, Allyn sent a static charge through a rift in the battle. The strange red electric charge sailed past Lukas and into the trees behind him. He was so far away. Lukas could dodge anything he threw at him. But he was reluctant to get much closer. Lukas was too fast, his attacks too quick for Allyn to dodge them up close.

He sent another static charge at Lukas then sent a second where he expected Lukas to be. Unlike fire, the charge's intensity didn't dissipate with distance. It continued to glow, twisting around itself with thin red threads that danced like lightning during a summer storm. The first missed wide, which Allyn had expected, but the second came surprisingly close. Lukas rolled at the last instant, and the charge streaked over the back of his head.

Allyn swelled with confidence.

Lukas stood, a fireball in his hands swelling to the size of a beach ball. He launched it over the battle toward Allyn. When it began its descent, it exploded, raining fire.

Allyn dove aside, curling up and protecting his head. Around him, fire was snuffed out by the moist earth. A few flames landed on him, burning his compression armor and blistering his skin. Anxiety replaced his confidence. Despite the distance between them, Lukas still had the advantage. *How do you kill someone stronger and faster than you?* Allyn was afraid to wield something more powerful. He felt it raging inside him, ready to be unleashed, but he didn't understand its consequences. And Jaxon said magic had consequences. Magic had its limits. No one knew what Allyn's limits were.

Lukas drew closer. Fire danced in his eyes. Lukas loved fire. He would have been the type of kid who burned his parents' house down while playing with matches. Allyn almost wondered if Lukas could wield anything else. Was he like Allyn and limited to only one element? Allyn suspected Lukas simply had his attack of choice—just like Jaxon preferred his air-aided punches. But air was replenishable. Fire wasn't.

That's it! If Allyn could force Lukas into wielding too much of a single element, Lukas would kill himself. *How do you kill someone stronger and faster than you? You outthink them. Create a new game. Change the rules.*

Lukas was only a few feet in front of him and continuing to draw ever closer. Allyn couldn't retreat. The warmth on his back told him he was as close to the burning manor as he wanted to get, so he circled Lukas. For every step Lukas took toward him, he took two to the side, working his way around until Lukas's back was at the manor.

Flames threatened to spread from the manor across the grassy field around it, but the wet ground contained the burning embers. Plants in large pots and small raised garden beds surrounding the exterior of the manor wilted under the heat.

A weak-yellow wall of fire six feet tall and nearly twice as wide grew in front of Lukas. It probably wasn't hot enough to kill Allyn, but he didn't want to find out. He didn't wait for it to finish forming. He threw a barrage of static charges through the firewall, aiming for where he thought Lukas was. Two. Three. Four. They shot through the fire like rocks through a waterfall.

Lukas grunted, and the firewall winked out. One of Allyn's static charges had hit its mark. Lukas toppled over a planter box, falling dangerously close to the flames that spilled out of the shattered manor windows. Allyn rushed forward. Lukas was on his hands and knees, dazed, hidden behind dark smoke that billowed out of the manor. Allyn shot more charges at him. They hit him in the side, rolling him onto his back and closer to the manor.

With Lukas partially hidden behind the planter box, Allyn's charges hit the ground around him, shattered potted plants, and disappeared into the manor. Lukas threw his arm toward Allyn.

Staring into the light of the fire, Allyn barely saw the ice blast flying toward his head. Instinctively, he *reached* for it. A coil of electricity stretched from his hand like a whip, snaring the ice out of the air. It burst into a shower of sparks. Lukas got to his feet, preparing to retreat.

No, Allyn thought. *Keep him engaged.* Allyn launched a charge in front of Lukas.

He planted his heels, sliding to a stop as the charge passed in front of him. He turned to Allyn with hatred in his eyes. Graeme had been a grand mage, and Jaxon was on his way to becoming one, but it was Allyn, a silent man who until only a few weeks ago had believed magic didn't exist, who had bested him. He'd nearly killed the man who'd orchestrated the attack at his condo, masterminded his sister's kidnapping, and destroyed the McCollum Manor. Lukas seemed infuriated to be beaten by his own creation.

Lukas attacked with a volley of fireballs. Burning white hot, they took longer to form but shot through the air faster than normal fireballs.

Allyn went to the ground to avoid the first. The rest missed high or wide, and one even hit the ground only a few feet in front of Lukas. Lukas unleashed another volley of fireballs. They still burned white, but a tinge of blue developed *inside*. The first burst halfway between them, the second closer to Allyn, and the third close enough to throw him onto his back.

This was a bad idea. He didn't know how much fire Lukas could wield before he snuffed himself out. And Allyn was forced to fight a defensive battle, which he was losing. One fireball could end him for good. He needed help.

Allyn caught a glimpse of Jaxon. He'd formed the remnants of their squads together into a cohesive unit that was maybe fifteen strong, matching Lukas's numbers. They fought a more organized battle, but as with most battles, once positions were secured and trenches dug, the battle slowed. While the McCollum Family had done an excellent job of using the early chaos to their advantage, the battle was still long from over. He was on his own.

A fireball shot past Allyn's head, singeing the tips of his hair.

Idiot! Pay attention!

Searing pain shot up his leg. His right leg was smoldering, and the pant leg was still on fire. Allyn rolled it in the moist earth, patting the fire out. Under the remains of his pant leg was torn flesh. Black, red, and blistered, it oozed white film. Fortunately, it wasn't bleeding—*the veins must be cauterized*. Smiling, Lukas stalked toward him. He believed the battle was over. Allyn tried to stand, but his leg buckled under him. He retreated, dragging his bad leg. Despite Lukas's methodical pace, he closed the distance between them. *This is it*, Allyn thought. *This is the end.* He tried to wield, but the pain acted as a barrier, a distraction. He couldn't find the torrent of energy inside him. Finally understanding Jaxon's exercises, Allyn laughed. Separating his mind from his body while finding the ability to ignore discomfort and pain could prove to be the difference between life and death.

Lukas stopped in front of Allyn. "What's funny?"

"Maybe my sister and I aren't so different, after all. We both have to learn the hard way."

Allyn was certain Lukas wouldn't understand the humor, but he smiled anyway as he knelt in front of Allyn.

He's right there. Waiting. Wield, and it's over. He won't have time to dodge it.

Allyn tried to ignore the pain and wield. He struggled to control his breathing and focus on something else— the blood running through his veins, the rhythmic beat of his heart, and the hair on his arms and legs standing up against the cool, gentle breeze. But the pain was too intense. Blood coated the remains of his pant leg. The veins were not entirely cauterized, after all. Sharp pains pulsed through him with the beat of his heart, and the tattered pant leg brushed against the wound as the wind blew. It all came back to the pain. He couldn't separate himself from it. He couldn't wield because of it.

Allyn's shoulders slumped as he sighed a final breath of resignation. White hot, two feet in diameter, and growing, a fireball formed in Lukas's hands. The air shimmered around it. Lukas wanted him to know there was no escape. Even if Allyn tried to roll out of the way, he couldn't roll far enough because the fireball was too large.

The gesture was also pointless. Lukas didn't know Allyn resigned himself to death. He expected Allyn to keep fighting.

He expects more of me than I do of myself. And why shouldn't he? Allyn had already lived up to Lukas's expectations. He was a new kind of magi who could wield. Lukas and Graeme both had expected him to change the magi community. Allyn had bested Lukas, saved Kendyl from his clutches, and largely destroyed his following.

I nearly killed him.

The fireball continued to grow.

He's afraid of me.

The realization stirred Allyn's desire to exceed those expectations. Knowing Lukas feared his potential gave him confidence. Allyn dove inside himself. The pain was still present, and growing worse as shock and adrenaline wore off, but instead of trying to wield around it, he accepted it. Embracing the pain, he poured it into the void.

And the void swelled with energy.

He pulled it to the surface, projecting it into his hands. His hands grew warm. He could *feel* the energy before he saw the red tendrils wrapping around his wrists like thin bolts of lightning.

Allyn threw up his hands, projecting the charge forward. Lukas's eyes opened wide. He threw hands in front of his face, and the fireball dissipated.

Red coils of electricity struck Lukas in the chest, but he wasn't thrown backward. The coils wrapped around Lukas, binding him in their clutches. His rigid body shook violently, his hair standing on end. His clothing caught fire, burning his skin, causing blisters to grow and pop. His skin melted, and eyeballs burst. As disgusting as it was, Allyn didn't let go. He let his pain and hatred flow into Lukas.

Let him feel my pain. It's time he understood the grief he's caused. Even if it kills him.

And kill him it did.

EPILOGUE

A LIGHT RAIN BEGAN. ALLYN LAY on the ground in front of Lukas, his eyes closed, allowing the cool rain to wash away the stink, the sweat, and the blood from his body and soul. Allyn didn't know how long he stayed there, but the rhythmic sounds of rain slowly replaced the violent sounds of battle. When he opened his eyes, the clouds had turned shades of purple and red. It made him think of all the death he'd seen and caused.

At some point, the manor had collapsed into an enormous mound of smoldering ash with only a single stone wall left standing. The once-cultivated lawn of the manor grounds was now a mud pit destroyed by battle.

"Allyn?" Nyla knelt over him, resting her hand on his chest.

Jaxon was beside her. His eyes shifted back and forth from Allyn to Lukas as though he perhaps expected the man to rise again. Lukas had made a habit of turning their carefully made plans against them and escaping when they thought they had him cornered. But he would never rise again.

"He's gone," Allyn said. His voice was oddly strained, raspy.

It was all Jaxon needed. Ignoring Lukas's remains, he pulled up Allyn's shredded pant leg, exposing his wound. He grimaced.

"That bad?" Allyn asked.

Nyla gently placed her hand over the wound, probing him. "It's hot to the touch and already showing signs of infection. We can't wait. If we do, we risk losing the leg."

Allyn leaned forward as far as Nyla would allow him to, barely getting a glimpse of what remained of his leg. The skin around the wound was an angry red. The rest was black, pink, and yellow. Allyn became flushed and dizzy, on the verge of passing out.

"Stay with me, Allyn." Nyla's voice was comforting. *Focus on that.*

Allyn locked eyes with Nyla. Her blue eyes were inviting and as comforting as her voice. They held him, keeping him calm. They didn't change or show any sign of pain as the tingling of her healing spread through his leg.

"That's all I can do now," she said only a few moments later. "The worst of it is better, and you should be able to walk. I wish I could do more, but there are so many wounded." She looked past him to the battlefield beyond, where too many bodies to count lay motionless. The McCollum Family was decimated. Only a handful of them remained alive, and their cries of pain and loss rang through the early morning.

"It's more than I deserve," Allyn said. "Thank you." He sat up, gingerly moving his leg, expecting pain. Nyla had done more than she'd let on. A thin layer of translucent skin covered the wound, creating a delicate barrier against the elements. His skin was still black, but that would heal in time.

Jaxon helped him up. He couldn't put his full weight on the leg, and he would walk with a limp, but he was mobile—and alive. Together, they slowly crossed the battlefield to where Graeme lay. Leira sat beside him, holding his hand and fighting back tears. She had closed his eyes and covered his wound with a coat. Except for his motionless chest, he looked as though he could be sleeping.

Liam charged out of the trees, coming to an abrupt halt several feet behind them. He was covered in blood, but he appeared uninjured. Had there been another battle somewhere else? Where were the ones he was supposed to be protecting?

Allyn took a small step toward him. "Liam—"

"What happened?"

"Liam, listen..." Allyn was suddenly at a loss for words, having flashbacks of telling Kendyl their mother had died. He wasn't sure if it was his place to tell Liam about his father. He turned to Jaxon and Nyla.

Jaxon exhaled deeply, then began to say something but stopped. Tears already welled in Nyla's eyes.

"What's wrong?" Liam asked. "Where is my father?"

Allyn deflated, his shoulders going slack. "Liam, I'm sorry. Your father... your father is gone."

"No," Liam said, shaking his head, face contorted in pain. "No... he's..." Liam rushed forward.

Jaxon stopped him with an arm and pulled him close in a tight embrace.

"Let me see him!" Liam shouted. "I need to see him!"

"Liam." Jaxon's deep voice was soft and tender.

His emotions making him stronger, Liam continued to fight, trying to shove Jaxon aside. "Why won't you let me see him? Let me see him!"

"Liam?" Leira stood.

Liam saw her, then the body at her feet. He fought savagely, kicking, stomping, and flailing. Jaxon let him go, and Liam raced toward Leira and the fallen body of his father. He slowed in front of the body. Leira's firm expression hid the torrent of emotions Allyn knew she must be feeling. She wore a mask for her little brother. Allyn knew the guise well.

Kneeling, Liam took his father's hand. "What happened?"

Leira circled her father, then dropped to her knees beside Liam. "He fought bravely."

Liam squeezed his father's hand hard enough that his own knuckles went white. "Was it quick?"

Leira stole a glance at Allyn and the others. "Quick enough." She wrapped an arm around him and pulled him close. Liam didn't fight it. Leira trembled slightly, her strength fading.

"We should bury him," Allyn said. "He deserves better than to be left here."

"They all do," Jaxon said, keeping one eye on the driveway as though he expected the police to arrive at any moment.

"I'll gather the rest. Go console her." Allyn nodded at Leira. Jaxon hesitated.

He's scared, Allyn realized. Jaxon could stare down a host of magi that intended to kill him, but consoling the woman he loved terrified him.

"She doesn't need you to say anything. Just be with her. Be her rock."

Jaxon nodded. He could do that. In many ways, he *was* a rock—a dense, stubborn boulder that wouldn't move for anyone else. He shuffled over and knelt behind Leira and Liam, awkwardly rubbing Leira's back. She leaned into him, resting her head on his chest.

That was when she broke down.

Half an hour later, distant sirens, still miles off, whined in unison. Too many to count, they echoed across the canyon.

Graeme lay across a hurriedly constructed funeral pyre in a small space within the manor that had been cleared of debris. His arms were crossed, and his white battle attire had been scrubbed as clean as possible. Allyn stood with the others around the pyre, humming softly. The other fallen magi had been burned where they fell, Lukas's magi included. For some, it was more than they deserved, but it was the magi way, and Graeme would have wanted it done.

Jaxon led the funeral procession, bringing the humming to a crescendo, then raised his hands to the sky and released a stream of fire. Thirty hands shot up, and those who could wield followed Jaxon's example. Allyn shot a series of jagged red static charges into the air. The display would likely be seen from the road, but it didn't matter anymore. They had been found.

The humming stopped, and Jaxon directed his fire at the pyre. The rest of the wielding magi did the same. Graeme disappeared among the flames. The pyre burned faster and hotter than it would have naturally, and Allyn was thankful he couldn't smell Graeme's burning flesh, though he did occasionally have to look away. Watching Graeme burn reminded him of Lukas's gruesome death.

As the sirens drew closer, Jaxon ordered them to move, leaving the pyre to smolder. Running at a steady pace, they fled the manor in an organized file, two men wide. Once they entered the forest, the pace slowed, but they continued, heading for the homestead, where Liam said the rest would be waiting.

Jaxon lagged behind, and Allyn fell into step with him. They stopped just beyond the tree line to watch as police cars screamed around the bend, up the driveway. The manor's remains obscured Allyn's view, but the red and blue lights pierced the early morning light. Earlier, the scene had been drastically different—an empty manor that had stood for decades and would stand for even longer.

Now it was laid to rubble, and dozens of faintly human bodies littered the grounds.

The police would conduct a full-scale investigation. They would call in the arson unit and other crime scene investigators. The coroner's office would be packed full of magi bodies that would have no dental or any other identifiable records. A morgue full of John and Jane Does would deepen the investigation. The library would be discovered. Its contents would be researched and catalogued. They would be exposed.

Then the real hunt would begin.

"What happens now?" Allyn asked.

Jaxon looked at him with fear in his eyes. "I don't know."

The hike back to the homestead was easier than the one from it to the manor. The sun hung low, and the first rays of morning cast light on exposed roots and sudden dropoffs. Wispy spider webs stretched from branch to branch, glistening in the light, as a black mass waited in the center of each, preparing for its prey. Chirping birds brought the forest to life, covering the sound of the traveling group's footfalls. What had taken them an hour in darkness took them half as long in the light of dawn.

The reunion was well underway by the time Allyn and Jaxon arrived at the homestead. There were hugs and tears for those returning and more for those who hadn't. A general sense of shock over the loss of the manor gripped everyone.

"Where are we going to go?" a young girl asked, clinging to her mother's leg.

All eyes turned to Jaxon. He stammered, searching for words, and rubbed the brands on his arms nervously.

"I know of a place," Allyn said.

"Where?" Jaxon asked, perhaps too eagerly to maintain his confident façade.

Allyn found Kendyl amid the expectant eyes. Her dark

hair glinted with a touch of red in the morning sun. She smiled. She knew what he was thinking. He smiled back, knowing that he would never hear the end of it. You can't put a price on everything. Having a place to call home was priceless.

"It's an old family property," Allyn said. "It's small, and it hasn't been used in years, but it's private, and nobody will harm us there."

"What about the police?" Jaxon asked. "Won't they know to look for us there?"

"How are you at pottery?" Kendyl asked, stepping forward, grinning.

Jaxon looked at her, confused.

"If anyone comes asking, you're a group of artists on a retreat. You rent rooms by the week, and you paid in cash."

"What about you?" Jaxon asked.

Allyn shrugged. "We'll take care not to be seen." When Jaxon didn't appear convinced, Allyn added, "Look, I know it's risky. And I understand if you don't like the idea, but it's only a temporary solution until we can regroup."

Jaxon pinched his forehead and thought for a moment. "We'll need IDs."

"Liam?" Allyn said.

"The physical IDs will be tough, but I can forge digital ones and create false identities. They won't hold up under close scrutiny but they'll buy us time."

"What do you think?" Allyn asked.

"I think it might just work," Jaxon said.

Relief spread through the group like a yawn. They knew that the McCollum Family would survive. They would endure. They would grow strong.

They just needed time.

The story continues in...

SPLINTER

The Machinists Series, Book Two
Coming Soon

For exclusive content follow Craig Andrews on
Facebook or sign up for the Mailing List.

http://eepurl.com/IEjIr
https://www.facebook.com/craigandrewsauthor

ACKNOWLEDGMENTS

I T'S SAID THAT WRITING IS a lonely enterprise, and while I agree with that statement, creating a book is a surprisingly collaborative endeavor. There were dozens of people who helped me turn this story from one that resided in my head to the book you hold in your hands.

It begins with my wife, Tiffany, whose unflinching support, never-ending enthusiasm, and occasional, well-timed verbal motivation kept me working. This book exists because she told me not to wait. Because she pushed me upstairs to write on the nights I thought I was too tired. Because she nudged me out of bed in the early mornings when I would have rather slept. And because she never complained or made me feel guilty that I sometimes spent more time with fictional Families than my own. If you ever get a chance to thank her, please do. The husbands, wives, and significant others of artists don't get enough credit for the achievements of their partners.

Special thanks also goes to my parents, Will and Lisa, who instilled in me a love for stories, and taught me that anything was possible. They told me to shoot for the stars, and helped me develop a work ethic to make sure I got there. I can never express how truly grateful I am to be their son.

To my own son, who while too young to know he was giving up his dad for the day, always welcomed me back with a smile and a hug. I want to inspire you the same way you inspire me.

To Gary and Gala Richey for raising such a loving, supportive daughter, and not laughing when I told them I was writing a book, but instead asked when they could read it.

To the team at Red Adept Publishing, headed by Lynn McNamee who patiently guided me through the editorial process. To Stefanie Spangler for her wonderful line-edits and continuously going above and beyond her initial job.

A huge thanks goes to all of my early readers: Tiffany (always my first reader), Will & Lisa Looney, Gary & Gala Richey, Mary Sharinghousen, Pamela Didier, Scott & Jami Hays, Anton Livingston, Tanner Vannett, Jehnna Pitts, Megan West, Abigail Winchester, Peter Arvidson, and Nick Hagen. Your excitement, kind words, and willingness to share the book with friends and family keep me going. Your advice and insights proved invaluable and this book is much better because of them.

And thank you lovely reader, for taking this journey with me. I hope I get the opportunity to do it again.

—Craig Andrews

CRAIG ANDREWS GRADUATED FROM PORTLAND State University with a Bachelors of Arts in English. Growing up on a healthy diet of fantasy and science fiction, some of his favorite childhood memories include being traumatized by the TV shows *Unsolved Mysteries* and *The X-Files*. He currently lives in a small, rural town outside of Portland, Oregon with his wife and two boys.

Say "hi" at any of the following:
craigandrewsauthor@yahoo.com
https://www.facebook.com/craigandrewsauthor
http://eepurl.com/IEjIr

www.ingramcontent.com/pod-product-compliance
Lightning Source LLC
Chambersburg PA
CBHW030023180626
46810CB00001B/175